DEATH IN THE FIELDS

—·—

BOOK ONE OF THE BLACK RIVER MYSTERIES

ERIC M. BISCHOFF

SHILSHOLE SHOPS, LLC

Book Cover by Mubashir Design

Ebook ISBN: 979-8-9927621-0-5

Print ISBN: 979-8-9927621-1-2

To My Three Girls:
Tonia, Brianna and Tori Rose

CONTENTS

— · —

ONE

Exhausted and too deep into sleep to escape it, the nightmare caught me again.

I'm standing at the foot of a bed: a hospital bed, but distorted, like in a Salvador Dali painting, too long and too narrow. There are beeps, distance voices and the antiseptically hollow smell of death. A phone is ringing. On the bed is the emaciated body of a woman, pale with shorn hair, eyes half open, staring blankly.

I can't figure out who it is. I step closer, between phantoms in hospital gowns. I let out a cry. It's my wife. Dead, surrounded by the detritus of a terminal cancer patient.

A voice calls from outside.

"You're too late."

I look out the window to see who it is, but all I see is a decrepit collection of cardboard shelters, ragged tents and discarded shopping carts.

Suddenly, I'm walking towards the shelters, following a policeman. He's talking, but I can't make out the words. Something about my name and a cell phone. Again, I hear a phone ringing.

The cop stops in front of a beat-up old tent that smells of spoiled fruit, cigarette smoke and human waste. He points.

"Why didn't you answer?" the policeman asks as he flips the tent door open to a pair of dead eyes staring out at me from a ragged sleeping bag. It takes my foggy brain a moment to realize it is an old friend, Sean, dead, yet crying for help.

The ringing is louder.

I cover my ears, turn and run, but now I'm running through a plowed field: a barren potato field with long rows stretching to the horizon. I focus, and in the distance, I see a hand, sticking up out of the ground. I'm stumbling through the uneven ground towards it. The hand is making slow, desperate grasping motions. I stop above it, watching the hand's movement. The ringing gets even louder. And then I hear a pounding noise.

I bend over and begin brushing dirt away from where the arm is emerging from the earth.

There was that pounding again.

I brush away more dirt. Long, blonde hair.

Pounding.

I brush. A forehead, eyebrows.

More pounding.

I clear away more dirt and see half a face, one eye staring up at me. A young woman with an expression of terror as she tries to speak. I know her.

"Help," the face says. "Help."

I don't understand.

Pounding.

"Hey!"

Pounding.

"Hey! You okay? Hey!"

I jerked awake, confused.

"Hey, mister," said a voice. "Are you okay?"

I looked around and saw that I was sitting in my old ragtop Jeep, parked at a truck stop. There was a woman, a girl actually, pounding on my driver's side door. I shook the sleep out of my head while I unzipped the Jeep's window.

"What's wrong?" I asked the girl. She was a waifish thing, late teens I guessed, in a frilly peasant blouse over ragged jeans and lugging an old, nylon backpack. Her long, wavy brown hair was gathered back in a ponytail, revealing small brown eyes and a long, thin face. The wrist she had been pounding on my door carried half a dozen homemade beaded bracelets. She looked like a refugee from a 60's hippie commune.

"You were like screaming and thrashing all over," she said. "I thought maybe you was having a seizure you know, or somethin'."

I shook my head. "Just a bad dream. Thanks."

"Okay. Sure," she said. She looked at me for a moment, almost stepped away then stopped. "You got any spare cash?"

Without thinking I shook my head. It was my default response. "No. Sorry."

She nodded, turned and walked away like someone who was used to hearing that. I watched as she strolled off. She looked a little bit like my daughter back in Bellingham. Just a lot skinnier. Like a young Fiona Apple.

"Thanks for waking me," I called after her. She just waved without turning, walked to a tractor trailer rig parked a few yards away and knocked. The door opened a crack, she said something to the person in the truck, listened to whatever the answer was and as the truck's door closed, she turned and walked towards the next vehicle. A lot lizard, I guessed, wandering from truck to truck to make a few dollars selling a little trucker comfort.

I climbed out of the Jeep and stretched my forty-eight year-old skeleton awake and tried to clear my fuzzy brain with a deep breath of the crisp, October morning air. The truck stop was at an eastbound interstate exit outside of Boise, Idaho. It was nearly six in the morning, which meant I had only gotten about four hours of sleep. And that's about what it felt like.

I needed coffee.

After a check of the Jeep and the utility trailer I was towing, I reached into the center console and grabbed a little bottle of pills, looked at it a moment then shook one out and swallowed it. I picked up my cell, made sure I was carrying my wallet and headed to the little café beyond the rows of gas pumps.

Emerging from the john after taking a morning pee, I noticed that the girl who had been knocking on my window had given up on the truckers and was sitting by herself at a table. She had a cup of hot water in front of her and was mindlessly dipping a teabag in and out of the mug. The kid looked a little hungry, but there was something else in her distant, unmoving gaze out the window. Depression?

Might have been me projecting my own feeling of depression on her. It was the big reason for me being on the road right now. The deaths of friends recently had begun haunting me, pushed further by the death of my wife two years ago. My frustration with work just added to it, making for a good case of clinical depression. My daughter pushed me to a therapist's couch.

"It is perfectly normal to feel these things after the passing of a wife," the therapist had said, which didn't make me feel any better. "And it is obvious," the therapist went on, "that you have unresolved guilt over the deaths of these friends that came to light after your wife was gone." Blah, blah, blah.

She had offered therapy and pills. I took the pills. She pushed me to schedule appointments so that she could help me more.

I decided that this road trip would be my attempt at therapy. Might work. Might not. But it was cheaper than a weekly visit with a psychiatrist.

I watched the girl sipping at her hot tea. She looked so much like my daughter. I debated, then went to the counter to order.

"Give me a couple of those breakfast sandwiches, a couple orders of tater tots and a couple bear claws."

The old, fat guy behind the counter, whose apron struggled to contain his gut, wiped his greasy fingers off and tapped the order onto his screen.

"Drink?" he asked.

"Two big coffees with room for cream."

I paid, he handed me the coffee and said he'd bring the order out in a few minutes. I added cream and sugars to the two coffees, went to the girl's table and dropped into the seat across from her. She looked up startled. I handed her one of the coffees.

"Hope you like cream and sugar," I said.

The shocked look on her face morphed to skepticism. After a few seconds staring at me, remembering me from the Jeep, she glanced down at the steaming cup of caffeine, then back up at me. Her expression relaxed, then she reached out and took the coffee. A faint smile appeared on her lips, then disappeared to be replaced by a mumbled "Thanks."

I raised my cup in a sort of toast towards her. "It looked like you needed this as much as I did," I said. "I hope that's okay."

The kid guzzled a couple big swallows and nodded at me. I pointed to the bracelets on her wrist.

"Make those?"

She glanced at the colorful beads decorating her forearm, then back up at me, nodding.

"Nice," I said. After a few more moments of awkward quiet, I pointed to myself.

"Richard," I said. "Rich."

With a quick, hesitant smile she said "Zandy."

"Hi Zandy." I took a few sips of the brew. "Where you heading?"

Zandy shrugged.

It looked like I needed to start things off. "I'm heading east. Eastern Idaho."

She nodded and gulped some more coffee. Silence.

"A little town called Black River," I said.

She just nodded and swallowed more coffee.

I took another sip.

"This coffee sucks, doesn't it?" I said.

I finally got a little laugh out of her. And a nod.

We continued drinking.

"Portland," she said, setting her cup down, giving another faint smile. "Where I'm going."

"Got family there?"

She shrugged. "Sorta."

The fat guy waddled over with a tray of food and a skeptical look and set the tray down between us. I thanked him and he walked off, still giving the girl a suspicious stare. Zandy looked wide-eyed at the food.

"It looked like you were hungry," I said, "and I wanted to thank you for getting me out of that nightmare I was having, so dig in." I got that skeptical look from her again. "Really. No strings attached."

She grabbed a sandwich and tots and starting scarfing them down.

"Thanks, mister," she said with a mouthful of sausage and cheese.

"Rich."

"Yeah. Thanks."

She had a tattoo on her left arm, a furry little dog of some kind. I pointed to it. She swallowed another mouthful of sandwich.

"A dog I had when I was little," she said. "Scooter. He was my best buddy." Her eyes watered a little.

I nodded, nibbled on my sandwich and watched her relax a little, her neck and shoulders loosening up as she took another big bite and then downed the last of her coffee.

"I'll get you some more," I said standing and going towards the counter.

"Could I just have a coke?" she asked.

I came back to the table with the biggest cup of icy cola I could get from the fountain. She poured some down her throat, followed by some tater tots.

"My stepdad's in Portland," she said. "that's why I'm trying to get there. Going to start over there." She shot a thumb towards the trucks. "Trying to make a few extra bucks along the way. Didn't bring much."

"Where'd you come from?" I asked.

"My mom and I were in Detroit, but it was getting really shitty there. And my mom's an asshole."

I gave her a reassuring smile.

"Why are you going to . . . what was the name of that town?" she asked.

"Black River," I said. "It's where I was born."

"You got a trailer full of shit. Moving there?"

"I don't think so."

"You ain't sure?"

I shrugged. "Taking care of some old business."

"Where you coming from?" she asked.

"Bellingham. In Washington."

"Got a job?"

"Yeah. Police department."

She stopped chewing. "You're a cop?"

I laughed. "No. No cop. Computer nerd. I work in the forensics department. No badge."

"You get fired or something?" she asked.

"Nope. Taking a few weeks off."

She went back to gobbling down her food. I pushed my remaining tots to her side of the table and she scooped them out after a head bob of thanks.

Without looking at me, she asked "What were you dreaming out there when I woke you up? Looked pretty scary."

"Yeah, sorry," I said. "Weird dreams. Things that happened a long time ago."

"In that town you're going to?"

"Black River, yeah," I said, then paused and gave a half-nod.

"Never heard of Black River," she said.

"It's just a little farming town. I grew up on a small potato farm near there."

"You got family there?"

I shook my head. "Not anymore."

We ate in silence for a few minutes as truckers wandered in buying beer, coffee, sugary pastries and candy bars. Zandy watched the men going in and out of the place, with them occasionally giving her a look and then giving me a wink as they walked out.

"Why is it that all truckers seem to be old, fat white guys?" she asked.

I laughed. "That's a good question."

"You know, they all think you're a john," she said.

"I know," I said.

"Is that why you bought this food for me?" she asked.

I smiled. "No. You looked hungry and I just . . ." I was struggling to find the right words. "I just saw you were hungry and I wanted to do something. Sorry. It's a father thing." I gave a shrug and a little smirk. "So, as a result, you get a fat-soaked breakfast sandwich and nutritionally useless caffeine drinks."

Zandy laughed. She had a good laugh, a real laugh. I liked it.

I stood and stretched.

"Well, Zandy," I said, "I've got to get going. I've got five more hours on the road." I pointed to the food that she was finishing up. "Need anything else?"

"Thanks, I'm okay."

"Alright. Good luck with your new life." She smiled, nodded.

"Good luck with your old life," she said.

I laughed, nodded and headed out to the parking lot, drove the Jeep over to the gas pumps and filled up. I was back into the driver's seat, buckling up when Zandy ran up to the door. I zipped the window open.

She reached in and handed me one of the bracelets she had been wearing.

"Thanks for the grub," she said and turned to go.

"Hey," I called out. She turned and I pulled a fifty out of my wallet and handed it to her. "Why don't you try to hitch into Boise and use this to buy a bus ticket? Should be enough to get you to Portland."

She looked at the bill, puzzled, and then took it. She nodded a thank you at me, but it was like she wasn't sure how to handle a simple gift. "You want like a hand job or something for this?"

I laughed and shook my head. "Just get to Portland, okay."

She looked down at the bill and nodded. "Thanks," she said, without looking up. "Really." She turned and walked off.

I started up the Jeep and turned out of the truck stop. In the mirror I saw Zandy walking up to a Kenworth and knocking on the driver's door. I just smiled to myself. Oh, well.

My cell rang.

Glancing at the screen as it sat in its charging cradle on my dash, I saw the caller was Jessie.

I stared at the phone, a finger poised over the answer button. I had known this call would be coming and I should have been better prepared, but it was too late. If I didn't answer, she'd keep calling until I did.

I pressed it.

"Hi Jessie," I said.

"Dad, what the fuck are you doing in Idaho?"

Damn. I had forgotten that I had set up the Find My Phone app on our phones in case one of us lost a phone.

"How you doing, Jess?" I asked

"Dad?"

"Yeah?"

"I tried to call you at work," she said. "They told me you were on vacation. What are you doing, Dad?"

"Taking some time off, Jess," I said.

"To do . . .?" she left the question dangling.

"A couple things. Finish up my mom's estate stuff and get things sold. Clean up some other things."

"Like what?" she asked. "Dad, I'm worried. These last few months you've seemed so down about things and I know you're frustrated with work and stuff."

"I'm fine," I said, knowing she wouldn't believe me.

"Does this have something to do with that buddy of yours that died?" she asked.

I decided not to let her continue. "Look, I'm about to jump onto the freeway. I'll give you a call when I get set up in Black River, okay? Love you. Bye."

I disconnected, hit the gas and pulled onto I-84 heading east.

Two

Southern Idaho is a high desert, a plain sandwiched between mountains north, south and east. The elevation is above five thousand feet in most areas, making for hot, dry summers and cold, snowy winters. That climate, along with the unique makeup of the soil, made this part of the state perfect farmland, evident as I raced along the quiet freeway, half-way across the south end of the state. Freshly harvested fields of wheat, hay and potatoes bordered both sides of the interstate and I zipped the window of the Jeep down to take in that dusty, sweet earthy air, the same kind of air I had known growing up.

Harvest air.

I had to think a moment. It was the first week of October. Most of the wheat would have been harvested, third, maybe even fourth crop hay would have been baled and some potatoes harvested. There would probably be another three weeks of harvesting before the winter freezes started, then winter would shut it all down.

I loved this time of year in Eastern Idaho: crisp mountain air, deep blue skies, leisurely drifting clouds. Except for occasional visits, I had been gone for almost thirty years. That was hard for me to believe.

I passed the city of Twin Falls, then a couple hours later, north of Pocatello, I entered the Fort Lincoln Indian Reservation, land set aside for the Shoshone-Bannock tribes, forced into its confines more than a hundred-fifty years ago. It was mostly farmland, a few houses, the skeleton of an old Indian School and now, at every exit, a casino.

The freeway turned northeast, left reservation land and up ahead was my home town.

Black River was a typical little farm town of maybe nine thousand. The only building with more than three floors was the hospital with four. Like most Eastern Idaho towns, Black River's culture was conservative and heavily populated by members of the LDS church, The Church of Jesus Christ of Latter Day Saints, though there were a few Lutherans, Methodists and even a few Catholics, like my family, scattered around. The town bordered on its namesake river, which, a mile downstream, emptied into the Snake River, eventually flowing into the Columbia and then out to the Pacific Ocean. The Black River was given its name by early settlers who discovered its headwaters emerging from ancient lava beds in the hills east of town, whose dark rock blackened the water.

Other than the many giant agri-business farms in the area and the remaining smaller, private farms, the main employer in the town and the county was United States Potato, a huge potato processing plant that occupied more than a hundred acres of property on the western outskirts of the town. At the factory, potatoes were stored, processed and frozen to be used all over the country as fries, hash browns, tater tots and even just plain potatoes. Nearly everyone in Black River had either worked at USP at one time or knew someone who had.

It was late morning when I took the exit into Black River. It curved down and around onto Main, the town's central artery. It was bordered on both sides by fast food franchises, cheap motels and over-priced gas stations. I drove past these and after a quarter mile, I turned into a large, mostly empty parking lot in front of what had once been a decent sized strip mall, but was now a collection of nail salons, tattoo parlors, a dollar store and a take-out pizza joint. The mall had been built on a large, semicircular chunk of land that had been carved out of a little hillside, which the buildings butted up against. At the east end of the lot, standing alone, was a larger, two story building of weathered, brown clapboard siding and a red tiled roof. A big, occasionally flashing neon sign mounted on the roof announced the place as Marty's Tavern. There was a worn, maroon awning extending over the front of the building shading a porch that held a few worn tables and chairs for outdoor dining. A large A-frame sandwich board sat next to the entrance describing coffee drinks, pastries and breakfast specials.

I pulled in next to the only three cars parked there and got out. After stretching four hours of driving stiffness out of my old body, I walked into Marty's.

I was immediately hit by the smell of frying eggs and steaming coffee and the garbled sound of country music coming from cracked speakers high up on the walls. There were tables bordering the walls except on the west side where a tiny, apparently unused stage area was cluttered with cases of beer and soft drinks. The south side held the big old-fashion bar and some stools beyond which I could see the kitchen and a cook, barely visible through a cloud of greasy steam. To the right of the bar, there was a hallway leading down to what the sign said were bathrooms.

Even though there were twenty or so wooden tables in the space, only two were occupied. A big, middle-aged man sat alone with his laptop and a coffee in one corner and an old couple sat further away, drinking their coffee and reading a newspaper. A young woman was setting a plate with a couple muffins down in front of them. She pulled a ticket out of an apron pocket, dropped it onto the table, turned and hurried back towards the bar.

"Be with you in a sec," she said, passing me. The green-eyed, slender woman had long, naturally red hair tied up in a ponytail that fell to the middle of her back. She was in tight, faded jeans and a light, button up blouse. A black apron was tied up around her waist. She went around the bar and then to a point-of-sale screen where she entered something.

I followed her to the bar and sat on a stool there as she finished what she was doing. After pressing a button on the screen, she pulled a pad and pen out of her apron and turned to me.

"What can we get you?" she asked. She had a little bit of an accent, Eastern European maybe. She had a cute, narrow nose, strong eyebrows over almond shaped eyes and perfect porcelain skin. I figured she must only be in her mid-twenties. God, I was feeling old.

I realized she was looking at me with those clear green eyes, waiting.

"Sorry," I said. I glanced at the menu posted above the bar. "Can I get the egg and pancake special? And a large latte?"

"Anything else," she asked. I shook my head. "Have a seat. It'll be just a few minutes."

"Thanks," I said.

I dropped my jacket onto a table in the corner next to the stage and then headed down the hall to the men's room. After a leak and taking a few minutes at the sink to wash the sleep off me, I want back out where a steaming cup of coffee was waiting for me. I sat, sipped some down, took a deep breath and felt myself starting to relax from the long drive.

I hadn't been in the place in ten years but there were the same tables and chairs, same neutral tan paint on the walls and the same, worn hardwood floors. There was a new LED TV up in one corner facing out, silently showing some national newscast. And there was a security camera mounted in another corner that I didn't remember being there before. The kitchen that was visible beyond the bar was bigger than it had been with more ovens and coolers than it used to have.

The cook, a tall, skinny, kid with a curly pointy beard put a steaming plate of pancakes, eggs and bacon on the bar, took his earbuds out and said something to the redhead. She inspected the plate as she picked it up, added a napkin and utensils and then headed my way. The cook popped music back into his ears and danced back to the grill.

The redhead brought the plate back over to me, set it down and made sure I didn't need anything else.

I didn't.

On her way back towards the bar, the big man who was sitting by himself working on his laptop called out "Miss?"

He said the word with a sarcastic tone which made me take another look at the guy. He was one of those guys that might have once been handsome, but the graying skin on his face, the wrinkles and bags around his lightly bulging eyes hinted at way too many vodkas and cigarettes. In the next ten years he would age twenty.

"Miss?" he said again.

There was an odd look of frustration tinged with anger on the redhead's face as she stopped and turned towards him, putting on a face of forced politeness. He waved her to come to his table. It was clear that she didn't want to but she went to him anyway. He reached out to take her hand but she pulled it away. Then he said something that I couldn't hear which elicited a terse response from her, after which she turned and walked back behind the bar. I saw the bearded kid lean over the service counter and give her that "you okay?" look, to which she nodded. But as she went over to the point-of-sale screen at the end of the bar, the man got up from his table and went to the bar where she was working. When she saw him, she shook her head but he stood there saying something quietly, but forcefully to her, with strong, firm gestures. The bearded kid leaned over the kitchen bar and said something to the man but he pointed an angry finger at him, said something and the kid turned back to whatever he was frying.

The man turned to the girl to say something but she turned away. Angrily, he reached out and grabbed an arm to stop her. She turned back to him and tried to shake his arm off.

I didn't like what I was seeing, so I got up from my table, walked up to the bar and plopped myself down onto the stool next to where the big man was standing. When he realized I was there, he released his grip on her arm. The girl looked at me, then him.

"How are you doing," I asked her.

Before she could answer, the big man broke in.

"We were having a private conversation," he said in an accent that seemed similar to hers. "Private."

I looked at him.

"Well, it didn't look to me like she wanted to have that conversation," I said.

"She did."

She waved a palm at me. "It's okay," she said quietly.

I looked at him. "Is that why you had to grab her arm? Because she wanted to have this conversation?"

"This is between me and her," he said. "Now, I want you to leave so we can finish this."

"Actually," I said firmly, but politely, "I want you to leave. Right now. Gather up your laptop and your jacket and get out of here."

He stared at me, open-mouthed.

"What the fuck?" he said.

"Pack up and leave or I call the cops to drag you out."

The woman tried to interrupt. "Please, it's okay."

"Shut the fuck up, Jia," the man said to her. Then he was back to me. "Who the hell do you think you are, ordering me around. You aren't the boss here."

"Actually," I said, "I am. I own this place."

The kid in the kitchen stopped working and turned to look and the girl stared wide-eyed at me.

"Mr. Willis?" she asked.

I shot her a smile and a nod, then turned to the obnoxious fat man and put on a polite smile.

"Now," I said, "get the fuck out of here before I have the police drag your lard ass out for me."

Angry silence.

He glared at her, then back at me.

I stiffened.

I may be close to six feet tall, but the big guy had at least sixty pounds on me and would likely clobber me in a fist fight. Luckily for me, he just shot me an angry look, gave the girl a stare and stomped out the door with all his stuff. We could hear the angry squeal of his wheels as he screamed out of the parking lot.

The kid in the kitchen let out a big sigh.

I turned to the young woman and extended my hand. "You must be Jia Lash," I said. "Rich Willis."

She shook my hand.

"Nice to finally meet you, Mr. Willis," she said. "This is Tyler." She indicated the beard in the kitchen. He came to the kitchen window and flashed a wave. He was twenty pounds lighter than me but two inches taller. His thick, curly beard matched his hair and he had the pale skin of a game console jockey. His small eyes, though, had a mischievous glint.

"Hi Tyler," I said. "And guys, call me Rich, okay?"

"So what the hell's goin' on," Tyler asked.

I explained that my mother bought Marty's Tavern twenty years ago. Called The Den at that time, it was a seedy, rundown joint that my father would frequent after his shift at the US Potato processing plant that was outside of town. She didn't buy it as a favor to my dad, though, she bought it so she could keep an eye on him, fixing it up and naming it after him. He went to his grave hating the place ten years ago and then my mom died six years later, leaving the place to me along with our old farmhouse and a small house in town, both rented out now. Jia already knew most of that, but I gave Tyler the Reader's Digest version.

"So where you been?" Tyler asked. "Jia didn't even recognize you and she's been running this place for like a year."

"I live up in Washington, north of Seattle," I said. "Mom's estate attorney has been handling this place, the rentals and the hiring."

Jia said to Tyler "We've emailed and texted back and forth but we had never met."

"Until now," Tyler said. "And just in time to chase off that fat fuck."

"Yeah," I said. "What's up with that guy, Jia?"

"Volkov," Tyler said.

"Volkov," I repeated. "What's he want?"

She shook her head. "It's just a personal thing. He's not really a problem."

"He Russian or something?" I asked.

"Ukrainian. Like me," she said.

"The guy's been here a few times," Tyler said to me. "I don't like him."

"Please," Jia insisted to both of us. "I'll take care of it."

I could tell it was more of a problem than Jia wanted to admit, but it was also clear she didn't want to talk about it, so I let it go.

I pointed up. "Is there still a little apartment on the second floor?"

Jia nodded. "It's got boxes and shit all over but it's there."

"Good," I said. "If you don't mind, I'm going to move in for a little while."

Jia was surprised and was about to ask something, but Tyler was quicker.

"That's awesome! How long you staying?" Tyler asked.

I shrugged. "Don't know for sure. Depends on some of the estate stuff I want to finish up."

"I'll get the key," Jia said going back into the kitchen, "and I'll walk you up there."

She emerged with a small ring of keys.

"Marie and Lee should be here shortly," she said to Tyler. "I'll be back down in a few minutes."

He gave her a thumbs up and me a wave as Jia came around the bar and waved at me to follow her down the long, cave-like hall.

"In the morning it's just me and Tyler," she said while I followed behind. "Marie and Lee come in to help with the lunch crowd. Marie on the tables, Lee on the stove."

We passed two rest room doors on the right and could see a marked exit at the end of the hall.

"That goes out to the dumpsters," she said.

Just to the left of the exit door, there was a doorway and then creaking, wooden stairs that cut back and up to the second floor. I followed her up and at the top of the stairs she indicated a door to her left.

"That's still a storeroom. Just paper goods, cleaners and shit like the security camera, the WIFI thing and some other electrical stuff that I don't know anything about."

She unlocked the door that was to our right and handed me the key. I walked in. The dusty little studio apartment was about like I remembered and as Jia described, littered with boxes, broken chairs and old furniture. In front of me was the tiny kitchenette and off to my left was a small living room area with windows that looked out over the parking lot. To the right was the old double bed my dad sometimes slept in when he was too drunk to drive. There was also a door to a closet and another door to the tiny little bathroom. I turned back to Jia who was standing inside the door.

"This will work fine," I said. "Can I park my Jeep around back to unload?"

"You can keep it back there. No one else parks there." she said. "Want some help cleaning this up?"

"I think I can handle it."

She nodded, started to go and then stopped. "Can I ask you something?"

"Of course," I said.

A pause. Then a deep breath.

"Are you here to sell this place?"

Jia was good at coming to the point.

"I hope you aren't," she continued. "I really like Marty's," she said. "I have good employees and great customers. And, to be honest, I can't afford to lose this job. I have a mother I'm taking care of and jobs in this town are hard to find. Really hard. So I'd appreciate knowing what you have in mind."

I wanted to make her feel better and say that nothing was going to change, but I liked Jia and thought she should know where I stood. She had a simple sincerity about her that was refreshing.

"Jia," I started haltingly, "To be honest, I really don't know. I came here to clean a few things up and my mom's estate is one of those. That includes Marty's and her two houses. So . . . do I keep all this that you have here and try to manage things like rentals, employees and taxes from Bellingham or sell them all?" I shrugged. "I just don't know yet, but look, I promise that I'll let you know just as soon as I have it figured out."

"Okay," she said. "But I want you to know, I have put a lot of work into this place. I've got the menu tweaked just right, I've got a reliable kitchen staff, good servers and I'm starting to make a life here in Black River for me and my mother." She swallowed and took a deep breath. "So, if you do decide to sell, could you maybe talk about selling it to me?"

I was a little startled.

"You?"

She nodded. "I don't know where I'd find the money or even how, but if there was a way, I'd do it."

I looked at the young redhead. I could see determination in her eyes and a strength to her voice. What could it hurt to give her the first shot when it came time to sell? I gave her a smile and a nod.

"That's a deal."

Jia seemed a little surprised that I agreed so easily and replied with a grateful "Thank you."

"I better get back for the lunch rush," she said after a moment and started toward the stairs. "Let me know if you need anything."

I called after her. "Thanks, Jia."

As her footsteps trailed down the noisy stairs, I looked around the place. Though dusty, junk filled and smelling faintly of the fried bar food that was cooking directly below, with some work, I thought I could make it livable for the short stay I had planned. I could toss most of the junk into the storeroom across the hall before I pulled the Jeep and trailer around and got all my things in. That should only take a couple hours.

After that, I was going to go visit my parents.

Then Jeannie.

Tomorrow, the sheriff.

THREE

Driving through Black River was like driving through a ghost town. Not a town full of empty buildings, but a town full of the ghosts of people and places that weren't there anymore. The music store where I bought my first album and where I took my first guitar lessons is a nail salon. The J.C. Penney's where mom took me to buy school clothes every year is a thrift shop. And the drug store where I bought my first Superman comic book has that same façade but now hawks tequila instead of Tylenol.

I took a left on Main to head out of town passing the ghosts of ten-year-old me being chased across the street by Jeannie Sorenson and the shadows of my grade school buddies walking from the public Junior High School to the little Catholic school we attended.

Ghosts.

Half a mile outside the north end of town and across the railroad tracks I turned into the Black River Cemetery, a large grass and tree covered park that could have passed for a picnic area and playground except for the granite blocks, crosses and statuettes popping up every ten feet.

I guided the Jeep along the dirt roads around the rectangular sections of the cemetery, some graves decorated with flowers or flags. In an older section, I drove by the graves of my father's parents, who I never met, along with dead aunts and uncles, long forgotten. Nearby, were the graves of my parents beneath a black granite monument announcing "WILLIS" in a bold, deeply carved script. I pulled off to the side of the road and laid some flowers at the base of the headstone, taking a few moments there, as i had every time I visited. Even though i wasn't remotely religious, something about the ritual of laying flowers and spending a moment remembering them was . . . comforting. After a few minutes, I turned to go back to the Jeep and stopped, recognizing a name on a headstone: a classmate from high school, Shannon Baumgartner. She had drowned early in our senior year and had been one of my teammates on the tennis team. I hadn't known her well, but seeing a gravestone of someone I had been in school with was a mortality reminder.

Back in the Jeep and after another turn, I pulled off to the side of the road near a little kiosk inside a three-sided shelter next the sexton's office. I went inside, where there was a display screen, keyboard and thumb wheel below a sign that read "Cemetery Directory". I punched a key and the screen came to life with a search prompt. I typed.

After a second, the screen filled with a list of Sorenson's buried here, their first names, a burial date and a grid number that indicated their location in the cemetery. I scrolled down the list and finally found Jeannie, her parents, her older brother and her older sister who had all passed away before her. They were located together in one section. A map of the grounds had been tacked to the wall next to the terminal. I ran a finger to the Sorenson location, jumped in the Jeep and drove to that section.

Between a pair of small poplars, I found the simple headstone for Jeannie's parents, showing the years they were born and the years they died. On each side of the larger headstone were two low, small granite markers for the two older siblings.

But where was Jeannie? I didn't see a headstone for her, but saw a brass plate half hidden in the un-mowed grass. I pushed the grass away and saw the name: Jean Marie Sorenson.

Seeing her name, I couldn't keep the images of the girl I grew up with out of my head. In fact, one of my first memories is of me and Jeannie, two four year-old kids, out in the middle of a pasture surrounded by curious cows while in the distance I could hear my mother calling out our names trying to find us.

I had had some kind of argument with my mother and so Jeannie and I decided to run away. We gathered up some graham crackers and a kid's canteen full of milk and took off across the fields. I don't remember how far we got or how we ended up there, but somehow Jeannie and I ended up in a cow pasture where my mother saw us amidst a herd of docile bovines. She pushed her way between the animals and dragged us back to the house where I got a serious spanking.

The image of Jeannie standing and looking at me as my mother delivered her punishment morphed back to the image of that same girl, buried in a potato field.

I shook my head and rubbed my eyes to clear the vision away, but no matter what I did, the picture of Jeannie, a friend I grew up with, lying dead and alone in a field was burned into my brain.

"I'm so, so sorry, Jeannie," I said. "I should have stayed connected. Should have been here."

I stopped.

Nothing I could say or think or do could help Jeannie now. Nothing.

What I was going to do was going to be for me. Maybe it was penance, maybe it was closure, maybe it was to pay a debt. It didn't matter. I had to do it. I had to find out who did this to Jeannie.

FOUR

"I'd like to speak to someone about accessing a cold case file."

I stood at the desk of a Brannon County clerk, who's dusty name plate announced was Geraldine Honas. A gapped-toothed, middle-aged matronly woman wearing an out-of-style flowered dress and a permanent frown, she smelled of too much deodorant and too much hairspray. She looked me up and down, set down what must have been her second cup of morning coffee and lowered the paperback book she was reading.

"A what? A cold case file?" she asked. "From here?"

I nodded. "I understand that in this state, cold case files are available to the general public."

She was still confused. "How old is this case?"

"Twenty-eight years."

"I'm gonna have to check with the sheriff on this. Name?" she asked.

"Richard Willis."

She pointed to a row of old metal chairs against one wall. "Sit. I'll see what we can do. Coffee over there, if you want."

I did want.

I grabbed a watery, lukewarm latte from the little coffee machine in the corner and sat myself down. It had been a rough night and I needed the caffeine.

It had been that dream again, except it had been more graphic than the night before.

There I was again, running down a dream hall that never seems to end, heart monitors beeping, daughter yelling at me to hurry, my friend Sean's emaciated face staring desperately, phones ringing, more angry voices, then a dirty hand thrusting up at me out of the ground, Jeannie's voice asking "Where did you go Richie?"

I took a long swallow of bad courthouse coffee to shake off the dream.

My pocket buzzed at me.

Yanking the phone out and looking at the screen I could see it was Jessie again.

"Hey Jess."

"I thought you were gonna call me back yesterday Dad," she said.

"Sorry. It took me a little longer to get settled and then it was getting late."

"So where are you now?"

"At the county courthouse here in Black River."

"You thinking about doing some work for them?"

I laughed. "I doubt this little town needs a computer forensics tech for much."

"Under arrest?" she joked.

"Trying to see if I can look at a cold case file here. A neighbor girl that I grew up with, a girl that was murdered here a long time ago."

"Oh, I'm so sorry, Dad. Was it someone I knew?"

"It was before you were born, a couple years after I graduated high school and was off at college. I had lost touch with her and then found out she had been killed. They never found out who did it or why."

"So sad," she said. "They'll let you look at the case?"

"In most jurisdictions they allow civilians to review cold case files. Some have even been solved after a civilian or even a family member took an interest in an old case."

"Dad, you aren't thinking you— "

"Just curious," I interrupted. "Nothing more."

The clerk came around the corner from the hall followed by a short, heavy-set man in a light brown sheriff's uniform. He had a massive pile of thick brown hair over a wide, jowly face, decorated with small, lively brown eyes, a narrow pointy nose and a nearly lipless mouth. She pointed towards me, said something and then waddled back to her desk. The uniformed man folded his arms and leaned against the door jamb looking at me, with a weird half-smile.

"Gotta go, Jess," I said, clicking off and getting to my feet.

"Richie Willis," he said.

I stared back at him. He let out a big laugh and came at me with an extended hand.

"Don't you recognize me?" he asked. "Gil. Gil Froman."

"Gil?" And it hit me. "Gilly?"

He nodded.

"Gilly!" I ignored his extended hand and we embraced like old friends. "Gilly! How the hell are you?"

"Just great, Richie," he said.

"You work for the sheriff now?" I asked.

"He is the sheriff," interrupted Geraldine.

"Are you shitting me?" I asked.

He pointed to the brass on his shirt. "Even got a real badge."

I laughed.

Gil turned to the clerk. "I was a sergeant and this guy was my captain," he said.

"In the Army?" she asked.

"Oh no, much worse than the Army. Catholic school," I said.

The woman just stared at us, eyes shifting back and forth between us.

Gil laughed. "It was between like first and what, maybe third grade? We always played army at recess."

"An army of about a dozen kids," I tossed in. "We would have battles, take prisoners, plan campaigns."

"Richie was the captain," Gil said. "I was sergeant. Jerry something was lieutenant, right? We would plan out our campaigns at the morning recess and at the noon recess, battle 'em out."

"Who was the enemy? The public schools?" she asked.

"Germans," Gil said. "We were watching too many war movies on TV. The kids a grade below usually played the Nazis. They always lost the battles."

"We more or less grew out of the playing army stage," I said, "and then Gil transferred to a public school and we lost touch. You moved somewhere, right?"

"Yeah," he said. "My dad got a job up in Montana."

Gil explained that after a six-year stint in the army, he came back to Black River and joined the sheriff's department. It took a while, but he rose through the ranks and finally got himself elected sheriff. That had been ten years earlier.

"Come on back to my office," Gill said pointing back down the hall. "We'll catch up and then talk about cold cases."

Gil's office was about what I expected from an eighty-year-old municipal structure: retrofitted AC, out-of-place double-pane windows and high ceilings that dangled ugly fluorescent fixtures giving the space a greenish glow.

Gil plopped into his chair behind his too modern desk and I settled into an uncomfortable vinyl and metal visitor's chair. We talked about school, old friends, the changes in the town where we were born. I told him about being a computer forensics technician for the Bellingham police department and he seemed surprised.

"I'm a little surprised too," I said. "I was going to be an actor or writer. Turned out I was better at writing computer programs than epic novels so I became a programmer, then a hacker and then--"

"A computer hacker?" Gil asked.

"Let us call it a security consultant, okay?"

Gil laughed.

"I started a little company that did data security work and we were occasionally asked by local law enforcement to assist in things like data recovery, unlocking cell phones, cracking passcodes. That kind of stuff. Then the Bellingham police department asked me if I would like to become an employee and create a data forensics department for them. The short version is that I liked the idea, sold my business to my daughter and joined the police department."

"Geraldine said you wanted to look at an old case," Gil said. "Is that for something up in Washington?"

"No," I said, "this is a personal thing. I'm taking some time off to clean up my mother's estate and while I'm here I wanted to see what had happened in this case."

"What kind of case was it?" he asked.

"Murder."

"Oh."

"She was a good friend that was killed after I went off to college." I snapped my fingers as I remembered something. "In fact, you knew her."

"I did?"

"Yes. She went to St. Mary's just like you and me. Jeannie Sorenson. She was in our class."

He shook his head. "Not sure I remember her."

"Sure you do," I said. I stood and went around to his side of his desk. "Can I use your computer?"

"Uh . . ." I had already swiveled his computer screen around towards me and reached for the keyboard. Gil was a little startled. "Sure. Go ahead."

I typed in the URL for my online data storage and logged into it. I navigated to where I had been storing images.

"I've been scanning old pictures and saving them here. Give me a second."

I navigated through some folders and finally found what I wanted, brought it up on the screen and swiveled it back. Gil stared at a black and white image showing a couple dozen little second graders, all dressed in white, holding candles and catechisms, standing in front of a church's altar, flanked by a priest on one side and some nuns on the other.

"Our first communion picture?" he asked.

I pointed to a skinny little kid in the front row looking terrified.

"There you are," I said.

"Holy shit," he murmured. He pointed to another shy looking kid in the middle of the pack. "You, right?"

"Yup." I started pointing out friends. "There's Joey, remember him? There's Barry Hatch, his dad owned the Rexall Drug Store, I think." My finger next landed on a tall, skinny girl with long, thick curly hair in an obviously handed-down, ill-fitting, frilly white dress. "That's Jeannie."

"Oh yeah. I remember her," he said. "She was the girl you said you were gonna marry." He laughed.

"That was in first grade, Gilly."

"Still funny." He stared at the picture for a moment. "Yeah. Jeannie. She was so cute. So, what happened to her?"

"Well. . . "I stood and sat myself back down in the visitor's chair.

"Two years after high school, Jeannie's body was found half-buried in an old potato field. Beaten to death."

"Shit."

"Somewhere in high school, I drifted away and lost touch with Jeannie and then I was off to college. I guess I was a sophomore in college when my mother called and told me about her being found. They never caught anyone, never even found out why she had been killed."

"That was like twenty-eight years ago?"

"This year is supposed to be our thirty-year class reunion. On the class Facebook page, someone posted a scan of the newspaper article about it and the fact that her killer was never found. That's part of what sparked this visit."

"You aren't thinking you are going to play detective and solve this, are you?" he asked.

"Gil, do I look like a detective?" I asked. "I'm just a computer nerd. A computer nerd who feels deep guilt for losing touch with a friend. I'd just like to know more about what happened."

"Sure, I get that." He leaned on his elbows and folded his hands looking at me. "As far as I know, we've never had anyone ask to look at a cold case before and because we are usually pretty short-handed, we don't dig into them as much as we should. But I can't think of a reason not to let you take a peek."

"Records haven't been computerized?" I asked.

"We've been working on it," Gil said. "We are only eighteen or nineteen years back so far, though. Scanning things in from newest cases to oldest. This one is probably still sitting in an old cardboard box downstairs."

"I'd love to take a look, if I could."

Gil pounded a few keys into his computer, navigated and typed more until he had the page he wanted, mouse-scrolling down a long list. He found what he was looking for, reached for his office phone and pressed a button. Over the phone's speaker came a thin voice.

"Hey Gil," the voice said.

"Wesley, can you bring an old case up to the conference room?" Gil asked. "Case number 85-1009-21M."

"That's an old one, Gil," the voice said. "It's gonna be buried at the bottom of a fuckin' pile."

"Yeah. So, unearth it and bring it up."

"Now?"

"I'll be waiting."

Gil ended the call and lifted his heft out of his chair. "Wes is a lazy asshole. Come on. I'll show you where the conference room is."

"Thanks Gil," I said. "I really appreciate this."

"Anything for you, Captain!" Gil slapped me on the shoulder and we made our way back out to Geraldine's desk.

"Swapping grade school war stories?" she asked not looking up from her work.

"Comparing scars," I said.

"Richie here is going to look through an old case," Gil said to Geraldine, who displayed a little surprise. "Wes is gonna bring it up to the conference room in a few minutes. Show my friend here where that is. And give him anything he needs, okay? He knows a little bit about how things are handled. He works for a police department out in Washington."

Geraldine reluctantly dropped what she was working on, stood and turned towards another hallway. "Fine. Follow me," she said.

Gil gave me a big bear hug.

"Good to see you, old buddy," he said. "Let's get together one of these nights. Maybe I can have you over for dinner?"

"That sounds great."

"I've got to meet some people downtown right now, but you take your time with the file and if you can't get through it all today, you can come back anytime. Just don't take anything home."

"Of course," I said. "Thanks, Gilly."

With a wave, he was gone.

"Come along, Captain," Geraldine said.

I turned and followed her down a plaster-walled, fluorescently glowing hall to where she stopped, opened a door and flipped on more old fluorescents to reveal a small conference room that was probably fifteen feet by fifteen feet with a large, fake oak conference table and chairs in the center.

She waved an arm at the table as though she was bestowing a prize on me. "Here you go!"

As Geraldine bumped around the room grumbling about sloppy men and removing a few discarded coffee cups and papers from the table, I asked "Gil a pretty good sheriff?"

She tossed some moldy paper cups into the corner trash can.

"He's a good guy."

"A good sheriff, though," I said.

She stopped and looked at me. A smile. "He's a good guy."

My puzzlement was obvious and she came a little closer and spoke in a slightly hushed voice.

"Between you and me, he's not the most ambitious guy around. Likes the job, shows up every day, schmoozes with everyone and keeps everyone happy."

"Ah."

"But he's not gonna go out and find more work, like in a cold case. He just does what he needs to do. But a good guy."

A gawky and balding, older man came in breathing heavily and dropped a small, dusty, brown cardboard box on the table.

"There ya' go," he said in a gravelly, cigarette-aged voice. "Not a big file." He winked at the clerk and handed me a piece of paper. "Sign that, will ya'?

The paper indicated the case number I was checking out with the date and time. I set it on the table, printed my name, phone number and email address and signed it. The man grabbed it.

"Thanks," he said. "Later, Geraldine." He vanished down the hall.

I slipped into a chair in front of the box and took a long, deep breath. Geraldine finished cleaning and saw the look on my face.

"You okay there?" she asked.

I just nodded.

"Okay, then. Looks like you're set," she said.

"Thanks."

The woman worked her way around the table gathering up the last bits of meeting detritus before exiting to the hall and closing the door.

I stared at that old box for a long time then brushed the dust off the lid, opened the box and started through the box's contents: vacuum sealed bags of clothing, envelopes of photo negatives, detective's notes, coroner reports, crime scene photos and lots of paper. It took me hours to go through things, interrupted only by Geraldine checking on me under the guise of coffee refills, but I finally had an outline of what had happened.

After graduating high school, Jeannie had stayed in Black River to help on her parents' farm, but then her father was killed in a farming accident, after which her mother decided she couldn't run the farm without her husband and leased it out, dying not long after that. That forced Jeannie and her little sister, Julie, to get jobs in town at US Potato. She had been working there for more than a year when on Friday, October 2nd, she disappeared. On the following Monday, a farmer named Turkel, who was leasing the ground, was tilling up a potato field when he noticed a bright red shoe in front of his tractor and a pile of dirt that didn't look right. He stopped and jumped off to take a look. He grabbed the shoe but realized it was on a foot that was sticking up out of the ground. He let go and jumped back, tripping and falling flat on his ass. That's when he noticed that at the other side of the mound, a woman's hand was sticking out of the ground. The closest phone was in the Sorenson house. Turkel ran to the house and called the sheriff, who at that time, was Roland Katzendorf. I remembered him because he had gone to school with my mother and the Katzendorfs went to the same church. I made a note to see if he was still around.

After that, it looked like Katzendorf had gone by the book. They had taped off the area, took hundreds of photos, scoured the ground for any item that might be evidence and when the medical examiner arrived, they slowly uncovered the body of a woman, apparently beaten to death and then buried.

Over the next few days the investigation by detectives and the medical examiner determined that Jeannie had probably been killed late the Friday night before or early Saturday morning. Because Turkel had been tilling the field, any footprints or drag marks were gone, but due to blood found around the area, it was theorized that she had been chased to that spot where she was then beaten and buried. The M.E. didn't believe that a weapon had been used, but that the killer had beaten and kicked her and then had buried her in the plowed field.

The most horrific part of the whole thing was the M.E.'s determination that Jeannie had been alive when the killer buried her.

Deputies interviewed family, friends, coworkers and neighbors. There were interviews with her two surviving siblings, older brother Pete and younger sister, Julie, but no interview with any boyfriend in the file, nothing in there about money problems, nothing about enemies, but also nothing about close friends. Reading through the detective interviews, it was becoming clear that no one seemed to know her very well at all.

Why had Jeannie become so isolated, seemingly so estranged from everyone? Who in the world would want to kill her and then bury her alive in her own parents' potato field?

Digging through the remaining detective notes and interview statements didn't help at all. After about six months, the notes became fewer and sketchier. Since there had been no new information, there had been less and less activity. Eventually, case notes only appeared every few years. Being an open case, a detective might pull the file once or twice a year, make a few phone calls, scribble a few notes and then move on to something more interesting. With every passing year and no apparent change, Jeannie's death became more distant, less important. Law enforcement would move on to more immediate, more resolvable cases. Jeannie would be forgotten.

Not by me.

Not this time.

I snapped pictures of everything I figured I'd need, then carefully repacked the dusty cardboard box and took it out to Geraldine, who was entering some long document into her computer.

"All done?" she asked without looking up.

"I think so. Thank Gil for me, will you?"

"Yeah."

I was at the door of the office, but stopped and turned.

"Hey Geraldine," I said. She kept typing.

"Uh huh?"

"How long have you lived in Black River?"

She stopped typing and looked at me, doing the math. "Well . . .my dad moved us here when I was eight." She did more math, then brightened when she figured out the answer. "I guess we've been here forty-nine years. Wow. Why?"

"You went to Black River High?"

"Sure."

"Did you know any of the Sorenson kids? They lived out on Marsh Road, on the other side of the river."

"I knew who they were," she said. "Small town, small high school, but I didn't really know 'em."

"This case I was reading," I started, "Jeannie Sorenson. It mentions that her parents had died and there are interviews with one brother and one sister but not the two older Sorenson kids who had already died. Any idea what happened to them?"

Geraldine thought a moment.

"Car accident, I think," she said. "Let me look it up. Sorenson with an 'O' or with an 'E'?"

"O."

She began typing. "Was her sister named Joannie?"

"Jackie," I answered.

"Oh yeah, that's right."

Geraldine typed the name in, waited, typed a bit more, then tapped a manicured nail on the screen. "There it is. Sorenson. One car traffic accident."

She was reading a report from the screen, then summarized it for me.

"It looks like Jackie, John and a third person, Richard Sato—know him?" I shook my head, and she continued. "On the way back to Black River from Idaho Falls they ran off the freeway at a high rate of speed out north of town."

"Where all the lava rocks are?"

She nodded. "The car hit some of the rocks head-on. They were all killed instantly." She was still reading. "No sign that they even tried to brake. Just wham! Straight into the rocks at 90."

"Damn," I said to myself. "What year was that?"

She scrolled down searching. "The year before Jeannie Sorenson was killed."

I stared at her. That meant that in the two years before she died, she lost her parents and a brother and a sister.

Geraldine was still reading.

"Listen. It looks like the brother was driving and the toxicology report says he had a blood alcohol level of 0.22 along with strong traces of cocaine and meth."

"What?"

"That's what it says." She stopped reading and looked around the office. "You know, I'm not supposed to be reading you all this." But then she just shrugged and went back to reading.

"John? Meth?" I said. "I had always thought of him as such a straight, sober guy. What the hell happened to him?"

"No clue, but the tox screens show that it wasn't just him. They were all pretty drunk and all probably pretty high. Must have been quite a party in I.F."

"What the hell . . ." I said. Geraldine saw the confusion on my face. I shook my head at her. "It's just me. I had grown up with the Sorenson family, we all went to the same school and I just had this image in my head of John Sorenson, the altar boy, John Sorenson the boy scout. I guess I just forgot that things happen and people change. The kids I knew just changed."

"Or," she said, "maybe the kids you knew, were never the kids you knew."

FIVE

By early afternoon, I was back out at a table at Marty's, transferring notes and images from my phone to my laptop. A bigger crew was working the place and Jia introduced them. Marie Morales was a short, wide woman in her early twenties with a cute smile and infectious high pitched laugh. With her big plastic glasses and lavender tinted hair, she reminded me of a chubby little Looney Tunes mouse as she waddled around tables, bracelets jangling on each wrist and a crucifix bouncing on her substantial chest, dangling from a silver chain necklace. Lee Hidalgo, in his early forties, red-nosed, with a swollen face and belly was working with Tyler in the kitchen, hopefully cooking up the patty melt and fries I had ordered twenty minutes before.

While waiting, I dug into my contacts and dialed an old high school buddy. Out of a cacophony of machine noises and distant voices I heard "Hello?"

"Sam the man!" I said.

It took him a minute.

"Rich?" he asked.

"How ya' doin' buddy?" I asked. Sam Seeger had gone off to college after high school like me, but had moved back to Black River a few years later to teach at the local elementary school. "What's all that noise?"

"Milking time," he said. "Helping my brother out. He's short-handed on his place this week. How ya been?"

We exchanged all the usual chatter that goes on between friends who haven't heard from each other in a while, talking about jobs, kids, wives and girlfriends. While we were going through this ritual, Jia brought my sandwich and fries over and then sat herself down across from me, snagged one of my fries and scarfed it down. I gave her a what-the-hell look and she just winked at me.

"Hey Sam," I said after we had finished all the catching up, "I'm trying to find somebody. Do you remember the guy who was sheriff when we were in school? He lived out on your side of town, I think."

"Uh . . . Katzendorf?" Sam asked.

"Yeah. Is he still around?"

"Still around," he said.

"Know where he lives?" I asked.

"You remember the old Cook place down the road past my folks' house?"

"Oh yeah. I used to date Emily Cook. Her dad was an asshole. Didn't like me."

"Katzendorf bought their place after he lost re-election a few years ago," Sam said. "Why would you want to see that old guy?"

"I wanted to ask him about an old case he handled. Remember Jeannie Sorenson?" I asked.

"Jeannie . . . oh wow . . . of course I remember. We rode the same school bus into town every day. From first grade to sometime during high school when I started driving. Maybe when I was a sophomore? So sad. She was so smart. I remember she always had her face buried in a book. Like from second grade on. Smarter than all the rest of us."

"How do ya' mean?"

"Helped with homework. Mine especially. I had a hard time in school. Once, maybe fourth or fifth grade, I was going to get an 'F' in History and the teacher gave me one chance to redeem myself with some sort of two-page essay about the Oregon Trail. In the course of one bus ride home, Jeannie dictated an essay about what was called the Utter Party Massacre on the trail by where Twin Falls is now. Got a 'C' out of that. Saved my butt. They never caught the guy, did they?"

"Unsolved case," I said, glaring at Jia who had managed to steal another fry.

"Jeannie was a sweet kid," he said. " She had such thick, long, curly blonde hair. A bubbly, happy laugh, I remember. Her brother was just the opposite of her."

"Peter?"

"Yeah. Unhappy kid. Rough and tumble, fighting a lot. Always a little banged up."

"I didn't remember that," I said. Jia was stealing another fry. "Hey Sam, I've gotta go. Maybe—."

"Are you in town?" he asked.

"Uh huh."

"Did you bring your guitar?"

"I always have my guitar," I said

"That's great! Let's get the guys together and jam one of these nights."

"I'd really like that," I said. "We could even do it here at Marty's."

"Your mom's place?"

"Yeah. Decent little stage here, enough room for the whole band."

"Let's do it," Sam said. "I'll try to get hold of the guys."

"That would be cool," I agreed, then thought of something. "Look, if you are free Sunday night, bring your guitar and you and I can sing and play a little here."

"I'll check with my wife to make sure she hasn't got anything planned for us. I'll let you know about Sunday night. Good talking with you Rich," he said.

"Same."

I clicked off, sat the phone down and looked at the thief sitting across from me.

"Hear everything you needed to hear?" I asked.

She picked up another fry. "You have a band?"

"Had. Before college. We just get together every few years to jam."

"But you play?"

"Not well."

"You should play here," she said pointing to the stage with my French fry. "Like every Friday and Saturday night."

"What?"

"Live music is a big draw," Jia said. "You guys could play here."

I stopped her with a head shake.

"I may not be here that long," I said, "and what if whoever buys this place doesn't want live music?" I closed up my laptop and pulled the sandwich and fries over as Jia snagged another fry off.

"So you still think you might sell it?" she asked chomping on my fry.

"I've only been here a day," I said. "Give me some time, but yeah, probably."

She nodded taking another one of my fries. "Well . . . just remember to give me a shot at this place first." She swallowed the fry and eyed the basket. "So what's that about a murdered girl?"

I pushed the stringy spuds towards her. "Would you like a fry?"

"Sure, thanks!" she said and took the whole basket and started scarfing the rest of the fries down. "I never get time to eat here. Too busy," she said.

I gave up on the fries and started in on my sandwich, just to keep her from getting it. She gestured at me with a French fry.

"Murdered girl," she reminded me.

"A friend of mine," I said. "Long time ago. Almost 30 years."

"Who did it?"

I shrugged. "Never caught anyone."

Jia pushed the loose red hair out of her eyes and gave me a puzzled look. "You're digging into it?"

I didn't look at her, just kept eating. But she didn't give up.

"Well? The story?"

I looked up. Again, something about her face and those green eyes said honesty was best. I took a deep breath. I took a few bites of my sandwich, chewed, swallowed and then started.

"Like a lot of people around here," I said, "I grew up on a farm. I was an only child. My parents were very close friends with our neighbors at another farm, the Sorenson's. They had five kids and since they were just across the field, went to the same school and went to the same church, they became my closest friends. Jeannie was the second youngest and she was my age, so we did almost everything together growing up. She was like a sister to me, a best buddy, someone who I told everything to and who told me everything. We went to Catholic school, had first communion together, confirmation, all the Catholic shit you're supposed to do. We hit puberty at the same time. We each had our first kiss in the loft of her parents' barn." I stopped and shook my head. "God, I had forgotten about that."

"Sounds like a perfect friendship," Jia said.

I nodded. "Growing up on a farm that's way out in the country can be an isolated upbringing, even when you have a lot of brothers and sisters, so Jeannie and I were the closest of friends. Our Catholic school was really small and insulated from the rest of this mostly Mormon town and so, it kept us all close. Close from kindergarten all the way through eighth grade. But when we hit ninth grade we moved on to the public high school. God, what a difference. There were so many activities that we hadn't had before. There was sports and art and music and dances and parties and other kids. Hundreds of kids. I got involved in sports and drama and then we started a band and we were really busy playing at dances and parties. And there were girls. A lot of girls, a lot of dating."

"You drifted apart," Jia said.

"There was so much to do. So many new things, but Jeannie never got into any of those and I was too self-absorbed to notice, even when she tried to say something. The real split happened in the beginning of our sophomore year. She invited me to the annual Sadie Hawkins dance."

"Sadie Hawkins?"

"I don't know if they even have those anymore. It's named after some cartoon character and it's a dance where the girls ask the boys to the dance."

Jia gave me a look of complete confusion which made me laugh.

"Now you know how old I am," I said. "Back then, culture required guys to ask the girls out. The Sadie Hawkins dance was the one set aside where the girls were supposed to do the asking."

"You Americans are weird," she said.

"No argument there."

"So what happened at this dance?" she asked.

"I was an idiot. The dance was in the school gym and I spent most of dance focusing on the band and talking to my friends. Jeannie and I had a big fight out in the lobby and she drove away. I had to bum a ride home from a friend."

"What was the fight about?"

"About us, about me not being around. About her loneliness. Not seeming to be friends anymore. And I didn't want to talk about it, didn't understand it. It was really the last time we talked."

"Sorry."

"I was just too stupid. She tried to talk to me later, left me notes, called once in a while and I just ignored her. Then I was off to college. She sent me a couple of letters. That was before email, but I never wrote back. Again, I was too busy. Then, a couple years later, my mom calls to tell me that Jeannie had been murdered."

"What did you do?" she asked.

"Nothing. I didn't know what to do. I froze. Didn't even go to the funeral." My voice trailed off. "Things I should have done . . ."

"I'm sorry," she said. "But it's not your fault."

"Hey lady," I said, "I was raised Catholic. Everything is my fault."

The door to the tavern opened startling Jia into a frightened look that relaxed once she saw it was just an elderly couple coming in for lunch.

"Did that Volkov guy come back?" I asked.

She shook her head. "Not in here, but I think I saw him in a car across the street when I got here this morning." She checked the time on her phone, got up and walked over to a window to look out at the parking lot.

"Why don't you call the police on the guy?" I asked. Jia shook her head. "Why not?"

"I just can't."

"Are you saving the security camera tapes, in case you need them?" I pointed to the camera high up in a corner covering the eating and bar area.

"That camera doesn't work," she said. "Tyler tried to figure it out, but I think he just made it worse."

"Let's see if we can get it working, okay?" I went up to the bar and waved to get Tyler's attention as he flipped someone's burger patty and boogied to music playing through his ear buds. He looked at me and plucked a bud out of one ear. "I understand you took a shot at getting the security camera working," I said.

"I couldn't figure it out," he said, pointing to the camera with one hand while burger flipping with the other. "Let me finish these and I'll show you."

A few minutes later, I was following Tyler up the stairs to the room across from mine. The small, windowless space was a jumble of huge boxes, broken chairs and worn out kitchen equipment. It smelled of dust and a lot of mold. Against one wall a beige CRT monitor and an old VHS tape recording device sat on a thrift-store desk beside a column of VHS tapes, a dusty keyboard and a mouse.

Tyler powered up the monitor, displaying a control screen with options and settings. At the top of the screen was an empty square box where the camera's view should have been seen.

"It acts like it knows there's a camera there," he said, "but nothing." He gave a helpless shrug.

I pulled up a chair, sat and leaned close, Tyler looking over my shoulder. The tape spindles were moving. "Sounds like it's recording," I said.

"I looked at the tape. It shows a time and date but no picture," Tyler said. He pointed to one button on the screen labeled System. "When I try to click on that, it asks for a password so I couldn't get any further."

"Does Jia know the password?" I asked.

He shook his head and pointed to a faded sticker on the recorder with a company name and number. "And the guys that put this in are long gone."

The desk had one wide, shallow drawer at the center and three smaller drawers to the right. I began opening the smaller drawers. The three little drawers were empty except for an occasional pen, pencil or dried mouse droppings.

"I couldn't find a manual," Tyler said.

"Not looking for a manual," I replied. "My years of doing this kind of thing has taught me that most people suck at security."

I opened the center drawer as far as I could and pulled out sheets of paper, business cards, boxes of staples, adhesive tape and a pad of sticky notes. I reached into the drawer, feeling around inside at the back and the sides and the top.

And there it was. I took a hold of it and pulled out a square sticky note that had one word scribbled on it in ball point pen. I showed it to Tyler, who smiled.

I clicked on the System button, typed in the word that was on the sticky note and the screen changed to a page of settings and information.

"Nine times out of ten," I said, "people just write down their password and hide it somewhere. In the work I do, I rarely have to rely on password cracking."

"You a hacker?" Tyler asked.

"It's sorta how I got into the business," I said.

"Cool," he said, appearing impressed.

The software was a decade old, but I managed to find a command screen and a list of commands that I began to work with.

"The system date and time is 24 hours off," I said. "The computer thinks it's tomorrow. I'll fix that later." With a few more commands, I could see that the recorder detected a camera so I sent some commands to that port, but after a wait the screen displayed an error message.

"Connection problem," I said. I turned the recorder around so I could see the connections on the back. There was a power connection, keyboard, mouse, monitor and four Ethernet ports, only one in use. "I'm guessing this is the camera." I disconnected the one Ethernet cable. It was dust and mold covered. So was the port it plugged into.

"Tyler, can you find me some rubbing alcohol and a Q-Tip?"

He stared at me then snapped his fingers. "First-Aid cabinet."

Tyler ran down the stairs and came back with alcohol wipes and some cotton swabs.

"No rubbing alcohol," he said.

I took the wipes. "These will work."

Soaking the swab with alcohol from the wipes, I cleaned out the port, plugged the cable back in and turned the recorder back where it was. I exited the system settings page and when the control screen came back up, there was a sharp, black and white image of the tavern displayed at the top of the screen.

"You did it!" Tyler said as we high-fived each other.

"Sometimes, it is something that simple," I said. "Just a dirty, mold-covered port. Good to have it working in case that guy hassles Jia again. You know anything about that guy?"

"She won't tell me nothin'," Tyler said. "Don't think he's a stalker dude. He seems like someone she knows, but doesn't like anymore. Old boyfriend maybe?"

"Too old to be a boyfriend."

"Too old and too fat," Tyler said.

"Gotta be something else."

"But she doesn't want to talk about it. Like she don't want any help."

"She probably doesn't need any," I said, "but let's you and me be ready to help if she asks, okay?"

"Deal," Tyler said. We fist bumped.

Back down at the bar, Tyler explained to Jia what we had done.

"Better be careful. This guy's a computer hacker," Tyler said stepping back into the kitchen. "And change the passcode on your phone before he hacks into it. And don't write it down on a sticky note." He gave me a wink.

"Hacker?" Jia asked.

I laughed. "I do computer forensics for law enforcement up in Bellingham. Not a hacker." I pointed up at the camera. "At least now we have a working camera. The date is screwed up on the computer, but I can fix that later. The point is to have a camera running in case your friend causes any problems and we have to call the police."

"No police," she said. "Please. Do not call them."

I looked at her hoping for an explanation, but none came. I raised my hands in surrender. "If I can do anything, you'll ask, won't you?"

She touched my arm. "Thank you," she said, then grabbed two menus to take to a couple that had just walked in.

I looked over at Tyler. We shrugged. He went back to cooking and I headed out the back door to see if I could find an old cop.

Six

The old sheriff's rundown, clapboard ranch style house was plopped down in a rural neighborhood more than three miles from downtown Black River in a large grass and tree lined lot, surrounded by a short welded-wire fence and other nearly identical houses planted in neighboring lots. A puffy, ruddy-faced Katzendorf, in a worn flannel shirt tucked into baggy jeans with garish suspenders that were attempting in vain to keep his pants up and his belly in, was pushing an old smoke-belching lawn mower around his front lawn. He took note of me as I came to the gate and stopped mowing, puffing away at a cigarette that was putting out as much smoke as his Briggs and Stratton.

"Whaddya need?" he yelled over the rattling old engine.

He couldn't hear my response and finally tossed the cigarette down and shut the mower off.

"What?" he asked like I was an annoying neighbor kid.

"Mr. Katzendorf," I said, "you probably don't remember me. Rich Willis. I'm Wilma Blessinger's son. You went to school with her."

He scratched at the gray stubble decorating both chins sorting out ancient memories. When he finished, he gave me a nod and pointed a short, thick finger at me.

"Yeah, I remember you," he said, coming to the fence where I was standing. "Your dad had a farm over by the reservation, right?"

I nodded.

"Heard that your mom died a couple years back," he said. "Sorry to hear that."

"Thanks."

He looked at me expectantly. "What do you need?" he asked. "I gotta sit down." He waved at me to follow him, dropping his heft down on the stoop at the front door, breathing hard and lighting another cigarette.

"I wanted to ask you about a case," I said.

"I ain't sheriff no more, you know," he said.

"I know. This is an old one, never solved. Jeannie Sorenson. About thirty years ago."

"Shit, thirty years?" He stared at me, then looked away, deep brow furrowed. Several puffs on his cigarette, a mumble of her name, then a faint look of sadness and a nod. "The girl in the potato field."

"Out on Marsh Road," I said.

"Yeah, I remember. Tough one. Pretty girl, left out in that field." He shook his head. "Never figured that one out."

"I know," I said. "That's why I came out here."

"Talk to the sheriff."

"I've been there already," I said. "And I read the case file."

"Great. Whaddya need me for?" he asked. "You one of them YouTube crime-solving assholes?"

"No," I said. "Jeannie was a friend. A good friend."

"Well, I'm sorry about that," he said, "but you've read the case file," he said. "That's all there is. Don't think there's any more I can tell you."

"Look, Mr. Katzendorf, I'm not a cop," I said, "but I work along-side them up in Bellingham. I know that the facts, the information, the evidence are all in the case file. But I also know that there is a lot that doesn't get put onto paper."

"What the hell you talking about, kid?"

I stifled a smile. Kid?

"I'm talking about what's in your gut," I said. "What suspicions did you have that you couldn't put down on paper? Who couldn't you interview and what did you think about the people you did?"

"Think about them? A thirty-year old case?" he asked. "Are you fuckin' kidding me?" Katzendorf grunted, managed to stand and started towards his mower. "I've got work to do."

"Please, Mr. Katzendorf. Can you just think back on it for a sec-ond?" I asked, chasing after him. "You interviewed friends, family and neighbors. You lived here. You knew the area. What isn't in the case file?"

He was at the mower, posed to pull the starter rope.

"Could you just take a minute?" I asked.

Katzendorf stared at me, then released his grip on the mower, turned and stalked angrily a few feet away, then back. He stopped, stared down at the grass for a minute, taking drags off his cigarette as he thought. His gaze came back up and he looked at me intently.

"Okay," he said grudgingly, "Maybe a couple things." He took a few more puffs. "Thinking back, I wish we had looked harder at the family. I don't remember why anymore, but there was something wrong there."

"Wrong? Like what?" I asked. "I grew up with her family. They were good people. I do understand one of her older brothers might have had a drug problem, but--" I stopped.

He gave me an astonished look.

"What?" I asked

"Don't remember details no more, been too long, but I remember they wasn't no Ozzie and Harriet family. I mean, c'mon, her dad killed himself drinking."

I stared at him disbelieving. "No, that's not true. It was a farm accident. His tractor flipped over."

Katzendorf answered with a snort. "The man was baling hay while he was so drunk he could barely stand. He fell off his tractor and ran over himself, probably too wasted to know what hit him." He looked hard at me. "You didn't know that?"

I shook my head.

"Porter Sorenson was a raging drunk, kid," he said. "And his wife wasn't much better."

I just stared at him.

"That's not how I remember them," I said.

"Then my gut tells me you better go back and ask the family about this and not me."

"Not many around anymore," I stammered. "Her folks are dead. And an older brother and sister are dead, but she has another brother who's still alive."

The old sheriff's face contorted as he tried to pull more memories out. "Paul. No. Peter, right? Older than the girl."

I nodded. Pete. His nickname was PeeWee. Sadly, we had a falling out early in grade school and had never connected after that.

"Yeah, that asshole was a piece of work. Never figured him out. Something wrong there, though. And I do remember a little sister. Living at home then. Jan? Jackie?"

"Julie."

He nodded.

"Was her brother Pete ever a suspect?" I asked.

Katzendorf thought a minute, shook his head. "Just an asshole."

"Nobody else you talked to? No other --."

"Thirty years, kid," he interrupted. "Know how long that is? Know how many fuckin' cases I had? All I remember is what I told you. Tell that lazy-ass sheriff they got to help you now. Or you do it. You go find those people and talk to 'em. I'm done with that shit."

"Okay."

He gave the mower starter rope a pull, it puttered, but didn't start. Then he looked at me.

"If I was you, I'd talk to the sister and the asshole brother and maybe find some friends of theirs. Go back and check newspapers. There was a lot happening back then. I got work to do."

Another starter pull, another puff of smoke and nothing.

"And why the hell does all this shit matter to you?" he asked. "It was thirty years ago."

"I owe her," I said.

He just shook his head. "Don't think that'll matter anymore to her."

With that and a pull of the starter rope, the lawn mower finally smoked to life and Katzendorf pushed the old machine away from me across the lawn.

I stared after him for a while, then went back to my Jeep.

I had to find Pete and Julie, but who would know how to find them?

I smiled.

Sally Burke.

I pulled up in front of a tiny little house in an old residential part of Black River. A low wooden fence surrounded a perfectly mown lawn dotted with maple trees. One side of the yard was bordered by lilac bushes that were as overgrown and fragrant as I remembered. A narrow sidewalk ran up to old fashioned, covered porch and a weathered front door.

As I stepped up onto the porch, the big screen door flew open and a big, pear-shaped woman in an oversized, flowered housecoat emerged, holding a dirty garden trowel in one gloved hand and a middling-sized ceramic pot in the other. Her large, round face, topped by perfectly curled and thick gray hair was partially hidden by thick plastic glasses. Her voice boomed.

"Where the fuck have you been, asshole?" she said.

"Nice to see you too, Mrs. Burke," I replied with a smile and a hug. I loved the old lady. She knew it. And she loved me. But she would never, ever admit it.

When I pulled back from the embrace with the woman, she aimed the trowel at a wicker chair to my left.

"Sit your fat ass down there," she said, "and tell me why the hell you have been in town for two days without coming here." She dropped the pot and tool onto a small table and stripped off her gloves.

"How did you know I was in town?" I asked.

She looked at me like I had just asked the dumbest question ever asked. I suppose I had.

Every small town had one and Black River had Mrs. Burke. She was the woman who knew everybody and knew everything. She kept up on the latest gossip, kept up on the latest news, knew who was coming, who was going, what city councilman had just been pulled over on a DUI and which fireman was sleeping with which deputy's wife. Having been the Black River High School English teacher for fifty years, most of the people still living in town had sat in her classroom at least once. Some for all four years. And she remembered every one of them. Including me. As gruff as she was, she was probably my favorite teacher and I think I was one of her favorite students. We had never lost touch and I always stopped to visit her whenever I was in town.

She squeezed her body into a chair next to me and I handed her a white paper bag with a half dozen maple bars that I had picked up on the way to her house.

"What the hell is this?" she asked as she opened the bag and pulled one of the maple glazed pastries out. She took a massive bite. "Why the fuck would you bring me these? Don't you know I'm not supposed to eat these?"

"I know."

She took two more bites. "These'll kill me if I keep eating them." Another bite. "Is that what you want?" She took another bite.

I smiled.

"I'm not eating any more of these," she said as she finished the first bar, pulled out another and took a bite. "Never bring me these again, okay?"

"Yes, Mrs. Burke," I said with an overly-obedient look.

She bit off another quarter of the bar. "You didn't answer my question."

It took me a second to remember what her question had been.

"Well, for one thing, I'm here to close up all my mom's estate stuff," I said.

"About damn time, Richard," she said. "Wilma's been gone for five years."

"Yeah. Been busy."

"Right. Gonna sell her houses?"

"Probably Marty's too."

"That piece of shit tavern? No one will buy that."

"It's not a piece of shit," I mumbled defensively.

"You oughta keep it."

I was shocked.

"Keep it? Why?"

"Income, shithead. You're gonna be old and decrepit in a couple more years and I'm sure you GenZers don't have any pension. Social security will be fucked by then, so you are gonna need the income. Keep it."

I shrugged.

"Move back here and live off the local drunks. It might be an LDS town, but you could make a decent living off those that aren't following all their weird little commandments."

"I'll think about."

"You? Thinking? That's a good one."

"I will think about it," I said. "I promise."

"Good. Now what else are you doing in town?"

"I came to see you," I said with a smile.

"Go to hell."

I laughed and watched as another maple bar disappeared into her mouth.

"Well?" she asked.

I cleared my throat. "You remember Jean Sorenson?"

"Sorenson?"

"Same age as me."

"That old?" she asked with a glare. She was working it. "Jean Sorenson. Yeah, I remember. Smart girl. Quiet." Then she remembered more. "Shit. She was murdered wasn't she? A year or two after high school?"

"Yeah."

"Never caught anyone either. Damn shame," she said. "So young." She looked at me. "Why?"

"I'm trying to find her brother Pete and her younger sister, Julie. I think they may still be around here, but I don't know where. I've Googled, searched Facebook, Twitter and Instagram. Every social media platform I could find."

"Social media," Mrs. Burke snorted. "Worth about as much as a phone book, which isn't worth shit anymore."

"And that's why I came to you," I said. "You are better than all those things."

"Damn right I am. Why are you trying to find them?"

"Trying to understand what happened," I shrugged, being vague. "She was a friend I lost touch with. Just wanna know."

"Catholic guilt got you, huh?"

"That's part of it."

"Serves you right for going to a fucking Catholic school."

"I blame my parents," I said, smiling. "So do you know anything about where Pete or Julie might be nowadays?"

"Well, the last I heard, Peter was driving truck for some cheap little outfit in Idaho Falls. Let me think." She paused, then snapped her fat fingers. "Olsen Trucking. Right off the highway outside of Idaho Falls, I think."

"I thought you might know."

"You're welcome."

"Any idea what happened to Julie Sorenson?"

She munched away on another maple bar. Then stood, holding up a finger.

"Wait."

She marched into the house, the screen door slamming behind her. It was quiet, then from inside I heard her talking with someone on the phone. I couldn't make out what she was saying but resisted the temptation to go to the door and listen.

A minute later she came out, shoving her cell phone into the pocket of her housecoat. She plopped back into her chair.

"You couldn't find her because she's been married a couple times and changed her name. Just talked to one of the gals on my bowling team. First she was Julie Blenken, now she's a Fincher, but apparently divorced again and on her own. She's in Pocatello, working at some hair salon. I don't know which one. Sounds like she's as fucked up as her mom was."

I don't know what expression suddenly appeared on my face but Mrs. Burke took it be surprise or shock.

"What? You didn't know?" she asked.

"No . . ."

"Messed up woman. OD'd on her pain meds."

"Pain pills?"

"She had those giant boobs, remember? They wreak havoc on a small woman's back, so the doc prescribed the pills for her back pain after she gave birth to all those kids and she got hooked on 'em. Kept needing more and more. Never got off that tiger. A year after the old man got killed, Jeannie found her mom dead in her bed."

"Not suicide?" I asked.

"No. She just fucked up and took too many pills."

I stood and walked a few steps to the other end of the porch trying to figure things out.

"Was Jeannie's dad really a drunk?" I asked.

"Oh yeah," she said.

I shook my head, and leaned on the porch railing looking out on her lawn. Mrs. Burke could see the puzzled look on my face.

"You didn't know any of this, did you?" she asked.

I just stared out.

"None of this shit is new, you know," she said.

"I didn't know any of it."

"Then you were a bigger idiot than I thought. You lived here for what, eighteen-plus years? This girl was your BFF?"

"At one time." I was not looking at her.

"Where the fuck was your head while all this stuff was going on?"

"I don't know," I mumbled. "I don't know."

I started down the steps and onto the sidewalk. "Thanks, Mrs. Burke."

She hefted herself out of her chair and came to the edge of the porch.

"Richard."

I stopped, but didn't turn.

"Richard, take a breath. Take some time. You'll need to adjust your perspective on your little village here. It may be a small town, but that only means that a smaller number of people are suffering. But they're still suffering, struggling, winning, losing, getting lost and getting found. Just like in your big towns."

I nodded.

"And don't let that Catholic guilt shit get to you."

"Too late," I said. "Thanks, again." I started for my Jeep.

"Okay, then asshole," she called after me. "Don't come by here again. And when you don't come by, don't bring me any more maple bars. Especially don't bring me any from the Albertson's bakery, just because their maple glaze is better than Walmart's."

I smiled back and waved as I jumped into the Jeep and started her up. "I promise. Love you."

"Love you too, shithead."

SEVEN

Marty's was packed for the dinner hour when I got back. Jia and her crew were running back and forth sending food orders to Tyler and Lee in the kitchen and drink orders to an overwhelmed Marie at the bar. I gave the two cooks a wave, each of them with ear buds, dancing to different music as they flipped burgers and dumped potatoes into the sizzling hot fryer. The air was filled with the aromas of onions, grease and spilled beer while obscure Grateful Dead tunes played overhead.

I got a slap on my arm and turned to see Jia standing there, her long red hair in a ponytail.

"Know how to cook?" she asked.

"Uh . . .not really," I stammered.

"Mix drinks?"

I shook my head.

"Shit," she muttered, then reached over the bar, pulled an apron and order pad off a shelf and slammed them into my belly.

"Go take orders," she said painting to the far wall. "You take those six tables over there." She started off.

"Why's it so busy?" I asked.

Jia gave me the same look of exasperation Mrs. Burke gave me earlier.

"Friday night," she said. "It's always like this. Now get going."

She was gone.

And with that, over the next two hours, I learned how to be something I'd never been: a waiter. I screwed up a few orders, dropped a few plates to a round of applause, but managed to make it to almost ten when the crowd finally became manageable by Marie, Camila and Jia. Lee had gone home, leaving Tyler alone in the kitchen, bouncing between fryer and grill.

I hadn't met Camila Ardelean before. A bright-eyed, slender woman in her mid-thirties with an easy smile but a reticent laugh, she was Laurel to Marie's Hardy. With thin, dishwater blonde hair tucked under a Black River Lions ball cap she flitted among the tables much faster than the lumbering Marie, who was chatting with a couple about to leave. Camila carried an armload of dirty dishes into the kitchen and began spraying them down.

I took my apron off and plopped myself onto a bar stool.

Jia, behind the bar, came over and handed me a glass of ice water that I desperately needed.

"We've been short-handed for months," Jia said, "and we've been dreading these weekends. It was great to have an extra hand tonight. I'll think we'll hire you."

"No thanks," I said. "I'm not qualified. Can't balance drink cups, can't remember customers' names and I look silly in an apron."

"You look great," Tyler yelled from the kitchen.

"Who asked you?" I yelled back with a wink.

"I should warn you," Jia said as Marie came over dropping off dirty drink glasses. "This is just a short pause. It will pick up again in a little while."

"There were some high school football games tonight," Marie said. "People will start coming in from them. And from movies."

The door opened and a half dozen college age kids came in and settled into a table near the stage.

"Shit," Jia said.

"What?" I asked.

She tilted her head towards the door.

Behind the herd of kids, a fat, middle-age man came in. Volkov again. He paused, looked in Jia's direction a minute, glanced angrily at me, then went to a table at the other end of the tavern, pulling out a laptop and plopping into a chair.

I looked at Jia.

"Want me to— "

"No," she said. "It's fine." She caught Camila's eye at the dish pit and pointed to Volkov. Camila nodded, pulled out her order pad and went to his table. "Going to take a break."

She dropped her apron on the bar and walked down the hall and out the back door. Marie snagged an order pad and was heading to the tables with the kids, but I touched her arm and pointed a thumb towards Volkov.

"Know anything about what's going on with her and that guy?" I asked.

"No idea," she said.

"How long has this guy been here?"

"He showed up day before yesterday. At first, I thought maybe he was her father or something 'cuz he's got that same accent, but she just laughed at me when I suggested that."

"Ukrainian mafia," Tyler whispered at us.

"Are you always listening to every conversation?" I asked.

"Of course," he said.

"Don't you have a burger to flip or something?"

"They're flipped."

"Well, flip 'em again, will ya'?" I said.

With palms up in a sign of surrender, Tyler went back to his work. Marie leaned toward me.

"Is there such a thing as Ukrainian mafia?" she asked.

"I have no idea," I said. "Even if there was such a thing, while the hell would they be in Black River, Idaho? Must be something else."

I took a deep breath and strolled over to where Volkov was typing on his computer. He looked up at me, tensing.

"Are we going to have any problems tonight?" I asked.

He stared for a moment. Then indicated his laptop.

"I am simply doing some work and enjoying the fine food and drink at your establishment," he said. "Is there any problem with that?"

"No."

"Then, my friend," he said, "we are not going to have any problems tonight."

"Can you tell me something? What's your issue with Jia?" I asked.

At that moment, Camila returned with a beer the man had ordered.

"You'll please excuse me," Volkov said. "My drink is here and I have work to do."

"Anything else I can get you?" Camila asked.

Volkov looked at me, then Camila with a smile.

"A double cheeseburger and fries, please," he said. "And, of course, peace and quiet."

Camila and I looked at each other and I gave the man a nod. We walked away.

As we did, Camila whispered to me.

"The guy creeps me out."

I was about to agree when Camila's eyes went to the parking lot. I followed her gaze to see a vintage fifties Willys Jeep with no doors or top pull in with four kids loaded onto it. They jumped out and came in, grabbing an empty table by the stage. As they did, another pack of rambunctious teens burst in and planted themselves at empty tables.

"Football game's out," Camila said watching another small group come in and settle at a table. She headed their way. "Can you take care of the kids by the stage?" she asked. "I'll get these others."

Grabbing an order pad I went over to the four college kids chattering noisily around their table. Two boys were reading lines to each other from playscripts, while the two girls were going over a menu. A tall, black kid looked up at me then turned to his buddy in glasses and a faded Star Wars shirt.

"Methinks the waiter doth approach," he said in a bad English accent.

"Oh no," I said as I reached them. "Theatre majors. Idaho State?" I asked. ISU was in Pocatello, about thirty miles south.

The redhead looking at the menu said "We just got out of rehearsal."

"Needed to get out of town," her companion said.

"What show are you guys doing?" I asked.

"Romeo and Juliet," the black kid said.

"Who's playing who?" I asked.

The redhead raised a hand. "The nurse," she said.

"Costumes," said the other girl.

"Benvolio," said the glasses kid, then pointed to his black friend. "Reggie's playing Tybalt."

"Ah, Tybalt, you rat catcher!" I said. The kids laughed. "I did the show in college. Played Mercutio."

"We do the show next month," the redhead said. "You should come and see it."

"If I'm still in town, I will," I said. Then I pointed out towards the parking lot. "Who's old Jeep is that?"

"My dad's," said Reggie.

"Great car. CJ-5?"

"CJ-3B" Reggie said. "You got one?"

I shook my head. "I wish I did. Got a Wrangler. Needed something that could do freeway speeds. That CJ series could barely do fifty."

"I know. I asked my dad to put a new engine and tranny in it to get that speed, but he said no way he was gonna get rid of that four-cylinder Hurricane."

"Good for him," I said. I introduced myself and we geeked out for a few more minutes on old Jeeps, then I took their order and dropped it off at the service counter.

"Hey Richie!"

I turned to see Gil Forman, still in his sheriff's uniform, walking in. In my peripheral vision, I noticed Volkov perking up and staring at the cop, thinking I called them. I smiled, imagining his discomfort.

"Gil!" I said approaching the sheriff. We shook hands. "Want a table?"

"Actually, I just wanted to talk to you," he said. "I'd like to get your help."

"Mine?"

"Can we sit?" he asked.

I pointed to a couple stools at the far end of the bar. "Over there. Want a drink or something?"

"Coke?"

I nodded and called out to Marie. "Could we get a couple cokes?" She nodded. Gil and I settled onto the stools as she brought drinks over. I took a sip.

"What's up, Gil?"

"I called your boss up in Bellingham."

"Uh oh."

"After talking shit about you," Gil said smiling, "he said you were a damn good computer forensics guy."

"Okay," I said, "why would you call him?"

"Little old Black River can't afford to employ a computer guy," he said, "so when we need one, we contract a guy out of Idaho Falls." After a swallow of coke, he looked around and lowered his voice. "A warrant is going to be served on a guy selling kiddie porn who works at a local bank."

"Okay," I said, hoping he'd get to the point soon.

"The forensics guy we wanted isn't available and we have to seize and search computer systems the moment we serve the warrant. We didn't have anyone who could do it until you walked through my door yesterday."

"Gil," I said a little shocked, "There must be someone else."

"There would be," he said, "if we had known that the computer guy was going to bail on us. We didn't and if we don't make this bust this week, we may lose our target."

"Man . . ."

"Look, Richie," he said, "it shouldn't take that much time. We just need two systems frozen, copied, decrypted and then data pulled off. You would have full access to our system and all our tools. I'd get a desk set up for you where you could work. And let me tell you," he continued, "these guys that peddle this shit are the scum of the earth. When I come across these guys, they go directly to jail and I throw away the key."

I took a few sips of my coke. I had been involved in pornography cases like this before, but I needed the time for what I wanted to do and was just about to decline when I had a thought. I realized that I might like having access to the local law enforcement's computer system.

There would be databases, names, addresses and police reports. I could use them. For Jeannie.

"I'd have access to databases for cross referencing and storage for the data retrieval?" I asked.

"Full access," he said. He could see me mulling it. "We'll get you whatever you need. You could set your own schedule."

I thought another moment, then smiled and nodded.

"So, we have a deal?" he asked.

"Deal."

Gil slapped me on the arm. "That's a huge weight off my shoulders." He poured the last of his coke down and stood. "Thanks, buddy."

I followed him to the door.

"I'll get the paperwork to get you set up as a contractor and get you a desk."

We were at the door.

"I really do appreciate this, Richie," he said.

I nodded and we shook hands.

"Come in Monday morning. You can sign the paperwork and we'll show you where everything is."

"I have my own tools for cases like this," I said. "You okay with that?"

"That's no problem. They're probably better than the shit we have." We shook hands. "Thanks again, Richie. This is a big help."

He walked out and I started back towards the bar. The kid I had been talking to called out as I passed.

"You a cop?" Reggie asked.

I laughed, turning to him. "No, he's just an old school buddy."

"I heard him say he was giving you a desk? Sure you're not a cop."

"Just a computer guy. Helping out," I said.

"Okay, if you say so." He looked around, stood and came up to me. "Hey, I noticed you guys are really busy here and short-handed. Any chance you're hiring?"

"Funny you should ask that. We could use help," I said, "but aren't you down in Pocatello?"

"It's not that far," he said. "No jobs in Poky." He gave me a pleading look and he seemed like a good kid, so I nodded.

"I'll tell Jia you're interested. She's the manager," I said. I dug a business card out of my wallet and handed it to him. "Email me a resume if you have one and I'll get it to her."

Reggie looked at the card. "Bellingham Police Department? And you say you're not a cop?"

"I do computer stuff for them, that's all. No badge. No gun."

"Okay." He pocketed the card, still skeptical.

"Email me, Reggie."

"I will, officer," he said with a smile.

I laughed, patted him on the shoulder and turned to see that Jia was behind the bar talking to Marie, who was sitting and chomping on a thick sandwich. I jumped onto a stool next to her and tipped my head towards the college kids.

"The kid over there wants a job," I said to Jia.

She glanced over at him "Why hire anyone? We've got you," she said with a smirk.

Marie laughed.

"I suck at taking orders," I said, "and I can't cook."

Jia gave me that cute, crooked smile, then nodded.

"Maybe."

"So, what is with the sheriff?" Marie asked between mouthfuls of deli meat and bread.

"Sheriff?" Jia asked, suddenly tensing.

"That man he was talking to is the sheriff."

"Is there trouble?" she asked pointing a thumb in Volkov's direction. "You didn't . . . "

"No," I reassured her. "The sheriff's an old buddy. He came here to ask me to do a little work for them next week."

She relaxed.

The door opened and a dozen new customers flowed in. Camila went to one table. Jia slapped an order pad into my hand, took one for herself and pointed to the crowd.

"Back to work, slacker!"

Just before we closed the bar for the night, Volkov gathered up his equipment and went to the door. He gave Jia a look, then glared at me as I helped clean tables and straighten chairs. When he was gone, Jia locked the door and let out a big sigh. I stopped and looked at her.

"You know, Jia, if we understood what was going on with that guy," I said to her, "we could help."

She went back to wiping down tables without saying anything.

Marie, Camila and Tyler finished their closing shift duties, said their goodnights and walked out the front door, Marie and Camila climbing into an old Toyota and Tyler puttering away on a little red scooter. I noticed that the parking lot was empty except for Jia's car and a large SUV. Its motor wasn't running, but the street lights were silhouetting a man at the wheel.

I called to Jia who was in back getting her things. "What color car does Volkov drive?"

"I don't know," she called back. "It's dark and it's one of those big SUV things." She emerged from the hall with a sweater and a bag. "Why?" Her tone had become apprehensive.

"That SUV parked out there," I said. "Might be your friend."

"Fuck," she murmured as she came to the door and opened it a crack. Then closed it. She threw her sweater and pouch onto a table. "God damn it."

It was him. I watched her trying to figure out how to handle it.

"How about I follow you home?" I asked. "My Jeep's out back."

"He'd follow us."

"He doesn't know where you live?"

"Not yet. And I don't want him to." She went to the door and took another peek, then sat herself down at a table. "I'll just wait here. He'll give up soon."

"Why don't you just spend the night upstairs," I said. "I'll grab my sleeping bag and sleep in the storage room. "He'll be gone by morning."

She shook her head.

"Thank you. You have been very kind. But I'm not going to make you sleep on the floor because of him. I'll wait until he goes away."

I was about to give in, when the obvious appeared to me.

"How about we sneak out the back and I drive you home?"

She turned to me.

"Leave your car here," I said. "After an hour or two, he'll get bored and go home."

"But tomorrow?" she asked. "And we live way out of town."

"I'll pick you up in the morning," I said. "We?"

"My mother," she said. "My mother lives with me."

"Does she have a car?" I asked.

"She doesn't drive."

"Then I'll pick you up before your shift starts, okay?"

Jia took another furtive look out the front. I heard a slow deep, frustrated sigh then she came back and grabbed her pouch and sweater.

"Let's do it. I'll get the lights."

"Leave 'em on," I said. "He'll think someone is still here."

We slipped out the back door and into my Jeep. Luckily, I hadn't taken the top or the doors off yet. I fired it up.

"Duck down in the seat," I said. "I'll drive out the front. He'll think I'm alone and won't follow me."

"Got it."

Jia slid the seat back as far as it would go, then tucked her small frame onto the passenger foot well.

"You are tiny," I said.

She slapped my leg.

"Shut up and drive before I cramp up."

"Wouldn't want that. And just so you know, the shocks on this Jeep suck."

"Great."

I pulled out from behind Marty's and drove across the lot passing near the SUV so that Volkov could see it was me leaving and assume Jia was still inside.

"I think it worked," I said. Jia tried to climb out of the foot well, but I pushed her back down. "Wait till we get a few blocks away, just in case."

She groaned.

At the parking lot exit, I took a right and headed into downtown. After going through a couple traffic lights and checking behind us, I tapped her on the head. She grunted and groaned until she had pulled herself up and onto the passenger seat.

"You should get a real car someday," she grumbled. "Instead of this piece of shit."

"I love this Jeep. Now, where am I going?"

Jia pointed to a traffic light ahead.

"Turn left there. That's the highway out of town."

After ten minutes and some lefts and rights onto side roads, she guided us into the gravel driveway of a small, square bungalow on a ragged little lot surrounded by trees and a few other small houses.

"That guy's not likely to find you out here," I said.

"He will eventually," she said with a sigh, opening the door to get out. I placed a hand on her arm.

"Anything I can do to help?" I asked.

"You just did," she said. She leaned in and planted a kiss on my cheek. "Thank you. But please, let me handle this."

I looked at her a moment, then nodded and she was out the door. A light came on over the front door and a stocky, older woman opened the door and let Jia in. The woman looked towards me, nodded, then closed the door. The light went off.

By the time I pulled back into the parking lot in front of Marty's, Volkov's SUV was gone, but as I drove past the tavern to park in back, I noticed the lights inside Marty's were off.

We had left them on.

I climbed out of the Jeep and moved quietly to the back door and pushed it open, listening. Beyond the hum of the refrigeration units in the kitchen and the AC, the place was silent. I closed and locked the door with a barely noticeable click and then stepped carefully down the hall, listening. The place seemed empty, the cash register hadn't been touched, the liquor case was locked and nothing was disturbed in the kitchen.

WTF?

Someone must have been inside while I was gone. Had Tyler come back for something?

I snapped my finger.

Camera.

I went upstairs to the security camera system, pulled up the play-back menu and scrolled back to about one o'clock, which is when Jia and I had left. I sped through the overhead view of the main eating area, watched Jia and I talking, her looking out the door, us heading towards the back exit.

Then nothing.

I kept running through the tape.

Nothing. Nothing.

Then, a few minutes after two, a figure entered the screen from the back hall. The big male figure leaned over the bar and looked, looked in the kitchen, then went to the front door to look out. Then he turned and walked towards the back and out of frame. Then the lights went out. When the camera lens adjusted to the reduced light, I could see that the place was empty and that our intruder had left.

It was Volkov.

EIGHT

I struggled to get a few hours sleep. It was the dream again: the hospital, the homeless camp, the empty field. This time I felt a shadow. I could only sense its presence there, somewhere beyond seeing. Then, as I stood in the plowed potato field, looking at the hand reaching up out of the dirt towards me, the shadow darkened. It loomed bigger, then closer, then bigger.

I forced myself awake.

Nine o'clock.

Saturday morning. I snatched the prescription bottle off the bed-stand and swallowed one.

After a long, hot shower, I grabbed a pair of caffeine laden lattes from Marty's kitchen and was out the back and in my Jeep by nine-thirty.

I surprised myself by being able to find my way back to Jia's isolated little neighborhood. When I pulled into the driveway, she was already standing outside waiting for me. I handed her a latte as soon as she was buckled into her seat and we were back on the road into town.

"Thanks again," she said. "I owe you."

"No, you don't. And if I can help with any of this thing that's happening with that guy, just ask, okay?"

She nodded. I opted not to mention that Volkov had visited the bar during the night. I knew that I could probably call the police, report the illegal entry and get him arrested for trespassing. But nothing was taken, nothing was broken. He would be in jail for a night, then back. And angry.

We made small talk as we drove and Jia told me a little about how she had gotten to this tiny little potato town. She and her mother had immigrated from Ukraine a year and a half before, leaving her father and older brother in Kiev. There was a small, but very strong Ukrainian community in this area, some of whom her mother knew, so they came to Black River to be around them. A couple months after arriving and moving into the rental they were now living in, she got a job at Marty's and quickly moved up to managing the place.

"My mother is still struggling with the language, which makes it hard for her to get a job," Jia said. "And her age. Hard to get a job in this country when you're sixty and speak only Ukrainian."

We pulled into the parking lot in front of Marty's and headed towards the back of the building.

"God damn it," Jia said.

I looked over at her and followed her gaze to the far end of the lot. An SUV was parked there.

"Him." I said.

She nodded.

We continued on and parked in the alley behind Marty's and she popped her door open.

When I didn't open my own, she asked, "Aren't you coming in?"

"I have some work to do," I said. "and I need to get to the library."

"Checking out a book?"

"Research," I said.

With a quizzical look, she closed the door and I drove off.

Black River's public library was located downtown in a two story, sandstone building that was originally a post office, built in the late twenties. It retained that stylish twenties look on the outside and even some of that institutional feel when you walked into the cavernous main lobby. The library itself only took up the first floor of the building, the rest being city offices and leased spaces.

I walked through the children's section to the checkout counter just as the librarian finished checking a small pile of kids' books out to a woman pushing two crying annoyances in a stroller. The librarian, in a loose baby blue blouse was a brown-skinned, woman, veering towards heavy, trying hard to disguise her middle-ageness with big glasses, over-permed hair, big earrings and too much perfume. Her small, dark eyes were tired, with bags under them that she had attempted to cover up with too much make-up. She had a sweater over her shoulders against the breeze from the air conditioner. She smiled politely in an offer to assist me and stood, an abundance of bracelets rattling.

"Hi," I said. "I understand that the old Black River News newspapers are archived here." The Black River News had been the city's only newspaper for more than eighty years, but Craigslist and internet news sites had first reduced it to a weekly advertiser and then killed it completely. If anyone even read a newspaper anymore, it was a regional paper.

"Yes, we have those here," she said. "We have the most recent going back about 12 years in the digital archive."

"I'm going back further than that."

"Those we have on Microfilm," she said. "They haven't been scanned into digital yet. Are you familiar with Microfilm?"

I smiled. "I'm that old, yeah."

"Good. What year are you looking for?"

I gave her the three years I wanted to look at: the year Jeannie was killed, the year before and the year after. She excused herself with a smile, stood, straightened a body-hugging skirt and slipped into a backroom. When she re-emerged she carried three wooden shoebox size containers.

"Each box is a year and you will find twelves rolls of film inside for each month of that year." She pulled a checkout form from a drawer, wrote down the years and slipped the paper to me, indicating a place for me to sign, which I did. She took the paper.

"These may not be taken out of the building," she instructed. "I'll need to hold your library card while you have these. I'll give it back when you return them."

"I don't have a library card, I'm afraid," I said. "I'm just visiting."

"Driver's license will work," she said, holding out her hand.

She was clipping my license to the checkout form, when she stopped and looked closely at it. Then she smiled and looked up at me.

"Richard Willis," she said. "Back in town."

Puzzled, I stepped back to look at the nameplate at her desk. It read Rosa Grazzano. She could tell I didn't recognize the name.

"All those years riding the same school bus and you don't remember me," she said with mock hurt.

I scrunched up my face in confusion, picked up the name plate and showed it to her.

"Married name," she said pointing to it. "Try Clawson."

I stood silent like an idiot for a moment, staring at her. Then it hit me.

"Rosa Clawson!" I said reaching out to shake her hand.

"Your punching bag's little sister," she said accepting the handshake. "How have you been?"

"Good," I said. I did remember her and I remembered her as the neighborhood party girl, partying with guys in back yards, back seats and even, on occasion, in the back of the school bus. I chose not to mention those things. "How about you, Rosa?" I asked. "Husband? Kids?"

"Husband long gone. Four kids, though. And even one grandbaby."

"Damn," I said, "you can't be old enough to be a grandmother."

"It's true. Grandma Rosa."

I shook my head. "Hard to believe. How's Robbie?"

Hearing the question, her eyes darkened for the briefest moment, "Oh, he's fine. Still the same, I'm afraid."

Rosa's older brother, Robbie, had been the same age as me and we rode the same bus to school from first grade until we each got cars in high school. For some long forgotten reason, we had never been able to get along. We got into fist fights when we were both in fourth grade, then again in seventh. He was a bit bigger than me then and I didn't fare well in those battles. But then I hit a growing spurt and by the time we were in high school, I had a little height advantage. In our junior year, one afternoon after basketball practice, I confronted him on the front lawn of the school about the way he had treated a freshman girl who had gone to the same Catholic school as I had. The conflict grew hotter, a crowd gathered and when I turned to say something to a friend, Robbie sucker-punched me. Angrier than I had ever been, I picked myself off the ground and we went at it. Before one of the teachers got out to break it up, I had broken his nose and cut up his lip so bad that blood was smeared all over his face and clothes. Needless to say, we were suspended for a few days. After that, we managed a grudging peace for the remainder of our high school years.

"He works at US Potato," Rosa said. "He does security there during the winter, but right now, when the spuds are coming in, he works in those giant cellars where they unload the potato trucks."

We chatted a few minutes more about kids we grew up with, men she had dated, neighbors who had died and teachers she hated. I had forgotten that Rosa was one of those people who would start talking and probably not stop for anything because every topic lead to another. I was finally able to get her to stop by indicating that I really needed to look at the microfilm she had brought me.

"Oh yeah," she said. "I know I can go on and on." She pointed to a corner at the far end of the room. "The reader is in that little reading room there. What are you looking for?"

"Do you remember Jean Sorenson?" I asked.

Rosa put a hand to her mouth recognizing the name. "Oh, that poor girl. I do remember her. I dated her older brother a couple times. Back in the day."

"You went out with Pete Sorenson?"

"A few times," she said dismissively. "Why are you looking into his sister's death? Didn't they close that case a long time ago?"

I told her I wanted to understand what happened and why the killer was never found, that I owed it to my old friend.

"Well...I hope there's something in there." She pointed to the film.

"Thanks Rosa," I said. "I hope so too."

The reading room was a quiet eight-by-eight space with one chair and a shallow shelf-like table that ran along the back wall. A dusty old microfilm reader sat on the table connected to a small laser printer. A few minutes of scrolling and I found the month of October, twenty-eight years ago and the day after my friend's body was discovered. There was the headline on the bottom of the front page: Woman's

Body Found in Field. I started reading and on the legal pad I brought with me, made notes of the people, places and times mentioned.

Reading the cold, impersonal case file had given me the basics of the investigation, but scouring the old newspaper articles, pictures and even letters to the editor, a fuller, more human story began emerging.

Jeannie had been working at US Potato and was living at her parents' old house with her sister, Julie, who also worked at USP. It was sunny that Friday in October. She and Julie left work around five in the afternoon and after a stop to have a quick drink with a co-worker, went home. An hour later, Jeannie told Julie that she was meeting a girlfriend at The Dump, an old burger joint, then going to a movie. Julie spent the night with a boyfriend at his house and when she returned the next afternoon Jeannie wasn't there. According to the newspaper, Julie claimed she didn't question Jeannie's absence then or even the next day, thinking that maybe she had gone to Reno or Jackson Hole for the weekend. Then on Monday, the farmer found her body.

The follow-up stories over the next months regurgitated much of what was in the case files. No one remembered seeing her at The Dump. No one went to a movie with Jeannie or saw her there, so the last time she was seen alive was when she left the house.

According to the medical examiner, she was likely killed late that same Friday night or early the next morning, hurriedly buried in the field and not discovered until the following Monday.

The stories got fewer and smaller as time went on, delegated to the back pages covering interviews, calls for anyone who might have information and occasional attempts at human interest stories around the murder and the Sorenson family. The usual tripe.

A month later, the first of two surprises showed up in a small page five article. Jeannie's older brother Peter was being held for assaulting a police officer and obstructing an ongoing investigation. I knew Pee-Wee had turned into an asshole, but I didn't know he had gotten this bad. Doing something to obstruct the investigation into his sister's murder?

The next surprise came the following December. A back page, follow-up article appeared covering how the surviving Sorenson family was doing. Little was said of Pete as it focused on Julie living all alone in the aftermath of her sister's death, but buried in a small paragraph near the end of the article was one sentence.

"Struggling for years with drug addiction," the article read, "Jean was on a path to full recovery and an optimistic future when her life was brutally taken from her."

I stared at the screen.

Jeannie and drugs?

I pulled out other rolls of film and searched for headlines. I had been so focused on stories concerning the killing I hadn't looked for anything else so I went back through the rolls and there they were: articles about drug busts, meth lab raids and overdose obituaries. Just like in the big cities, drugs had hit Black River.

I gathered up the rolls of microfilm and walked back to the front desk. Rosa must have heard the reading room door open and was quietly brushing her hair and touching up her face paint. As I came up to the desk I saw that she had dropped the sweater and loosened the top two buttons on her blouse exposing some serious cleavage. Thirty years later, she hadn't changed.

"Find what you needed?" she asked, taking the boxes of microfilm.

"More than I needed. Can I ask you something?"

"Sure," she said leaning over the counter to hand my license back and making sure I had the best view possible of her ample bosom. I forced my gaze back up to her eyes.

"When we were growing up, were there a lot of drugs around?"

Rosa's expression went oddly blank for just a moment and then morphed into curiosity.

"Some, I guess," she said. "I mean probably. Why?"

I pointed towards the boxes of microfilm.

"Stories in the Black River News," I said. "Drug busts, overdoses. Jeannie might have had some problems. And her brother, Pete. Did you notice anything when you were dating him?"

She raised her eyebrows and shook her head.

"Not that I saw, but like I said, we only dated a couple times."

I nodded.

"Your friend Jean might have been involved?" she asked, sitting back down.

I shrugged sadly. "Hard for me to believe it though. If it's true."

"Sorry."

"Thanks for the help, Rosa," I said.

Rosa got back up, leaned over, placed her hand on top of mine and took a breath to start saying something, but I stopped her.

"I'm going to have to get going," I said, feeling just a little uncomfortable as her hand pressed on mine. "I wanted to drive out to the old Sorenson place and then get to US Potato if I have time."

"USP?" she asked, seeming to be surprised. "Who you gonna see out there?"

"Jeannie's old boss."

"Oh."

"The guy is still there after all this time."

She smiled. "Look, how long are you going to be in town?"

"Longer than I planned, it looks like."

She smiled. "Good. Why don't we get together some night and maybe catch up?"

"Okay," I said, politely and pulled my hand out from under hers.

She scribbled her number on a sticky note.

"There's my cell. Give me a call. Or text me. We can meet some-where."

I nodded, stashing the note in my pocket.

"Thanks again, Rosa," I said, turning towards the door.

"Call me!"

I just waved and was out.

On the sidewalk, I pulled her note out of my pocket and looked at the number. I crumbled it up and tossed it into a trash can.

I shook my head thinking about the newspaper articles. Had I been too self-absorbed, too naïve back then? I guess that wouldn't surprise me. I sighed and looked up at the crisp October sky, then around me at the streets and buildings of the little town that I thought I knew.

It was time for me to do some more re-evaluating.

NINE

My phone buzzed and I glanced at the screen as I drove through town. It was my daughter.

"Hey, Jess."

"Dad."

It was that dad-you're-in-trouble voice.

"I called your boss at the station again and — "

"Why the hell did you do that?" I asked.

"Because I was worried about you."

"Don't you have other things to be worrying about?"

"No."

"Well, find something," I said.

"You aren't on vacation," she said.

"I'm not?"

"Your boss said you were taking two more weeks leave and that you might decide to quit. Is that true?"

It was true. The depression I was feeling and a combination of burnout, the death of my wife, death of a dear old college buddy and the arrival of middle age was pushing me to make a change in my life. I had already taken two weeks leave, but had asked for two more to think about quitting. I explained that to her.

"So, what are you gonna do, Dad?" Jess asked.

"Don't know, Jess, but I think I've got to make a change."

"Sell grandma's houses yet?" she asked.

"Meeting a realtor on Monday," I said.

"And the bar?"

"Working on that."

"What about your friend's murder?"

I decided not to give her much detail on that subject and she was going to keep asking questions that I didn't have time to answer. "I'll have to call you back. I'm going to lose you in a second 'cuz I'm heading into a tunnel."

"Okay," she said. I heard her start to say something, then stop. "Wait! I've been there. There aren't any tunnels in Black River."

"Bye Jess!"

I punched off.

A moment later, my phone beeped and I looked over to see a middle finger emoji from her. I smiled.

Two miles out of town put me in the farm country where I grew up. I took an unmarked left off the road and started down a wide gravel road. Where another road ran off to the right, a half mile away was the Sorenson farm. I turned down the road to the old Sorenson place. The home, the shops, barn and two large potato cellars had covered three acres and had been surrounded by fields and pastures. The fields were still there, but the crumbling, old, two-story home stood empty and all that was left of the buildings that had been there were a few sad walls barely hanging on to rock and concrete foundations.

I pulled into the dusty, overgrown yard, stopped and got out of the Jeep to look around. I hadn't been on the Sorenson's property since early high school and it was sad to see what it was now. What had been a lawn, was a ragged field of dried weeds. The old front porch was collapsing, barely clinging onto the house. Windows were broken, mortar was falling from between bricks and half of the chimney was in a pile on the ground.

The Sorenson kids who were closest to my age, Pete and Jeannie, were my buddies growing up. It was usually me and PeeWee teasing, chasing and battling Jeannie. As we neared pubescence, though, Pete changed for some reason, so it was more Jeannie and I together and less of PeeWee.

I walked towards where the skeletal remains of the barn stood. I saw Jeannie and I walking through the building, talking about school, of futures, of plans. We were feeling the first hints of puberty and I watched how clumsily we taught ourselves how to kiss, how I had to explain to her the weird hardness in my pants and she had to explain menstruation to me. I could see the thin, yellow-haired girl laughing at me with her big, loud, toothy laugh as I struggled to understand.

Two friends. Just learning and exploring.

The picture faded.

I walked across the cracked concrete pad that had been the floor of the barn to the large, five-acre field that spread out before me. I walked past some posts where a fence used to be and then stepped into the field. It had been harvested of its potatoes a couple weeks before and the rows had been tilled. Birds were dive bombing to catch worms and spiders and some leftover rotting potatoes were trying to sprout again. I picked up a handful of the plowed up dirt, closed my eyes and smelled its richness. For a brief moment, I was ten years old again.

This was the field where my friend died, beaten and buried alive. Half-way to the other side is where the neighbor had found her.

I asked myself why she would have been there. Could the killer have carried her there? No, I didn't think so. Jeannie was not a small woman and to carry someone through loose disturbed dirt to dump her in the middle of the field seemed like it would be too difficult.

Instead of being carried there, was she running there? Being chased by someone? What happened?

I needed to go back to people mentioned in the case file.

I went back to my Jeep and checked the time on my phone. It was late afternoon. Though US Potato would be unloading trucks for many hours more, the administration offices would close at five and I wanted to talk to someone there.

The United States Potato Processing Company occupied a massive chunk of land west of Black River, the area covered by massive potato cellars, giant, billowing smokestacks, frozen storage warehouses, office buildings and acres and acres of parking for visitors, workers, trucks bringing potatoes in and trucks carrying product out.

Various parts of the complex were making and shipping products: frozen products for grocers, frozen products for fast food restaurant chains, products going to other food processing companies, starches, and even bagged Grade A, Number One baking spuds being shipped off to fresh food markets.

I located the main office building and slipped into a slot reserved for visitors. The two story, concrete and glass, foggy grey monstrosity made no pretense of beauty or elegance. It was simply a giant box holding offices.

The empty lobby was similarly nondescript, with nothing but a giant, framed directory of offices on the wall. I searched for Kurt Windham's name, found the location and headed up to the third floor and down a long hallway until I found Suite 112.

Suite was a generous term for the office Windham occupied. It was a small, mostly glass office space in a row of other glassed office spaces. He noticed me, then did a double-take as he recognized me, rose from his desk and enthusiastically waved me in, coming around to shake hands

"Richard Willis? Holy cow!" he said indicating a chair, that I dropped into. "Haven't seen you since you graduated. How ya' been?"

He dropped back behind his desk and we spent a few minutes talking about school, old friends, people who had died in car wrecks, which old girlfriends married which high school football stars and how the little town of seven thousand people now had almost nine thousand. The office was simple, uncluttered, meticulously arranged. The proper number of neatly framed photos mounted on the off-white walls and the expected family photos arranged neatly on his small, faux-wood desk. The room smelled of Pine-Sol and Windex.

Kurt Windham was exactly what I imagined he would look when he hit middle-age: neatly pressed slacks, starched blue dress shirt and perfectly trimmed, short blonde hair. All that was missing was a tie. Maybe LDS church members didn't wear them on Saturdays. Windham had been a year younger than me in school but had been sort of the unofficial manager of our high school rock band. He did get us a few gigs, but mostly he schlepped amps around, put up posters and ran the sound board.

He was also one of the last people to see Jeannie Sorenson alive.

"Wow," he said, "I haven't thought about that in a while. That was like twenty years ago?"

"Twenty-eight," I said. Windham had been one of Jeannie's co-workers at the time, working on the processing line. Now he was managing one of the distribution channels. I explained to him that I had just wanted to find out what happened to an old friend.

"Feels weird talking about it after this long," he said.

"How long had you worked with her out here?"

He looked around the little office thinking. "Well, I started here part time my last year at high school. Then I went full time. I guess it was a year after that that she came to work. She had dropped out of college, I think."

"Did she say why?"

"She said it was money. She had been getting some kind of survivor benefits because her parents died, but that might not have been enough."

"Wasn't she getting income from leasing the farm out?" I asked.

"I don't remember that, but even if she was, that wouldn't be enough to pay for school and support her and Julie."

He said that Jeannie's sister Julie came to work at USP a few months later and the three were among others working the processing line, which was an entry level job of sorting, weighing and cleaning potatoes. It was a tedious, repetitive job and they sang, talked and gossiped most of the day. People got to know each other pretty well on the line.

"What do you remember about her there?" I asked.

"It was a long time ago."

He leaned back in his office chair, staring off to the side, then smiled, looking back at me.

"She was always nice, always friendly, and could be fun, but also, kind of. . ." He searched for a word. "Distant, I guess. And she called in sick a lot." A pause. "And I remember her and Julie always talking about ways to meet guys."

"You ever go out with either of them?"

He snorted a laugh. "My mom would have been scandalized if I had dated someone outside the church."

I laughed, too.

"I do remember her and Julie talking about their older brother."

"Pete?"

"Yeah, him. Something bad there. He was a truck driver or something and had moved away, leaving them to deal with the house and the farm. I guess she was mad about that."

He went on to explain how they would sometimes all go out for a drink after work. He remembered that Friday twenty-eight years ago well because of the questioning by the cops at the time. As usual, their group had met up for a drink after work.

"No one else met there that night? Just you three?"

"Just us three. We'd get something to drink, something to eat and then they'd leave." He smiled. "I usually stayed and ate because I was trying to figure out a way to ask the counter girl out. Never did."

"So, that night, you stayed and Julie and Jeannie left?"

"Yup."

"Together. They just drove off."

"Well, after a few minutes. Jeannie had stopped to talk to some people who were coming in. Her sister was already in the car and had honked at her a couple times." He laughed. "Jeannie just flipped her off."

"Who was she talking to?"

"Dunno."

"Guy or gal?"

"Both. She was talking to a couple people. Don't know who. I only glanced that way when her sister honked at her. I was too busy watching the counter girl. You remember Tiffany Mayer? The short little brunette cheerleader with the gorgeous smile?"

"She was beautiful," I said.

"Man, I wish she woulda gone out with me."

"Do you remember anything else after that? I mean about Jeannie," I asked.

He shook his head.

"So when Jeannie left, whoever she had been talking to must have come in. Did you recognize who it was then?"

Windham shook his head.

"I'm afraid my focus was on Tiffany," he said, letting out a sigh. I smiled back and nodded.

"Yeah. Tiffany."

We talked more, but he didn't have anything to add. We talked a few minutes more about what we had been doing since school and how he had worked his way up at USP. When our topics finally dried up, I stood and reached out a hand. "Thanks Kurt. I gotta get back to Marty's."

Windham stood and we shook.

"You think you're gonna find anything new about Jeannie's death after thirty years?" he asked.

I shrugged.

"Gotta try," I said.

He sighed and nodded.

"It was good seeing you again, man," he said. "Maybe we can get together while you're in town. Maybe have you over for dinner?"

"That'd be great, Kurt. Thanks!"

I made my way back down to the lobby and out the main doors. I had started down the steps to the parking lot when a voice stopped me.

"Hey, Wilbur."

At the bottom of the stairs, there was a man leaning against a battered, mid-seventies Chevy Corvette that was covered in grey primer and sanded down fiberglass repairs. It took me a few seconds to recognize him, but it was Robbie Clawson, who my dad used to refer to as my arch-enemy. He had lost weight over the years but had grown a bit of a pot belly and his dark hair was thinning on the top. Dressed in worn, gray work overalls and heavy work boots, he was giving me that crooked smile of his that communicated disdain and maybe polite hatred. His faced had aged harder than mine. Deep creases in his forehead and around his eyes that had settled deeper into their sockets, seeming to shrink and dried, pock-marked skin was evidence of a rough passage of time for him.

Wilbur was an insult-name assigned to me in Cub Scouts during a typical childish battle with other kids trying to come up with rude variations of their names as an insult. They had a hard time finding one for me until someone came up with Wilbur, thinking the name conveyed dopiness or something. Most of the kids forgot about the insult-names later, but Robbie remembered mine and used it whenever he felt like annoying me. I didn't remember what his insult-name had been. Wish I could.

I moved to shake his hand but he turned it into a very awkward, back-slapping embrace that took me by surprise, because we had never really been friends.

"Been a while, huh, Robbie?" I asked after breaking away.

"Couple years," he said.

"Nice old Vette," I said pointing to the car.

"It will be if I ever finish the body work."

"I ran into your sister a few hours ago," I said. "She mentioned you worked here."

"During the busy season," he said. "Got my own business I run the rest of the time."

"What's your business?"

"Security shit. Cameras, monitoring. That kind of stuff."

"Live in town?"

"Out on Howell Road, north of town."

"How'd you know I was back? Rosa tell you?"

He nodded. "Then I happened to see you go in there." He pointed to the administration building. "And I thought I'd catch you on the way out. See how you're doing."

"Just in town to close out some of my mom's estate stuff."

"Say, didn't she own Marty's? That bar in town?"

I nodded.

"So now you own it, right?"

"Yeah, all mine," I said. "Haven't decided what to do about it. One of the employees might be interested in buying it."

"How much you want for it?' he asked.

That surprised me.

"Uh, well, I haven't figured that out either yet. Why?"

"Well . . . I've been thinking about giving up the security business and getting into something else. Marty's is a nice place."

"It seems to be."

"So, how much?"

Still a little weirded-out, I shrugged. "If I decide to sell the place and can come up with a price, I'll let you know," I said.

We spent a few more minutes on polite, awkward chit-chat. I didn't want to go into detail about why I was at USP, so I just said I was there visiting an old school buddy, mentioning that Kurt had been involved in the band I played with in high school. After a few more minutes, we shook hands, he slipped into the Corvette and I took off towards the Jeep.

That was one of the few times he and I had ever parted ways without blood dripping off one of us.

TEN

It was going to be a busy Saturday night at Marty's. The parking lot was busy, cars coming and going and as I pulled into the lot and headed towards the back of the building, I noticed Reggie, the college kid who had been there the night before, standing next to his old Willys Jeep talking to two girls, who looked to be college-age like Reggie and seemingly smitten by the handsome young man. I slipped my Jeep in next to his.

"Hey Reggie," I said as I stepped out.

"Hi, Mr. Willis," he said.

"Rich," I corrected. "Hey girls."

The two threw me a cursory hello and told Reggie they'd see him inside. As they disappeared, I walked around his old Willys, checking it out.

"You do much on the body?" I asked.

"My dad and I had to patch holes and pound out some dents," he said, pointing to various places around the old Jeep.

"Nice job."

"We had to weld in a new floorboard. The original was all rusted out."

Reggie popped the hood and we talked about the rebuild of the motor, finding old parts and using 3D printers to replace some parts.

"You still interested in a job?" I asked as he latched the hood back into place.

"Shit, yeah," he said. "Gotta earn enough money to buy this thing from my Dad."

I slapped him on the shoulder. "Come on then. Let's go talk to Jia."

The place was jumping. Three fourths of the tables were occupied, Maroon Five was blasting out of the speakers and the air was filled with the smoky smell of the burgers and onions Tyler was burning on the grill. We walked up to the bar and when Jia returned from a table passing an order to Tyler, I touched her arm. She stopped.

"Jia," I said, "this is Reggie. He's looking for a job."

She looked him over. "Any serving experience?" she asked.

"Just running the register at my dad's car shop," he said. "I'm a fast learner, though."

Jia looked around. "I don't know. We need help, but I was hoping for someone with experience who was a lot better than this guy here," she said with a thumb towards me.

"Come on," I said. "Why not give him a try?"

Jia paused and looked around again. Then nodded to herself. She leaned over the bar and grabbed an apron, handing it to Reggie.

"How about we try you out tonight?" she said.

"Okay," he said.

"Put the apron on." He did. Reggie could clear and clean the tables when the customers left. As he got more comfortable with things, she said, he could start doing more. And at the end of the night, she would decide about keeping him on.

"How's that sound?" she said.

"Works for me," he said.

Jia waved at Marie who waddled over and introduced her to Reggie. "Show him where things are and then start him on some tables."

"Got it. C'mon Reggie."

Reggie gave me a smile, a "Thanks, Rich!" and then he was off after Marie.

Jia tapped me on my arm. "Yeah, thanks Rich. I owe you again if this kid works out. We really need the help."

"Seems like a good kid," I said. "I think he'll be okay." Jia went off to help a customer, I gave Tyler a wave and headed upstairs. I went into the storage room to check the security camera. I could hear the tape running in the vintage recorder and the monitor displayed the eating area. The system date was still off, though, so the monitor was displaying the right time but it was displaying tomorrow's date. I'd have to fix that. Not now. I didn't want to deal with powering down the system, getting into the BIOS, changing the date and rebooting.

Feeling lazy.

So I put it off.

In my room, I sat down on the edge of the bed, exchanged a few quick texts with my daughter and then pulled out my guitar and amp to play, which always seemed to refresh me. I spent a few minutes getting the thing tuned and then started plucking out a few notes, a few chords. From the bar, I heard St. Vincent's song Huey Newton playing and played along with it, then a Foo Fighters tune came on and I tried playing that one.

A text message interrupted my playing. My old band buddy, Sam, had contacted the other members about getting together at Marty's. We would try to gather the old band together on Marty's little stage.

That meant I really needed to practice because I was rusty,

"Kiss Me" by the Struts was now blasting up from the bar so I did my best to strum along. It was tough.

I kept this up as more songs played downstairs until the tips of my fingers felt raw. I gave up, dropped my guitar onto the floor and flopped back onto the bed, exhausted.

I sat up from there, looked at the clock realizing I had fallen asleep. It was closing in on midnight. I stretched, rubbed my aching fingers and headed downstairs.

The place was about half full. Camila and Lee had already taken off and Reggie was clearing tables. I found Jia behind the bar, going through receipts.

"The kid doing okay?" I asked.

Jia held up a finger while she finished counting, then dropped the receipts into a box under the bar.

"He's great," she said. "Good with customers, works hard. I'd say he's a keeper."

Then something happened.

The last thing I remember was Jia looking behind me.

Then a surprised expression.

Worry.

Alarm.

An open mouth to say something.

Then there was blackness.

I learned later what had happened.

Jia saw the door behind me open as we were talking and Volkov's angry bulk moving towards us.

Realizing what was happening, she tried to warn me, but a wicked right fist from Volkov smashed hard above my cheek and I dropped like a puppet released from ts strings.

He hit me again as I went down and kicked me in the gut and Jia was yelling and then Reggie was there and he threw Volkov back towards the door and Volkov charged again, but Reggie had the reach on him and bashed him hard in the face and then Volkov was down and Reggie was kneeling on his chest, pinning him.

Jia ran over and Tyler came out and Reggie said to call 911.

I mumbled the words "No. No police."

"We need the police," Reggie said, struggling to keep the big angry man down.

Jia put an arm on Reggie. "Please. No cops."

Reggie looked at her. Looked at the fat man. Looked at me. I muttered something like "No cops, Reg."

"Please," Jia said.

Reggie sighed, looked at Volkov and cocked a fist. "You gonna get the fuck outa here?"

Volkov stared. Glaring, furious. A glance at Jia's pleading face. Then a restrained, but angry nod at Reggie.

The black kid stood and kept an eye on the man as he stood, stepping back. He pointed towards me, still out of it on the ground and in a tight, low voice said "Tell him to stay away from her."

Volkov turned and walked out.

As Reggie turned to look at Jia, she followed Volkov out, exchanged some words and ran back in to help Reggie who was trying to get me to stand. I was still out of it, but waving off the suggestion of an ambulance.

"Let's get him upstairs," Jia said.

This was where my brain began working. I became aware of the massive ache where Volkov had sucker-punched me. Then the pain in my side where he had kicked me. I was glad he wore tennis shoes and not pointed leather loafers.

With an effort, I was able to walk up the stairs with Reggie and Jia balancing me and they guided me to my room and got me to the bed. Tyler appeared with a plastic bag of ice and I pressed it to my face.

I managed a feeble smile.

They gave me a quick rundown about what had just happened.

"Thanks guys. I'll be okay now."

"You took quite a hit there," Tyler said.

"I'll be fine. You guys can head back down. Let me rest."

They looked at each and agreed, moving towards the door.

"I'll check on you," Jia said.

I nodded and they were gone.

I dozed off. I remember Tyler coming up with more ice once. Jia came up a couple times, checking on me. By a little after one in the morning, my head had finally cleared up. The music from the bar had stopped. I heard plates clanging in the dish sink, heard garbage being hauled out, heard doors open and close. I guessed that the evening was over, so I stripped down to my boxers. In the bathroom, I looked at my face in the mirror and could see that I was going to have a bruise.

I swallowed about a half dozen ibuprofen tablets, killed the lights and crawled painfully into my bed.

I heard footsteps on the stairs and then a light tap on the door.

It swung open and Jia walked quietly into the room. I flipped on the lamp at the bedside table and half sat up.

"Wanted to see if you're still okay," she said.

"Just sore."

"Got a bruise starting," she said pointing to my eye.

I nodded. Then gave her a hard look. "So, what the hell was that about?"

She let out a heavy exhale, then gave me her crooked, sad smile.

"What?" I asked.

"Volkov thinks we slept together last night. When you snuck me out of here. He says he broke in, couldn't find me or you and then figured we had gone to a hotel. Or your house."

"My house?"

"He doesn't know you're staying upstairs. Doesn't know you actually live in another state."

"That's it?" I said. I struggled off the bed. Stood. "The guy sucker-punched me because he thought I was screwing you?" A nod. "Why?"

She backed up a step. "He just does. . .."

"Is he your dad?"

"No!" She was emphatic.

"Brother? Ex-boyfriend? Stalker?"

"No. No. No."

"Is he a fruitcake?"

"No," she said finally. "He's my husband."

Well, that stopped me.

"It's a fucking mess," she said. Taking a deep breath, Jia paced in my little studio giving me the story.

Her father had been a member of a crime family in Kyiv that got caught up in a vicious turf war between families. Last year, her father was forced to make a deal with the other major crime family. The same way royal families once made arranged marriages to merge countries or end wars, the crime families agreed to a truce if he would agree to marry his daughter to the son of the other family.

"Volkov," I said. "And you agreed?"

"Fuck no," she said. "But people were getting killed. Friends, neighbors. It was awful. My father pushed hard."

Her mother figured a way out and they agreed to the marriage. Keeping Jia's father in the dark and using her mother's contacts in Moldova, they arranged an escape. The wedding went as planned. Vows, toasts and promises of peace were made and the reception dinner was a raucous, drunken, crowded mess in which Jia and her mother disappeared. Using false passports to get thru Moldova, Romania and Bulgaria, they made it into the US.

"My mother had some very distant relatives in the Ukrainian community here and thought this might be the best place to hide and start over. And it was. Perfect. Until a few days ago. That's when Volkov showed up."

Volkov wanted to convince her to come back to Ukraine with him, Jia explained. He didn't know where she lived yet, but he would eventually find out.

"You can't call the police because they would find out you have a bogus passport," I said. "Your mother too, right?"

"We'd get deported back to Kyiv. Volkov can't kidnap me and take me back by gunpoint, but if he finds where I live and finds my mother, he may have a way to force me back."

She was in a tough place.

"What are you going to do?" I asked.

She just shook her head.

"Then, you figure out what you can do and I'll do everything I can to help. Okay?"

She gave me that cute, crooked smile. "Okay. That's one more thing I owe you, I guess."

She moved to the door and I laid back down on the bed. Instead of leaving though, Jia went to the door and closed it. Then she walked back over to the foot of the bed kicking off her shoes and unbuttoning her blouse.

I sat up, staring.

Jia was smiling at me, slipping the blouse off her shoulders to the floor. She reached behind her back and unsnapped her bra which joined her blouse on the floor.

"I'm way too old for you, you know," I said.

"And I'm way too young for you," she said unsnapping, unzipping and slithering out of her jeans. "But I owe you."

"Owe me?"

"You have done more for me the last two days than anyone has done in years."

Her panties dropped and she stepped out of them, standing completely naked there at the foot of the bed: perfect porcelain skin and a slender, smooth torso, small youthful breasts and that long, now loose red hair, draping over her shoulders.

"You don't owe me a thing," I stuttered.

"Well then, think of it as a 'thank you' for taking punches for me."

"No need to thank me."

She crawled onto the bed.

"Okay," she said, straddling me and looking at me mischievously with those big green eyes. "Look at it this way: I haven't been laid in a year and a half and I really need a fuck. How's that?"

I reached over to the lamp and turned it off..

"I'm good with that."

—·—

ELEVEN

Sunday.

I awoke to a scent I hadn't smelled in years: a delicate perfume, sweet perspiration and the odor of sex. Something made my nose itchy and I smiled, realizing it was a long stray red hair from the sleeping redhead next to me. I rolled to my side and propped myself up on one elbow.

Jia was on her side, back to me, the blankets pushed down to her waist. Her bare back was firm, covered with soft, unblemished skin and when I placed my hands against it, all I could think of was how old I was.

"'bout time you woke up," Jia said, rolling over to face me. "I wanted to get you up an hour ago."

"You should have," I said. "What time is it?"

"Almost nine. You had such a restless night I didn't want to wake you."

"Tossing and turning?"

"And talking. A lot."

"These dreams I've been having lately . . ." I started.

"Who's Bess?" Jia asked.

"Bess was my wife."

"Something happen?"

"Died two years ago."

"Sorry. You kept saying 'Wait, wait' or something."

"I have this recurring nightmare about her in the hospital where she was dying. Me begging her not to go, to wait, that I had things to say, things to fix."

"And you mentioned a Sean?"

"I did?"

Jia nodded.

"Sean was my best buddy all through college. A couple months ago, they found him dead in a homeless encampment in Seattle."

"Oh god . . ."

"I had to identify the body. They found a business card with my name on it."

"Did they find him in a field or something?"

"A field?"

"You mumbled about digging something out. You were getting frantic and moving all over the bed. I gave you a shove and you stopped."

"That's my friend that was killed here in Black River. She was found in a field."

"You have these dreams a lot?"

"Yeah."

"You should see somebody. That sounds a little fucked up."

"It is fucked up. I'm a little fucked up."

"So did you see anyone?" she asked.

"You mean a shrink? Yeah. I went to one."

"And?"

"And what?"

She frowned at me. "What did the head doctor say?"

"Said I was depressed and gave me those pills," I said, pointing the bottle on the bedstand.

"That's it?"

"Not gonna bore you with the rest," I said.

Jia gave me an annoyed growl, threw the blankets off and straddled me.

"You know," I said, "we can't do this anymore."

"I know," she said. "And that's why you can bother me with all that, because it will never leave this room. I want to know what your wife and two friends dying have to do with you and why you're here and what it has to do with an uncle."

"Did I say something about an uncle, too?"

"That's what it sounded like," she said. Then Jia put her hands on my shoulders and leaned down so that we were almost nose to nose, her clear emerald eyes looking intently into mine.

It's hard not to be honest when you have a beautiful naked woman on top of you.

I pushed her off and sat on the side of the bed facing the wall. Jia came up and sat behind me, her legs on both sides, her hands on my shoulders, her breasts pressed against my back.

"Go ahead," she said gently.

I took a deep breath.

"It's a depression, I suppose," I said, trying to verbalize things that had been mostly abstract. "Mixed with a little self-loathing 'cuz I have not been a good friend or good husband. Maybe not a good person."

"Bullshit," she said. "What gives you that idea?"

"It started three years ago," I said, "when my wife was diagnosed with cancer."

The diagnosis was like a slap in the face, I explained. It woke me up. I had been obsessed by career, pushing everything else aside, even friends and family until that diagnosis. I had so much I should have given her of my time and love and I didn't. Then she was gone, along with the chance to fix it. After that, I did my best to repair the things with my daughter that I had screwed up. I felt like I had been absent during her struggles dealing with her mother's death.

"But these friends who died," Jia said, "they still haunt you?"

"Yeah."

I got up and went into the bathroom, ran some water and splashed it on my face. I came back as I toweled off.

Jia was sitting on the side of the bed watching me.

"For an old dude," she said with her crooked smile, "you still have a passable body."

I threw the towel into her face and plopped back down on my back on top of the bed. Jia straddled my waist and reached back between my legs.

"And for an old dude," she said, "the equipment seems to be in pretty good working order."

"Didn't I say something about not doing this anymore?" I asked.

"Yes, you did." Jia smiled as she pressed her lips over mine.

Later, both of us sweating hard and panting, she rolled off onto her back next to me.

"Thanks," she said after we had both caught our breath. "That should keep me for a few months. At least until I find someone my own age."

"Glad I could help," I said.

"So," she said after a few minutes, propping herself up on an elbow, looking at me. "Those dreams."

"Let's not do that," I said. I got up and sat on the corner of the bed to get dressed

"I think I've figured you out. These three people that died show up in your dreams because you think you failed them."

"Do we really need— "

"You're trying to make up for it, right?"

I slipped my boxers on. Jia slid up next to me.

"And that first day when you got here and you chased off Volkov. You helped me. You helped me like you hadn't helped your buddy."

I slipped my pants on and stood and walked to the little closet and grabbed a t-shirt.

"Right?" Jia asked.

I looked at her.

"So, you helped me."

I nodded.

"And now you are trying to repay that other friend by helping the police find her killer?"

"Not helping them, helping me. Paying a debt."

"A debt? To who?"

"Jeannie. I owe her."

Jia stood. "Owe her?"

"Sorry. I gotta get going," I said. "Do you want me to sneak you out of here?"

"No," she said. "I parked three blocks away, behind Kepler's Market. He won't know anything." She grabbed my arm. "What do you owe her?"

I turned to her, bent down and gently kissed her.

"You know," I said, with a little sadness. "We really can't do this again."

"Yes, the boss-employee thing," she said, "and I don't want a real relationship right now." She gave me that crooked smile. "And, like I said, you're too old for me."

I gave her a look of mock disappointment and turned for the door.

"You didn't answer me," she said. "Why do you owe your friend? And what about your uncle?"

With a wave, I was out and down the stairs. I went down to the bar and was surprised to see it empty. It hit me that it was Sunday. I went to the front door and looked at the little sign that specified when the place was open and closed. On Sundays, Marty's doesn't open until eleven. I guessed that was so everyone could get to church before going out for brunch.

I checked out the parking lot for any suspicious SUV's. None. Volkov must have figured Jia stayed home or something. He'd be back though.

I had told Jia I'd stay out of her business with him, but it was no longer just her business. The guy had sucker-punched me into unconsciousness and that made him my business. I knew I couldn't call the cops about what was going on between him and Jia, but maybe I could take care of Volkov in a way that didn't involve her..

It was time to go shopping.

I headed towards Idaho Falls, the biggest city in that part of the state, because I needed thrift stores and pawn shops.

The LDS and Catholic thrift stores turned out to be closed – I had forgotten that it was Sunday – but the Goodwill, Value Village and Salvation Army shops were open. I hit the stores heading to their electronics sections. After visiting three, I was still empty-handed except for a vintage WIFI router that I needed.

My fourth stop, a small Goodwill store in the old part of downtown looked to be fruitless as well. I scoured the electronics section with no luck. Giving up and turning to go, a conversation caught my attention. I paused and pretended to be looking at used kitchen gadgets so I could listen in.

A short, massively fat man in jeans and a flannel shirt that barely held his massive belly in was talking about a guitar.

"Kid," he was saying, "if ya' gotta buy a used axe, go to the right fuckin' pawn shop. Not here. The best one for instruments is Main Pawn and Loan. It's four blocks down that street." He pointed out the window. "But don't buy an amplifier there. That asshole doesn't know a good amp from a bad radio. You want an amp? Jerry's Pawn out at Westgate is the best place."

"Okay," was all the kid said before leaving.

"Fuckin' idiot," the man mumbled.

"Excuse me," I said walking over to the man. He turned.

"Yeah?"

The man smelled of sweat, grease and cigarette smoke. Nicotine stained the beard below his mouth and his teeth were almost orange from a lifetime of Marlboros.

"I heard you talking to that kid about pawn shops," I said, "and it seemed like you knew what you were talking about."

"I do," he said, "not that it mattered to that little asshole."

"Where's the best place to get used electronics?" I asked.

"What kind? Stereos? Phones?"

"Computers."

"Mary's," he said without a second's hesitation.

"Sorry. New to town. What's Mary's?" I asked.

"Mary's Pawn and Loan. Out on Yellowstone. They got a shitload of computer crap there. College kids come down to hock their shit when money from mommy runs out and they need beer cash."

"Mary knows her stuff?"

"Ain't no Mary there. It's Les. He's the owner. Mary was his second . . . no, third wife. Les used to work for one of those big computer companies that was in Utah. Can't remember its name. Came here after they went tits up. Knows his shit."

I said my thanks and was out of there.

Mary's was on the old Yellowstone Highway that ran north out of Idaho Falls. I pulled up to the building which looked to have once been a convenience store: lots of glass in an unimaginative old concrete structure. Inside, the rows of shelves were piled high with used tools, stereos, some musical instruments and against one wall, a huge assortment of battered laptops, towers, monitors, keyboards and bins holding cables, mice, trackballs and more.

It looked like the place would have what I needed. I began going through the laptops, plugging them in, booting them up until I found an old Dell laptop that would be good enough. I took it the counter where a thin little Asian man was quietly waiting.

"Do you have any thumb drives?"

He pointed to a shelf in the display case. There were dozens of USB thumb drives. I pointed at two tiny ones and he pulled them out.

He rang me up and I gathered up the equipment thanking him. "You're Les, right?" I asked.

He nodded.

"You don't talk much," I said.

He gave me a surprised look. "Really? Huh. My old lady says I never shut up."

Stashing my new equipment into the backpack I had in the Jeep, I went in search of a coffee shop where I could sit and get the laptop set up. I stumbled across a Walmart in my search and decided to take advantage of it. I ran in and with cash, spent three hundred dollars for a prepaid VISA card so I could make some anonymous online purchases. It didn't take me too much longer to find a coffee shop that claimed to have WIFI. And I liked its name: Bean There, Bun That.

The coffee shop was small and dark, but laid out with nice wood grain tables, comfy chairs, a few couches and not many customers. It smelled of burnt milk, coffee and sugary pastries. There was only one barista handling the early afternoon clientele, a very tall, slender woman whose hair hung down her back below her waist. A name tag indicated Emaline was her name. Big, colorful earrings dangled from her ears and her wrists jangled with metal bracelets when she handed me my latte and scone.

I thanked her. Then, after getting the WIFI password, I settled myself into a tiny, corner table, pulled out the Dell laptop that I had just purchased and went to work.

Over the course of the next two hours, I installed a new operating system on the laptop along with all the security programs and utilities I would be needing. It felt like the laptop was ready for what I would be using it for. I packed up and on my way out, stopped at the counter.

"Hey Emaline," I said, "do you happen to know where Olson Trucking is? It's supposed to be around here somewhere."

"Yeah," she said. "I pass it on my way into work. Well, I pass a sign at least. About a mile north." She pointed that way. "As you are heading out, there's a bunch of old warehouses on the left. There's an Olson Trucking sign there, like maybe they have an office somewhere in those old buildings."

It seemed odd that she would remember a sign pointing to a little trucking company, so I asked her why.

"Oh . . . you'll see."

She was right. You couldn't miss the sign. It had Olson Trucking written on it and an arrow pointing to the offices. What you couldn't miss, though, was above the arrow: the giant image of smiling, winking blonde beauty showing more cleavage than Dolly Parton. Next to her face it read: "We Truck All Night".

I turned into the cluster of old buildings and warehouses and found a small building that looked like it was tacked onto the warehouse behind it. I pulled up to the door just as a woman was stepping out, turning and locking the door. I realized that I had lost track of time. It was almost six at night.

I stepped out of the Jeep as the woman was opening the door to her car.

"Excuse me," I said.

She turned with the look of someone that had no interest in talking to anyone, let alone a stranger. She was a big, square woman, looking to be at least sixty, in a large, flowered dress. She glared over the top of her reading glasses at me.

"What?" she said.

"I'm looking for Pete Sorenson," I said. "Does he still work here?"

"Yeah," she said. "Why? He in trouble again?"

"Trouble? Not that I know of," I said. "I'm an old school mate of his."

"Not a cop?" she asked.

I was a little puzzled. "Cop? No. Why would you think I'm a cop?"

She looked at me a moment and then must have decided I wasn't a policeman. "He's on a run to Salt Lake tonight. He'll be back tomorrow afternoon." She was about to slip into her car.

"He'll be here?"

She shrugged. "Maybe. But it'll be his Friday so he'll probably be at Red Deer's."

"Red Deer?"

"It's a bar. His watering hole."

She climbed into her car, shut the door and was soon on her way, me staring after her.

She was worried that Pete was in trouble again? That I was a cop?

What kind of trouble had PeeWee been in?

It looked like I was going to have to do some digging and by tomorrow, I should have access to everything I'd need to do that.

— · —

TWELVE

Tyler was hanging out behind Marty's when I pulled in, vaping something that smelled faintly of raspberry.

"Quiet tonight?" I asked.

"Sundays are slow," he said. He pointed his pen at the back door. "There's a guy at the bar waiting for you."

"Volkov?"

He shook his head. "Some other guy. He was talking to Jia. I couldn't hear nothing."

I nodded and turned to go in and he stopped me.

"What?"

"Volkov's in there too. Corner table, on his laptop."

"Okay."

"Gonna beat him up?"

I just laughed.

"Throw him out?"

"No," I said. "Don't want to do that."

"Why not?"

I just smiled and Tyler put his vape pen away and followed me through the back door. He slipped into the kitchen and I walked out to the bar where Jia was cleaning glasses and Camila was working the tables. Volkov looked up from his computer as I came in and we locked stares for a few seconds. Then he made a little derisive smirk and went back to what he was doing. He knew that Jia wouldn't let me get the authorities involved in what was going on between them.

"Wilbur!"

That voice again.

I glanced down towards the other end of the bar.

Robbie Clawson was the guy waiting for me.

"Hey Rob," I said, slightly confused.

He was propped on a stool nursing a glass of beer which he lifted in the gesture of a toast towards me. It didn't look like it was his first of the evening. I pulled up a stool next to him.

"Buy you a drink?" he said jokingly.

I called down to Jia. "Could I get a cider, please?" She nodded and I turned to Clawson. "What's up?"

He took a gulp of his beer.

"I was serious when I said I might be interested in buying this place," he said.

"If I decide to sell, you mean?"

"Yeah. I could do a lot here." He waved an arm at the room like a magician casting a spell. "Lots of potential. And you aren't even using that stage. You know what you could do with that?"

Jia set a glass and a cold can of cider in front of me.

"Here ya' go, Wilbur," she said with a more-crooked-than-usual smile.

I gave her frown.

"What's he talking about? Do with what?" she asked.

I jabbed a thumb towards Clawson. "He claims he wants to buy the place." I said with a wink he couldn't see. She narrowed her eyes at me then turned towards Clawson.

"Oh yeah?"

"Yup," he said. "I'd get different beers in here, toss out a few things and get a pool table. Maybe pinball machines?"

"Pinball?" Jia asked, scrunching up her face.

"Yeah." He pointed to the stage. "and get some bands or maybe get some dancers up there. That'd bring people in."

"Yes, it would," Jia said wryly. She gave me a sideways glance and went back to the other end of the bar, Clawson watching her.

"She's got a great ass," he said quietly. "I'd keep her around."

"Look, about this place," I started.

"How much you think you want?"

"I have no idea. I'm not even sure yet that I want to sell it."

"But you might?"

"Might. Do you even have the money?"

He suddenly got a little evasive. "I'm pretty sure I can raise it. I might have to do a contract thing with you or something. You're going back to Seattle, though, right?"

"Bellingham," I corrected. "After I finish a few things."

"Oh, yeah, Rosa said you was looking at some old murder?"

"Your sister told you about that?" I asked.

"Said it was someone we used to go to school with?"

"Jean Sorenson," I said.

"Shit!" he said. "I remember that. That was fuckin' awful." He shook his head sympathetically. "Why are you looking at that? That's the sheriff's job."

"Just curious about what happened to an old friend," I said.

Clawson nodded, staring at me.

"I remember that happening," he said, taking another drink. "I remember telling Rosa that they oughta look at Jean's brother." He looked away, thinking. "What was his name?"

"Pete."

He snapped his fingers, turning back to me. "Yeah, him. I told Rosa the lazy ass sheriff's people oughta be lookin' at him."

"Why?" I asked.

He took a swig and went into a loud whisper. "Cuz I think he was beating her. He was one mean asshole." Another swallow. "And I'll bet he was doing more than that, if you catch my drift."

"What makes you say that?" I asked.

"Just what people were saying back then. I'd look at him. I'll bet they got in some kinda fight and he beat her to death and buried her in that field."

I stared at Clawson. He looked back at me.

"Seriously," he said. "Check him out. Fucked up dude. Never liked him."

He chugged that last of his beer and stood, patting me on the shoulder.

"Off to work," he said.

I turned to him, surprised. "This late?"

"Back on the night shift for the next two weeks," he said. "Let me know when you come up with a price for this dump and we'll work out a deal."

I just nodded.

Clawson waved and I watched him wobble a little as he went out the door.

I stared after him, going over everything he said, until Jia interrupted me.

"You aren't going to sell this place to him, are you?" she asked.

I waved my hand towards the door dismissively. "He'll never get the money and even if he ever did, I would never sell to him."

"Why not?" she asked.

"He and I have a history. And it's not a good history."

"Sounds like a story I'd like to hear," she said.

"A story I'll tell you one of these days." I pointed upstairs. "Gotta go get my guitar. An old band buddy is coming by. We're gonna try a couple songs."

Before I snagged my guitar, I was going to do a test run at Volkov's laptop.

Upstairs, I powered on the Dell laptop I had set up that afternoon and logged into my bogus profile. I launched an app which searched the place's wireless network and gave me a list of everything connected to it. Luckily, there were only a few and I could eliminate the phones, the point-of-sale system and the computer I was on. After a few minutes, I found the device I was looking for: Volkov's laptop.

I launched another app and examined data traffic running back and forth on Volkov's machine. By looking at the data packets, I could tell he was browsing an Eastern European website, streaming music via Pandora and running an email program. Volkov was a sloppy computer user. He wasn't using any serious security software, he was browsing with an old internet browser and he was running a computer with an outdated operating system.

Hackers love users like Volkov.

I followed the flow of data packets going back and forth between his computer and the website he was on and injected a tiny executable program into the stream. Getting into that stream was like wading out into a river and then setting a special package in the river to float down with the current to a destination: his laptop. Volkov didn't notice anything as his old browser ran the little executable and installed a tiny program that would let me in.

I waited a few minutes, then I launched a program on my computer and connected to the program I had just snuck onto his machine.

I was in with full access to all the files on Volkov's computer.

I smiled to myself, shut the app down and closed the laptop I was using. I was set up. If things worked the way I hoped, in a few days, Volkov would be out of Jia's life. I was going to sucker-punch him back.

Digitally speaking.

Sam would be showing up soon so I grabbed my guitar, music sheets and my small amplifier and went back down to the bar and onto the stage, taking a good look at the performance area for the first time. It was more like a dark, messy cave than a stage. It was maybe twenty feet wide and ten feet deep cluttered with boxes, chairs and broken tables, all covered in a patina of dust and hamburger grease.

Jia was behind the bar mixing a drink and I called out to her. "You okay if I move this stuff up to the storeroom?"

She gave me a thumbs up. "Want help?"

"I got it."

After thirty minutes I had half the junk upstairs when Sam walked in the door and jumped up on the stage. We embraced. He was a little shorter than me, a square man with a friendly oval face who had put on a little weight over the years. He had always reminded me of George, that character on the old Seinfeld TV show.

"How ya' doin' Sam?" I asked.

"Not bad, buddy," he said, "just hope my old fingers can still work this guitar."

"Probably better than my fingers. Give me a few minutes. I'm trying to clear some of this crap off so we have room to play," I said grabbing two old chairs.

"I'll help," he said.

We talked as we moved some things up to the storeroom and took others out back.

"Did you get a hold of Katzendorf the other day?" he asked as he threw an old lamp into the dumpster. "About Jean Sorenson?"

"Found him."

"Did he remember her? The guy's pretty ancient."

"He remembered the case," I said. "Which brings up a question I want to ask you."

Sam's family had lived out in the same farming area. All the families knew each other, worked and played together, rode the same buses to the same schools.

"Rob Clawson was just in here," I started.

"Clawson?" Sam seemed surprised.

"Yeah. He mentioned Jeannie's brother, Pete. Do you remember him?"

Sam stopped and leaned back against the wall.

"Pete," he started, remembering something. "I remember him. We called him PeeWee when we were kids, right?"

I nodded. We went back inside to the stage to grab more junk.

"Yeah. He'd been fun and a friend, I guess," Sam said, "but at some point, I dunno, maybe it was when he hit puberty, he changed. Got mean." He thought a moment. "Angry might be a better word. Got in some fights. You know about that, right? Even a fight with me."

I was a little shocked. "You? In a fight? Hard to imagine." Sam was a mellow, easy-going guy and thinking of him being in a fist fight was a stretch for me.

We hauled the last of the junk to the trash, which left the little stage cleared off except for a pair of chairs. Sam pulled out his guitar, I powered up the little amplifier and we plugged in to tune up.

Camila heard me failing to get my 'E' string tuned to 'E' and came up to the stage looking at us as if we were the class troublemakers.

"You two ain't gonna embarrass us are you? In front of all these people?" She indicated the half dozen people scattered around.

"Probably just embarrass ourselves," I said.

"Probably," she said walking back to the bar to drop an order. I couldn't tell if she was joking, Sam was sure she wasn't.

As we finally got our instruments into the same key, I looked up to see that Volkov had gathered up his laptop and was walking towards us.

"Shit," I muttered.

Sam gave me a puzzled look.

I stood, set my guitar down and walked to the edge of the stage. Stepping down off it I walked towards him, tensed up, ready to start swinging. Camila turned to watch, Tyler came over the service counter and Jia ran around the bar to come over, then stopped next to Camila when Volkov reached out to shake my hand.

I stared at it.

He looked at his hand, then up at me.

"I am sorry," he said. He didn't sound like he was sorry I got hurt but more like he was apologizing for a social misstep, like farting in an elevator.

"What?"

"I am sorry," he repeated. "I should not have hit you. It was a misunderstanding."

"Yeah?"

"I thought that you and--" he nodded towards Jia, "that night. . . but I was wrong."

Lucky for me he didn't know about the next night.

"So I should apologize to you," he said, his hand still out to me.

I hesitated, looked at Jia who seemed totally baffled, then grudgingly took his hand and shook.

"Good," he said. He turned, but I called out. "How about Jia?"

Volkov stopped, stiffened and didn't look at me. "Not your concern." He walked out of the tavern.

I watched him for a moment, feeling like I should go after him. But a glance towards Jia who gave me a quick shake of the head stopped me. I sighed, nodded and turned back towards the stage.

"Why didn't you kick his ass?" Tyler called out.

"Not the right time," I said. Tyler growled, Camila scowled and then everyone went back to work. Sam and I picked up our guitars, him giving me a curious look.

"Disgruntled customer?"

I laughed.

"Jealous husband?"

I chose not to tell him how close to the truth that was.

"A little disagreement with one of the employees," I said sitting. "So what are we gonna play?"

Sam set up an iPad with some music he had found for us and for the next hour we struggled through some old songs by John Mayer and Bruce Cockburn and even tried our hand at some early Springsteen tunes until our fingertips were sore and our voices were wearing out. Happy to have gotten a smattering of smiles and occasional applause from listeners, we decided to call it a night before we completely ruined our aging vocal cords.

As we put our music and guitars away, Camila walked past on her way to a table.

"Well," she said. "at least you guys don't suck."

I gave her the evil eye, Sam gave her a WTF gesture and she moved on.

"We still harmonize nicely," Sam said.

"Yeah, I think we do," I said. "Thanks for doing this, Sam. I really needed it. I haven't been able to sit down to play and sing in years. I missed it."

"You still sound decent."

"Maybe, but my fingers don't seem to work the chords as well as they used to."

"Seemed good enough to me," he said. "Can we get some of the band together here sometime?"

"This was too much fun. We've got to do it."

"Awesome," Sam said, stepping off the little stage. "I'll get on the phone and get them here."

He started to the door then turned back to me. "Too bad you can't hang around here for a few years. Playing in a band again would be a hoot."

"Yes, it would."

He waved and was gone.

I grabbed my guitar and amp. I dropped off the stage and set them down in front of the bar where Jia was pouring a beer for someone. I plopped onto a stool.

"You are good," she said.

"Thanks. A bit rusty and my throat is raw. Haven't sung that much in a long time."

"Just a minute," she said. She pulled a bottle of ice tea from the cooler, poured it into a glass with some ice, lemon juice and honey, and handed it to me. "Throat soother."

I took a swallow.

"Oh, yeah. That feels good. Thanks."

I heard the door open behind me. It closed.

"Hey, sweet cheeks."

Her voice.

I hadn't heard that voice in more than twenty years, but it was unmistakable. I smiled. Without turning to see, I spoke.

"Of all the gin joints in all the towns in all the world--"

"I walked into yours," the voice said.

I swiveled around on the stool to see a beautiful ghost from my past standing in the doorway.

Eleanor.

Eleanor Fife was just as I remembered her. Tall, with long, straight dark hair that fell across her wide shoulders most of the way down her back. She was a strong, but slender woman with long legs, a big toothy smile and small, but piercing, clear blue eyes that still twinkled. With her long face, wide cheeks, thin lips and strong dark eyebrows, Eleanor was not what might be described as beautiful, but she was incredibly attractive. Wearing a loose t-shirt, tight jeans and sandals, a big pouch hanging from a shoulder, it didn't look like she had gained a pound since I had seen her last, just a few more wrinkles and smile lines.

I stood and went to her, meeting halfway in a happy embrace, tears welling in both our eyes. I pulled back and she gave me a light kiss on the cheek.

"What the hell are you doing here?" I asked.

She laughed.

I hadn't forgotten her laugh. It was a big, open mouth laugh. Not delicate, cute or feminine, but a great laugh.

"Reggie," she said.

"Huh?"

She patted my cheek. "How's your head?"

It took me a minute.

"Oh! That Reggie," I said. "You know him?"

"He's one of my students."

I pointed a finger at her, as I figured it out. "You're directing Romeo and Juliet."

A nod. "I teach at Idaho State now," she said.

Ellie and I had met in college, the University of Utah, both active in the theatre department. I was there on a scholarship and she was there because she lived in Salt Lake City. She was a little older than me and far more talented. During a production of Neil Simon's Star Spangled Girl that we were in, I fell hard for her and by that summer, we had moved in together. It had been a fun and passionate relationship, really my first serious one and I learned a lot from her.

"Reggie told me he got a job here," she said. "Then he told me about someone coming in and flattening the owner. I asked him who the owner was and here I am."

I had a big smile on my face.

I pointed to a table. "Got time to sit? It's late but—"

"Sure." She hung her pouch on the back of a chair and sat herself at the table.

"Can I get you a drink?" I asked.

"Any light beer?"

I nodded and turned to the bar. Jia and Camila had been watching and listening with amusement and Jia had drawn a beer for Eleanor before I got to the bar.

She handed it to me with a big teasing smile, Camila joining in.

"Thanks," I said sarcastically taking the beer and my glass of ice tea back to the table.

"What's that?" Eleanor asked.

"Tea with honey and lemon," I said. "For my throat. A friend and I were singing and playing guitars a little while ago."

"You still play?"

"Play is a generous term."

"Never went back to doing theatre?" she asked.

I shook my head.

Approaching our last year at school, I had realized that I didn't have what it would take to make it in the world of theatre and had been moving more into computer science while Ellie blossomed in the dramatic arts. I found myself spending more and more time in the computer lab and less with Eleanor, who became busier than ever with her stage productions. I guess I was drifting away from her and was too stupid to see what I was losing. With her graduation approaching, she had decided to get her Master's and had received a grant to attend a graduate school in Wisconsin. She wanted me to go along, finish my BA there, but I decided I would go for my Master's in computer science up in Seattle and wanted her to come with me.

"How'd you end up at Idaho State?" I asked.

"After I got my Master's, I studied for another year in London, then came back and taught at a little junior college in New Hampshire. Then at Oregon State, then Idaho State. I've been at ISU for twelve years now. The chairman of the department is retiring at the end of the next semester and I am in line to take over."

"Congratulations," I said. "Chairman of the Theatre Arts Department. Not bad."

She smiled.

In that last year of college, we argued more and more with our opposing careers and about halfway through the last semester, she basically threw me out of the apartment we shared.

"How come you're here?" she asked. "Last I heard, you were doing computer stuff in Seattle or something."

"Bellingham."

"Reggie says you're a cop," she said with a mischievous smile.

My eyes rolled.

I explained what my work was and that I had come back to Black River to wrap up my mother's estate and that I had been asked to help the local sheriff, who was an old friend.

"Cop," she teased.

"Asshole."

She laughed. Then I did. There was a pause as we both sipped on our drinks, then Eleanor looked around the bar.

"So, will you sell this place?"

I shrugged. "Still don't know."

"If he sells it, Jia is buying it," Tyler called out.

"Are you listening to our conversation, Tyler?" I said, swiveling in my chair to look at him.

"Of course I am."

I flipped him the finger. He laughed, turned back to the grill and I turned back to Ellie.

"If you sell it, you'll head back to Washington?" she asked.

"I guess so."

She looked at me. Paused. Nodded.

We talked and I was able to get a few tidbits of her story from her. She had married a physics professor she met when she was teaching at Oregon State and they had a son, who was now teaching at a high school in Sacramento.

"So, what's your name now?" I asked. "Take his name?"

"Hell, no," she said. "His last name is Smith-Fitzpatrick. No way I was gonna be a hyphenate. I kept my name and he didn't mind."

Eleanor continued saying that while she was at Oregon State, she got a job offer from ISU. It offered more money and was closer to her family, who still lived in Salt Lake City. She took the job and moved to Pocatello. A year later, he followed, getting hired to head the Physics Department.

"That's good that you two get to work together like that," I said.

She nodded.

We spent another two hours talking about old friends, dead parents and all the work she had done to get where she was. Conversation flowed easily between us. I had forgotten what that was like.

Eleanor finally glanced at her phone, chugged down the last of her second beer and stood, grabbing her pouch.

"I've got to get back to Pocatello, Rich," she said. "Three lectures tomorrow morning."

I stood. We walked towards the door and out onto the narrow patio at the front of the tavern.

The air was cool, crisp. We both took deep breaths. She looked at me. She looked for a long moment, then gave me a gentle, almost sad kiss on the cheek.

"It was so good seeing you again," she said. "Thanks for the beers."

She paused for a brief moment, then went to her car and drove away as I stood on the porch watching.

Ellie.

THIRTEEN

It was after eight the next morning when I walked into the lobby of the sheriff's office, but the place was empty. Was everybody at a meeting? I sat myself down into one of the visitor chairs outside the office to wait.

After twenty minutes, Geraldine dragged herself through the door, holding a giant cup of coffee and lugging a purse that was as big as my backpack. She acknowledged my presence with a sigh while unlocking the door to the office and walking in to her desk. I followed her in.

"You need those files again?" she asked without looking at me.

"No. Gil asked me to come in this morning."

She glanced up at me as she sat at her desk and snorted a laugh.

"Gil's morning doesn't start until ten," she said. "He's no early bird."

"Great."

"I'll have the coffee machine set up in a few minutes or you can go down to the coffee shop at the other end of the building. They've got donuts."

I nodded.

"I'll be back," I said.

The little coffee shop was about as big as a large living room, old, institutional, with three small tables in front of a glass counter displaying various pre-made pastries. Three deputies sat around one table discussing the weekend's football games. The counter-girl was tiny and mousey looking with tiny dark eyes that were constantly scouring the area like a frightened squirrel.

I ordered a latte and two scones.

"Thought this kind of place would be busier on a Monday morning," I said while she prepped my order.

"Never is," she said. "Nuthin' seems to start around her 'til like ten."

"Why?" I asked.

She shrugged.

I pointed to the deputies that were laughing away about something.

"They been here for half an hour. Same every day. They hang around for like two hours every morning. Not much to do, I guess."

"Huh."

She handed me a paper cup with my drink and a bag with my pastries.

When I got back to the sheriff's office, I gave one of the scones to Geraldine, who was politely grateful, but gave me the distinct impression she would have preferred something filled with jelly. I sat to scarf mine down. I had just swallowed the first mouthful when Gil walked through the door.

"Richie! You made it."

"I'm here," I said.

"Good."

"Well," Geraldine said with theatrical astonishment, "good morning America! How the hell did you manage to get here before nine?"

"Appointment with my friend here," he said. He threw a pair of folders on her desk and jerked a thumb in my direction. "We're going to be contracting Richie to help with this Wendover thing. Get those forms we used when we contracted that other computer guy."

Geraldine nodded, opening a cabinet and searching through folders.

"We'll set him up in Navarro's old office," Gil said.

"That room is so full of boxes that there's no place to work," Geraldine said.

"Then clear it out. And get him a key and a security card. We'll be in my office." He waved at me. "C'mon in."

Gil tossed his cap onto one of the chairs in his office, sat himself down behind his desk and leaned back, feet on the desk. I slipped into a visitor's chair.

"What's the story on this guy you're busting?" I asked.

"Name's Austin Wendover," Gil said with half a laugh. "Austin Wendover. A name like that, he's gotta work at a bank, right? Works at First Idaho Savings, lives out on Hall Road. Know where that is?"

"Somewhere east of here, right? The foothills."

"Yeah. Seems he's been downloading and selling this pedophile shit for a while."

"How'd you find out about him?"

Gil smiled. "Angry girlfriend."

Wendover's girlfriend, Alyssa Schnelz, found it on his laptop, Gil explained. She was freaked out but afraid to confront him so she told her grandmother who brought it to the sheriff. Using a court ordered tap on his phones and internet service, they found out he was selling pictures and videos online.

"Why was the girlfriend angry?" I asked.

"Well," he started, "Wendover is thirty-one. Alyssa is barely eighteen and she told her grandmother that she was mad at him because he was spending a lot more time on his laptop and she wanted to see what he was doing, because their sex life was getting . . .weird."

"Weird?"

"Granny told us Wendover was making the kid wear schoolgirl clothes and had asked her to shave."

"Shave? What? She have a beard?"

"Shave her pubic hair."

"Oh . . . to look younger," I said.

"Fuck, Richie," Gil said, "his girlfriend already looked like she was fourteen. Petite, tiny little tits, long blonde hair. Grandma figured out something was totally fucked up and came to us. The kid doesn't know about that part."

Gil went on to explain that the detectives monitoring Wendover's online activity found he was using the servers at his bank to store the encrypted images and videos. Then he would upload to a website where people would buy them.

"We believe that he searched for new material online at home, then he would download it to an external drive, take it to work and load it into a hidden folder at the bank."

"That way there was nothing incriminating on his home computer," I said.

Gil nodded. "And if they found it on the bank's servers, they wouldn't know who put it there."

"How'd he do the money?" I asked.

"He used a program call Cash App to collect money, usually Bitcoin. We were able to match up transactions on the app with transactions on the dark web server."

I knew from experience that after Wendover was arrested, evidence collected and data decrypted, he would get handed over to federal agents because the sales had been both over state lines and across international borders, but Gil wanted the bust.

"When is it going down?" I asked.

"Tomorrow morning. After Wendover gets to work, we hit his house. After we nail that down, PD takes him at work."

"The bank's gonna hate that," I said with a wry smile.

"Fuck 'em," Gil said.

Geraldine came in with a small handful of papers, plopped them on the desk in front of Gil.

"Contract, W-9, Service Scope Agreement," she said. She handed me a key. "The office Gil wants you to use."

"Thanks."

To Gil she said "Sandy is on her way up with his security card. She – I mean – they will get him logged in."

Gil nodded an acknowledgement, Geraldine turned and left.

"Who's Sandy?" I asked.

"Sandy is our IT department."

"Sandy can't handle the Wendover search?"

Gil rolled his eyes. "Sandy is basically desktop support. They – she decided she didn't like the female pronoun – they are not qualified or interested in being anything more. Ever see that movie, Office Space?"

I nodded.

"Sandy's like that stapler guy."

Gil sorted through the forms and slid them across the desk to me as his phone beeped.

"Damn," he mumbled, glancing at the phone. "Fill these out."

He grabbed the phone and I did the paperwork while Gil talked to some downtown merchant complaining about graffiti. I finished at the same time Gil finished with the caller and handed the papers back. He did a quick scan and nodded at me.

"Looks good," he said.

There was a door tap and a chubby, round, big-eyed face topped with a dishwater shag of hair appeared in the doorway. Gil waved her in and a stocky but not unattractive woman who was working hard at hiding her gender walked in. She was in high top Keds, baggy, khaki cargo shorts and a t-shirt under an unbuttoned short-sleeved, collared shirt. Her small, dark eyes gave me a quick once-over as she stopped just inside the door. One arm was a solid sleeve of tattoos.

"Sandy," Gill said. "This is Rich Willis. The forensics guy from Bellingham."

"Hey," Sandy said. She handed me a credit card size piece of plastic. "Your security card. This will get you into almost any department door in the building."

"Thanks."

"Sandy," Gil said, "show him where things are and make sure he gets logged into our system and all the databases he'll need for tomorrow."

"Got it."

I stood and we started to the door, but Gil stopped us.

"Hey Rich."

I turned. "Yeah?"

"You got a gun?" he asked.

I was a little surprised. "A gun? No, why?"

"Making sure," he said. "Didn't want you showing up tomorrow with a pistol in your pants."

I had to laugh. "No gun." My dad had taught me how to use a gun, but I hadn't touched one since I was fourteen. I knew how they worked and had been passable with a pistol and rifle when I was younger, but I had no desire to even touch one.

"Good. Get settled, get into the system and then meet the detectives down in the squad room tomorrow morning at eight before the raid."

"Sounds good," I said, grabbing my laptop bag.

"This way," Sandy said.

With me following, Sandy lumbered down the hall and down to the basement where a set of old metal doors opened into the sheriff department's small squad room, a stale, poorly lit space that looked to have been built before the second world war but partitioned off with a dozen half-wall cubicles. The room wreaked of burnt coffee, spoiled microwave burritos and men who hadn't showered in a week. I could hear keyboards rattling and one-sided phone conversations. Sandy gave the room a sweep of an arm.

"I present the brains of the Brannon County sheriff's department," Sandy said snidely.

"Hey guys," a voice called out from a cubicle. "IT's here. Hide your porn!"

"Shut the fuck up, Yankovic," Sandy said.

A chorus of sneers arose from invisible males.

"Assholes," Sandy called out, leading me to the non-windowed wall of the squad room where Sandy unlocked the small corner office and walked in.

Standing in the doorway to the little space, I shot a thumb back to the room. "You don't like those guys?" I asked.

"Like I said, assholes," Sandy said. "I hate 'em all."

I shook my head. "Then why do you work here?"

"Easiest job I ever had, dude. Nothin' much ever happens around here, good pay and good bennies. For work, I just tell these morons to reboot their shitty computers and everything is fixed. Easy. All I have to do is put up with a bunch of wacko, right-wing Neanderthal deputies."

"And I'll bet they hate your pronoun choice," I said.

Sandy got closer and in a quiet voice said "I tell 'em I'm non-binary and that I want to use 'they' instead of 'she' for my pronouns just to fuck with 'em. I'm happy with who I am." She reached up and cupped her hands over her breasts. "I'm a she, see? Tits and all. I just like to see those morons squirm. And it also keeps them from comin' on to me if they think I might possibly be packing a cock and a couple balls."

I had to laugh. I liked her.

The small office held two chairs, a desk, an old tower computer and monitor and a telephone. In one corner, apparently bolted into the floor was a small safe. Sandy handed me a key.

"This is for the evidence locker," she said pointing to the safe. "Only you and the lead investigator on this case have keys."

Sandy explained that this office had last been used by the computer forensics guy they hired before. He was cracking some cell phones and a pair of laptops grabbed during a meth bust. To ensure the chain of evidence, after the raid in the morning, Wendover's computer drives, cell phone and any other electronic devices would be locked here while they were being examined or decrypted. After that, they would go to the county prosecutor.

Sandy sat herself at the desk and powered up the computer. She pulled out a scrap of paper from a pocket and read something off it to log into the system. She handed me the paper.

"That's your login and password," she said. "Pull up a chair."

Sliding the other office chair next to her, I watched as she gave me a guided tour of the system, showing where I would store the drive's contents. She also showed me the messaging system I would use, the local and state crime databases and access to the national criminal database, NCIC, and Homeland Security.

"You probably won't need the databases," Sandy said, "but you have access, just in case. Okay?"

"Yeah, not too different from where I've been working."

"Good."

"I prefer to use my own laptop, though," I said. "All my tools are on it. Any problem with that?"

"Nope," Sandy said, waving off the old computer that was on the desk like an annoying fly. "I wouldn't want to use this piece of shit PC either. It's only really good for running a thirty-year-old version of Doom." She pointed to the top drawer in the desk. "You should find a couple big, portable hard drives you can use."

"Perfect. I should be okay here then," I said. "Thanks."

"No problem."

"I'll get settled, check a few things out and then be back tomorrow morning."

"Okay." She turned to go.

"Hey Sandy," I said stopping her. "Who's the lead investigator I'll be dealing with on this?"

She scratched the side of her nose looking out into the squad room. Then came back.

"Probably Yankovic," she said.

"Decent guy?"

"Decent detective," she said with a sneer. "Asshole human. His world is good and bad, black and white. Nuthin' in between. That's why I love fuckin' with him. My world is a rainbow."

I laughed and Sandy was gone.

The little space was stuffy, so I propped the door open, then sat and pulled out my laptop to log into the system. I found the folder I'd be using and created a password protected subfolder there. Next, I checked out all the tools on my laptop that I would need: password hacking, drive mirroring and decryption apps.

With everything ready for what I would need to do after the morning's raid, I decided to take advantage of my access to the local law enforcement database.

I wanted to know if what people have been saying about Jeannie's brother, Peter, even resembled the truth so I did a record search for his name. The system exploded with hits.

"Holy shit," I mumbled looking at the readout. As an adult, there were at least four DUI's, three assaults, firearm charges and numerous other complaints on Pete's record. His juvenile cases listed driving charges and two other assault charges, the oldest going back to when he was in high school and another just a few months before Jeannie was killed. I clicked on the link to look at the details of that one. The assault complaint had been filed by Jeannie saying that Peter had come home drunk, gotten into an argument with Julie and then when Jeannie had intervened, he beat her up. After he passed out, she called the sheriff's department and PeeWee was arrested. Then thirty days in county lockup.

A knock at the door startled me and I looked to see a short, stocky and hard man in jeans and a light blue dress shirt leaning against the door. Bullet-headed with deep set, dark eyes, topped with marine cut hair.

"You Willard?" he asked.

I turned my chair to face him.

"Willis."

"Yankovic," he said.

He didn't offer a hand, so neither did I.

"Sheriff says you've done this before," he said.

"A few times."

"Good," he said, "but let me explain how I do things." I gave him the nod to go ahead. "I run the raid on the house. You stay in the car until I call you to come in. You will be taken by my men to Wendover's computer. You'll copy the drive, then we will take the computer away. If there's a cell phone or iPad or anything, we will bring those to you and you'll copy those. Everything gets marked and sealed in evidence bags and brought back here to be cataloged. After that, you get the copies of the drives and you start your work."

"About the same as we've done out our way," I said.

"Just want to make sure we are straight on things here," he said.

"We're straight," I said.

"Good. Be here tomorrow at eight. It will be me, some deputies and you."

"No Gil?"

Yankovic snorted. "Gil? No. He'll supervise from his office." He put the word supervise in air quotes.

"Okay."

"In the morning," Yankovic said, turning and walking back into the rat's maze of cubicles.

As I watched him go, I decided that I probably wasn't going to like him.

I turned back to the laptop's screen,, looking at all the entries for my one-time buddy, PeeWee.

What happened to him?

I stared at the screen for a long time, then snapped the laptop shut.

After leaving here, I had one stop to make. Then after that, I was going to find Pete Sorenson.

FOURTEEN

I managed to slide my Jeep into a parking place in front of Lion Realty in what used to be the hub of Black River's downtown business district. Once the interstate highway on the west edge of the town was finished though, the businesses either abandoned their old downtown locations or closed up completely.

Lion Realty was a one-man operation run by Randy Bronco and located in one of the retail spaces in a single floor office building that had once contained a jeweler, an eye doctor and a music store. Those places were now occupied by a tattoo parlor, a nail salon and a karate studio.

As soon as I was out of the Jeep, the real estate office door burst open and Randy Bronco's massive bulk burst out from it, raising his arms in an enthusiastic welcome as though he were greeting someone coming back from a long war.

"Richie!" he exclaimed, wrapping his big, flabby arms around me. Randy was Shoshone-Bannock, with thick, black hair on top of a pumpkin shaped, sun baked head which sat on top of a huge, round body. Cowboy boots, oversized, suspendered jeans and a button up blue, long sleeve shirt completed his work uniform. He had been a scrawny little kid, but success as a realtor had gone straight to his waistline. In school, he had been a beady-eyed, back-stabbing little sneak. Now he was a beady-eyed, back-stabbing little realtor and I didn't really like or trust him but, for some reason, my mother did and so I was stuck with him. He had been managing her two rental properties as well as Marty's for decades.

"How ya' been?" he asked, an arm around my shoulder, guiding me into his office and indicating a visitor's chair in front of his desk. The small office was furnished with two desks, one being for his assistant I guessed. There were comfortable chairs scattered about and a coffee table littered with real estate and home improvement magazines. The walls were covered with pictures of houses, businesses and farms that I assumed Randy was trying to sell. Mixed alongside the houses, were items boosting the Black River High School Lions: a calendar, newspaper articles, Lions pennants, and various team pictures.

"I've been good," I said. "Looks like you are doing okay."

"Can't complain, my friend," he said. "Can't complain." He filled a mug from a little automatic coffee maker he had on a credenza and set it on his desk. He held up another mug as an offer to me. I nodded and he filled it. "Anything?"

"Cream," I said.

"Even though the economy seems all fucked up," he was saying as he handed me the mug, "real estate is pretty decent around here." He waddled around his desk and squeezed into his chair.

"Oh yeah?"

"Housing is booming here 'cuz I.F. and Pocatello are so fucking expensive. We're turning into a little bedroom community."

"Good for you," I said.

"And maybe good for you, my friend."

"That's what I want to talk to you about," I said. "I think I'm ready to unload those two rental houses my mother owned."

I was sure I saw big green dollar signs pop into his eyes.

"Excellent. Do you have a number in mind?"

"I don't know real estate prices here. I'd like to get an appraiser to take a look at them and then maybe go with what they think."

He nodded in agreement. "I can get an appraiser out to look at them right away and get the houses listed online in a day or two and I could get them into the multiple listing service by the end of this week. On the old farmhouse, the family that lives there might actually opt to buy, which would be sweet. They've been good tenants. The renters at the older house on Maple probably won't buy the place. I don't think they make enough to get a home loan. Young couple."

"Okay."

"I'll let 'em know though, just in case they got a rich uncle or something."

I nodded.

Randy leaned forward on his desk, hands clasped. "Now, what about Marty's. How much do you want to try to sell that for?"

"You know," I started, "I'm not sure yet that I want to sell it."

He was surprised. He sat back in his chair staring at me. I could see the green fading from his eyes.

"Dude!" he said, "this would be the perfect time to unload that old building."

"It would?"

"Hell yeah. It sits on an ideal lot. Thirty seconds from the freeway. Lots of parking. Frontage. Any smart investor would snap that up in a heartbeat. Knock that shitty building down, put in a nice big sporting goods store. Or a hardware store. You could make a fortune on that sale."

"And you'd do okay too," I said wryly.

"Hey! A guys gotta make a living, right?" he said. "I got mouths to feed."

Mostly his own, I guessed looking at him.

"For now, I'd like to hang on to it," I said. "I like it being there. And people like having a little tavern."

"People like having a little money, too," he said. "Especially me." The dollar signs were back.

"For now, no," I said. "And if I do decide to sell, I want to give the manager the first shot at it."

"Jia?"

"She told me she would be interested. And she seems like a smart lady. I'll bet she could do it. How'd you find her?" In managing the property, Randy had hired Jia to manage the bar.

"She and her mom moved into one of my rentals and she asked about a job at about the same time we were losing that guy that used to manage it. Can't remember his name. Anyway, Jia said she had some experience running a place like that, so I tried her out."

"Good choice," I said.

"Would it change your mind if I gave up my commission on the place?"

I shook my head. He might give up his commission, but he would replace it with a kickback from the buyer.

"If I do change my mind, I'll let you know." I stood and held out a hand. "Thanks Randy. Let me know about the appraisal when it comes in."

He pushed himself out of his chair and took my hand.

"How long you gonna be in town?" he asked.

I shrugged. "Not sure yet. Depends." I started to the door, noticing again all the school stuff on the walls. I turned back to him. "You never left town after high school, right?"

"Didn't run off to college like you did," he said. "I still live in the house I grew up in. Bought it from my mom when she moved to Phoenix."

"What was it like after that, after high school?"

"Whaddya mean?"

"The town, the area. Did it change much?"

Randy rubbed his chin and sat down, staring at a wall, trying to go back in time thirty years. He shook his head slowly as he tried to recall. "Population didn't change too much. A lot of small farms got consolidated into a lot of big ones. US Potato got bigger. A lot of Mexicans moved in."

"How about drugs?"

"Yeah," he said, "but that was already starting when we were in school."

"Do you remember the Sorenson's? Jeannie or Peter?" I asked.

Randy thought a moment. "I remember Pete, I think. He was a troublemaker. Seemed to always be in a fight."

"Was he a drug dealer?"

Randy stared blankly for a second, then shook his head.

"I don't think so. He was a drunk. A serious drunk. Why?"

"The Sorenson's were neighbors and his sister Jeannie was my best friend growing up, but I lost track of them. Somehow. And it's looking like the Sorenson's had a lot of problems that I had totally missed. I guess drugs were one of them."

Randy shook his head. "Drugs were a problem for a lot of families. Still are. But I don't know about the Sorenson's."

I nodded and thanked him.

"Let me know about the appraisals," I said. With a wave, I was out.

Instead of hitting the freeway for Idaho Falls, I decided to take Old Highway 91. It was slower and rougher on an old Jeep with crappy shocks, but having taken the doors and top off, the pleasant air of freshly harvested hay and tilled earth followed me all the way to I.F. and into Olsen Trucking's half full parking lot.

Inside the office behind a low counter, I found the same woman I had talked to the day before, looking just as grumpy as the day before and wearing the same baggy, flowered dress as the day before. She looked up from the keyboard she was typing on, not remembering me.

"Yeah?"

"Pete Sorenson around?" I asked.

She remembered me then. "Dunno," she said.

The woman picked up her desk phone and pressed a button that must have put her on a loudspeaker in the warehouse behind the office because I heard it echoing her voice. "Pete. Front office." She sat the handset back in its cradle. She pointed to a set of worn, green leather chairs set against the wall behind me.

"Have a seat," she said.

Before I could get to the chairs though, a scratchy voice spoke through the speaker on her phone.

"Aggie," the male voice said, "Pete's gone already. Probably at the Deer."

I stepped back up to the counter.

"At the Red Deer?" I remembered what she had said yesterday.

"Know where that is?"

I shook my head.

"Head back towards town. It's on the left after you pass the golf course."

I thanked her and within five minutes, I was parked between a big, dirty Ford F250 and a Chevy Tahoe at the side of The Red Deer. It was an old, concrete block building; single story, flat roof, ugly beige paint. There were three big windows and one big wooden door facing the road. Old neon beer signs advertising Budweiser, Coors and Pabst hung in the windows along with aged posters hawking lottery tickets and local sporting events.

It was dark and busy inside The Deer. The bar that ran along the wall to my right as I walked in had a half dozen guys on the stools nursing beers and whiskeys. The booths along two of the walls were occupied as were most of the tables. There were two pool tables in the back, players working on both. A dart board hung on the far wall. Except for the three or four waitresses or bartenders, I could only see two other women in the place. This was a guy bar, an old fashioned working man's bar, a place guys went to after work before they had to go home.

I stepped to the bar and ordered a beer from the short, chubby, bottle-blonde who showed me a bottle and a glass. I dropped a bill on the bar, grabbed the bottle and glass and took a seat at a table in the back where I could watch the pool game.

It had been a long time since I had seen Pete Sorenson, which made me worry that I might not even recognize him. I looked around. The guys sitting at the bar watching a football game on a monitor seemed too old. No one sitting at a table or one of the booths looked quite right, so I watched the dozen or so guys around the pool tables as they talked, laughed and played. At the nearest table, the game was almost over. A tall, thin man was taking a shot. He was wearing carpenter's jeans, a faded Carhartt t-shirt and a billed hat. I couldn't see his face. The faded lettering on the back of the t-shirt read Olsen Trucking.

The guy took his shot but his ball took a wrong bounce and the eight ball went in ending the game. He let out flurry of angry curses at the table.

That's when I recognized him.

I actually didn't recognize Pete so much as I recognized his father's face: the long nose, the thick-lipped, crooked, cigar smoker's mouth and the deep-set eyes. He was slimmer than his dad had been and when he flipped off his hat to wipe his brow, I saw he had a full head of thick, curly hair while his father had been nearly bald at the same age.

Pete exchanged a few words then angrily handed the winner a couple of bills out of his wallet. He snatched a bottle of half-finished Bud Light off a side table, searched for an empty booth, found one, signaling a waitress to bring him another beer.

The same big blonde that gave me my drinks, sat a bottle in front of him, chatting away. When he reached out and put a hand on her butt and gave a squeeze, she pulled his hand off and shook her head, giving him the exasperated look that she had probably given him before. She turned and Pete watched her tight jeans wiggle their way back to the bar.

Pete had tilted his head back to gulp from the new bottle when I set my glass on the table and took the seat across from him, taking in his completely inked arms.

"Nice tats," I said.

He swallowed a mouthful of beer, looked at me and set the bottle down, puzzling at me through bleary, watery eyes.

"Pete Sorenson," I said.

"Yeah," he said slowly. "Why?"

Now he was more suspicious than puzzled.

"PeeWee," I said, "it's Rich Willis."

His brain wasn't running on all cylinders so it took him a couple beats, but recognition finally came to him along with a tentative smile.

"Richie," he said. He lifted his bottle as a toast and I tapped it with my glass. We both took swallows. "Richie Willis. Well, shit. Thought you was outa here forever."

I shook my head. "I come back once in a while. How ya' been?"

"Okay, I guess," he said. "Aren't you living like in Portland or Seattle?"

"Bellingham."

"Bellingham, yeah," he said. "That's what I heard. Staying with your mom here?"

"No. She's gone."

"Oh, sorry."

"Yeah. Just camping out at Marty's for a week or so."

"Oh yeah, Marty's," he said, remembering. "Your mom owned that."

I nodded and we each took a drink. "I was watching your game," I said

"Recreating. Just got back from a long run," he said.

He went on to talk about all the different trucking companies he had worked for since high school; quitting some, some going out of business, some firing him.

"Asshole managers," he said bitterly.

He had been married to a woman who already had a couple kids, but said she ran off with them. I didn't ask why. I mentioned that I had heard that his sister Jackie and brother John had been killed in a car accident.

"Long time ago," he said, looking down at his beer.

"I was sorry to hear that," I said. "I didn't realize John had a drug problem."

Pete's head jerked up and he looked at me.

"Who told you that?" he asked.

It took longer to answer than it should have. "Just heard it from someone," I stammered.

He eyeballed me for a few moments as if trying to come up with something to say, then gave up and looked away.

"Sorry, just asking," I said, defensively. "You ever get sucked into drugs?" I asked.

He turned back and gulped down a couple swallows of beer.

"I prefer my drugs in a glass," he said.

"How about Jeannie?"

"What?"

"I had heard that maybe she had gotten into some bad stuff before she died."

The hand that had been holding his beer tensed into a fist and his eyes narrowed.

"I don't talk about Jeannie," he said in a tight voice.

I was about to press a little harder when a huge shadow appeared at the table.

"Petey!" a man said shoving his way into the booth next to Pete and setting two full bottles of Bud on the table. "Brought you a refill."

The man was a truck driving cliché, with baggy jeans, a faded Allman Brothers Band t-shirt that was failing to hold the man's massive gut and a ragged John Deere cap. The fat man reeked of beer, grease and tobacco and he extended a thick, battered hand over the table.

"Reese," he said in a big booming voice.

"Rich," I said shaking hands.

"You a driver?" he asked.

"Old friend of PeeWee's," I said. "We grew up together."

"PeeWee?" he asked looking at Pete.

"Pete," I corrected. "It was just a dumb nickname from grade school. We all had stupid nicknames. Me too. My last name is Willis, so the kids called me Wilbur. I think it was after some guy in an old TV show about a talking mule or horse or something."

"Wilbur," Pete muttered.

"I had one too," Reese said. "Pieces."

"Pieces?"

"My last name is Peters," he said.

It took me a second, then I smiled and nodded. "Reese Peters, Reese's Pieces."

"Yup." He took a swig.

"We were mean when we were kids," I said.

"Wilbur," Pete muttered again.

"We were just catching up on things," I said after an uncomfortable silence. "Haven't seen Pete in years. Asking about his family."

Reese tried to put on the best sympathetic face someone could who had put down too many beers. "Oh yeah, sad about them. Parents, brother. That older sister. And then the one sister being, you know . . . killed."

"I was just asking if drugs might have been a problem for his younger sister."

Reese shook his head. "Pete wouldn't have let that happen."

"He wouldn't?"

Pete looked like he was about to burst. "Why do I feel like I'm getting the third degree, Richie?" he asked.

Reese stepped in. "I'm sure he's not doing that, Petey. Hey, how about another beer, guys?" He signaled the blonde waitress. "Have you see the ass on that woman? Love to take her home some night and show here my big tractor."

"Your wife wouldn't like that," Pete said, happy to be moving on to a new topic.

"Fuck her," Reese said.

The waitress stepped up to the table. "What can I get you guys," she asked.

Reese smiled and put a hand on her waist. "Three buds and you."

"Three beers," she said, then leaned close to Reese's ear. "And take your fuckin' hands off me or I'll have my wife come down here and jam that bud up your ass. Got it?"

Reese put his hands up as though warding off a blow as the woman turned, walked away and Pete and I laughed.

"That's something I'd like to see," Pete said, patting Reese on the shoulders. "You getting beat up by a gang of lezbos."

Reese turned, started to say something, but was interrupted.

"You found him."

A figure appeared at the table. It was the woman I had talked to at the trucking company office.

"Hey, Aggie," Reese said looking up at the big woman.

She looked at Pete and pointed at me. "This guy's been in the office a couple times looking for you."

Pete glared towards me. "He has?"

Aggie nodded. "Yeah. Glad he finally found you." She playfully slapped Reese on the chin. "Keep your hands off the ladies here, asshole."

She walked off and joined a man at the bar.

"You've been lookin' for me?" Pete asked, anger building. "I thought this was just some accident running into me. What the fuck are you doing, Richie?"

"Look, Pete . . ." I started.

"All these questions? No wonder I'm feeling like I'm being . . . interrogated."

I took a deep breath. "I just want to know what happened to Jeannie, that's all."

"Jeannie? Why the hell is that any of your business anymore?"

"She was my friend, Pete and I . . ."

"Go to hell," Pete said, pushing on Reese to get out of the booth.

"Hey guys . . ." Reese said trying to slow things down.

"Get out of the fuckin' way, Reese," Pete said pushing him out.

"What happened between you and Jeannie?" I blurted out.

Pete was out, swiveling towards me. "What?" he snarled.

I scrambled out of the booth and stood facing him, wishing I hadn't said that. But it was too late. "Thirty years ago. Did you do something to Jeannie?"

Pete angrily grabbed my shirt in both hands, his face six inches from mine. "Stay out of my way or I'll pound your face in." With both hands he shoved me back into the booth.

Reese stepped in front of Pete.

"C'mon guys," he said.

Pete pointed over Reese's shoulder at me. "Stay away from me. And don't you go near Julie, either. Go back to Seattle or wherever the fuck you're from. I don't wanna see that fuckin' face of yours around here. Okay?"

Pete stalked out the tavern's door. I tried to stand and go after him, but Reese pushed me back into the booth.

"Sit down," he said. "You go after him and he'll tear you a new asshole. And you know he can do it."

I pushed myself back out of the booth. "Yeah."

"Then why you doin' this?" Reese asked.

I started towards the door, but Reese grabbed my arm. I turned angrily.

"Why?" he asked.

I pulled my arm loose.

"Peace of mind, righting an old wrong, penance. Whatever the hell you want to call it."

I threw a couple twenties on the table and was out the door into the late afternoon sun but Pete was nowhere to be seen.

I don't know if I was angry or relieved not to see him, but I decided to give up looking for him and headed for my Jeep. As I passed a big truck, like a bull charging out of the gates, Pete bolted out from behind one of them, rammed into me and smashed me into the concrete wall of the bar.

The back of my head bashed against the concrete and everything became blur of activity. A fist came from my left, but I got an arm up to block it, and then a fist from the right and I blocked that one and then there was Pete's furious, spitting face, yelling something at me and then a wild right hit me and then a left caught my ear and I tried to twist away but a kick landed hard between my legs. Then there was blinding pain and I couldn't see and I dropped to my knees as a fist smashed into my left cheek and then my right and I was dazed and I slid down the wall onto my side, moaning.

"Pete, stop," I moaned raising arm to stop the pounding, but a steel boot crashed into my ribs causing an explosion of pain and knocking the air out of me and I felt something pop in my chest. I rolled into a fetal position.

Then I heard a scramble in the gravel and Reese's voice.

"Stop it Pete!"

Reese was pulling him back.

"That's enough!" Reese said. He twisted Pete's body away from me and shoved him towards an old truck.

"Get outa here, Pete," he said. "Before someone calls the cops on you again."

"Stay away from me, Willis," Pete snarled at me. "Stay away."

I heard a truck door open and close. An engine started. Then spinning gravel as a truck roared out of the parking lot.

I tried to get up, but slipped back down on my butt against the wall, struggling to catch my breath. I could taste blood. I reached up, felt a cut next to my left eye and I could feel my lip bleeding. As my vision cleared I could see someone standing above me. Reese.

"You alright? Want me to call someone?" he asked.

I shook my head. "Just help me up." I put my hand up and Reese pulled me to my feet. I let out a moan of pain and leaned back against the wall. I grabbed at my chest.

"God damn that hurts," I growled. "I think the asshole cracked a rib."

"Better get to the ER," he said.

"They can't do anything with a cracked rib." I pushed myself away from the wall. "Just going home."

I stumbled to the front of my Jeep and leaned against it, making my way toward the driver's seat. Pain.

"You really pissed him off," Reese said. "You better back away from all that shit about his sister."

With an effort, I pulled myself into the Jeep and sat with a moan. I dropped my head. Took a deep breath. Looked back up at Reese.

"I think something may have happened between Pete and his sister."

"Like what?"

I stared at him and then just shook my head and drove off.

FIFTEEN

After leaving The Red Deer, I freaked out several Walgreen's customers when I stopped there and snagged some antiseptic wash and
cotton pads to clean up the cuts and bruises on my face and an Ace
bandage. The pony-tailed cashier gave me a suspicious stare when she
handed me my purchase.

"Wife beat me up," I explained. "She asked me if her new outfit
made her look fat. Guess I gave her the wrong answer."

I spent a few minutes in the parking lot cleaning up the blood
and cuts on my face before leaving, pulling in behind Marty's thirty
minutes later.

I grabbed the Walgreen's bag and turned to get out of the Jeep, but
the pain in my ribs ripped through me like an electric shock and I
doubled over just as Tyler came out the back door with an overstuffed
plastic trash bag destined for the dumpster. He dropped the bag and
ran over to me.

"You okay, dude?" he asked. "What happened?"

He grabbed me by the elbow to help me out of the Jeep. Once my
feet were on the ground, I bent over and leaned back against the car.

"Did that Ukrainian guy do this?"

I shook my head.

He patted me on the shoulder. "Hang on." Tyler turned and trotted towards the back door. "Someone's here looking for you."

"What?"

He disappeared inside while I tried to catch my breath which wasn't easy because any deep breath I took, shot a lightning bolt of agony to my brain. After a few shallow breaths, I was finally able to straighten up. Tyler came back down the steps followed by a tall woman in jeans and a loose, sleeveless button blouse. Eleanor stopped when she saw me leaning against the Jeep.

"What the hell happened this time?" she asked running to my side.

"Ran into an old school buddy," I said when she grabbed my left arm in one hand, put another arm around my waist.

"Face first?" she asked. She shook her head at the cuts and started me towards the back door.

"Funny as ever, Ellie."

"Let's get you upstairs," Tyler said. "Got any pain pills up there?"

I thought a minute.

"Tylenol."

He made a derisive snort and looked to Eleanor. "You?"

She shook her head while guiding me up the three steps to the door. Tyler sighed in exasperation.

"I'll get you some," he said. Once inside, Tyler jogged toward the kitchen, pointing to the stairs on the right. "Take him up there."

"I'm really okay," I said turning to go up the steep, narrow stairs.

"Yeah, you look great," she said with unconcealed sarcasm. "Just walk up, I'll be right behind you."

"To cushion my fall?"

"Hell no. You start falling? I get the hell out of the way."

"Ah, she still loves me."

"Just shut-up and get up the stairs."

In my room, she sat me down on the bed, then pulled a chair over from the kitchen area, sat facing me and grabbed the Walgreen's bag out of my hand.

"You gonna tell me what happened?" She poured the contents of the bag onto her lap. "Washcloth?"

I pointed behind her, to her right. "Bathroom. Under the sink."

"You never seemed like the barroom brawler type to me," she said going to the bathroom. I heard her running water.

"Funny you should say that," I said.

"What?" She poked her head around the corner. "You were in a bar fight?"

"Well, technically not in a bar," I said, emphasizing the 'in'. Eleanor returned with a wet washcloth, sat and started cleaning my cuts. "And technically, not a fight."

I could hear footsteps running up the stairs and Tyler came in carrying a little orange prescription bottle and handed it to me. The label had been scraped off. I showed Eleanor.

"What's in there?" she asked warily.

"Pain meds," Tyler said.

"What kind?"

"Uh . . . Oxycodone."

"Where'd you get these?" I asked.

Tyler's eyes slid back and forth between me and Eleanor. "Is that important?"

Eleanor looked at me and sighed. "Probably not."

I smiled. "Thanks Tyler, but I don't think I need these."

Eleanor, gave me a look, pressed a hand to my side and gave a little push, a hammer of pain morphed into a scream.

"Okay," I gasped. "I guess I do need them."

Tyler disappeared into the bathroom.

"So tell me," he said coming back with a glass of water for me.

"He says he was in a bar fight that wasn't in a bar and wasn't a fight," Eleanor said.

I started to laugh, but it turned into a moan of pain. "Don't make me laugh. I think I have a cracked rib." I took the glass of water and drank down two of the pills.

Tyler started to say something.

"What?" I asked handing back the glass.

"Uh . . . you probably should only have taken one of those."

Eleanor and I stared at him.

He looked back and forth between us, a little scared, then tried to be reassuring.

"Don't worry," he said. "Probably just knock you out."

Eleanor gave him a worried look, not quite believing him.

"Really," he said.

Jia stepped into the room, holding two small plastic bags filled with ice cubes and looked at me, wide-eyed. Eleanor took the bags and laid them on the bed.

"God," Jia said. "What happened?"

"A bar fight that wasn't a bar fight," Tyler said.

"Huh?"

"We're trying to get him to tell us." Eleanor said.

"It was in the parking lot outside a bar. In Idaho Falls. A guy jumped me."

"Mugged?" Tyler asked.

I shook my head.

"An old schoolmate," I said. "He was a little drunk and a little pissed off and we had a disagreement. I left, but he caught me in the parking lot."

"That's it?" Tyler was skeptical.

"Yeah, pretty much," I said.

"Shit," he said. "I was hoping for a better story."

"Best I could do," I said. "Give me a few hours, though. I'll see if I can think of one that's more interesting."

"Please do," Tyler said.

"You going to be okay?" Jia asked.

I nodded. "Not as bad as it looks."

She was skeptical but nodded, then smiled. "Good. Then while you're up here, fix that damn security camera clock. It still thinks it's tomorrow."

"I'll get right on it." I smiled back at her.

"C'mon Tyler," she said turning him towards the door. "People need their dead cow meat."

"Rest, dude," Tyler said. Then the two were gone and Eleanor turned back to me with that you-poor dumb-slob look.

"Let's get that shirt off," she said grabbing the material of the shirt at my waist. With a scream of pain followed by multiple curses, I raised my arms as far as I could, letting her get it over my head and off. She looked at my left side and gently touched my ribs. I jerked back.

"You're all red right here," she said, "but I don't see any bones pushing out like they're broken. Maybe cracked. Maybe just bruised. Gonna look like shit in a day or two."

"Feels like shit now," I said.

She picked up one of the Ace bandages.

"Let's get you wrapped and then get some ice on it."

Eleanor gently wrapped my chest as tightly as she could, apologizing every time I let out a moan.

"Why are you back here tonight?" I asked as she worked.

She shrugged, avoided my eyes. "It was nice seeing you again and I realized that I did all the talking last night and I wanted to hear more about what you've been doing. Besides getting in non-bar-fight bar fights, of course."

"Please don't make me laugh," I said. "It hurts."

"You know, I could always tell when you were lying. Or when you were muddying up the truth."

I sighed. Yes, she could.

"So what really happened today?"

I relented and told her what had happened with Pete and why I had been looking for him.

The story surprised her and she stared at me, looking me over, seeing someone she hadn't seen before, processing the story.

"So this Pete hurt his sister back then?" she asked.

"Possibly."

"And might have been involved in her death?" She turned away and shook her head like someone trying to wake up. "So freaky to be asking that kind of question."

I smiled and almost laughed, but I grabbed my chest and just nodded.

"This Jeannie was that good of a friend?" Eleanor asked, still trying to wrap her head around the story.

"She was."

"That was thirty years ago, Rich. Are the police still working on it?"

"It's an open case," I said. "Any unsolved murder is left open, but unless something new comes up, the cases eventually end up as shelved dust magnets. And without some kind of push from someone, no one is going to wipe the dust off."

"You said the sheriff is an old friend? Can't you push him to look at it?"

"Only if I find something tangible. The big problem is that the sheriff's department here is not the most ambitious I've ever dealt with."

"Tell them about her brother," Eleanor said.

"They knew about him back then, knew what he was like, but had nothing to tie him to what happened to Jeannie."

"No one else?" she asked.

I sighed. Shook my head. "Pete and their little sister Julie are the only ones left and as far as I've seen looking at the files, they haven't shown any interest in looking into it. They may have good reason. I'm finding out that that family was more messed up than I ever knew."

"Then why you?"

Eleanor tied off the last of the bandages she had wrapped around my chest and helped me lay back on the bed. She pressed the ice bags against my ribs.

"Thanks, Ellie."

"Why you, Rich?" she repeated.

I reached over to the little table next to the bed and grabbed a small prescription bottle from a drawer and handed it to her. She gave me a puzzled look, then glanced at the label.

"Fluoxetine?"

"Anti-depressant," I said. "Prozac."

She was even more puzzled. Maybe even a little shocked.

"Ellie, ever sit down and look back at your life, at the choices you've made, the paths you've chosen?"

She shook her head. "Haven't had the time, I guess."

"Death can make a person take a second look at things," I said.

"Jeannie's death?"

I took a deep breath. Shook my head. "No, my wife's death."

Eleanor nodded, remembering. "Two years ago, you said."

"It was a long illness," I explained. "Cancer. And I wasn't there at the end. She was in the hospital and I was in Portland when my daughter called me in a panic, saying that her mother had slipped into a coma. I raced back up to Bellingham, but I was too late."

I told her that that was what started my slide into a depression. More than my wife's death, more than my not being there at the end, it was that maybe I had never been there. I wasn't a good husband, I told Ellie. I didn't cheat on her, didn't beat her, helped around the house, changed baby diapers, fixed meals.

"But I wasn't there," I said. "I was obsessed with work, with my career, with me. I was in a movie about me and everyone else was a bit player. I hadn't given her the attention she deserved."

Eleanor nodded.

"I was selfish and self-absorbed. Focused on my life, not our life. It didn't register with me then, but after my wife died and I started looking back at things, I saw it."

"That put you in a depression?" she asked.

"I think I was already on the slide, but that gave me another push, along with something else. You remember our old college buddy, Sean?"

"Of course. Always going to write that great American novel. Never finishing."

"He moved up to Seattle after college, still trying. We kept in touch over the years. I helped him out from time to time. He lived off his mother's estate for a while, but he was spiraling down. I got busy with my work. Sean would call and talk, hinting that he needed help. I helped when I could, but it was when my wife was sick. And I was getting frustrated with my work, looking at changing. He called more often and I picked up less often. Then I stopped picking up."

I pushed myself up on my elbows to look at her.

"A few months ago," I said, "I got a call from Seattle PD." Eleanor sucked in a gasp of air. "He had been living in a homeless tent camp for a year when they found his body. The only recent number on his phone had been mine. Someone had to ID him."

"Poor Sean." Eleanor turned back towards me.

"I was already going down and Sean's death just pushed me further down that slide . . . into . . . that hole."

"Can't imagine."

"Laying there, in that dark hole of self-pity, like a good recovering Catholic, I assumed being in that hole was my fault so I looked to see where I had gone wrong."

"Now that's fucked up." Eleanor shook her head and rolled her eyes.

"Of course it is," I said. "But I decided I needed help."

"Not something I ever heard from you."

"My daughter actually forced me to see it one night during a silly little argument about something she wanted to have of her mother's. She needed it and like the idiot father that I was, I was pressing her on why she needed it. That set her off and she was blasting me about my not understanding that some people actually needed things, actually needed others and that some people actually needed to be needed and how I had failed to understand that my whole life."

I looked up at Eleanor.

"You remember the last thing you said to me when I moved out of our apartment? Just before you closed the door you said to me that it was probably best that you and I ended it, because I had never really needed you. Remember that?"

Eleanor looked at me a moment, then turned away. I think I saw sadness in her eyes.

"I remember," she said.

The room was quiet, just the muffled sounds from the bar below us. Some old Dan Fogelberg song was playing over the café speakers and I could smell the onions Tyler was frying.

I explained that my daughter helped me get in touch with a shrink. With that help and my daughter's support, I started crawling out of the hole. And like a guy in a twelve-step program, I needed to make amends.

"How?"

"First, I opened up to my daughter. It was hard for me, but it was the right thing to do and it turned out to be what she needed."

I explained that my next step was to do something to make up for what I felt I had done to Sean, by not being there. I went through all his notebooks of little stories that he must have been writing as background pieces to that great American novel he never wrote. It turned out, those were perfect short stories so I assembled them together in a book called "Tales from the Homeless Canal" and put it up on Amazon under Sean's name. It would never sell much, but it meant that Sean was finally published.

"I had a little extra money," I said, "so I arranged to have Sean's body shipped back to his hometown in Utah and have him buried there. I had a headstone made for him. It reads 'Sean Dayton – Author'."

Eleanor gave me a nod and a sad smile. "He would have loved that." She sniffed and wiped an eye. After a moment, she frowned. "And then this Jeannie, this friend of yours?"

I started to go over that whole story, but the pain pills were hitting me hard. I laid back on the bed.

"Tyler was right," I said. "I shouldn't have taken two of those."

"Why don't you sleep for a while?" Eleanor said. She patted me gently on the arm, almost a caress, then stood to go. I nodded at her and then nodded off.

It was a few hours later and I was drifting in and out of the oxy fog. There were voices and steps on the stairs. It was Jia and Eleanor.

"It's so true," Jia was saying, "Ukraine is an old country with an old patriarchal culture."

"You're shitting me," Eleanor said. "It looks so modern when I see it on CNN."

"The buildings, the businesses, the machines are all modern, but they are being run by old country men and to those men in my country, women are still property. We are like pets and I'm a pet that got off the leash."

"Men are assholes," Eleanor said.

"Most," Jia agreed. "Rich isn't."

"He was," Eleanor said. "In a lot of ways. But he's changed, I think."

"You loved him?" Jia asked.

"A long time ago."

The door opened as Jia led Eleanor into the room and I forced myself up to a sitting position on the end of the bed. I probably looked like shit.

"You look like shit," Eleanor confirmed.

"Thanks, Ellie." I tried to shake the tangles out of my head. "What time is it?"

"Almost one," Jia said. "He's out there again."

I looked at Eleanor, then Jia. "Volkov?"

She nodded. "I explained to Eleanor what you did the other night and she has offered to sneak me home the same way."

I stood unsteadily. Eleanor placed a hand on my chest and gently pushed me back down.

"You're about to say that you could do it," she said. "You can't do it. You've got so much oxycodone in your system, you'd drive your car into a ditch and never feel it when your head went through the windshield. I'll do it."

I smiled and gave up.

"Where's my phone?" I asked.

Both looked around the room until Jia pointed to the floor next to the bed stand. I must have knocked it over while I slept. I turned to retrieve it but Jia stopped me. She grabbed it and handed it to me.

"Thanks," I said. "Gotta set the alarm."

"Why?" Eleanor asked.

"I have to be at the sheriff's office by eight." I saw the concern on their faces. "My head will be clear by morning and I'll take like half a pill so that I can function with minimal pain. I have to be there."

They reluctantly agreed and I laid back down on the bed, not even bothering to cover up and was asleep before they even left the room.

An oxy sleep is a fitful, dream-filled and hazy sleep. Flashes of images from the last few days, dreams of the past, of tomorrow's raids, of Volkov out in the parking lot. I thought I felt the bed moving, shaking. Then there was something else that I could sense through the fog in my head. What was that? A smell? Yes. What was it? Something sweet. Faint. The aroma. What?

Coconut.

SIXTEEN

The dream again.

The hospital, the homeless camp, the plowed field, but a little different this time. Things were fuzzier, like I was looking at them through a dirty, broken window that distorted what I was seeing.

I was running from the pleading face staring up out of the ground. I was running. Running. Falling. Getting up. Running.

At the edge of the field, I collapsed. Exhausted. On my back, breathing hard. Gasping. Inhaling.

I stopped.

A whiff of something.

What was it?

I took a breath.

Something familiar. It was sweet.

Lavender? Vanilla?

No. I took a breath.

Coconut?

Yes, it was coconut. Another breath. Another. Slowing. Slowing. A deep inhale.

I opened my eyes. I was on the bed looking up at the ceiling where the reddish-yellow morning light was glowing.

But there was that coconut smell again. And I felt an arm laying across my chest.

Eleanor.

She was asleep, next to me, fully clothed like I was, breathing softly. I turned to look at her. She was as beautiful to me as she had been in college, her long hair splayed out over her face and shoulders. I reached over and lifted the hair away from her face.

She felt my movement and stirred.

"You still use coconut shampoo," I whispered.

She opened her eyes and looked up at me with those clear blues.

"And you still snore," she said, rolling onto her back and sitting up. "How do you feel?"

"Tell you after I sit up. Jia get home okay?"

She nodded. "Got a brush here somewhere?"

She got up, stretched and headed towards the bathroom.

"Ellie," I said quietly. "What are you doing here?"

From in the bathroom, "After I dropped your girl off, I came back to check on you. It was late and I thought I would lay down for just a minute and I guess I fell asleep."

With a lot of effort and some quiet moaning, I managed to get myself upright, then rolled my feet off the side of the bed and sat. I rubbed my chest where the Ace bandage was wrapped. The feeling was now more of a deep ache then a sharp pain. I glanced over at the bottle of Oxy, grabbed it and shook one pill out into my hand. I had to function. Today was the raid on the banker and I didn't want to have a screwed up head. I swallowed the Oxy and one of my happy pills without water, hoping there wasn't a problem mixing the two medications.

The toilet flushed and Eleanor emerged brushing that gorgeous long hair of hers. She saw me sitting up, came over and sat next to me as she brushed.

"How is it?" she asked indicating my rib cage.

"I think it'll be okay today," I said. "Just took one Oxy."

"Can't just lay here this morning?"

"They are busting that guy this morning and I have to be there."

"What are they going to say when they see those scrapes and bruises on your face?"

I shrugged. "What should I tell them?"

"That you're an idiot?" she said with a smirk.

"Thanks," I said. I gently pushed myself up from the bed. "Gotta pee."

"Jia seems like a nice kid," Eleanor said while I was in the bathroom. "We talked a lot on the drive to her place. She's really gotten herself into a fix with that Volkov. I offered to help, but she won't take it."

"Yeah."

"She hasn't figured out what to do and the longer that guy is here, the harder it's gonna be."

"I know," I said coming out of the bathroom. Eleanor was gathering up her sweater and pouch. "I may be able to find a solution downtown."

"Your old buddy the sheriff?"

"Maybe," I said.

"It better be soon," Eleanor said, "Jia thinks that in another few days, this Volkov will do something drastic."

"Yeah." I went to my tiny closet and pulled out a long sleeved dress shirt. I managed to get it tucked in but it was hurting to try to button it. Eleanor stepped over and helped.

"What about getting Jia a green card?" she asked buttoning my shirt. "Or worker's visa? Or whatever?"

"Can't. She and her mom snuck into the country," I said. "They are actually illegal aliens. One call to Homeland Security and they'd get hauled off to some federal detention camp."

"Shit," Eleanor said. "That would be too bad. She's a good kid. I like her."

"Something will work out."

She finished buttoning my shirt, then began gathering up her stuff.

"Aren't there going to be questions about you being here, spending the night in an old boyfriend's bed?" I asked.

"On an old boyfriend's bed," she said, "not in it. And I'm going home now. You see, I was just helping an old friend after she had a rough night."

"I do see," I said. "She's lucky to have such a good friend."

She looked at me a moment. "Very lucky," she said.

Eleanor was at the door and glanced back at me. "You sure you're gonna be okay?" she asked.

I nodded. "Pill is kicking in. I should be okay."

She gave me a quick smile and a nod, then without a word, headed down the stairs.

Just before eight, I stepped into the old squad room in the basement of the Brannon County courthouse. Yankovic in street clothes and two uniformed sheriff deputies were gathered around a third's tiny cubicle, staring at his computer's screen. Yankovic waved me over. The cubicle was big enough for a desk and a couple chairs, but nothing else. The three walls were skewered by hundreds of colorful thumbtacks, holding up high school sports calendars, faded newspaper articles, and photos of kids fishing, swimming, opening presents and playing sports. The desk was covered in framed family pictures, more kids, parents, church events and, in one picture, a young woman and a man in wedding attire standing outside the LDS temple in Idaho Falls.

Yankovic pointed to my face as I neared the group.

I shook my head at him. "Don't ask," I said.

He rolled his eyes and shrugged. He turned to the uniforms.

"This is Willis, the forensics guy," he said. He pointed to the three men with him. "Thorpe, Cruikshank and Alden."

They glanced at me, nodded and went back to the screen, where the third cop, Alden, a skinny, mousy-looking guy trying hard to look like Tom Cruise, was pointing to a spot on a satellite photo on Google Earth. He was indicating a house that was on the end of a long, half-mile dirt road. Then the deputy pointed to a spot near where that half-mile road split away from the main road. There was a wide spot or turn-out in the road there.

"Jackie's parked there in his old Buick. When he sees Wendover leave for work, he'll call and you'll head in. Yank and Shank in one squad and Thorpe and . . ." He pointed at me.

"Willis," I said.

"Thorpe and Willis in the other. Willis stays in the car 'til the place is secured. Jackie says the girl is there, so this is just a knock and serve. No door bashing."

"The girl's not gonna give us trouble?" Cruikshank asked.

"She's just a kid," Yankovic said. "She doesn't know that her grandmother called us in."

"Not arresting her?" I asked.

"Just going scare her," Yankovic said, "encouraging cooperation. We'll take her to grandma's when it's all over." He looked toward me and then the deputies. "Any questions?" Heads shook. "You got what you need here, Willis?"

"Everything is in here," I said, indicating my backpack.

There was a beep from Yankovic's pocket. He pulled out his phone and looked at the screen.

"Time to go," he said, putting the phone away.

He tapped Cruikshank on the arm and I stepped aside letting the two brush by me, followed by Thorpe who pointed after the others.

"Cars are out back," he said. I followed Thorpe through the main squad room door and then out to the parking lot. Four big, blue, Brannon County Sheriff's Department SUV's with light bars were lined up next to the building. Cruikshank took the wheel of one as Yankovic climbed into the passenger seat. Before he closed his door, he called out to Thorpe.

"No lights," he said. "And no hurry. We'll take side-roads out of town, just so we don't get noticed by Wendover as he's driving in to work."

Thorpe gave the thumbs-up and he jumped into another SUV. I went around to the passenger side and worked hard to hide how much it hurt to climb up into that beast. We followed them out of the parking lot.

Thorpe could see I was in pain.

"What happened?" he asked pointing to the cuts on my face.

"Got into a disagreement with an old school buddy."

"Looks like he beat the crap out of you. Ribs?"

"Kicked me when I was down," I said.

"You didn't fight back?"

"It was an ambush. Didn't get the chance."

Thorpe just shook his head and we drove on in silence. I opted for useless small talk.

"You grow up here?" I asked.

"West of here," Thorpe said. "Yank said you were born here?"

"Born here, but I live in Bellingham. Came back to close out my mother's estate. I'm staying upstairs at Marty's. Mom owned it."

"Marty's, yeah," he said. "I've been there quite a few times. I've got a crush on that cute redhead that works there."

"Jia."

"Man, if only I was single," he said, "And if only my wife wasn't so good with her forty-five."

We were on a long, straight stretch of two-lane road that ran east out of town towards Wendover's place when we reached the turn-off. The cop who had been in the Buick waiting there, flashed his headlights at us and we pulled off the pavement and onto the gravel driveway.

Cruikshank and Yankovic pulled into the driveway and parked in front of the garage and we pulled up behind them. It was a medium sized, ranch-style house, with a red brick façade around the lower part of the house and brown clapboard from there to the roof. A narrow sidewalk ran from the driveway to the front door.

Thorpe stepped out of the SUV as the other two did, then leaned back in towards me. "Wait in here. I'll get you after it's locked down."

I watched the three men, Yankovic in the lead, march up the sidewalk to the front entrance. There was a heavy wooden door behind an aluminum screen door. He rang the doorbell. Nothing happened. He knocked. Then they all three backed up a step, apparently hearing a sound from inside. Cruikshank and Thorpe's hands drifted unconsciously down to their side arms.

The door opened and a small figure appeared behind the screen. She looked startled to see three men at her door and she backed up a step. Yankovic said something and she was shaking her head, looking nervously back and forth between Yankovic and the two uniforms. She backed away reaching for the door to close it and Yankovic pulled the screen door open before she could react and grabbed her arm and pulled her away from the door pulling her outside to Thorpe who wrapped a big hand around a tiny bicep while the other two men went in. She struggled, but Thorpe held on and was saying something to calm her. She was a tiny woman, maybe five feet tall and petite in baby blue shorts and a loose, faded pink tank-top. Her long, straw-colored hair was loose and unkempt, as if she had just gotten out of bed. It all made her look dangerously young.

Thorpe led her back inside the house.

It would be a while before they needed me so I slumped down in the passenger seat of the SUV and closed my eyes. With the oxycodone in my system, it didn't take long for me to drift off.

A tap on the window woke me.

Thorpe's massive shape was there.

"We're ready for you," he said, starting back up the walk. I glanced at the clock on the dash. Thirty-minute nap. Not bad.

I rubbed the sleep out of my eyes and moaned in pain as I grabbed my backpack and slipped carefully out of the car, following Thorpe up the sidewalk and slipping on disposable gloves.

The front door opened into a small foyer which continued on to a glassed living room overlooking a small backyard, bordered by the bushes we saw from Google Earth. To the left of the foyer was a sitting room that led to a dining room and kitchen and then out to the garage. To the right, a carpeted hallway led down to what I assumed were bedrooms and bathrooms. Thorpe led me that way to the last door. It opened into a room that was originally a bedroom but had been converted into a home office.

A huge LED monitor and a PlayStation sat on top of a big, solid oak desk. There had been a wide drawer at the center of the desk and three big drawers running down its left side, but they were scattered on the floor where they were tossed after being searched. A tower computer hummed along on the floor next to the desk and a very expensive office chair was parked at the desk. An older office chair sat by the small window that looked out over the front lawn.

The walls were bare, no photos, posters, calendars or anything. There was no TV, receiver, DVD or CD player anywhere in the room. I'd seen that before. He was one of those guys who got everything through their computer: music, movies and news. His computer was his window to the world.

Thorpe waved at the room.

"This seems to be it," Thorpe said. "So far, no computers, phones, tablets, or drives found anywhere else."

I dropped my pack to the floor and lowered myself into the desk chair.

There were voices down the hall.

"Asshole!"

It was the girl and she wasn't happy. Thorpe disappeared.

More voices and some scuffling and protests from the girl. Then Yankovic appeared in the doorway, pulling the girl by the arm, her wrists cuffed behind her. Yankovic had a bloody scratch on his left cheek.

He pulled her through the door and to the other office chair. He un-cuffed a skinny right wrist, pushed her down into the chair, then cuffed her to it.

"Didn't have to do that," she growled at him.

"Didn't have to scratch me, either," he said.

"Asshole."

"Shut-up kid," Yankovic snarled. "Or you'll get tossed into jail with your boyfriend."

She mumbled something, but Yankovic ignored her, turning to me.

"Gotta leave the kid while we finish up," he said. "You can get started on the computer."

I nodded, a questioning glance towards the kid.

"She gives you any problem," he said, "you are authorized to kick the shit out of her."

She mumbled. "Motherfucker."

Yankovic headed towards the door.

"And watch out," he said. "She's got serious nails."

Then he was gone.

She started rolling her chair towards the door, but I backed mine up to block her.

"Just hang here," I said.

She glared at me.

"It's going to be fine," I said, using as calm a tone as I could. "Between you and me, Yankovic is just doing the bad cop thing to keep you out of his way while he does his job."

"And you're the good cop," she said sarcastically.

"Not a cop."

She tilted her head, shook it with a smirk.

"Really," I said. "Just a hired hand."

"Yeah, right." She was angry, but some of the steam was dissipating.

"Really," I said. "I've done this before. You are going to be fine."

"That asshole says he's gonna bust me," she half-snarled.

I shook my head. "When they are done searching, and when I've copied off all the drives, these guys will un-cuff you and drive you to your grandmother's. Probably buy you a cheeseburger on the way."

She gave me a raspberry, but was cooling a little more.

"My name's Rich," I said holding out a hand.

She stared at it.

"Alyssa, right?" I asked.

A nod. She reached out with her free hand and we shook.

I set my laptop onto Wendover's desk to work, talking to keep her calm. I didn't want to get the same fingernail-across-the-cheek treatment Yankovic got. "I'm sorry about your boyfriend. They explained what's going on?"

Another nod. "Something about pictures."

"Kiddie porn."

The girl stared at me.

"Selling it," I said.

Alyssa nodded towards the computer. "You're gonna look for it?"

"That's my job."

"It's password protected, right?"

"I'm not logging into the computer," I said.

She looked.

"I'm running an app that will make an exact copy of his computer. I'll search the copy. I don't want to try to log into his computer."

"Why not?"

"If you don't want someone to get to something in your computer, you set a trap. If they attempt to log in and fail a certain number of times, it sets off a program that wipes out the drive. Erases possible evidence."

"Booby trap," she said.

"That's why I copy the drive. Helps me bypass the trap."

My app had begun copying the computer's drives and anything left in the computer's memory.

"So you think he's hiding stuff?" she asked.

"On here," I said pointing to the computer, "and at the bank. And maybe other places."

Calm now, pre-occupied, she rolled her chair away from me and against the windowed wall.

"He downloads the stuff from the dark web," I said, "then sells them on Asian and European sites. There's a chance he may even be creating some original stuff and selling it."

That got her attention. I kept going.

"Ever see anyone else, any young girls here?" I asked.

A head shake.

"Ever see him stashing any external drives like this around any-where?" I pointed to one of the external hard drives I had with me.

She looked a moment, then shook her head.

"How about one of these?" I held up a couple of USB thumb drives, one about the size of my thumb and the other a smaller rectangular one. She pointed to it.

"That little thing is for storing stuff?" she asked.

"You can store thousands of pictures on these," I said. "Ever see him with any of these?"

Her eyes slid away for just the briefest of moments and then came back to me. "I don't think so."

She was too young to be a good liar.

"He could hide pictures on little drives like this, stick them in a pocket, take them to the bank and then upload them to a server to sell. Made money that way."

"A lot?"

"Some people will pay big bucks for pictures of young girls." I said, deciding to keep pushing. "Has he got a nice camera?"

She shrugged, but I could see the gears working.

"Did he take any pictures here?" I asked.

That brought her eyes back up to mine.

"If he did," I continued, "they'd now be up on some Asian website selling for a nice chunk of money." She swiveled her chair around to look out the window and I decided to take a shot at what I think happened. "Alyssa, did Wendover take pictures of you?"

She was silent.

I could hear the cops moving things around in other parts of the house. Where I was, there was only the sound of computer fans and the click of my drives copying. And Alyssa's heavy, rapid breathing.

"That fucking piece of shit," she mumbled.

Alyssa turned her chair back towards me. The blood had drained from her face.

So, he had taken pictures of her.

"He told me I was gonna be a model." She said it more to herself than to me. "He promised me no one would see them."

"I'm sorry," I said.

Alyssa was looking around the room, not looking at me, calculating.

I kept quiet and watched.

After a few moments, she came back to me.

"He had a bunch of those little drive things," she said. "I remember seeing them. I thought he just threw them in those drawers." She pointed to the four drawers that were laying around.

I went to the drawers, picking up the largest of the side drawers and looked through it. Nothing. I took it back to the desk and slid it into its slot. I did the same with the other two side drawers. Then I picked up the big center drawer and dug around. Paper clips, pencils, erasers, staples, all the usual office flotsam. I set it on its track to slide back into the desk, but it jammed, an inch from going all the way in. I pulled it back out, thinking something inside was catching. Nothing. I tried to slide it in again. It still wouldn't go all the way in. I pulled the drawer out, looked inside, tried again.

Alyssa was watching me struggle. The drawer still wouldn't slide all the way in.

"There." Alyssa said pointing. "Something's sticking out."

The drawer face was an inch-thick piece of oak. From her angle, Alyssa could see three tiny black rectangles in the wood on the side of the drawer facing her. I looked closer.

There they were. Tiny USB drives.

Wendover had made little slots in the side of the drawer for holding the little drives. Anyone looking at it would just assume they were part of the drawer. One had gotten knocked loose when the cops where throwing them around and it was keeping the drawer from closing.

Alyssa reached out to touch it. I pushed her hand away.

"Yankovic," I called.

"What?" came the angry yell back.

"I need baggies and tweezers," I yelled back. "Or needle nose pliers."

There was a scrambling of feet.

Thorpe came in, followed by Yankovic.

I pulled the drawer all the way out and flipped it over, dumping everything out. I turned the side toward the two cops and pointed to where the USB drives were buried in the wood.

"Thumb drives," I said.

"Holy fuck," Thorpe said.

"You touch 'em?" Yankovic asked.

"No."

"How'd you find those?" Thorpe asked.

"Alyssa spotted them."

We all turned to look at her, but the girl was bent over, her face in her hands, weeping uncontrollably.

I turned back to the two guys. "She just realized Wendover's been selling pictures of her," I said quietly.

Thorpe looked at the girl and sighed, sincere sadness on his face.

"No surprise, I guess," Thorpe said. "Damn."

After the drives and computer were copied and bagged up, Yankovic put on the good cop mask and gently un-cuffed Alyssa, apologizing for upsetting her, explaining it was just part of the job. He turned to me.

"How soon can you get into those drives?"

"Depends," I said.

"Whaddya mean?" Thorpe asked.

"If this guy had half a brain," I said, "he will have encrypted the drives to protect them. I can crack the drives, but it might take a day or two."

Yankovic nodded. "Well, get it as fast as you can. I want to get this stuff into the feds' hands as soon as possible."

He was gone.

Thorpe touched Alyssa's arm.

"C'mon kid," he said, gently. "Let's get you to grandma's."

Seventeen

By early afternoon, I was back at the courthouse and had finished filling out all the usual evidence forms and incident reports on the morning's raid. By tomorrow, the drives would be ready for me to start working on them.

I looked around, trying to remember where I had stashed my Jeep. I found it and ten minutes later, I was pulling into the parking lot at Marty's while a familiar looking SUV was leaving. The vehicle passed by and the driver gave me a scary, cat-that-ate-the-canary smile.

Volkov.

Something had happened.

I pulled into the back of the bar, dropped my backpack full of gear upstairs in my room and then came back down to the bar where Camila was huddled with Tyler, speaking in low, worried tones.

"We have to call the police," Camila was saying.

"She says no," Tyler was insisting.

"We could get in trouble if we don't," Camila said.

"But if we do call the cops, they'll find out she's illegal and they'll send her back to Ukraine," Tyler said.

They turned to me as I came around the corner.

"What happened?" I asked.

Both of them were trying to decide whether to say anything or even what to say.

"What?" I asked.

"Volkov," Tyler said finally.

I looked around. "Where's Jia?"

Tyler shot a thumb back down the hall towards the women's restroom. I put a hand out for them to stay there and went to the restroom door and listened. I could hear snuffling from inside. Crying. I quietly tapped on the door.

"Jia?" I said.

Nothing.

"Jia?" Still no answer. "Okay, I'm coming in."

I waited a moment, then opened the door and walked in.

The women's restroom was pretty small, just three old wooden stalls along one wall and a counter with three sinks under a tall, wide and worn mirror on the opposite wall. Jia was sitting on the counter, staring at the phone she was holding in her hands. She didn't look up at me.

"He's going to turn me in," she said, wiping her eyes. "If my mother and I don't fly back to Ukraine with him next week, he will turn himself and me and my mother into Homeland Security and we will all be deported." She looked up at me. "I don't want to leave. My mother doesn't want to leave." She sniffed. "We love it here."

"He's turning you in today?" I asked.

She shook her head.

"Friday. Unless I agree to go with him before then. But I would have to leave my mother here and . . . and what would she do? How could she get by?"

I pulled a few paper towels from the dispenser and went to her, heaving myself up to sit on the counter next to her. I handed her the towels. She wiped her eyes.

"I don't know what to do," she said, looking back down to her phone. "Call my mother? Call the police? Call Volkov?"

I placed my hand over her phone.

"You want to stay," I said. "I want you to stay. Everyone here wants you to stay."

"Yes, but. . ."

"Volkov still hasn't found out where you live? Hasn't found your mother?"

"Not yet."

"Good," I said. I looked her straight in the eye. "Jia, do you trust me?"

She looked back up at me, eyes red, searching mine. Then she gave me a gentle nod.

"I have come up with something that I think can fix this for you," I said.

Her brows furrowed, questioning.

"I can get Volkov sent back to Ukraine and out of your life."

She stared. "How?"

"Will you trust me?"

"I said I would. Why? What are you going to do?""

I held up a hand and shook my head to stop her from asking any more questions.

"Just trust me on this."

"I don't understand."

"You will. But for this to work, it's better that you don't know anything about it right now."

She looked at me for a long beat, wiping the last of her tears away and I placed a hand on hers. "Don't call your mother, the police or Volkov."

She was still staring at me, deciding.

"Jia, I promise you that Volkov will be gone by Friday." I put on a look of strong, self-confidence, but it was stronger and more self-confident than I really felt.

A faint smile showed up on her face, then, with her eyes watering up again, she nodded.

I smiled, gave her hand an it's-gonna-be-alright squeeze and slipped off the counter.

I left her in the bathroom to recover and went out to Camila who was stacking glasses at the counter and waved Tyler over.

"Guys," I started when Tyler got there, "I have something in mind to help this situation for Jia, but I'm gonna need your help. Game?"

Camila nodded.

"Oh, yeah," Tyler said. "What do we do?"

"First, don't call the police about Volkov, okay?"

Camila looked like she was going to argue, but finally decided to go along. Tyler nodded.

"Good. You both gonna be here Thursday night?" I asked.

They nodded.

"And Volkov's been here every night since he got in town?"

"Every night," Camila said.

"Good. Now . . . you can't tell a soul about this. No one. Not Jia." I looked at Camila, then Tyler. "Not Marie and not Lee. Marie is a little too . . .uh . . . ethical for what I'm going to suggest and it would only take two beers for Lee to tell everyone in the bar all about it. So, deal?"

Tyler and Camila looked at each other a moment, then nodded. Tyler attempted a cross-my-heart gesture followed by what he thought was a Boy Scout sign, but it looked more like a cross between a peace gesture and flipping me off.

"Okay," I said. "Here's what I want to do."

Without giving them too much detail, I explained what I wanted to do and what I needed them to do to help. Without hesitation, they agreed and after getting another vow of silence from them both, Tyler went back into the kitchen and Camila resumed stacking glasses just as Jia returned from the bathroom, eyes dry, but red.

She gave me a sad smile of reassurance as she passed me and went around behind the bar.

"If you don't think you need me," I said, "I'm going to Pocatello this afternoon."

Jia looked around the bar at the half dozen patrons scarfing down burgers and fries and shook her head. "We're fine."

"Okay."

"Thanks again, Rich," Jia said.

I smiled and nodded and started towards the back.

A voice behind me at the door stopped me.

"Hey, sweet cheeks."

I turned to see Eleanor entering, dressed in tennis shoes, faded jeans and a loose beige blouse, her long hair loose down over her shoulders. And that big, toothy grin. For a flash of a moment, looking at her, I was back in college again. I forced myself back to the present.

"Ellie," I said teasingly, "isn't this like three days in a row?"

"Girl's gotta eat, you know," she said. "I was at a regional meeting in Idaho Falls and I'm on my way back to Poky, but I thought I'd stop and grab lunch here. Did you know that Marty's is the only non-franchise burger joint near the freeway exit?"

"Really? That's great. We could sell our location to Appleby's and make a fortune, right?"

"Hell no," she said. "The world doesn't need another Appleby's."

A thought hit me.

"You're heading to Pocatello," I said.

She nodded. "Why?"

"I'm trying to find someone and she works at some hair salon in Pocatello, but I don't know which one. Doing anything? Wanna help me track her down?"

"An old girlfriend?"

I shook my head. "The sister of my friend that was killed."

"The sister of the guy that beat you up?" she asked with a smirk.

"He didn't beat me up," I protested. "He jumped me."

She smiled. "And then he beat you up."

I gave up. "Okay, okay. He beat me up, Alright?"

"Okay," Ellie said with a sly smile. "Is his sister going to beat you up too?"

"Look," I said in mock anger, "you wanna help or not?"

She gave me that big toothy smile again. "Buy me a burger?"

"Deal. Meet somewhere in Poky?"

"Hell no," she said. "It's a gorgeous day. Let's take your Jeep. The doors and top are off, right? You can bring me back later and I'll get my car."

"I like that idea," I said. "Need anything out of your car?"

She indicated the pouch that was hung over her left shoulder. "Got all I need right here."

"Then let's go."

Out the back door, strapped into the Jeep, we took off, making a quick stop at a Macdonald's drive-thru for a pair of quarter-pounders.

"Feel guilty getting a burger here instead of Marty's?" Ellie asked, her mouth full of processed bread, meat and cheese.

"Not one bit," I said. "The nice thing about these quarter-pounders is that you can one hand 'em while steering and shifting gears. Try doing that with one of the burgers from Marty's and it will fall apart on you."

"Wow," she said in mock amazement. "Who would have thought you could have put so much thought into something so stupid."

With both of us laughing, I pulled out onto the main road. Turning left would take us to the freeway. I looked to the right.

"Wanna take a shortcut?" I asked.

"A shortcut to get to Pocatello?"

I smiled, turned right and started through town.

"It's not exactly a shortcut," I said, "that's just what my mom called it. She liked to shop in Pocatello 'cuz she didn't like the stores in Black River. And she hated taking the freeway. All the cars driving fast scared her, so she told me we were taking a shortcut."

"So it's a longcut?"

"Any problem with that?"

Ellie flipped her hair up so that the breeze blew it back, held up her quarter-pounder and looked up at the cloudless blue sky.

"On a day like this? No problem at all."

We were off.

There was an old, two-lane highway that used to run between Idaho Falls, Black River, Pocatello and a few other small communities. It followed the Black River to the foothills where it ran north and south. It was a winding, narrow, potholed old road, but running along the foothills, it presented a perfect view of the gorgeous, wide, flat valley floor of Eastern Idaho.

As we drove south, we talked about Marty's, about what I had been doing, about her classes and her department and the satisfaction of teaching.

We were speeding around corners in the open Jeep, shifting up and down the gears, wind blowing our hair every which way. I looked over at Ellie and she had her eyes closed, feeling the wind. She wore a big smile. She felt me looking at her.

"Know what this reminds me of?" she asked.

I shook my head.

"Remember that POS motorcycle you had in college?"

"The Honda," I said remembering. "Honda 185, I think."

"Reminds me of all those times we used to race from Salt Lake to Ogden to that arthouse movie theatre on your bike. Froze my ass off on some of those rides."

"But you loved it," I said.

"Hell, yeah!" She laughed. "Did we wear helmets then?"

"I don't think so."

"We were idiots."

We were emerging from a turn and I grabbed the gear shift to drop down a notch and Ellie placed a hand on mine as I shifted.

"Yes, we were idiots," she said. I looked at her a moment. She was just looking down at her hand, lost in a memory. She smiled to herself, a slightly sad sort of smile. Then she removed her hand and turned to look out at the valley racing past us.

We rode in silence for a few more miles.

"Why didn't you just google a list of salons and call them?" she asked.

"You'd rather sit in some dark coffee shop making blind calls to a bunch of hairdressers?"

Ellie just laughed, pulled out her phone and started googling. After scrolling through a few screens, tapping in a few more search terms and cursing AT&T's lousy cell coverage, she showed me a screen of salon listings.

"Great," I said. "But where do we start?"

She held up a finger and she thumbed through the listings, thought a moment and then thumbed through some more and finally nodded to herself.

"Okay," she said. "Where's this road come out when it hits Pocatello?"

"Uh . . . I don't know the name of the street." I said. "It goes under the freeway, kinda southeast of town, then . . . around a curve." I had to picture it in my head. "There's an old Baskin-Robbins on the right, then a bunch of houses and like a block or two away on the left is the MiniDome. I mean Holt Arena or whatever they call it now."

"Oh yeah," Ellie said. "That sounds like Terry Street, right by the college." She went back into her phone, scrolling and thumbing and scrolling some more. Then she stopped, looked out to the passing scenery, then back to me. "Figured it out. Stay on the road until you hit Fifth Street, then hang a right. We'll start there."

"Great," I said. "You guide, I drive."

Ellie led me through the streets until we came to the first salon on her list and we pulled into the parking lot of what must have once been a convenience store but now displayed a huge, hand-carved wooden sign that identified it as Harry's Hair. Two old cars were already parked there and we slipped in next to them.

"You sure this is the best way to find this girl you're looking for?" Ellie asked, stepping out of the Jeep.

"I tried every social media platform I could find," I said. "She's either changed her name again or doesn't use any of those services."

"Phone book?" she asked with a wry smile.

I stared at her.

"When was the last time you even saw a phone book?"

A bunch of crude little bells that were hanging on the inside of the door jingled as we entered Harry's Hair. Based on the place's name, I thought we would be walking into a barbershop. We weren't. It was a hair and nail salon with an open floor layout, worn beige linoleum under six old salon chairs laid out in two rows. Two middle-age ladies were lounging in them as their hair was being worked over by two younger women. The smell of shampoo, burnt hair and something that smelled like paint thinner circulated the entire space.

At the front door, a large Native American woman sat behind a counter working on a computer. She wore a bright, multi-colored frock that was failing to hide the fact that she was carrying a hundred and fifty pounds more than she should be. Her wrists, ears and thick black hair were decorated with chains, stones, beads and handmade copper and tin trinkets. She jingled with every move of her hands over the keyboard.

"Appointment?" she asked, without looking up, jingling.

"No," I said. "Is Harry around?"

The woman looked up from the screen. "I'm Harry."

I felt Eleanor stifling a laugh behind me.

"Harriet," the woman said. "Whaddya want?"

"I'm trying to find a woman," I said. "She's supposed to be working at a hair place here in town."

"You a cop or something?" she asked, looking at me, more annoyed than suspicious.

"No."

"Why's your face all beat up?" she asked.

I heard Ellie stifle another laugh. I glanced back her way and she put on a serious face. Her eyes were still laughing though.

"Bar fight," Ellie said.

I gave her another look, then back to Harry. "It wasn't a bar fight. A guy jumped me in a parking lot."

The woman lifted her huge frame out of her chair and leaned forward to get a better look.

"This girl you're lookin' for in trouble?"

"No. She's the sister of a friend of mine who died a few years ago."

Harry looked at me, blinking her heavy eyelids a few times, glanced at Eleanor, maybe for reassurance, then came back to me.

"She Indian?" Harry asked.

I shook my head.

"She gotta name?"

"Julie," I said. "Julie Sorenson, but I guess she's been married and divorced a couple times, so it might be Julie Blenken or maybe Fincher."

Harry glanced off to the side, looking like she was searching for something. Looking, thinking. Then a head shake and she came back to me.

"Name don't ring bells for me," she said. With a grunt, she shifted around to look towards the salon chairs. With a booming voice that would never need a bullhorn to amplify it, she called down to the women. "You two know a Julie Blenken or Fincher or . . .." She looked at me. "what was the other name?"

"Sorenson," Ellie said.

"Sorenson," Harry said.

The two beauticians looked at each other and then each looked back at Harry, shaking their heads. Harry nodded and turned back to me. Then one of the clients, a small woman whose big, puffy, curly grey hair was getting re-curled called out.

"You know," puffy-hair said, "there used to be a Julie working at Rosie's, down in Chubbuck. I think she was a Fincher."

"How do I get to Rosie's?" I asked puffy-hair.

"You don't," Harry said. I turned back to her. "It's a Chevron now. Bulldozed that whole strip mall about five years ago."

"Shit," I muttered.

The girl working on puffy-hair spoke up.

"A lot of them that worked at Rosie's moved over to Fox Cut Salon. You could try there."

"It's down at the other end of Yellowstone Avenue," Harry said. "Near the Goodwill."

"Fox Cut Salon?" I asked.

"Yeah."

"Thanks. We'll check there."

I turned to go and gave puffy-hair a wave of thanks.

Ellie turned to follow me out, but Harry stopped her pointing to Ellie's long, straight black hair.

"You should let that go," she said.

Ellie stopped and turned back to the big woman.

"Huh?" she asked.

"You should stop coloring your hair," Harry said. "Let that grey come out. It'll give you a mature classiness."

Eleanor's mouth moved, looking for something to say, but nothing came out until finally she was able to say defensively "I don't color my hair. This is my real color."

Harry snorted.

"And my real weight is a hundred and ten."

It was my turn to laugh and I let out a big one as I exited the salon, Ellie kicking me in the butt as she followed me out.

That started an entire afternoon of us following the bread crumbs of Julie's employment trail. Near the end of the day, the trail dropped us at a worn little strip mall near the airport, west of the city. The long concrete block structure housed the usual strip mall inhabitants: a smoke shop, a Domino's Pizza, a tattoo parlor, a nail salon, public restrooms and, at the end of the building, Linh's, the hair salon that Julie may have worked in.

We parked in front of Linh's and looked at the run down little place, windows covered with faded posters showing various women's hair designs and a neon sign that occasionally clicked off like it had a short in it. There was an old plastic "Yes, We're Open" sign dangling at an angle in the window of the salon's door.

Ellie looked at me shaking her head.

"It's like we are following someone's slow descent into hell," she said. "This is the worst looking one yet. What do think was happening to her?"

"I wish I knew," I said. I pointed over at the restrooms. "Isn't it weird to see public restrooms at a shitty little strip mall?"

Eleanor nodded. "Because none of these little shops has a bathroom in it. The building is too small and old."

"Could be right."

"And I, for one, am glad they have it." She jumped out of the Jeep. "Be right back."

She dashed into the restroom and I got out to stretch my legs. The landscape was typical high desert, flat, very few trees and bare foothills beyond the freeway where a scattering of cars and trucks whizzed by on their way to better places.

Ellie came out with a big sigh.

"I needed that," she said. She shot a thumb toward the hair salon. "Shall we?"

A buzzer buzzed when we walked into Linh's and we were immediately hit by flowery smells so strong it was like walking into a greenhouse full of lavender. There were four salon chairs in the tiny place, all occupied by women in various stages of beautification.

An older Vietnamese woman eyed us, whispered something to the woman whose hair she was trimming, then came over. She was tiny, wearing an old-fashioned, form fitting, single piece flowered dress that ran down below her knees. Her thick black hair was bundled tightly with large jade pins to highlight a thin, pale and worn face, a face that hadn't smiled in years.

"We close. Fifteen minutes," she said in heavily accented English. "You got appointment?"

"Are you Linh?" I asked.

She nodded. "Appointment?"

"No," I said, "I just wanted to ask a question."

She just stared waiting.

"I'm trying to find an old friend who might have worked here. Julie Fincher or maybe Blenken?"

"You bill collector?" she asked.

I smiled and shook my head.

"Cop?"

Eleanor looked at me. "Why does everyone think you're a cop?"

"I wish I knew."

"No Julie here," the woman said.

"Damn," I said. "Did she ever work here?"

At the nearest chair, a much younger Asian girl was working on a client's hair.

"Did you say Julie?" she asked in a quiet voice. The older woman turned quickly to the girl with a stern glare.

I turned to the girl. "Yes, Julie Fincher. Know her?"

"No Julie here," the older woman said harshly staring at the young girl. "No Julie."

The girl stared at the woman, then glanced up at me quickly before going back to her client's hair. "Sorry," she said. "Thought you said Judy."

The older woman then placed herself between us and the girl, arms folded in front of her.

"No Julie here."

Her look said get out and we did, with a brief thanks after a glance at the girl, who tried hard not to look our way.

We climbed into the Jeep.

"Well," Ellie said, "that was fuckin' weird."

"It certainly was."

"What now?" she asked.

"Don't know," I said. I had put the key in the ignition to start the engine when the door to Linh's opened and the girl that had spoken up came out, gave us a very brief look and then disappeared into the women's restroom.

Ellie patted me on the knee.

"Wait here."

She jumped out and followed the girl.

A few minutes later, Ellie came back out of the bathroom and came over to the driver's side.

"Your friend works at that nail salon right there," she pointed to the little shop called Bonjour Nails. I was about to get out but Eleanor stopped me. "She's not there today. The girl says it's her day off, but she'll be back tomorrow."

I looked back at Linh's front door. "Why?"

"The girl says Julie used to work at Linh's, but there was a falling out," Ellie said. "Apparently the old lady there isn't the most honest business owner in this strip mall and was skimming off Julie's tips. They fought and Julie left."

"I see."

"We can catch her at the nail salon tomorrow."

"We?"

Eleanor grabbed my arm and tugged on it like she wanted to get me out of the Jeep.

"Let me drive," she said.

I smiled and nodded. She jumped into the driver's seat and I strapped in as shotgun.

"Thanks for going in there and talking to that girl," I said as Ellie backed us out of the parking lot and headed back towards town.

"Hang on!" she said flooring the Jeep.

She raced around corners and hit every bump and pothole she could, letting go with her big toothy smile and laugh every time the Jeep's lousy shocks bounced us off our seats.

"Feel like a milkshake?" she asked.

"Yes," I said, "the way you're driving."

"I mean a milkshake to drink, asshole. My treat," she said. "There's an old ice cream shop up here a couple miles. Used to go there with my son after school. Real ice cream."

Five minutes later, Ellie slid us to a stop in a gravel parking lot next to a little clapboard building off the side of the road. The place looked like it was one of those small, postwar cottages that were built for the baby boomers, but with a pair of take-out windows and a drive-thru, it had morphed into a little burger joint. Above the two take-out windows, a giant, pink, neon sign read "Fanci Frosteez" in a swirly, flashing script. I started to get out, but she stopped me.

"Wait here."

Eleanor jumped out of the Jeep and went to one of the take-out windows. When she turned back towards me a few minutes later, she had a drink in one hand but was hiding something behind her back with the other.

"Close your eyes," she said, a sneaky smile on her face.

"Huh?"

"Come on. Close 'em."

"Is this gonna hurt?" I asked.

"Not much," she said. "Shut-up and close your eyes."

"Okay, okay."

I closed them.

"And keep 'em closed."

I nodded.

"Hold your hands out," she instructed, which I did. She slid what felt like a cold plastic cup into my hand. "Take it. Eyes still closed."

I took it.

"There's a straw at the top."

I found the straw.

"Take a sip."

Pretty sure I wasn't going to get poisoned, but slightly worried that she had given me a ghost pepper milkshake, I took a tentative draw. And a taste.

Ellie laughed as I opened my eyes wide with an excited smile and took a bigger swallow.

"Ironport and Cream!" I boomed after it had cleared my throat on its way to my belly. "Ironport and cream!"

Ellie had a big, happy and proud look on her face watching me take another swig. Ironport was an old-fashioned soda that used to be big in Idaho, Utah and Wyoming, but had almost completely disappeared. It was like a cross between a root beer and a black cherry Dr. Pepper, but there were other spices in it. And then when mixed with vanilla ice cream and whipped cream, you had one yummy treat.

"I haven't had one of these in like thirty years," I said, swallowing more.

"I remembered you talking about it," Ellie said. "Remember us hunting all over Salt Lake, Provo and Ogden trying to find it?"

"On that old crappy motorcycle."

"Yup."

"And we never found any." I was almost halfway through my drink by the time Ellie slipped in behind the steering wheel.

"Thanks Ellie," I said. "Wow."

We sat there in the Jeep for another half hour, sipping and talking. When I mentioned that I was afraid that her hanging out with me all day was going to cause her grief with her husband, she just shrugged it off.

"He and I are busy people," she said. "He's got his life and I have mine."

She said he had become head of the Physics department at the school and that the department was apparently doing serious work in conjunction with the Nuclear Engineering Lab in Arco.

"And you're looking to be the head of your department," I said.

I got a quick smile from her and a nod.

"If I get the chairmanship, I'll have that on my CV which will make it easier to get hired in a state that actually supports the Arts."

"Another state?" I asked. "You'd actually move?" She nodded. "Then wouldn't your husband have to give up his chair to go with you?"

Ellie looked at her watch and fired up the Jeep.

"We better get back to Marty's," she said.

With gravel flying everywhere, she backed us out of the parking lot, back onto the road and pointed the Jeep towards Black River. I worked on my drink and looked over at Ellie who seemed a little lost in thought as she drove, sipping on her milkshake. She was staring at the road blankly, working something over in her head and I noticed a tear appearing. She turned away from me and rubbed her eyes. I knew enough not to ask any more questions and we drove on in silence.

Eleanor got us back to Black River, pulled into the parking lot in front of Marty's, stopped near a blue Toyota 4Runner and killed the engine. It was early evening.

"This is my stop," she said, climbing out.

I slowly got out of the Jeep, having stiffened up from sitting so long and with my ribs starting to hurt again. I groaned and held my side.

"Pills wearing off?" she asked as she came around.

I nodded.

Ellie walked around to the driver's door of her car and I followed her.

"Ellie, I can't thank you enough for today."

She stopped at the door and turned to me, smiling and nodding.

"I haven't had this much fun in years," she said. "Sunny day, running around in that old Jeep, chasing your friend all over Poky, scarfing down milkshakes." She shook her head. "Great day, Richie. Great day."

She beeped her car and the door unlocked. She turned to open it, then paused. She stared at the door for a second, then turned her head to look at me.

"What?" I asked.

"Richie . . . I need to try something," she said.

"Uh huh?"

Eleanor moved close to me, placed her hands on my waist, leaned in and pressed her lips to mine. A little startled at first, I finally returned the kiss, wrapping my arms around her.

Then, gently, she pushed herself away, not looking at me, and turned back to her car.

"I had to find something out," she said as she opened the door.

"Find what out?"

She slipped into her seat and closed the door. She looked up at me. There was a hint of a smile. And then she was gone.

—•—

EIGHTEEN

Wednesday morning.

The Bannon County Court House was as sleepy as it had seemed every other day. The halls were quiet, the same handful of people were in the cafeteria and no front desks seemed occupied, so after I had a latte in one hand and a bear claw in the other, I made for the small office I had been given.

Two older policemen that I had met but whose names I didn't remember, waved at me as I unlocked the office door and went in.

I set myself down in the not-very-comfortable office chair and between swallows of caffeine and mouthfuls of sugary dough, fired up my laptop and the desktop computer that would give me access to the local databases as well as NCIC and Homeland Security. I logged in then turned around and opened the evidence locker.

Yesterday's team had put the bags with each of the drives inside. I pulled one out, locked the safe back up and set the bag on my desk. Attached to the top of each bag was a brown envelope, labeled for that drive. It contained an evidence log. These were filled out by anyone who touched the evidence and was necessary to show chain of custody when the case came to trial. The first entry was from the day before and described the custody of the evidence from where I had copied it, handed it to an officer and then through other hands until it was locked in my office.

I started a new entry, indicated the date and noted that my task was to decrypt and inventory the contents.

With that, I opened the bag and plugged the drive into my laptop, running an app to check drive size, verify drive integrity and check for drive partitions without changing anything. That done, finding only one partition, I ran a preliminary inventory app on the drive and found out it wasn't encrypted at all. This was Wendover's boot drive, running an older version of the Windows operating system, and it had only one user folder. I dug out an old command-line app and ran it to reset the Administrator and user passwords which was easy to do.

Next, I did a quick scan through the files, but it was just the basic operating system, not even any temp files. It booted up Windows so Wendover could log on, connect to the internet and his other drives. My guess was that Wendover had kept the temp files, browser cache, kiddie porn and the main apps on the other drives in his computer, or maybe only the thumb drives so that they could be hidden or disposed of, if necessary. I dumped a complete file inventory of the boot drive to the printer and put the list in the envelope. I added my notes to the evidence log, unplugged the drive from my computer, put it back in the bag and then put the bag and envelope in the locker. I pulled out the next bag, which contained one of the little USB drives I had found hidden in the side of the desk drawer.

I started an entry in the drive's attached evidence log and then plugged the little thumb drive into my laptop. This drive was, as I suspected it would be, encrypted. I fired up my decrypting app and it began working on the little drive. I sat back and let it work. It would search the files and attempt to figure out the encryption key.

There was a light tap at the door, I opened it to see Sandy there holding a Diet Coke and some kind of savory muffin.

"Wanted to see if you got going okay," she said.

"So far," I said. "I'm working on the drives now."

"Good. Need anything?"

"I might need more printer paper," I said.

Sandy pointed down to the end of the room where tall, gray metal lockers stood against the wall.

"In there," she said. "Paper, pencils, staples or any of the other office shit you might need."

"Thanks."

Sandy felt someone come up behind her and turned to see Yankovic there.

"Hey, Yank," she said. "Later, Willis," Sandy squirmed past the man and out the door.

"Done yet?" Yankovic asked, He pointed to my laptop screen, which was scrolling numbers and letters and commands as it worked.

"Just started. First drive was a simple boot drive. Nothing on it, no encryption." I pointed to the USB drive and then my screen. "This was one of the hidden drives and it is encrypted. I'm trying to decrypt it now."

"Gonna work?" There was more than a subtle hint of skepticism in his question.

I nodded.

"How long?"

"Depends on the encryption. If he was smart and used a really long encryption key, it could take a while."

Yankovic just shook his head and gave a dismissive shrug. He didn't understand the process and wasn't going to pretend that he did.

"Okay," he said finally. "Let me know."

He turned and was gone, letting the door close as he left.

I turned back to my laptop to see it still working on the drive, so I decided to do a little work on my other project. I switched to the desktop computer and logged into the law enforcement database to do a search of incidents in the years just before and just after Jeannie's death. I punched in the criteria and watched the screen fill with columns of names, dates and infractions.

Scrolling through the list, I recognized a few names: classmates, neighbors and even a couple relatives. I wasn't too surprised to see Rob Clawson's name pop up. He showed up with a few drug-related arrests, a DUI and one dismissed assault charge during that period, but nothing in the last twenty years which made me happy to think that maybe he had finally gotten his act together.

Searching on, I found Pete Sorenson's arrests in that period. There were two DUI's and three assaults. Looking at the details of the incidents, two of those assaults looked like they had been bar fights that turned into assault charges.

Digging deeper, I found two other surprises: Jeannie was charged with a DUI a month before she died and Julie was arrested after an accidental drug overdose. That happened a month after Jeannie was killed.

Some bad stuff in that family.

I dumped the search results off to my printer and was stuffing them into my backpack when the laptop beeped at me.

My app had worked out the encryption key and had unlocked the USB drive.

Opening the drive with a file explorer, I found what we expected to find: hundreds of computer images and dozens of video files. I pulled one of the images up to confirm my suspicions and then closed it, disgusted. Kiddie porn. That was the evidence that would seal the deal and send Wendover away for a long time.

I dumped a complete file listing to the printer and then attached it to the evidence log. I added an entry in the log with the time and date and the description of what I had done along with the decryption key my app had used.

I stopped.

The place was quiet, so I reached into my pocket and pulled out my keys. On the key ring, there was a small plastic trinket I had made on my 3D printer: a miniature Mac Classic computer. It fit with my whole nerd vibe, but the best thing about it was the tiny little slot I had built into the bottom of it. I pressed on it and out popped a very tiny USB drive.

I plugged the drive into another port on my laptop, then went to Wendover's thumb drive, found the files I wanted and copied them from his drive to mine. When the copy process was complete, I put my little drive back into its hiding place on the key ring. Unplugging Wendover's drive from my laptop, I stuffed it back into its evidence bag and had just sealed it when the door opened, startling me.

Gil.

He saw me jump and then yelp with pain. My ribs still hurt. I tried to massage the pain away.

"Sorry," he said. "Didn't mean to scare you." He saw my grimace and took in the cuts on my face. "What the hell happened? Car accident?"

"No. Long story."

"I got time," Gil said. He stepped closer looking at the marks on my face. "You know I've been doin' this job for quite a while, right?"

I nodded.

"I know what cuts and bruises from a fall look like, what they look like after an auto accident and what they look like after a fight."

"Yeah," I sighed.

"Who?" He stepped back, leaned against the wall and folded his arms. There was a smirk on his face.

"I made the mistake of trying to ask Pete Sorenson about his sister."

Gil smiled and shook his head. "Silly fuck. You at least landed a few yourself, right?"

"Didn't have the chance," I said. "He jumped me in a parking lot and I was down on the ground with him kicking me before I knew what was happening."

"Shit," Gil said.

"Really nailed me hard in the ribs," I said touching my side.

"You could get him for assault."

I shook my head. "No witnesses."

"Want me to go after him?"

"No," I said, "Out of your jurisdiction anyway. Happened in I.F."

He nodded, but pointed at the cut on my face. "Need anything for that?"

"It'll be okay," I said with a wave. With a tiny grunt of pain, I spun around in the chair and put the drive back in the evidence locker and pulled out the next one.

"Progress?" Gil asked, pointing to the drive.

"I was able to get into one of the thumb drives we found hidden in Wendover's desk."

"And?"

"You got him."

Gil pumped a fist into the air. "Yes!"

"I still have all the other drives to go through and we'll probably find more stuff on them."

"Find any names or email addresses we can go after?"

"Not yet," I said. "If there are any, they'll be on the data drive we pulled off his home computer."

Gil patted me on the shoulder.

"This is great, Richie," he said. "You know, I can deal with thieves, drunks and even one or two murderers. I can talk to them. Even been friendly with one or two. But pedophiles like Wendover?" Gil shook his head. "I throw 'em in a hole and forget about 'em. They are the lowest of the lowest." He pointed to the drives. "One more pedophile into the hole. Great job, Richie."

"Thanks."

He was about to leave, but I stopped him.

"Gil?"

He turned back.

"Yeah?"

"I've been talking to some other people about Jeannie. It looks like there was a lot of shit going on with the Sorenson family back then and everybody seems to be pointing at her brother Pete."

"Yeah?" he said, not communicating a lot of enthusiasm.

"What would it take to get one of your guys to take a closer look at the case?"

"Did you find something?"

"You mean like a direct link?"

He nodded.

"No direct link."

Gil gave me a sympathetic look, but shook his head. "If I had more guys, if this hadn't been worked to death almost thirty years ago, if you had something more, we could take a look. But right now? No."

"Okay," I said. I was disappointed, but not surprised. It wasn't that he was understaffed, it wasn't that they were too busy. After being in the office a few times over the past week, I had come to the conclusion that this was a department just coasting along, doing what it had to do, not motivated to do any more and that came from the top on down. From Gil.

"Sorry," he said pushing himself away from the wall. "But let me know if you need anything for this Wendover thing."

"Right."

"And hey, if you wanna do lunch, come up and get me."

I gave him a wave and a nod and he was out.

With a resigned sigh, I opened the next bag, made my log notes, plugged in the drive and went to work on it.

By early afternoon, the decryption was complete. This was the data drive off Wendover's home computer and the encryption was a lot stronger, though still not great. Wendover was barely more than an amateur at computer security.

On the drive I found the URL's to sites where he had found the kiddie porn, found images in the browser cache that he failed to delete and was able to crack his email system to pull down names and email addresses of buyers and sellers.

Again, I noted the work in the evidence log and printed out a complete file inventory.

Separately, I sorted and dumped out the names and email addresses I was finding and copied them to the desktop computer where I up-loaded the names to NCIC and Homeland Security where they could be cross matched for any possible felonies.

While on the DHS site, I searched around for some forms I would be needing for another little side project. When I found them, I copied them onto my computer and filled them out. I dug into my backpack and put a couple sheets of the card stock paper I bought a few days ago into the printer and printed what I had done.

When the printing completed, I stashed the printouts in my backpack and closed down the department computer.

Deep breath.

After making further notes in the evidence log, I put Wendover's data drive back in the bag and locked it up.

I noticed that Yankovic had come back into the squad room with what must have been his fifth cup of coffee. He saw me stand up and stretch and came my way. He came in without a knock.

"Done?"

I shook my head. "Three done. They're back in the locker. Four more to go."

I shut down my laptop, picked up my backpack and shoved the computer into it. Yankovic raised an eyebrow at me.

"Can't finish today?"

I shook my head.

"Don't have time to decrypt any more today."

"We're paying you to get this done, Willis," he grumped.

"In my spare time, Yankovic," I said. "And I've used up today's spare time." I saw him start to puff up and I put my hands up, palms out to stop him. "Another day or two, that's all. You got the guy locked up. We've got his kiddie porn. We have the proof he was selling it. Game over. We're just cleaning up now."

Yankovic was still fuming and not happy with me, but I could see him come to the realization that there wasn't a damn thing he could do about it. After a minute, he let out an angry sigh and slight nod.

"I want you back here tomorrow."

I nodded.

"I'll try to get the rest of the drives decrypted tomorrow," I said. "Then you can pack them all off to the prosecutor and stuff Wendover into a cozy little prison cell."

"Tomorrow," he said, then turned and walked back towards his desk in the squad room.

I watched him go. Brusque and impatient, he was like a lot of the detectives I knew, but that was probably part of what made a good detective.

Made me glad I wasn't one.

A few minutes later, I was out the door, down the hall and making my way down the steps of the court house when I saw Rosa Grazzano, the librarian and Robbie Clawson's little sister. Since I had been back, I had only seen her sitting at the library desk and seeing her coming up the steps, I realized that I had forgotten how short she was. She was wearing tight maroon slacks that were failing to contain a body that was experiencing middle-age spread and an autumn leaf print button up blouse that she appeared to keep as unbuttoned as possible to make sure that her heavy cleavage was noticed by everyone.

It was.

"Hey cutie," she said in a flirtatious tone that didn't sound right coming from a woman closing in on fifty. "You haven't called."

"Hi Rosa."

"Lose my number?" she asked.

"No, no" I said. "Just been crazy busy. Mom's houses, Marty's."

She pointed up towards the building I was leaving. "At the assessor's office?"

I shook my head.

"Helping the sheriff on something."

"What?" she said in surprise.

Without going into detail, I just explained my background and that the sheriff was an old buddy who asked me for some help.

"Help with that Sorenson murder you were talking about?"

"No, a different case."

"Oh."

"But that brings up a question. You stayed here in town after high school, right?"

"Never left." It sounded like there was a tinge of regret in that answer.

"What was it like here, after I left town?"

"Thirty years ago," she said, looking up at the building, frowning, thinking. "Why?"

I let out a sigh and leaned back against the railing, jabbing a thumb back towards the court house. "I've been digging into old arrest reports. Lots of DUI arrests, drug arrests, burglaries, fights, assaults . . . More than I expected."

"Yeah."

"Not how I remember things."

"Things changed. Jobs dried up, with Mexicans taking a bunch of them. Walmart came in and chased out all the little stores. Shit, Rich, kids didn't have anything to do but hangout, get drunk or get high."

"It looks like the Sorenson family had some drug and alcohol problems. Remember anything about that?"

"I remember Julie drank," Rosa said, "and probably too much, but I don't remember the drug thing with them."

"And your brother."

She was surprised. "Robbie?"

"Going through the reports in there," I said tilting my head towards the court house, "it looks like your brother spent a few nights here during that period."

Rosa's eyes slid away for a moment, then came back. A sigh and a shrug.

"He had a few run-ins," she said. "You remember how he was. That wicked temper? Liking to fight? Got him in jail a time or two."

"Drug possession too," I said. "A couple of times."

She tried to say something, then shrugged and looked up towards the building. "He was just trying stuff, I guess. It was a crazy time." She looked back at me. "But he's been good. For years, now."

"Married, kids and everything?"

"Well . . ." she started. "Was married. Two kids. They split up, though and she moved to Montana somewhere."

"By the way, did you know that Robbie came to the bar the other night and told me that he thought Jeannie's brother had something to do with what happened to her."

Rosa just stared at me for a moment. "Really?"

"His theory is that Pete maybe got mad about something and beat her to death."

Rosa looked away again, then shook her head and came back. "I'll bet he just heard that from someone and was repeating it. I'm not sure he even knew the Sorenson family that well."

"Robbie acted like he knew Pete," I said.

"I wouldn't know about that," she said.

"Maybe I'll catch up with Robbie later and ask him."

She nodded.

"He at USP today?"

"I think he's doing the late shift, in the cellars, helping unload spud trucks and then doing security or something."

"Thanks," I said. I took a step down, but Rosa grabbed my arm and gave me that flirty eye flutter again, pressing herself against me and making sure I got a healthy glimpse down her blouse. "So, you gonna give me a call one of these nights while you're in town?"

I struggled, but finally managed to pull my eyes back up to hers.

"Of course," I said. "After I'm finished with this stuff here."

"Sweet," she said. "Don't forget."

She twiddled her fingers at me and started up the stairs towards the main doors.

"Hey," I said. "I forgot to ask. What are you doing here?"

Rosa smiled and held up a handful of envelopes. "Parking tickets."

I laughed, she laughed, then she turned and walked into the building.

NINETEEN

After I left the Brannon County Courthouse and was nearing the little strip mall outside of Pocatello where Bonjour Nails was located, I saw sets of flashing lights ahead in the small, gravel parking lot.

A brown-uniformed cop got out of his cruiser, hiked a thick leather belt up over his bulging gut, climbed up the two steps to the wide, covered walkway that spanned the strip mall and then marched straight into the nail salon where a flustered, young Asian girl was holding the door open for him.

I stopped the Jeep next to a huge, ugly, beet red SUV. A deputy emerged from the salon as I slipped out of the Jeep, followed by a little, very round, middle-aged woman who looked to be Filipino. She was in a baggy, overly-flowered blue smock that fell below her knees and was gesturing angrily at the cop, both arms waving in the air, pointing occasionally to something or someone inside the salon. The cop stood facing her, making notes on a pad and nodding patiently as the woman raved.

A small crowd from the other businesses in the strip mall were gathering around to watch and I slipped in among them. The woman shouting at the cop was getting angrier. I couldn't catch every word of her mangled English, but it sounded like there was a drunk woman inside attacking an employee and destroying equipment. The cop was managing to keep his cool even as the woman showered him with angry spittle.

There was a noise from inside and the cop pulled the screaming Filipina away from the door as another deputy dragged a handcuffed woman out. The tall, thin woman he was leading, with ragged shoulder length hair wasn't a customer, but an employee because I could see she had a nametag pinned above a pocket. She gave the older woman an angry, drunken glare as she passed by. She had a long, pale face, a thin line of blood trailing from one nostril. Deep sunk eyes, thin lips and a long thin nose. It took me a moment, then I realized . . . it was Jeannie's little sister, Julie, visibly drunk and angry, struggling with the cop who was leading her out.

The deputy with the notepad stopped them and I could hear him tell the other officer to get a camera out of his cruiser to get some pictures of the damage inside the salon. The second officer nodded, dragged Julie to the corner of the walkway where a thin, rusted metal pole supported the awning. He reached behind her and cuffed her to the pole, giving her a warning about not moving, then went to his SUV.

The crowd was focused on the flowered smock woman annoying the notepad cop, so I wiggled in and around them until I was close to where Julie sat angrily staring at the ground, muttering to herself. She felt me approach, looked up, squinted through her reddened eyes at me, then dropped her gaze back down. A few seconds later, though, she raised her eyes back up to mine with a curious, hazy, searching look. She realized that she should know me.

"Hi Julie," I said quietly.

"Uh . . . . who?" she started. Another moment, then her watery eyes widened a little. "Richie?"

I nodded, then watched as waves of expressions washed across her face: recognition as she saw someone she hadn't seen in decades, sadness that she was so drunk, then embarrassment as she realized the situation he was seeing her in. She bent her head away.

What do you say to a woman who's drunk, bloody and handcuffed to a pole? All I got out was "Julie. . ."

She turned her face back up towards me.

"What are you doing here?" she said in a hoarse whisper, blowing a stray strand of hair off her face.

"Came to talk to you," I said.

"Fuckin' timing sucks, Richie," she said.

"No shit. What did you do?"

She struggled to hold back tears.

She jerked her head towards the smock woman. "She's ripping me off. Fucking bitch. Got tired of it. Starting yelling at her then one of her little minions tried to shut me up. So, I guess I shut her up instead." She raised a cuffed fist, showing her bloody knuckles. "Then I went a little nuts." She shook her head, looking away. "God damn it."

I glanced at the uniforms.

"They gonna let you go after things calm down?"

Julie glanced up as a young Indian woman walked out the door, holding a blood soaked towel to her face. With that much blood, I knew Julie had broken the woman's nose.

With a subtle, thin smile, then a sigh of sadness and regret, Julie shook her head.

"Not this time," she growled. "Shit."

I looked at the angry woman and the bloody young girl and nodded.

"These guys are county cops and they're gonna end up taking you to the Bannock County lockup. You got anybody to bail you out?"

"Fuck no," she said.

I stared at her for a few moments.

"You'll probably get arraigned later today or in the morning and they'll set bail."

She gave me a quizzical look, then "Whatever..."

"You got any cash?"

Julie just snorted.

"Anybody I can contact?" A head shake.

"Okay," I said with a sigh. "I'll see what I can do."

She stared up at me, confused. "Huh?"

The cop who had gone to his SUV was coming back with a camera and noticed me talking to Julie. He angled our way.

"Just don't worry about it," I whispered. "I'll figure something out."

The deputy came over, stepping between me and Julie.

"Step back, please sir," he said in his rehearsed cop voice.

"I'm an old friend," I stuttered, coming up with an angle. "I told Julie I would get her car home, but I need her keys. Would that be okay?" Julie flashed a puzzled look my way, figured it out, then nodded at the cop.

"Where are your keys, Miss?" he asked.

She jerked her head towards the door of the salon. "Purse. Lavender. Behind the counter."

"Just a minute," the deputy said, holding up a finger. He stepped up to the door, whispered to the notepad cop and then went inside.

"What's your address?" I whispered. "I'll get a friend to help me and we'll get your car there."

Julie was still in a confused drunken state, but managed to give me an address.

"It's just a shitty little house out on the edge of town," she said. "No garage. Just park it in the driveway."

I nodded and glanced at the door as the deputy emerged with Julie's big, ragged purse, dangling a noisy keyring with a half dozen keys. He held it up.

"This it?" he asked her.

Julie nodded.

The deputy tossed me the keyring. "What's your name?"

"Richard Willis," I said and stuffed the keys in my pocket.

He took out his own small notepad and made a note of my name and cell number. He nodded as the other cop came over, having finished with the smock woman. He jabbed a thumb back at the salon.

"Go in there and get some pictures of what our guest did," he said. "And for God's sake, don't start a conversation with that crazy woman. She'll tear your head off."

The deputy nodded and disappeared into the salon.

The notepad cop went to Julie, unlocked one handcuff and then gently, but firmly, stood her up.

"Hands behind your back, please," he said. She stifled a cry and let him cuff her wrists behind her back. She glanced at me, embarrassed, then looked away. He took her arm and half-supporting, half guiding, started towards his cruiser.

"She'll be at county," he said to me over his shoulder.

A moment later, she was in the back seat of his SUV and on her way to the county lockup.

The gawkers thinned out when the two sheriff's cars took off, so I walked back to my Jeep and jumped in.

How was I going to get her car home? Her house was nearly ten miles away so I wasn't going to drive her car there and walk back and get my Jeep.

I decided to drive back to Black River and get Jia or Tyler to lend a hand. I cranked up the motor and headed down the road and onto the freeway, pushing the Jeep into the fast lane until the speedometer was pushing into the eighties, but then I had a thought. Eleanor was in Pocatello, at the college, which was just a few miles ahead. Maybe she could help me.

I made a sudden lurch into the slow lane, getting flipped off by an angry trucker and slid to a stop at the side of the freeway. I flipped my emergency flashers on and used my phone to search for the ISU website and found a number for the Department of Theatre and Dance. I punched it in.

"Theatre and Dance," came a young woman's voice, who I guessed was a student working the office phones because she sounded young and bored.

"Hi," I said, "I'm trying to reached Eleanor Fife. Is she in today?"

I heard what sounded like pages turning and the girl talking to herself. Then she was back on.

"Uh, she finished her last class for the day about an hour ago," the woman said.

I was afraid I missed her.

"She's gone home then?"

"No, I think she's down in the theatre," she said.

"What theatre?"

"It's the Black Box Theatre," she said. "Know where that is? They're going to be doing Romeo and Juliet there in three weeks."

I didn't know about the Black Box Theatre but she gave me directions, I thanked her and clicked off.

Within ten minutes, I was inside the very dark, cavernous, basketball court size Black Box Theatre. Three sides of the rectangular space had rows of theatre seats forming a "U" around the raised performance area at the center, which was cluttered with chairs, tables, metal stage lights and a giant folding ladder extending up twenty feet to a grid of pipes over the stage where dozens of stage lights were mounted. A few of the lights were on, splashing down onto the performance area.

A small, but muscular young kid, probably a student, was at the top of the ladder attaching a heavy old black Fresnel lamp to the grid. At the bottom of the ladder, her back to me, was Eleanor, pointing to where she wanted the light mounted. She was in paint-splattered white coveralls with her hair tucked up under an ISU Bengals ball cap. She hadn't heard me come in.

To my left, students were lounging in the theatre seats and I recognized the tall black kid nearest me, so I quietly went that way, dropping into the seat next to him.

"Hey Reggie," I said quietly, giving him a gentle slap on the back.

Reggie, the kid I had hired to work at Marty's had a script and notepad on his lap as he watched Ellie guide the placement of the lights and was surprised to see me.

"Rich!" he said. "What are you doing here?"

I pointed to the ladder. "Waiting to talk to your teacher there. This where your show's gonna be?"

He nodded and held up his script. "Working on my lines."

"How is she as a director?"

"Frickin' awesome," he said. "The cast loves her."

I watched as the kid on the ladder finished attaching the light and dropped down to Ellie who handed him another instrument and pointed to another spot on the lighting grid. He started back up the ladder as a door opened at the far end of the room and a man entered, closing the door behind him.

He walked towards the ladder and into the light. I could see he was a slightly chunky man, medium height in khaki slacks and a light blue, long-sleeved button shirt. He was gray haired, with a matching gray beard, both perfect and neatly trimmed. He had a wide face, and strikingly thick eyebrows over small, dark eyes. He was carrying a folder in one hand and had a small backpack and a sports jacket slung over a shoulder.

He glanced up at the guy at the top of the ladder and then down to where Eleanor was standing and went that way. She had seen him come in and took a few steps towards him.

"Who's that?" I whispered to Reggie. "Department head?"

Reggie shook his head. "Her husband."

"Oh."

I suddenly realized what an idiot I was thinking that Ellie would be able to drop everything to help me.

"He's a physics professor," Reggie continued. "Never seen him come to a play. I don't think he even likes theatre."

I watched the man hand Ellie the folder he had been carrying. She nodded, they exchanged a few words, then he turned and left, leaving her standing looking through some things in the folder.

"I better get going," I whispered to Reggie and stood, but as stood, Ellie turned back towards the ladder and noticed me.

"Richie?" she said in surprise.

I raised a hand as she started my way.

"Hey, Ellie."

"Miss Fife," the kid on the ladder called down. "Where do you want this light focused?" Ellie held up a finger signaling me to wait and went back to the stage, found a spot and looked up at the kid.

"Right here," she said.

I gave Reggie a wave and stepped through the seats and onto the stage area while the kid on the ladder carefully adjusted the heavy lighting instrument to aim at where Ellie was standing.

"Up a little," Ellie said.

The kid loosened a bolt and angled the light up a little.

"Perfect," she said to him as I reached where she was standing.

She smiled as I stepped to the ladder watching her.

"How long has it been since you walked onto a stage?" she asked.

I looked around the performance area and took a whiff of dusty old lamps heating up, sawdust and drying paint.

"Wow," I said. "Long time. The last show I was in was at The Pioneer, twenty some years ago."

"What brought you up here?"

Ellie went to the stage lights on the table and picked one up, stepping to the ladder.

"I was trying to catch up with that woman we were looking for yesterday."

"Julie." The kid came halfway down the ladder and Ellie handed him the instrument, pointing to a different spot on the lighting grid.

"Yeah. Julie," I said. "I found her."

"Good."

"But there was a . . . complication."

She looked at me, tilted her head and furrowed her brow at me.

"I came by to see if you had an hour or two to spare to help me un-complicate it. I can see now that that was a little presumptuous of me." She could see I was getting ready to walk out.

"Hang on there, detective," she said. "Is it an interesting complication?"

I stopped and smiled slyly. "Give me a couple hours of your time and I'll tell you."

Ellie put her hands on her hips and gave me that look: the look of someone who knew they were getting maneuvered, but liking the idea.

After a moment she said, "If you help us get these last lights up, I'll have a few hours free."

I was about to answer, but she stopped me.

"And you have to buy me a burger. I haven't eaten since breakfast and I'm starving."

I held out my hand. "And I'll even throw in some fries." We shook.

After thirty minutes of my handing lights up to the kid on the ladder, moving the ladder around and focusing the instruments, all at Ellie's direction, we finished up and bowed to a round of applause from Reggie and the two other actors sitting with him as we headed out of the theatre. As we neared the Jeep, Ellie nudged me aside and jumped into the driver's seat. Again.

"Hey!" I protested.

"I know where the hamburgers are," she said. "It's faster if I drive."

"Sure," I said sarcastically going around and jumping in to ride shotgun.

"Besides," she said, "I'm gonna take advantage of every chance I get to drive a top-down, doors-off old Jeep."

"Fine."

She held out her hand.

"Keys?"

Ellie drove us to a little hamburger shop that looked like it had been built in the sixties and never remodeled. I explained what happened with Julie as we waited in the drive-thru lane for her avocado burger and fried mushrooms, telling her that I had promised to drive Julie's car home for her.

"That Julie sounds like one screwed up lady," Ellie said.

I nodded.

"With what she has been through, how could you not be a little screwed up?" I asked. "Father dead in a farm accident, mother dead by drug overdose, brother and sister killed in a car accident and another sister murdered."

"All that." Ellie shook her head. "Poor girl."

When she pulled up to the pay window, I passed my card to her and she retrieved her burger and fries and my Diet Coke. With her one-handedly scarfing down her burger, we headed out of town and I told her all I had learned so far about the Sorenson family tragedies.

"That is way too much for someone to handle without serious therapy," Ellie said.

"Or serious medication," I said.

"Sounds like she's already doing some serious self-medicating."

We drove along for a bit with Ellie juggling fried mushrooms, bites of her burger and gulps of my Coke until I broke the quiet.

"Reggie said that was your husband that you were talking to when you were hanging lights."

She nodded.

"He's off to Chicago for a physics conference."

"Reggie says he's not much of a playgoer," I said.

She laughed. "And I'm not into string theory so it balances out."

Ellie remembered the way to Bonjour Nails and when we got close, I told her to go around the building to the back. We crunched onto the gravel parking lot around the building where more than a dozen cars were parked.

"She said her car is an old, puke green Toyota Camry," I said.

Ellie pointed down to the opposite end of the lot. "Puke green," she said. I saw it, nodded and we slipped in next to it. Ellie killed the Jeep and I jumped out with Julie's keys in hand.

Her car was a piece of crap. A banged up old Camry, lots of dents, scrapes and nearly bald tires.

"Expired plates," I said.

"How far to her house?"

"Back through town," I said.

"Let's take back roads so you don't get pulled over."

"Good idea." I came back to the Jeep, pulled out my phone, clicked on Google Maps and punched in the home address Julie had given me. Ellie watched as I zoomed around the map. She pointed to a side road and then traced a route all the way to Julie's neighborhood.

"I can do that," I said.

"And I'll tag right behind you in case a cop appears. He won't be able to see the expired plates that way."

"He might arrest me anyway for driving a piece of unsafe junk."

Ellie patted me on the arm. "Don't worry. I'm sure someone will bail you out. Now let's get going."

I slipped in behind the Camry's steering wheel and with a puff of blue smoke, the car started.

"Burnin' some oil back there," Ellie said pointing to the cloud that was pouring out of the back.

"No surprise," I said pointing to the car's odometer. "She's got a hundred and seventy-five thousand miles on this thing."

"Then let's get this to her place before it blows up, okay?"

With her trailing close behind, we kicked up some gravel slipping out of the lot and started south.

Julie's house was a faded, pinkish clapboard cottage, fronted by a tiny brown lawn and small, matching junipers. Sheets of corrugated fiberglass covered a porch that ran along the front of the house. There were similar older houses to the left and right of Julie's, but behind them was a huge plowed field.

I pulled into the dirt driveway next to her house and Ellie drove in behind me. I got out, locked the car door and stood looking at the place. Ellie killed the Jeep, jumped out and came over to me as I walked down the side of the house looking.

"Shitty little place," she said.

"Could be okay if she would put some work into it," I said. "But it doesn't look like she has."

Ellie handed me the Jeep keys and we started back towards it until I stopped and looked back.

"What?" she asked.

I looked at the ring of Julie's keys. One of them was probably a house key.

"You have to pee, don't you?" I asked.

"Huh?"

"Since she gave me a key, I'm sure it will be okay for you to use her bathroom."

"What the hell are you talking about?"

I stepped onto the porch and went to the front door, holding up what I guessed was the right key.

"Richie," Ellie said quietly, "what are you doing?"

I smiled at her.

"Letting you in so you can use the bathroom."

"I don't need to use the bathroom."

"Of course you do," I said. With the key in the lock, I opened the door and held it for her. "You better hurry. Wouldn't want you to make a mess all over the seats in my Jeep."

Ellie paused, realized what I was doing, gave me that teacherly shake of her head and slipped inside, me right behind her.

The front door had opened directly into the sparse little living room, furnished, apparently, by the Salvation Army. There was an archway in front of me to the right leading to a small dining area and a smaller archway to the left leading back to what I guessed was the bathroom and bedroom. The place smelled of sour milk, microwave dinners and cigarettes.

"Isn't this breaking and entering?" Ellie asked.

"Of course not. She gave me a key. And you needed to use the bathroom. That's my story and I'm sticking to it. Let's look around."

"Why?"

I shrugged. "Maybe it will help me understand."

"Understand what?"

"Understand what I'm not understanding."

"Sometimes Willis, you are so full of shit. . . "

"I know." I smiled at her. "Indulge me. Just for a few minutes. Look around. Tell me what you think."

Ellie shook her head and started off towards the dining room area, looking at the floor, the walls, the furniture. I looked down the hall towards what I guessed was the bedroom.

"Third hand furniture," Ellie said. "Worn out throw rugs." There was a medium size LED TV sitting on a bookcase and an overstuffed chair facing it. She looked at the overflowing trash can beside the chair. "Looks like her diet consists of microwave popcorn, beer and a lot of vodka."

I slipped down the hall. The first door on my left was a tiny bathroom, barely big enough to hold a tub against the far wall as well as a sink and toilet on the adjoining wall. There was a mirrored medicine cabinet above the sink. I opened it. The shelves held most of the usual female stuff along with a handful of prescription medications like Xanax, Paxil and some kind of non-narcotic pain reliever. I closed the cabinet and went back out into the little hallway. I could hear Ellie opening and closing drawers in the dining area.

"She has an old computer on the dining room table," Ellie called out. "And the place is cluttered with folders and papers and what look like court documents." I could hear her shuffling papers around. "Eviction notices, notices to appear, judgements and lots of others.

The drawers are full of them. Some look like they are ten years old." I heard another drawer open.

"Shit," Ellie said.

"What?"

"A gun. She's got a gun in here."

"What kind of gun?"

I went to where Ellie was standing, looking into the shallow top drawer of a buffet cabinet. Inside was a dusty, black steel revolver next to an unmarked box of shells.

"I'm not much of a gun guy," I said, "that might be a twenty-two. You didn't touch it, did you?"

"No way," Ellie said. "I hate guns." She pointed at it. "Why does she have that? Protection?"

I shrugged. "Protection from what?"

Ellie returned the shrug.

"It's pretty old. Maybe something they had on their farm for dispatching animals." Ellie gave me a scrunched up, grossed out face. I just smiled. "Let's keep looking around." I said.

"Okay . . . I'm looking." Then I heard her mumble. "Still don't get what I'm looking for."

I smiled to myself as I went back to the hall at the other side of the house and then to the back room. The shades were pulled down over the two windows making the space dark and musty.

I flipped on a light to reveal an OCD nightmare. Piles of t-shirts, dirty panties, pajamas, books, magazines and shoes like stalagmites, marking a path from the door to an old, wooden-framed and unmade double bed. A bedstand, mirrored dresser and a chest of drawers were the only other furnishings in the room. Books and photo albums were stacked on top of the dresser.

I turned, hearing Ellie coming down the hall.

"Not much in the kitchen," she said "This girl is kind of a mess. Empty microwave dinner boxes and vodka bottles in the trash and nothing in the fridge but cold beer and ketchup. I did find a box of Lucky Charms. Maybe she poured beer over that for breakfast." She glanced around the bedroom, shaking her head. "Feeling really bad about this, Willis."

"Me too."

I went to the dresser and shuffled through the photo albums. Near the bottom of the mound, one scrapbook caught my attention. I opened it.

"Jeannie's photo album."

"Richie," she said, "this is wrong."

"I know."

"Then what do you--?"

She had just seen what I was seeing.

"What the hell?" Ellie asked pointing.

I shrugged and shook my head.

The old album held Polaroids, color and black and white Sorenson family pictures: her dad in the field, mom and dad together on the lawn, the whole family at a picnic, Julie and Jeannie with their parents, older siblings and other pictures.

In every one, the heads of her mom and dad had been cut out and discarded.

"Holy shit . . ." whispered Ellie. "Mommy and daddy issues you think?"

We both stared as I flipped through more pages of the album. The heads of her parents had been cut out of every photo in the book.

I closed the album and was putting it back where it was when a photo slipped out of it and onto the floor. Ellie grabbed it.

"Look at this," Ellie said. She handed me the grainy, five-by-seven photograph. "Is that you?"

I didn't remember ever seeing it before, but it was me. Twelve-year-old me.

In front of a haystack, I was staring at the camera in work jeans, torn t-shirt and scraggly hair, not happy about having my picture taken. Next to me, with her arm around my shoulders was a taller, leggy girl, long, curly corn-silk blonde hair flowing over her shoulders. Her clear and strong baby-blue eyes stared at the camera, a look on her face that was hard to define. Disdainful? Defiant? I pointed to her.

"Jeannie."

"What's that look?" Ellie asked. "With her arm around your shoulders like that, it's like she's being protective of you."

I nodded. It was true.

"This looks like she blew up an old photo of you two," Ellie said. "It's got that fuzzy sort of look to it."

"Like taken with an old Kodak or Polaroid."

As I held the picture, staring at it, Ellie snatched it out of my hand, cramming it back into the photo album.

"This is seriously messed up, Willis," she said. "And I can't tell which is more messed up: you digging through an old friend's family photos or that old friend cutting off the heads of her parents in all those pictures."

"Maybe we're both messed up," I said. "C'mon. Let's get outa here."

We started down the hall to leave, but Ellie suddenly stopped at the bathroom door and held up a hand. She twisted her mouth, glanced into the bathroom and then looked at me.

"Oh, shit."

"What?"

"God damn it."

"What's wrong?"

She stepped into the bathroom and slammed the door.

"I guess really do have to pee."

— · —

TWENTY

Eleanor was dropped off and I was in Black River as the sun was getting low in the west. It had been a long, busy day and I really just wanted to set myself down at a table at Marty's and have a burger and a beer, but I had questions gnawing at me and decided to take a detour to US Potato. Robbie Clawson's sister had said he was working the swing shift. Maybe he could answer some of those questions.

I drove into the sprawling USP campus and into the visitor's lot in front of the main office building.

Behind me, on the other side of the lot were the huge potato storage cellars. Trucks would come in from their farms fully loaded, get weighed, drive to one of the half-underground cellars, back down into it, unload their spuds then leave to get another load.

Rosa had said Rob was working the cellars so I headed in that direction.

A wide, asphalt roadway, wide enough for at least four giant rigs to pass, led down between the twelve cellars, six on each side, their huge openings facing the fairway. The cellars, almost two hundred feet long were identical A-frame concrete and metal structures, half underground with the apex of the roof nearly fifty feet above ground. The mammoth doors were wide enough to allow two trucks to back down into the cool cellar at the same time to drop off their cargo.

The trucks were lined up to unload at two of the cellars at the end of the row on the right of the fairway. An older man, probably in his sixties, making a note on a clipboard was standing at the top of the driveway that led down into one cellar and I went up to him. He was in work boots, dirty, heavy duty jeans and a plaid flannel shirt under a worn out ball cap with a Seattle Mariners logo on it.

"Yeah?" he said in a gruff, tired voice.

"I'm looking for Rob Clawson," I said. "Is he down here?"

The man snorted. "Clawson?"

I nodded and he pointed further down the road.

"Next cellar down." He turned away and went back to his clipboard as if I had never been there.

"Thanks," I muttered to the back of his head.

I dodged between two trucks and walked down into the cellar he had pointed to. It took my eyes a few moments to adjust to the darkness, but my nose knew right away where I was. The cool air flowing out carried the smell of dust, diesel exhaust and that earthy, almost nutty aroma coming from freshly dug root vegetables.

Potatoes.

Halfway down the length of the cellar, a truck was backed up against a wall of potatoes that towered above it, unloading spuds into a giant V-shaped bin that carried the potatoes up a long, conveyor belt that was like a firetruck's extension ladder, taking the potatoes high up and pouring them onto the growing pyramid of tubers where men were guiding the flow of spuds pouring out.

As I got closer, I recognized one of the men up on the mound of spuds as Robbie. He did a sort of double-take when he noticed me there and gave me a quick wave. After a word to another guy, he handed the man his shovel and slipped carefully down the side of the spud hill to the ground and came over to me, gloved hand reaching out to mine.

"What the hell you doing down here?" he asked, smiling, as we shook hands.

I gestured at the huge space.

"Remembering what this was like," I said. "I trucked a lot spuds down here."

"Me too," he said.

"What are you guys doing up there?" I asked pointing to where the waterfall of spuds was streaming off the conveyor belt.

"Making sure we get the spuds piled as high as possible but leaving plenty of room between them and the ceiling so that we have lots of air flowing over them." He pointed to the series of huge fans mounted in the sloping roof of the cellar. "We've got to keep the place cool and the air moving to minimize the chance of mold growing. Nothing in the world smells worse than a pile of moldy, rotting potatoes."

"No kidding," I said. "An odor not to be forgotten."

We both stared at the wall of tubers for a moment, then I started to say something but Clawson beat me to it.

"My sister said she saw you at the court house," Clawson said.

"It looks like she's going to have to take out a loan to pay off her parking tickets," I said, nodding.

"Still digging into what happened to Jean Sorenson?" he asked.

"Yeah," I said after a moment. "I wanted to ask you something about that."

"Me?" he asked.

"I dug into old police records to get a better handle on what happened and like you said, her brother Pete had a lot of problems with the police."

"Yeah . . . you know I had some too," he said.

"I don't care about those, Robbie" I said. "I was just hoping you might be able to tell me what it was like here then."

"Whaddya mean?"

"Where were people getting the drugs?" I asked. "I mean, I read about so many arrests, so many OD's. Where were people getting the stuff? Who was selling?"

Clawson stared blankly.

"Like, who did you buy from?" I asked.

Clawson shook his head. "I don't do that shit anymore."

"I know," I reassured him. "But back then?"

"You know," he said, shrugging, "I mostly just got it from friends. You know? We'd be at a party and I'd like snag some shit off a buddy. Or at work, a guy would have an extra baggy he'd sell me. Not like he was a dealer. I don't think I even knew any dealers."

"None?"

"Like I said the other day, the only guy I heard might be dealing was Pete."

"You think Pete Sorenson was a dealer?"

He gave a shrug and a half nod. "Maybe. That's probably where Jeannie got hers."

I blinked.

"So you knew Jeannie was doing drugs?" I asked.

"Well . . ."

"Why didn't you tell me that the other day?"

"I guess I wasn't really thinking about that," Clawson stammered.

I looked at him a minute.

"Okay," I said. "Can you think of who else was dealing or selling the stuff back then?"

Clawson had looked down thinking when a loud, gravelly voice boomed over the cacophony of the diesels, the gears and the yelling workers.

"Little Richie! That you?"

A truck door slammed, there was a thick, wet cough and I looked up the dark, sloping dirt driveway to see a tall, thin silhouette striding down towards us, tossing a cigarette to the ground as he walked. It only took me a second to figure out who it was.

Cousin Willy.

Seemingly enveloped in a cloud of dust, cigarette smoke and cheap whiskey, the old man wrapped his long arms around me in a way-to-manly bear hug.

"How the fuck you been, Little Richie?" he asked.

Willy – really Henry William Willis Jr. – was the son of my dad's much older half-brother, Henry, the product of an affair my grandfather had with a very young Shoshone woman.

I freed myself from the man's hold and took a look at him. I hadn't seen him since my mother's funeral and even then he was suffering from the ravages of cigarettes, whiskey and bad microwave food: boney arms and legs, a pot belly and a deathly gray pallor. At that time, I thought he had looked like a skeleton that had been dug up and dressed in a suit. Now he looked like a skeleton that had been dug up, reburied and dug up again. He was like the Keith Richards of Black River.

"How you doin', Willy?" I asked.

"Good," he said, letting loose with a few thick coughing hacks and pointing up the ramp to an idling diesel truck waiting to unload. "Driving for Sunset Farms." He extended a hand to Clawson. "Hey, Rob."

They shook and Willy wiggled a thumb in my direction.

"So you know this guy?" he asked.

"Went to school together," Clawson said.

"No shit?"

Willy threw an arm over my shoulders. "I thought you was a cop or something in Seattle or Portland."

"Not a cop, Willy," I said. "I'm back here trying to finish up mom's estate stuff."

"And you didn't have the time to give your cousin Willy a call?"

"I was going to," I lied. "Just got too busy with things."

He gave me an expression of mock hurt. "You had the time to catch up with this slacker, but not your favorite cousin?"

"I came down here to ask Robbie about an old friend who was killed."

"Recently?" he asked.

"No. Thirty years ago," Clawson said.

"Jean Sorenson," I said.

Willy thought for a moment, then wiggled a finger at me.

"The girl in the potato field, right?" he asked.

I nodded.

"You grew up with her?"

I nodded again. He looked at Clawson.

"You too. Didn't you date her or something?"

Clawson seemed jolted back by the question, but he shook his head.

"You sure?" Willy asked.

"You think I'd forget something like that?" Clawson asked. Willy focused back on me.

"Did they ever figure out what happened?" Willy asked.

"No," I said.

"That's why he's here," Clawson said. "Detective Willis."

"You said you wasn't a cop," Willy said.

"I'm not. Jeannie was a friend. A good friend that I . . . neglected. Just trying to understand what happened."

"That brings you here?"

Rob stepped in. "Jean might have been into drugs and Rich is asking if I knew who was dealing. I told him I didn't really know much about that."

"Seriously?" Willy asked. "C'mon, Rob, you remember." Rob shrugged.

I turned to Willy. "What do you know?"

"Well . . . a little."

"Like what?"

"As innocent as you might think I am," he started.

"Willy," I interrupted, "you have never been innocent."

"Fuck you," Willy said, slapping me again on the chest, which hurt like hell. He pointed a finger at Clawson. "You remember, Rob. They found that huge meth lab out west of town."

Clawson shook his head.

"So, meth was the problem?" I asked.

Willy coughed and shook his head. "Meth wasn't that big around here then. It was mostly pot, heroin and angel dust, you know, PCP. Came up through Nevada and Utah. Lyle Hendrix, remember him?"

Clawson shook his head but I nodded.

"PE teacher," I said.

"Yeah. He was dealing 'til he OD'd a few years after you left."

"Shit," I mumbled.

Clawson pointed towards the hill of spuds. "Guys, I really need gotta get back to work."

"Okay," I said. "See ya', Robbie."

"Okay. See ya' Willy," he called, starting up the hill of spuds.

I turned to Willy and pointed back up the ramp and we started towards the daylight.

"Fuckin' weird," Willy muttered as we walked up the dirt drive.

"What's weird?" I asked

"Rob. Not knowin' about drug dealers and stuff. I dunno. Maybe my memory's all fucked up, but I thought he hung out with some of those guys."

"Really?"

"Maybe. Ah, who the hell knows and, anyways, why are you bothering with something that happened a million years ago?" Willy asked, throwing his arm around my shoulders again like the protective uncle he wasn't.

"Guilt," I said. "For things I didn't do."

"Just what I thought," he said. "Your mother."

"My mother?"

"It's her fault."

"Huh?"

"She's the one that made you get raised Catholic, sending you to that Catholic school and mass every day. Planted guilt in you, man."

He was probably right.

I slipped out from under his arm and gave him a pat on the back.

"Come down to Marty's one of these nights," I said. "I'll buy you a burger. Clog up some arteries and maybe put some fat on those skinny bones of yours."

"I could go for a juicy burger."

"And I promise not to feel guilty about it."

At the top of the dirt ramp, just short of being blinded by daylight, I looked back down into the cellar to see Clawson back at the top of the pile. He was just standing up there, at the top of the potato pyramid leaning on his shovel, watching the waterfall of potatoes.

Tyler, Jia's main guy in the kitchen at Marty's was a bit of a doofus, but man, could he throw together a good burger. I was at a corner table with my open laptop in the middle of my third juicy bite when Marie dropped off the fried mushrooms I had ordered. She leaned in close to me and gave a nod to the far corner of the pub where Volkov was working on his laptop, guzzling black coffee.

"I cannot understand why the man has not turned Jia over to the Homeland people, already." she whispered.

"Too messy. It would throw them all into the morass of the immigration legal system: court orders, appeals, detentions. It could take months to get back to Ukraine that way. He'd probably rather not do that."

"Okay," she said, giving Volkov a sideways glance. "I'd still like to have my three brothers take him out back and explain things to him."

I smiled and shook my head as Marie walked away mumbling in Volkov's direction. "Bastardo . . ."

Between bites of my burger, I logged onto the old Dell laptop I had bought, using a fake profile.

I fished the keys out of my pocket and slipped the tiny little USB drive out of its holder and plugged it into the laptop, moving the files I had taken off Wendover's drive to the laptop and then I wiped the USB drive clean of any hint that those files had ever been there.

Just as I closed the laptop, Reggie walked in to start his evening shift. He gave me a quick nod on his way and I was surprised to see him followed in by Ellie. She saw me, gave me a smile and walked over to my table.

"Reggie's shitty old Jeep wouldn't start," she said, "so I gave him a ride."

"No Jeep is shitty," I said with indignation.

"You two are Jeep nerds."

"Wanna grab a burger and hang out 'til his shift is over?" I asked.

"The set's getting moved onto the stage tonight so I've gotta get back," she said, "but I will grab one bite."

She snagged the burger off my plate, took a big bite and then put it back.

"Thanks," she mumbled through a mouthful of bread, beef and lettuce. "Needs onions."

"Don't like onions," I said.

"I know. Your loss."

I pointed towards where Reggie was talking with Jia. "He need a ride back?"

Ellie shook her head. "I think he said his girlfriend was going to come and get him, but let me check."

She walked over to the bar and was talking to Reggie when Volkov got up from his laptop with his coffee cup and went to the bar where Jia was going over an order with Tyler. He dropped his mug onto the bar, startling Jia who turned and scowled at him. I couldn't hear what he said to her, but she answered with an expression of anger which caused him to lean over the bar, his own anger rising.

Ellie saw Volkov seeming to threaten Jia and stepped around Reggie going towards Volkov. He turned as Ellie stepped up to him.

"Whaddya need?" she asked Volkov.

He looked at her dismissively then back to Jia saying "She knows what I need." Then he looked toward Ellie. "Not your concern."

Ellie started to push against him and say something, but Jia put a hand up to stop her.

"You needed coffee, right?" Jia asked Volkov.

He stared at Ellie for a moment, then finally back to Jia.

"Coffee."

Jia hesitated but Tyler grabbed a carafe of coffee from behind her and filled his cup. Volkov glowered for a few more moments until he reached for his cup, looked at Tyler and then glared at Jia.

"Friday," he said.

He tramped back to his table.

"Asshole," Ellie said as I came up behind her.

"Jia, what the hell is this about Friday?" Ellie asked.

The redhead let out a sigh and leaned closer to Ellie, speaking quietly. "I have to agree to go back to Ukraine with him by Friday."

Ellie was shocked into silence.

"What?"

"Or else."

"Or else what? Jia, you don't have to do anything you don't want to do."

Jia was shaking her head.

"If I don't," she said, "he will turn my mother and me in."

"Turn you in? For what?"

"Turn her into Homeland Security," Tyler said.

"Because of what happened in Ukraine, Jia and her mom are not exactly here legally," I said.

"If he turns us in, we will be deported back to Ukraine," Jia said.

I quickly explained the situation to Ellie who seemed to grow angrier as I spoke.

"We can't let that happen," she said.

"It won't," I said.

Ellie frowned at me. "So what the hell are you going to do? Say please? Or maybe beat him up?" She pointed at my bruises. "Though you don't seem to be very good at that."

"Don't worry," I said. "Volkov will be gone by Friday."

"Gone by Friday? How the hell are you going to do that?"

I sighed and looked at Tyler who shook his head at me.

I wanted to explain it to her, explain it to Jia, but I couldn't. It could get them in trouble or potentially mess up what I had planned. I gave my head a small shake.

"I can't tell you right now."

"Why the hell not?" she asked, angrily.

I looked at her, then to Jia, then back. "Do you trust me?"

"Huh?"

"Ellie, can you trust me on this one? Please. It's really important. Trust me. I promise you'll understand when it's all over."

Ellie was about to shake her head, but Jia placed a hand on her arm.

"Eleanor," she said, "I trust him."

Ellie looked at Jia who nodded back at her. She looked over to Tyler, who nodded as well. And then Ellie looked at me. She stared into my eyes, searching intently for something. I'm not sure she found it, but finally, she let out a sigh.

"I'm not sure how you got these guys to give you this kind of trust," she said, "but it looks like you got it so I guess I'll have to go along."

She turned to Reggie.

"You sure you've got a ride back home, Reg?" she asked.

"Yeah."

She took a step to walk around me, then stopped and jabbed a finger into my chest. I winced.

"Don't screw it up," she said. She gave me a stern look and then was gone.

I sighed and rubbed my sore chest. I hoped like hell that I wouldn't screw it up.

TWENTY-ONE

A pounding startled me.

The door.

It was early Thursday morning and I was back in the barely occupied Brannon County Courthouse cracking the encryption of the first of the last four Wendover hard drives. I looked up from my computer screen as Yankovic opened the door to the miniature office where I was working and stepped in.

"Done yet?" he asked.

"Four drives left," I said, not looking at him.

He stepped annoyingly close behind me to look at the screen, which was running a series of numbers and letters as it worked. "My program is decrypting each file so we can see them."

"You mean see his kiddie stuff?"

"Yeah."

He waved me off like I had just farted and started for the door. "I sure as heck don't wanna see that. Just get it done."

I nodded.

"Today would be good," he said, meaning that yesterday would have been better.

Yankovic made for the door almost smashing into Sandy who was coming in with a mug of coffee in each hand.

"Watch it, nerd," he said slipping by her, then stopping and turning my way. "Today, Willis."

Then he was gone.

Sandy watched him go, then kicked the door closed behind her and set one of the mugs on the desk.

"These guys don't like you any better than they like me," Sandy said.

"Aren't we lucky?" I said wryly.

Sandy laughed and aimed a middle-finger salute at where Yankovic had been standing.

"Saw you were in early and thought some serious caffeine would be in order," she said.

"Thanks," I said. I pointed to the only other chair in the tiny office. "Have a seat."

Sandy nodded toward my computer screen. "Decrypting?"

"Almost done with this drive," I said. "Three more to go."

"How'd you learn to do all this?" she asked. "School?"

"Some. Mostly taught myself."

"No shit?"

"Before I went to work with the police up in Bellingham, I had a small computer security company. We also did a little forensic work for various police agencies and when the Bellingham City Police Department decided they needed their own forensics guy, they offered me the job."

"But why leave your company? The one you started."

"I started the company during the Wild West days of computing. It was exciting, dangerous, challenging." I shook my head dismissively. "Then corporations moved in, standardized, monopolized and centralized things. It got to the point where our company was just doing firewalls and site security. Boring stuff."

"What happened to your company? Sell?"

"To my daughter. She added website design and hosting to the security service. She has five or six employees now."

Sandy took a few sips of her morning brew, both of us watching the computer screen as images and video files were decrypted.

"Are you like a private detective too or something?" Sandy asked.

I let out a short laugh. "What?"

"I heard the sheriff and Geraldine talking," she said. "Couldn't hear all of it. Something about you trying to solve a cold case."

I shook my head and told her what I knew about Jeannie's death and what I was trying to find out.

"I'm not a cop or a detective or anything like that," I said. "I wouldn't want to be and I would suck at it. I just want to find out what happened to her."

"The cops never found anything?" Sandy asked.

"And I probably won't either. It's been almost thirty years." I shrugged. "But I have to look."

"Who have you been talking to about it?"

"Mostly trying to hunt down her brother and sister, to see what they know." I rubbed my sore ribs. "That hasn't been easy. Been searching arrest and court records too."

"Talk to her friends?"

"A few." I looked at my watch. "I'm going to see someone in a few hours that might be able to give me more names."

"Who?"

"I'm bailing Jeannie's little sister out of jail this afternoon."

Sandy just stared at me.

I gave a head shake. "Long story. And I've got to get these drives finished so I can get to Pocatello by one."

Sandy let out a sigh. She could see that I needed to get to work, so with a heavy grunt, she lifted herself out of her chair. "Well, when you have time, I'd love to hear about it."

"Thanks Sandy," I said. "I promise that as soon as I have time, I'll explain the whole thing."

"I'm counting on it," she said.

And then she was gone.

By eleven that morning, I had put the last of the now decrypted drives back in the safe, added my notes to the evidence log and locked them back up.

Yankovic must have been keeping an eye on me because as soon as I started packing up my gear, he came knocking at the door.

"You aren't quitting early again, are you?" he asked brusquely as he entered.

"Yeah," I said.

His brows furrowed.

"We needed those today. We--"

"They're done," I said, waving him off.

He stared.

"They are back in the safe, decrypted with all my notes."

"Good," he said finally.

I pulled my wallet out and extracted a business card, handing it to him.

"I left one of these attached to my notes in the safe, but here's my card if you need to ask me any questions about it. I assume you'll also need me back for the trial to prove chain of evidence or if the court has any questions concerning the decryption."

He was looking over the card while I threw the last of my computer gear into my shoulder bag.

"Anything else?" I asked.

He looked at me and shook his head. "Nope."

Without a "thank you" or anything, Yankovic turned and walked back to his desk.

Geraldine was standing at her desk gathering up her purse when I walked in. She turned and gave me a polite smile.

"Off to lunch?" I asked.

"A luncheon with the mayor and city council," she said. "Is there something you needed?"

"Gil around?"

A voice came from his office.

"Right here, Richie."

The sheriff emerged, putting on his jacket as he stepped out, his Brannon County Sheriff's Department cap in one hand.

"How's it going with those drives?" he asked as he approached me.

"All done."

"Great!"

"Could you come by Marty's later tonight?" I asked.

Gil looked at Geraldine, then me. "Sure. Why?"

"I want to talk to you about the drives and I'll give you a log and invoice for my hours."

"Sounds fine," he said. "Of course, you know, county government is slow to pay. Might take months to see a check."

I laughed. "No problem. Can you come by around eight? I probably won't be back 'til then."

"I can do that," he said, slapping my arm.

"See you tonight then," I said, waving, as he and Geraldine headed down the hall.

I had bailed my drunken dad out of jail more than once, so I knew the process for posting Julie Sorenson's bond and by mid-afternoon, it was done and I was sitting on a bench outside the detention center waiting for Julie to be released.

Taking longer than I had hoped, Julie Sorenson finally pushed out of the detention center's front door and squinted into the bright afternoon sun. She stopped and dug into her oversized purse until she found a pair of similarly oversized sunglasses and slipped them on. Then she pulled a cigarette pack out, stuck one in her mouth and lit it. Sucking it in deeply, she paused and then exhaled heavily. It was at that point that she noticed me. She seemed to pause a moment, thinking or maybe deciding something, then took a deep breath and started in my direction, puffing away.

"Richie Willis," she said stepping up to me, "it is you."

She was wearing the flowered smock over worn-out jeans from the day before and they were so wrinkled I guessed that she must have slept in them. Her long hair was matted and frayed. She noticed my gaze.

"A hell of mess, I know," she said trying to stretch out the wrinkles of her smock. She noticed that she still had a Bonjour Nails name tag pinned to her smock. "Shit." She ripped the tag off her smock and tossed it to the ground. She let out a sigh as if a weight had been tossed off and straightened herself up, giving me a wry smile. "Probably not gonna need that again."

"Don't think they'll hire you back?" I asked with a similar sarcastic smirk.

"Not this time."

"This time?"

Julie looked around and wrinkled her nose as if smelling something rotten. "Can we get the hell outa here?"

I pointed down the street to my doorless, topless four-wheeler.

"My Jeep awaits," I said, starting off.

She followed me quietly for a bit, but as we got closer, she cleared her throat.

"I . . .I was a bit fuzzy on things yesterday," she said. "I wasn't a hundred percent that someone was getting me out and I wasn't sure that the someone was you."

I laughed. "It was me."

I walked around to the driver's side and Julie slipped into the passenger seat, tossing her cigarette into the road. She snapped the seat belt in as I started the machine up.

"Why?" she asked.

"Huh?"

"I may be a drunk, Willis," she said, "and I may be hung-over, but I'm not an idiot. Why the fuck were you at Bonjour and why the fuck are you giving me a ride home? Me. Someone you haven't seen in twenty years."

"Closer to thirty," I said.

"Shit, Richie," she said sitting back as we pulled away from the curb. "Thirty?"

"Almost."

Julie looked off in the distance for a moment, then shook her head and slumped down in her seat, looking forward.

"Thirty fuckin' years," she mumbled.

We drove on silently for a while and I managed a few sideways glances in her direction. Time had not been good to Julie. She was a woman that life had broken. Her skin was pale and drawn tight around her face with deep wrinkles around her eyes and mouth and her teeth were long and stained. Her long thin fingers were scarred with old burns and cuts and her knuckles were a little oversized which likely meant she was experiencing the first pangs of arthritis. A stranger looking at her would have guessed her as sixty, but I knew she was probably forty-five or forty-six.

"You were gonna be like an actor or something, right?" she asked. "After high school?"

I rolled my eyes and laughed half-mockingly at myself. "Sounds pretty silly when you say it that way, but I guess maybe that's what I thought. Ended up in computers."

"Wow," she said. "Pretty fuckin' weird. From farm boy to actor to computer nerd."

I had to laugh. It was pretty weird.

"So I gotta ask again, Richie," she said. "Why were you out at Bonjour Nails? Getting your nails done?"

"Looking for you."

"I knew that, dumbass," she said, shaking her head at me. "Why?"

"I wanted to ask you about . . .Jeannie."

Her expression went blank and she turned to watch the buildings go by as we zipped along near the outskirts of Pocatello.

"A little late, don't you think?" she asked.

I nodded.

"So what's the point?" she asked.

"To understand."

Julie turned away for another moment, shrugged her shoulders and then glanced back at me. "What's to understand? She's dead."

"How did she get there?"

Julie gave me a puzzled look. "Get where?"

"To where she was in her life," I said. "Look. I know about the arrests and the drugs, Julie, but what was going on in her life that got her there? Did she have any friends or boyfriends or girlfriends?"

"Jeannie had a hard time making friends. If she had one, it was one at a time. You were that friend for a long time."

"I know."

"Looking back, I'm not sure she had any real friends until maybe she was a junior. She started hanging out with that Dreyson girl. Sally or Sandy or something."

I had to think a moment, trying to remember who that was.

"Celeste maybe? Dreyson or Deyson?" I asked.

"Maybe."

"She got her involved in drugs?"

Julie started to say something, stopped herself, looked down thinking and then came back to me, shaking her head and seeming to choose her words carefully. "Maybe she encouraged it. I dunno. 'Cuz, it loosened her up, relaxed her."

"Made it easier to make friends?" I asked.

"Something like that, I guess," she said, looking hard into the distance, thinking. "Part of something you never understood."

"What?"

"Loneliness."

I pulled the Jeep into the driveway of the little house Julie was living in, right behind her beat-up Camry. I pulled her keys out of my pocket and handed them to her.

"Julie," I started, "what happened that night Jeannie died?"

She stared at the keys in her hand for a moment, then spoke, spoke as though she was far away.

"USP," she said, "we were working there. It was a shit job. Better that than flipping burgers though. We didn't work in the same department, but our shifts were the same so we usually drove to and from work together. To save gas."

"Where was PeeWee?" I asked.

"Hell, Pete was already driving truck for some company and was living with a bunch of guys in a house north of town somewhere. Don't remember where."

She said that she and Jeannie met in the parking lot after their shifts ended and drove downtown to a little Mexican place called Taco Tex's for beer and tacos. She figured they were there for an hour, each having a couple beers and then they drove home. They were home for a few hours when Jeannie came downstairs where Julie was watching TV and said she had gotten a call and was going to go meet a friend at the Dump. She told Julie not to wait up.

"And that was the last time you saw her?"

Julie nodded.

"No idea who she was meeting?"

"How the fuck should I know?"

I shrugged and raised my hands defensively. "Just asking. According to the police records, you weren't concerned about her being--"

Julie jerked her head towards me.

"What do you mean, police records?" she demanded.

I was a little confused at her sudden shift in mood. "At the court house," I stammered, "I was looking through the case. . ."

Julie abruptly jumped out of Jeep and turned on me, gripping the door frames hard.

"Are you a cop?" she asked angrily.

"No," I said defensively.

"You're reading Jeannie's files?"

"Yes . . . but . . ."

"So this is like some interrogation?" she asked. "You interrogating me?" Julie was getting hotter and hotter. I waved my hands palm out in surrender, but she wouldn't stop. "Pretty shitty thing to do, Willis," she said, pushing away from the Jeep towards her house.

"I'm not interrogating, Julie. I'm not a cop and I'm not trying to hurt anyone."

She stopped and turned. "Then what the hell do you want?"

"I just want to know what happened."

"Why? Why now? Why thirty years later?"

"I owe her."

"Owe her?"

"A lot. I owe her more than I knew at the time."

"Owe her for what?"

I swallowed hard looking at Julie as she opened the door to her house, stopped and turned to me, waiting for an answer.

"Jeannie saved me," I said.

Julie just stared: confused, then angry, then anguished.

"Well, it's just too fuckin' bad that you weren't here thirty years ago to save her."

With that she went inside, slamming the door and raising a cloud of dust that swirled and then blew away with the afternoon breeze.

TWENTY-TWO

"He's not here yet, boss," Tyler whispered conspiratorially, leaning through the service window at Marty's. I was behind the bar filing some special papers in Jia's employee folders. Jia was at a table beside Camila talking with one of the regulars while Marie was coming back with an order from a well-dressed older couple. Volkov's usual corner table was unoccupied.

I turned back to Tyler, faking confidence.

"He'll be here," I said. "Been here every night, right?"

"So far."

"Good," I said, glancing at the wall clock. "We've got time."

Tyler nodded with a half-smile, looked around the bar with a slightly worried expression and then ducked back into the kitchen.

I finished filing and then went back upstairs to the little room that held the security monitor and server. I sat down in front of the server and pulled out the old Dell laptop that I had set up a few days before. I powered it up, made sure I had a good connection to the WIFI network and launched my little remote access app.

A movement from the security camera caught my eye and I was startled to see Eleanor enter Marty's. I hadn't expected her but then saw Reggie follow her in. He must have had car trouble again so she gave him a ride. As much as I wanted to see her, Ellie's presence might complicate what we were planning to do.

I headed back down to the bar where Reggie was strapping on his server's apron and Eleanor was settling onto a bar stool near him.

"Car trouble again?" I asked Reggie.

"I think it's the timing chain," he said. "My dad's gonna help me take it apart Saturday."

I stepped past him over to Eleanor.

"Hey Ellie, I didn't know you'd be here tonight," I said.

"Reg needed a ride. Again," she said elbowing the kid. "And, I needed to talk to you."

"Needed?"

"Okay. Wanted."

"Can it hold for a few minutes? I've got something to do."

She nodded.

I grabbed Reggie's arm and headed him down the hall toward the back door.

"Be back in a minute," I said.

I walked Reggie down the hall out of earshot.

"Tyler's ready. You still okay with all this?"

"Oh yeah," he said.

"And you haven't said anything to Eleanor, right?"

"Nope."

"Good. Wanted to make sure in case this whole thing goes sideways." I patted him on the shoulder and followed him back.

Jia was behind the bar, leaning across it, talking quietly to Ellie when we came back in. As soon as she spied Reggie with his apron on, she pointed to a table by the door where three men in dirty work clothes had just settled in.

"Get those guys some menus and take their orders, okay?"

Reggie headed their way.

"Where'd you two go?" Eleanor asked.

I was on the brink of inventing a reason when a sound drew my attention to the door.

Volkov had entered and was stopped just inside the door looking around, his gaze coming to a stop in Jia's direction. I heard a faint moan from Jia when he gave her what might have been a smile. He held up one finger.

One day.

Eleanor caught Jia's gaze and turned to see Volkov. She stiffened like she was going to stand but I placed a hand on her arm.

"Ellie," I said in a quiet, calm voice, "don't."

Volkov walked casually to his table and slipped into a chair, pulling out his laptop.

Ellie turned to me.

"Don't we have to do something?" she asked, looking first at me, then to Jia who turned to me with a silent, questioning look. I held her gaze and gave her as confident a nod as I could.

"It's just another night at Marty's," I said to her. "Have Marie go take his order."

Jia looked at me, calculating and then nodded. She went down to the other end of the bar to where Marie was writing down an order. I glanced over the service counter to Tyler who had been listening to all this. He arched his eyebrows questioning and I gave a tiny shake of my head. He nodded and went back to the fryer.

Ellie's eyes followed Jia over to Marie then followed Marie to Volkov's table where she stood taking an order. Ellie turned and was about to ask something.

"Just a sec," I said. I stood and waved a hand at Jia. "Could we get a couple ciders?"

Jia gave me a wave and a nod and I sat back down.

"Cider okay?" I asked Ellie.

"Yeah," she said hesitantly. "I suppose."

Jia came down to us with bottles of cider and ice filled glasses. Ellie saw Jia giving me a long look, then glanced up to see Tyler looking at me expectantly. Before Ellie looked in my direction, I gave Tyler a nod. Jia noticed it and looked back and forth between us.

"Hey boss," Tyler called out, a little louder than he should have. "Can you cover me here for a minute? I've gotta powder my nose."

"Sure," I said to him, standing. I touched Ellie on the shoulder. "Be right back."

"You're going to cook?" she asked incredulously.

I smiled. "Of course! Want me to make you something?"

"God, no!" she said.

I stepped around the other end of the bar and into the kitchen with Tyler. He pointed to two order sheets and then we turned our backs on the women and he pointed towards the grill like we were discussing how to flip a burger.

"It's the black Lexus SUV," I whispered. "Probably backed into a parking slot at the other end of the lot." I gave him the plate number. He nodded, pulled a small bundle out from under a cooler and headed out the back door while I slipped over to the grill and began flipping burgers and onions. Both Jia and Ellie stood and looked over the service counter watching. Ellie elbowed Jia.

"He's actually cooking?" she asked.

"I guess so," Jia said, shaking her head.

"While you're back there," Eleanor called over the counter to me, "maybe I'll chance an order of fries?"

I gave her a thumbs up, Jia laughed and I dumped a pile of frozen French fries into the fryer with a splattering sizzle. I was starting to feel like a real cook. I just hoped nobody ordered anything more exotic than a burger before Tyler got back.

Reggie appeared from the other end of the bar and joined the two women watching me.

"He's actually cooking?" he asked.

The two laughed. I turned and came to the service counter.

"Why is everyone so surprised to see that I can fry a hamburger or dump spuds into a vat of boiling oil?" I asked, heading back to the grill. After a few more minutes at the stove, I assembled a reasonable facsimile of a cheeseburger with onions and a side of fries and placed it on the service counter.

"I think you're supposed to say something like 'order up'," Eleanor said.

"Okay. Order up!"

Camila came over, gave me a you-shouldn't-be-cooking look, grabbed the plate off the service counter and took it to a customer, looking it over carefully as she went, making sure I hadn't screwed it up.

I yanked Ellie's fries out of their oil bath, dumped them into a paper basket and sprinkled on salt just as Tyler came back. He stuffed the bundle he was carrying back under a cooler and stepped over to me and gave me a nod. I returned the nod, slapped him on the back and let him take over.

I went back Eleanor with a basket of fries and settled onto a stool with the intention of sharing them when I heard the front door open behind me.

"Hey Rich," a voice called.

It was Gil Froman.

"Hey sheriff!" I responded loudly so everyone knew a cop had entered. I caught Volkov reacting as he saw a policeman walking into

Marty's. He stared as the uniformed man walked my way, shook hands with me and sat himself onto a stool on the other side of Ellie's. I noticed that Volkov relaxed.

"Gil, this is Eleanor Fife," I said. "Teaches at ISU. Ellie, Gil Froman, Brannon County Sheriff."

They shook hands.

"What can we get you, Gil?" I asked.

"Diet Coke?"

I leaned over to catch Reggie at the other end of the bar. "Reggie! Could you get the sheriff a Diet Coke?"

Gil was exchanging small talk with Ellie about going to school at Idaho State when Reggie set a glass with ice and a can of Diet Coke in front of Gil.

"Thanks," Gil said.

Reggie smiled, then looked in my direction. I gave him a nod. He nodded back.

Ellie saw the exchange and arched her eyebrows questioningly. I gave her a tiny head shake and the hint of a smile, then leaned past her to Gil.

"Gil, I've got my copy of the evidence log and some notes for you about the case," I said. "I'll go grab 'em."

I slipped off the stool and started down the back hall to the stairs. At the same time, in the corner of my eye, I saw Reggie head out the front door.

Game on.

Upstairs, I sat in front of the camera so I could watch what was happening down in the café. And with a deep breath, I powered up the used Dell laptop, launched my little remote access app and issued the command to connect to Volkov's laptop.

I watched the hourglass spinning, the app trying to connect.

Still spinning.

I felt myself tightening up. This had to work and it was taking too long.

Spinning.

If this didn't work, Jia would be forced to choose between two terrible options: going with Volkov or getting her and her mother deported by Homeland Security.

Spinning. . . spinning . . . spinning . . .

Connect.

Got him.

I was in.

I opened a new command window and located a batch file I had written and started it running.

The monitor was aimed down at the tables and I could see Volkov in the corner, back to the wall, gulping down some coffee and plugging away on his laptop.

The front door opened and Reggie stepped in.

"Anyone here have a black Lexus SUV?" he asked.

Volkov perked up.

"Anyone own a black Lexus?" he repeated loudly.

Volkov stood, said something and Reggie walked over to him. I knew that Reggie would be telling Volkov that someone had just backed into his car.

Volkov was furious, yelling at Reggie, gesturing wildly, indicating that he wanted Reggie to show him what happened and hurrying out the door, Reggie following.

The moment they were gone, I launched my program.

First, it disabled the keyboard and mouse on Volkov's computer. Next it disabled his screen saver and sleep timer to make sure the laptop display stayed on. The next process kicked in, moving files from my laptop into a folder on Volkov's. I watched the progress bar as the files moved to his machine and watched the door, hoping Reggie was keeping the Ukrainian outside.

Watching the door.

Watching the progress bar.

Watching the door.

Progress complete.

The last of the batch file commands launched a slideshow program on the desktop of Volkov's computer. Next, it killed the connection to my laptop and then it deleted the remote access program I had installed on his machine.

Fingers crossed, I pulled my phone out and texted one word to Camila.

"Go."

Looking up at the monitor, I saw Camila react as she got my text, then going to the bar, snagging a pitcher of water and going to Volkov's table to fill his water glass. I had given her a hint as to what she might see, but she wasn't fully prepared for what appeared on his laptop's screen. The horrified look on her face was real.

I had copied a few hundred files from the child porn dealer's computer onto Volkov's laptop and they were being displayed on his desktop in a non-stop slideshow. Though they were the tamest of the Wendover files I had decrypted, they were still incredibly disturbing. Her hand was over her mouth, her eyes were wide and staring.

I was sorry that she had to see those, but now she had to move. Had to move before Volkov came back in.

She stared.

I wanted to yell out at her.

Move!

After a moment, she shook the cobwebs out and quick-walked over to Marie. She whispered and pointed to Volkov's computer, then Marie followed her over to Volkov's table. When she went around the table and saw his computer screen, she let out a gasp and grabbed Camila's arm with both hands. She stared in shock for a moment and then said something to Camila, who nodded and Marie ran over to Gil and tapped him on the shoulder and then frantically grabbed his shirt and pulled at him, pointing to Volkov's table, her eyes wide with shock.

Gil stood and followed a very upset Marie across the room to the laptop. When he got around to the other side of the table and saw the screen, his face mirrored the two women's faces. He started asking questions and pointing and Marie was pointing out the door and that's when I knew I had to move. I shut down the old dell laptop I was using and with a grunt, tore the laptop screen off the body of the laptop at the hinges. Next I pulled the small hard drive out of the computer and with a pair of metal cutting shears I brought up from the Jeep, I cut the drive into little pieces and shoved them into a pocket. Finally, I flipped the body of the laptop over, opened it up and, using the shears, I cut every cable and wire I could reach and scraped off as many solders as I could as well as prying half a dozen chips off the motherboard.

These steps insured that no one would ever know what it had been used for and who had used it.

I gathered up the scraps of the laptop, grabbed the papers I had for Gil and ran back down the stairs and out the back pulling the tiny pieces of the hard drive out of my pocket, flinging them across the alley, scattering them among the weeds and bushes there. Then I buried the remnants of the laptop deep into the dumpster, knowing it was scheduled to be emptied in the morning.

I ran back inside Marty's, holding the folder like I was bringing it
to Gil, and stopped just inside the bar next to Ellie who was watching
the activity around Volkov's table.

"What's going on?" I asked, feigning surprise.

"Dunno," she said, not looking at me. Then she turned on her stool
towards me. "Something's going on with Volkov's computer."

"Oh yeah? What?"

Eleanor looked at me for a beat, then to the sheriff and Camila and
Marie and then slowly back to me with a suspicious look.

Before she could open her mouth to say anything, though, the door
burst open and an angry Volkov came in muttering about the damage
to his SUV, followed by Reggie, who gave me a wink and a tiny nod.
Volkov came up short when he saw three people at his table. He took
a few steps closer, his anger growing and Gil took a step towards him,
a hand out to stop him.

"What the fuck you doing?" Volkov asked, pushing, but Gil held
his ground.

"That your computer?" Gil asked.

"Of course it's my computer," he snarled. "Get away from it."

In a practiced move that was quicker than I had ever imagined
possible from Gil, he grabbed Volkov's right hand, spun him around,
pushed him hard against the wall and twisted the man's arm high up
behind his back, eliciting a scream of pain and in the same smooth
action snapped a handcuff on his right wrist.

By now, customers were backing away from the area in shock.

"Get the fuck off me," Volkov yelled.

"You are under arrest," Gil said as he snapped the cuff on his other
wrist, "You have the right to remain silent. . ." He started reciting the
Miranda warning.

"What the fuck for?" Volkov growled, "What are you doing."

Gil twisted Volkov around, still holding the cuffs and pointed him toward the laptop's screen where the slideshow was continuing.

"You are under arrest for the possession of child pornography."

Volkov gawked wide-eyed at the computer screen until Marie couldn't take it anymore and slammed the laptop closed. Camila took a very upset Marie by the arm and led her away, down the hall to the women's bathroom.

"That's not mine," Volkov said.

"It's your computer," Gil said, searching the man's pockets.

"Those aren't my pictures!" he cried. "Someone put them there."

Gil gave him a grim half-laugh. "You know how many times I've heard that?"

Volkov was stammering angrily in broken English and Ukrainian as Gil found the man's passport, opened it, looked at the picture then up to Volkov.

"Ukrainian, huh?" Gil said.

Inside the passport he found Volkov's B-2 Visitor Visa and waved it in his face."

"Well," Gil said, "I guess this means that this will be a Homeland Security problem, won't it?"

Volkov stared.

"You are in deep shit, buddy," Gil said. He turned toward where Jia, Ellie and I were standing and watching. "You got a big garbage bag and a pair of vinyl gloves?"

I nodded and looked at Jia.

"I'll get them," Jia said. She reached under the counter and pulled out fresh trash liner and a handful of disposable gloves, taking them to the sheriff.

"Put the gloves on," Gil said to Jia.

Volkov stared angrily at Jia. "You did this." He spat at her and Gil slammed him hard against the wall.

"Knock that off," Gil snarled.

"She did this to me!" he yelled.

Jia just stared back, wide-eyed, a little scared. She shook her head.

Gil pointed to the things on Volkov's table.

"Put all those things in the bag, please," he said.

"That little bitch planted all those pictures on my computer."

She stared up at him. "I did not. No!"

"Why the hell would she do that, Volkov?" Gil asked. "Huh?"

"She is trying to get rid of me."

"Trying to get rid of you?" Gil laughed. "Why?"

"So that I don't turn her into your immigration people," he snapped. "She's not supposed to be here. She is illegal."

Jia stared, eyes bouncing from the sheriff to Volkov and back to the sheriff.

"Illegal?" Gil asked.

"She's a hundred percent legal!" I called out loudly.

Everyone turned to me as I said that. I glanced at Jia who's expression was growing more frightened. I nodded at her, then to Gil.

"Got all her paperwork right here," I said. I reached over the bar and pulled Jia's folder out of the employee cabinet and walked over to Gil opening it up. Reaching in I pulled out a copy of her Employment Authorization Form, with her picture and the appropriate dates on it along with a photo copy of her passport and the Form I-94 work endorsement. All with official State Department and Homeland Security stamps and signatures. I handed them to Gil.

As he looked them over, I glanced over at Jia, who was frowning and searching my face for something. I gave her as reassuring and subtle a smile as I could manage. I then pulled out another official form.

"And here is the I-9 form we filed with the IRS, validating her legal status to work here."

Gil took the form

"She's illegal," Volkov was arguing. "Those are fake."

Gil shook his head.

Volkov tried to lunge at me, but Gil had a tight hold and slammed the man back against the wall again.

He spat something in Ukrainian at Gil then turned his ire on Jia spouting foulness only Jia could understand. She snarled curses back at him which I guessed were Ukrainian variants on "go to hell" and "fuck you".

Gil waved all the papers in front of Volkov's furious, beet-red face.

"They look real to me," Gil said. He handed them back to me. "Not that that even matters." Gil pointed to the items Jia had just finished bagging up. "Possessing and trafficking in stuff like you've got on your machine . . ." He was struggling to control his anger. He took a breath. "Let's just say people like you go away for a very long time." He took the trash bag of items from Jia. She gave Volkov one last glare, turned and walked back over to the bar, into the protective embrace of Camila and Marie and surrounded by Tyler, Reggie and Ellie like a herd guarding their young.

Gil grabbed Volkov's upper arm and pulled him toward the door. I moved ahead of them, customers stepping aside, staring at the enraged and still cursing man the sheriff was leading away and pulled the door open. Gil gave me a nod of thanks.

"I'll bring you my notes on the Wendover case tomorrow," I said as he passed by me. Volkov spat a few more words in my direction as he was yanked out the door, but Gil kept a tight hold as he guided him towards his cruiser. As he got to the back door of the sheriff's vehicle and Gil was unlocking the door, about to push the Ukrainian into the back seat, Volkov looked at me.

I just smiled.

His eyes narrowed and he bared his teeth, opening his mouth to say something, but Gil shoved him into the back seat and slammed the door before he could get anything out.

Jia and the others came out onto the porch of Marty's, standing around me. We watched Gil going around to the driver side to get in his cruiser. Jia grabbed my arm to pull me into a happy embrace but I stopped her.

"Just smile and wave folks," I said. "Smile and wave."

We all watched Gil start up the cruiser and pull out of his parking spot, waving as he passed in front of us. We all waved and smiled at the bloated and angry face staring at us from the back seat, waving until Gil reached the other end of the parking lot and disappeared.

On cue, everyone erupted into a cheer and into laughter. Reggie and Tyler and I exchanged handshakes and congratulatory pats on the back, everyone talking about what had happened in the last few minutes. I turned to look at Jia. She was standing, staring at where the cruiser had gone, tears flowing down her face. She twisted around in my direction, looking up at me, trying to speak, but a big, grateful smile was all she could manage. She threw her arms around me, crying like a baby, the stress of the last few days dissipating with every sob.

Ellie was behind me. She looked at Reggie and Tyler.

"You guys set all this up?" she asked.

"What?" Marie asked.

I nodded and smiled at her.

"Camila too," Tyler said, pride in his voice.

"So cool," Reggie said. "So, so cool."

I turned to Camila and Marie. "I'm sorry you had to see some of that stuff and Marie, I'm sorry that we didn't let you in on it, but it was important that your reactions were honest."

"But what about a trial," Jia asked. "And if he gets out on bail."

I shook my head.

"Won't be a trial."

"Huh?"

"Since he's here on a temporary visitor's visa and has apparently committed a very serious felony right in front of a sheriff who despises keepers of child porn, Volkov will be turned over to Homeland Security and then after a few weeks locked up somewhere, he'll be deported to Ukraine and never allowed back."

Tyler and Reggie laughed and high-fived each other.

"It's politically too messy to have a trial on something like this with a Ukrainian right now, so they'll just toss him out, send the evidence to Ukraine and let them deal with him."

Jia stood back and looked me. "How did you do it?" I smiled, shyly.

Tyler piped up. "Teamwork!"

Jia looked towards everyone and spread her arms wide, eyes still wet with tears. "Thank you, thank you all."

"Let's go celebrate!" Tyler said.

"Yeah!" Reggie chimed in.

Jia gave them all a faux stern look, pointing inside.

"No!" Jia said. "We have customers in there. Get to work you slackers, before I fire you all!"

Grudgingly, the guys followed Marie and Camila back into the bar, then Jia turned back to me and took my right hand in both of hers. She stared hard at them for a few moments and gave my hand a squeeze.

"I can never thank you enough for what you just did for me," she said. "And for my mother. I owe you."

"Pay me back by staying here and managing this run-down old hamburger joint."

She squeezed my hand again, still not looking at me and shaking her head. "I owe you."

She released me and disappeared into Marty's.

I relaxed my shoulders, relieved, turned and sat myself down onto the patio steps looking out at the parking lot. Ellie dropped down next to me and put an arm around my shoulders. We sat quietly for a few minutes until Eleanor finally spoke.

"How the hell did you do all that?"

I smiled. "Like Tyler said, it was a team effort." I glanced around to make sure no one was listening, then continued quietly, pointing to where Volkov's SUV was still parked. "A few minutes ago, instead of powdering his nose, Tyler took a towel and hammer out to Volkov's Lexus and quietly bashed in the headlights and the fender. Then Reggie went out and pretended to see someone back into it which got Volkov out of the building."

"And you hacked into his computer and installed all that . . . stuff."

I nodded.

"Stuff you got from that case you were helping the sheriff with, who just happened to have a meeting with you at Marty's at the same time."

"What a funny coincidence," I said with a smile.

She just shook her head at me. "What if you had been caught?"

"I wasn't."

"Having all that child porn, smashing his car, hacking into his computer. That's all illegal."

"Yes."

"And all those work permits and forms for Jia. Where'd they come from? Are they real?"

"Real as far as Gil knows and he'll never look any closer at them then he did tonight."

"Fake government documents."

I coughed.

"Also, a crime?"

I shrugged.

"Everything you guys did tonight was illegal. To help Jia."

"To save Jia," I corrected. "Sometimes, what may be the illegal thing, may also be the right thing."

Eleanor looked at me curiously, then laid her head on my shoulder as we watched an old Ford F-150 pull into a parking spot. The driver killed the engine and stepped out of the truck coming towards us. Eleanor felt me stiffen. It was a man walking a little unsteadily towards us through the dark lot. He stopped, still in shadows, about thirty feet away. I recognized him. Ellie and I stood.

"I think you cracked one of my ribs, PeeWee," I called out to the man.

"I'm sorry about that, Rich," Pete Sorenson said. "Didn't mean to hit you that hard."

"It was a kick, not a hit," I said.

He snorted a laugh and stepped a little closer until he was illuminated by the building's light. He was in beat-up work boots, dirty, worn jeans and an old Nickelback t-shirt.

Ellie leaned in towards me. "Is this your friend's brother?"

I nodded.

"You deserved it anyway," Pete said.

"I only wanted to talk to you, Pete."

"So I hear," he snarled. "You been tryin' to talk to Julie too, huh?"

"Yeah."

"Well, back off, Willis."

"What?"

"It's not your business."

"I want to know what happened, that's all. And for god's sake, she was your sister. Don't you want to know?"

"It was thirty years ago. Won't do anybody any good now to dig into it."

"Why?" I took a few steps in his direction.

"Old wounds, Rich. Leave 'em alone."

"Pete, can't we talk --"

"Leave it, Willis," he bellowed. "Don't come near me or Julie again. Leave us the hell alone!" Pete pointed an angry finger at me. "Don't talk to me or Julie ever again, understand? Jeannie is dead and buried. Leave her there."

He glared at me for a few more seconds, then turned and strode off to his old truck, firing it up and screeching out of the parking lot.

Ellie and I watched him go and then Ellie stepped down next to me.

"You're not going to let it go, are you?" she asked.

"Would you?"

She looked at me with a sad smile.

"C'mon," she said, "Let's get back inside."

We walked over to the bar where Reg, Marie and Camila were around Jia who was looking through the forms I had shown the sheriff.

"How'd you get these?" Jia asked, holding up the forms.

Reggie slapped me on my back.

"He's a hacker," Reggie said. "Didn't you know that?"

"Helping the sheriff with a case they are working on gave me access to government databases," I started, but Ellie interrupted me.

"Can I use your bathroom?"

"Sure," I said.

She nodded and headed down the hall toward the bathrooms.

I went on to explain how I had found the forms and documentation needed and how I had made them look official enough to fool a small town sheriff. I also explained to them that they can never talk to anyone about it because it would get us all in trouble. They all seem to agree with me and then scattered, getting back to work except for Jia, who waited until the others were farther away and stepped closer to me.

"Rich . . .would it be possible to get what I would need to get my mom and I permanent residency here? So we could sign up for social security? So I could get my mother on Medicare?"

"I'm not the best at forging those kinds of government . . . documents," I said, "but I started out as a hacker and I have had people who can do it. I'll contact them and see if it's possible."

Jia was working hard to keep from crying, wanting to thank me. I just touched her arm. She smiled, turned and went back to work.

Satisfied with what we had done, I went back down the hall to wait for Ellie, but heard the toilet upstairs in my little apartment flushing. She must have decided to use my bathroom instead of the tavern's, so I headed upstairs and into my room, just as Ellie came out of the bathroom.

"Thought you would be downstairs," I said.

Ellie walked up to me. She was in a loose, buttoned blouse and her usual tight jeans, but she had kicked her shoes off.

"What you guys did for Jia tonight was just amazing," she said.

"I was just trying to get back at him for sucker punching me," I said with fake modesty.

"Yeah, right."

Eleanor, the girl I had loved for so many years in college stepped up to me, wrapped her arms around me and engulfed me in a passionate kiss. I was stunned into helplessness for a few seconds, then relaxed and put my arms around her, pulling us into a tight embrace. After what seemed like forever, she broke off the kiss and leaned back, unbuttoning her blouse. I looked down at her long fingers as they finished with the buttons and she dropped the blouse to the floor. Then she grabbed my t-shirt at the waist, pulled it off over my head and kissed me softly on the lips.

"Another test?" I asked.

She nodded as she reached down to loosen my belt.

"What if I fail the test?" I asked.

She smiled. "Then you'll have to retake it."

"How many tries do I get?"

"As many as it takes," she said. "After all, we have all night."

TWENTY-THREE

The dream was different this time. It was like a video that was out of focus. The sound was muddled, but I could hear voices, could hear that I was talking but I couldn't understand what was being said.

Instead of feeling like I was in the dream, I seemed to be a passive viewer, without the feeling of desperation, of anxiousness to get somewhere or do something that I usually had in these dreams.

I was walking down a hospital corridor as usual, but leaving, not racing in. And then, when I found myself at the homeless encampment as I always did, it was empty; everything and everybody gone.

Then I was in that big, empty field again, night, no moon, slogging through the plowed-up earth towards a figure in the distance. I got closer and like before it was Jeannie, thick, curly blonde hair blowing in a dust churning wind, but this time, she was trying to claw her way out of the ground. When she saw me, she started frantically waving. I couldn't figure out what she was doing, but then realized that she was warning me to get back, to stay away, pointing towards a figure standing at the edge of the field.

A man. A big man, standing and watching.

Straining my eyes through the swirling dust storm to see who it was, I started walking in that direction. Getting closer, the figure grew taller and bigger and I kept getting smaller. The figure was familiar.

I stopped suddenly.

I knew. My heart started racing, I was breathing harder and harder. My uncle.

There was a sudden crash and my uncle disappeared into a cloud as an oversized trash dumpster was rushing at me, flipping over, the lid spreading and trash cascading over me.

I bolted awake.

Breathing hard.

Sweating.

But the sound. . .

I was awake, but I could still hear the crashing of a dumpster.

What the hell?

My head began to clear.

The dumpster. In back of Marty's. It was being emptied.

I rubbed my eyes, trying to shake the dream off, and then remembered that I wasn't alone. I looked to my left to see Ellie, laying on her side, propped up on one elbow looking at me. Her long, dark hair draped around her long neck and over her pillow, framing her face perfectly. She was beautiful.

"What?" I asked.

"What were you dreaming?"

"Did I say anything embarrassing?"

She smiled. "Lots of things." She pressed a hand to my bruised ribs. "A lot of moaning, too. Time for another one of Tyler's magic pills."

I nodded and made a motion to get up, but she pressed me back down.

"I'll get it," Ellie said, tossing the blankets off and getting up. She started towards the john. I couldn't help but admire her tall, slender naked body. There were a few small sags, some wrinkles and scars, but still an amazing body for a woman in her late forties.

"How do you do it?" I asked.

She stopped and turned and I stared, admiringly.

"What?"

"After twenty-five years, how do you still have such a perfect body?"

She waved me off with a snort and a backhanded swatting motion, heading into the bathroom.

"I'd love to say it's from hours at the gym," she said from inside, "and a healthy diet and eight hours of sleep." I could hear her opening the medicine cabinet and shaking out a pill. "But it's just genetic. I was very lucky. Inherited my Mediterranean mother's high metabolism and my Nordic father's strong body. Blame them." She came to the door of the bathroom. "Catch!" She tossed the little pill at me, which I, of course, missed, but eventually dug out from the blankets where it landed. "Be right back." She closed the door.

I threw the pill into my mouth along with one of my happy pills and guzzled the last of a glass of water that was sitting on the bed stand.

My phone flashed at me and I looked to see a text message from my daughter. It read: "Answer your phone!"

Then I saw that a call was coming in.

"Good morning, Jess," I said picking up.

"Where have you been?" she demanded without a hello or anything. "I've been calling for hours." I looked at the time.

"Sorry," I said. "My phone was on mute. And it's only eight o'clock, Jess. What's wrong?"

"I didn't hear from you yesterday."

"Crazy day yesterday," I said, sitting up and trying to slip into boxers while cradling the phone to an ear. "Something happen?"

"No."

I was a little relieved. "So, what's up?"

"Nothin' much, Dad," she said. "I just hadn't heard from you and was worried."

"No need to worry," I said. "I'm a big boy now."

Jesse let out a short snort of a laugh. "Right, Dad. Still plan on being back next week?"

"Uh . . ."

I heard Ellie flush the toilet and then the bathroom door opened.

"Wanna get dressed and go some breakfast?" Ellie asked.

She stopped cold when she saw I was talking on the phone and the surprise and the surprisingly embarrassed look on my face. Her eyes got big and the room went still. I have no idea why I should have been embarrassed. It was just a little weird to be talking to my daughter and have a naked woman walk into the room.

The room was silent.

The phone was silent.

I was silent.

There was a pause, then Jess's voice on the phone.

"Dad?"

A pause.

"Yeah?"

"Dad, I think I heard a woman ask if you wanted to get dressed and go get breakfast."

"She did?" I smiled and winked at Ellie as she tiptoed over and sat on the bed.

"I'm pretty sure she did, Dad."

"Yeah."

I could see Jess right now, smirking into the phone at me.

"Dad, I think you should go get some breakfast."

"Okay, Jess, I will."

"And Dad?"

"Yeah?"

"Get dressed first."

There was a giggle and she clicked off.

I shook my head, let out a short laugh and tossed the phone onto the bed.

"Daughter?" Eleanor asked grabbing her pile of clothes and sitting on the edge of the bed next to me.

I nodded.

Eleanor slipped on her panties and was untangling the bra that I had mangled when I ripped it off her last night.

"What was your daughter calling about?" Ellie asked. "What did you say her name was?"

"Jess," I said. "Just checking up on me." I took a breath. "Wants to know when I'll be back."

Ellie paused and looked at me. I could see she wanted to know what my answer had been, but changed her mind, nodded with a smile and finished unraveling the bra straps and slipped it on.

She got up and retrieved her blouse from where it had dropped onto the floor and we both continued dressing in silence. Eleanor sat down on a chair to put her shoes on.

"What were you dreaming about?" she asked.

"That nightmare I keep having," I said. I told her about the images of the hospital, the homeless encampment and the plowed up field where Jeannie's body had been found. "It was different this time. I didn't feel that panic I usually feel."

"You were mumbling things that sounded like you were scared or startled and said something about an uncle and then you bolted up awake. A little freaky."

"Sorry."

"What's with the uncle?"

The shadowy image from my dream flashed to mind, but I shook it off.

"Don't know what that was about," I said. She looked at me, knowing I was holding something back, but decided not to ask any more questions. I went to her as she stood and placed my hands on her waist.

"It's the recovered Catholic in me," I said, tilting my head toward the old bed, "but I'm feeling a little guilty about all this."

Eleanor looked at me with a tiny smile and a shake of her head. "Don't. This was all my doing."

"A test."

"Correct."

"Actually," I said, "I think there were a couple tests last night."

She smiled. "Yes, there were."

"So . . . how did I do?"

"I'll be grading papers later tonight and I'll let you know." She pulled me close, kissed me, then backed off. "C'mon. I've got to get back down to school this morning and I need sustenance. These tests are exhausting."

"Let's go," I said. "And then I need to pick up some maple bars."

Twenty-Four

"These are the worst fuckin' excuses for maple bars I've ever eaten," Sally Burke said through a mouthful of gooey, sweet dough sitting next to me on her rickety old porch swing. She pointed a chubby, arthritic finger at me. "And if this eighty-year old woman goes into insulin shock because you made her eat these, I'll take you out of my will."

"First," I said, "you're not eighty."

"Seventy-six," she piped in.

"Second, that's not how insulin shock works. Third, you can't go into insulin shock because you aren't diabetic and finally, you can't take me out of your will because you know full well I'm not in your will."

"Good," she said. "As fucked up as my old brain is, I was afraid I might've stuck you in." She stared at me expectantly. "So? You're here for pleasant conversation?"

I smiled.

"Thought so," she said without waiting for an answer. "So, what the hell do you want this time? Did you find those Sorenson kids?"

I nodded.

"But they weren't very interested in talking to me," I said.

Mrs. Burke pointed at the healing cut and bruise on my face.

"I see you found Peter."

"Yeah."

"You get a few punches in?"

"Didn't get a chance."

She gave me a disappointed head shake. "So you came to me for boxing lessons?"

"No. . . ."

"Lesson number one: duck!"

"Darn, wish I'd thought of that."

"Did you find the little sister?" she asked.

"Yes and--"

"Did she beat you up too?"

I gave her a mock angry look.

"Are you gonna let me tell you why I'm here?"

She smiled. "Tell me what you need."

"Okay. Dreyson or Deyson. Those names familiar?"

"Deyson. You mean the Deysons?" she asked. "The farmers out on Lewis Lane?"

"I think so. A daughter. Julie said her name was Celeste. She was in school the same time I was."

I could see the woman was digging through old memory cells.

"Julie says she was friends with Jeannie."

"Not Celeste," Mrs. Burke said finally. "I think she means Sara. Sara Deyson. A solid 'B' student. Smart girl. And so pretty. Coulda been an 'A', but didn't have that kind of ambition. A good family, good money, but she had it too easy. I think she slipped into drugs or alcohol pretty early."

"Sara," I said. "Now I remember her. From the tennis team. We played mixed doubles at a few tennis matches. Totally forgot. She had a really funny laugh. We use to tease her about it."

"Not Deyson anymore," she said. "Married a Wilcox out of Idaho Falls"

"Sara Wilcox." I pulled out my phone and started googling.

"He's gone now, though," she continued. "Killed at work. Some heavy piece of equipment rolled over on him."

"Is she around?" Google wasn't giving me much.

"Moved back here after hubby died." She looked off into the distance. "Either didn't have much money or lost it all. I think she's living out west of town. A little messed up, I think."

"Whaddya mean?"

"Saw her a few months ago at the store. Looks pretty rough."

I stared at her for a moment, then tapped her lightly on the forehead.

"You know, I don't know why I bother with Google. You've got all the world's information right there."

"No, Google has the information, but I have the knowledge. Don't confuse the two."

"Any chance you know her address?"

"Do I look like a fuckin' phone book?"

"Sorry."

"I think she's on Turner Road."

"Turner Road. Isn't that out in the lava fields?"

She nodded.

The eastern part of Idaho had been covered by a lava flow seventy-thousand years ago, with thousands of acres of lava still exposed, but in many places, soil had taken hold and farms and houses had sprung up there where land was cheap. Turner Road meandered among some those lots west of Black River.

"Thanks Mrs. Burke."

"Look, kid," she said, "after you were skulking around here a few days ago asking about the Sorenson girl, I went down to the basement and dug through my school journals."

"You have a lot of stuff in there about Jeannie Sorenson?"

"Just the opposite."

"Huh?"

"Almost nothing about her. Or her brother. Or her sister."

"Really."

"I found a few notes from English class when she was a freshman. Stuff like: sits in the back, quiet, distant, wary."

"Wary?"

"No idea why the fuck I wrote that, but I did. She was plenty smart with good grades, but I don't remember her getting involved in any school activities. Do you?"

"No."

She looked me over.

"What happened between you two?" she asked.

"It was before high school," I said.

"What?"

I shrugged and stood, stepping away.

"I'm going to track Sara Wilcox down and see what she remembers."

"And you're not going to tell me what happened with you and Jean?"

"No, I'm not."

She stared at me, then sighed, shook her head and flicked her wrist at me dismissively.

"Go find that woman," she said. "And when you are ready to talk about what happened with Jean, I'll be here. Expecting maple bars."

I smiled.

"Deal. Thanks, Sally. You've been a huge help."

"You're welcome," she said with a smile, but then she put on her mock angry old lady face.

"Now, get the fuck off my lawn, before I call the cops."

"Yes, ma'am," I said with a wave.

Once out of the neighborhood, I tapped the nav screen on my Jeep and pulled up a road map to remind myself how to get to Turner Road. Locating it on the map, I dialed into the sheriff's office and asked for Sandy.

"Sandy," I said after she came on the line, "this is Rich Willis. Could I ask you to look something up for me?"

"Of course, sir," Sandy said in a weird formal tone. "Just a moment, please. Let me get logged onto our system."

I could hear muffled voices, then an office door closing. After a pause Sandy came back on.

"Sorry about that Rich," she said in a quiet voice. "Yankovic was in here. Had to get rid of the asshole. What do you need?"

"An address."

"For?"

"Wilcox out on Turner Road," I said. "It should be Sara Wilcox, but might also be under her dead husband's name."

"This about the Sorenson girl?" Sandy asked.

"I've been told that this Sara was a friend."

There was a pause, then she came back.

"Here it is: Wilcox. Sorry, no street address, just a box number."

"That's sounds right," I said. "It's outside of town. Probably has a route number with the box number."

"Yeah," she said. "How'd you know?"

"Growing up, out on a farm, our address was like that. What's the address?"

"Route seven, box twenty-eight," Sandy said.

"That means her mailbox is the twenty-eighth on the post office's route number seven. I should be able to find it."

"Cool."

"Thanks partner."

"Hey," Sandy said, "am I getting paid for this?"

"Free beer and burgers at Marty's, how's that?"

"Good enough for me," she said.

Turner Road was an old, pot-holed, but paved, county road that ran north off the highway. There were houses scattered along the ribbon of road in spots where actual soil covered the old lava bed enough to support a garden and yard. A few of the houses were newer with manicured lawns, but most were older, ranch style homes with either brown yards or none at all.

After only a mile, I found the mailbox labeled Box Twenty-Eight at the bottom of a driveway that ran up to a small, gray, L-shaped ranch house. The place had been decent at one time, but weather and lack of upkeep had left it looking tired and worn out. A wheelchair ramp led from the front door to the driveway where an old compact Chevy was parked in front of the closed garage. I pulled up behind it, killed the motor and heard a little dog yapping hysterically inside the house.

I stepped out of the Jeep as the screen door was pushed open by an old woman in a wheelchair. She was in a baggy, flowered housecoat over fuzzy slippers. A pair of clear tubes ran from an oxygen tank on the back of her chair over her matted gray hair to a nasal cannula under plastic rimmed glasses. As she pushed herself out, a short-haired mutt of indeterminate breed scooted out around her and raced towards me yapping. When the little monster got closer, I bent over and held out my hand for the dog. He stopped barking, took a whiff of my hand

and, seemingly satisfied that I wasn't going to hurt him, ran back to the woman in the chair who, I assumed, was Sara's mother.

"You lost?" the woman asked.

I took a step closer, about to answer when I realized the woman wasn't Sara's mother.

"Sara Deyson?" I asked, unfortunately not masking my shocked surprise very well.

She stared at me.

"Wilcox, yeah," she said. "Who are you?"

I was speechless for a beat, looking at what had been an old tennis teammate and someone who was the same age as me.

"Sara?" I said. "It's Richard Willis."

She stared.

"Black River High? Tennis team?"

Her eyes widened in recognition.

"Richie?" She said my name finally, but it came out with a tinge of sadness attached as she unconsciously compared her physical condition to mine. She did manage a smile.

"You're back in town?" she asked.

"Trying to close up my mother's estate," I said. "How've you been?" I immediately realized the stupidity of that question.

"I've been wonderful," she answered sarcastically. "How about you?"

I opened my mouth to apologize for the stupid question, but she raised a hand to stop me.

"What brings you out to this shithole?"

Though it wasn't a shithole, it might be on the rim of a shithole. But I didn't say that.

"I've been trying to get a handle on some old classmates and thought you might be able to help. Do you have a few minutes?"

"Well, I was going to go jogging," she said with a wry smile, "but I guess I can spare you a little of my time. Come on in."

I headed up the ramp and held the door open as she wheeled herself inside.

"Can I get you something to drink?" she asked without turning back to me.

"Thanks, no," I said.

The front door had opened into a tiny entryway, beyond which a medium size living room appeared to my left and a dining room was straight ahead. Sara wheeled herself to the cluttered, chrome-legged dining table and gestured for me to sit in a matching vinyl covered chair on the opposite side. A picture window over the table looked out on a backyard of wild brown grass where a lonely lawn mower lay rusting.

"Excuse the mess," she said, waving a thin hand at the stacks of papers and folders on the table. "I'm dealing with some Medicaid and insurance issues."

"Sorry." I didn't know what else to say. The young, athletic tennis player I remembered had morphed into this wheelchair-bound old woman.

"It's okay," she said in a voice sad and tired. "I know what it looks like."

"What happened?" I asked finally. "Accident?"

"I wish it was an accident," she said with a snort of a laugh. "Then I'd have someone else to blame." Just sitting there, she was working hard to catch her breath. "This is all on me."

She bent over and scratched the ears of the dog that had settled under the table to keep an eye on me.

"Choices," she said. She shook her head to change the subject, looked at me with a smile and asked how I had been doing. We spent a few minutes exchanging small talk and telling each other semi-truths about what we had been doing since our school years, talking about jobs, kids and old classmates.

"I was at the cemetery," I said "and passed by Shannon Baumgartner's grave. I had completely forgotten about what happened to her."

Sara seemed startled by the name, then grew sad and mumbled, "Shannon. . ." She looked over at me. "She and I played doubles. Should never have happened."

"Drowned, right?"

Sara didn't answer. Her lips were moving, and she looked so stricken, I was afraid maybe she had had a stroke until she went into a weak, wet coughing fit. When she had recovered and cleared her throat, she turned back to me.

"So, you are staying at Marty's," she said, "trying to find some kids from school and you end up out here?"

"Actually, just one kid," I admitted.

"Who?"

"Jean Sorenson."

She seemed stricken again.

"Jean. Yeah . . . murdered," Sara said.

"I know," I said.

Sara frowned and gave me a questioning look.

"What happened to her?" I asked. "How'd she end up beaten and buried like that?"

"Jean . . ."

"Weren't you and Jeannie friends?" I asked. "Her sister Julie mentioned it."

Turning towards the window, Sara shrugged.

"Maybe more friendly than actual friends," she said.

"You were still here in town then, right, when she was killed?"

Sara was struggling with something. She would turn, open her mouth almost to say something, then turn back to search out the window.

"It would really help me," I said. "She and I had been best friends and then we lost track of each other."

"I hated what happened to her," she said, still looking out the window. "It scared me."

Sara was quiet, but breathing hard, looking like she was trying to remember something. I waited and watched and then Sara took as deep a breath as she could take.

"It was hard to know Jean," she said. "I mean, I knew her: we would meet at The Dump for a burger, go to movies once in a while, be at Starview Lanes sometimes. But still, I never really knew her."

"Why not?"

"Wouldn't let anyone know her. She wouldn't let anyone get close to her. At least not that I ever saw. Kept people at arm's length."

"Even you?"

"Yeah. You could have fun doing things, laughing about news, talking about people, but she would never talk about herself or her family."

"Ever go to her house?" I asked.

"Tried to invite myself over once or twice but she would always find a way out." She was remembering more details. "And then there was her brother."

"Pete."

"Serious asshole. Never could figure that out."

"What do you mean?" I asked.

She looked away again. Then she shook her head and shrugged. "I dunno."

"Did he do something? Say something?"

She didn't look at me. "Just . . . scared me." She took a breath. "I'm not sure how to explain it, I mean, it was years ago."

"Please try."

She turned to me, puzzled. "He was mean, I guess you could say. Angry. Serious temper. Especially when it came to his sisters. Maybe angry at them? Maybe protective? I don't know."

I pushed harder. "Is there a chance he did something to Jeannie?"

She sat up straighter, placing her hands on the wheels of her chair like she was going to move and frowned at me.

"What do you mean?" she said.

"Could he have been hurting her?"

She shrank back into her chair shaking her head. "I don't like these kinds of questions," she said, unlocking the wheels on her chair.

"Please. . . "

Sara reached for her wheels to move away, but I leaned forward and as gently as possible, placed my hands on the arms of her chair and used the softest tone of voice I could manage.

"Sara . . . many years ago, Jeannie did something for me. At that time, I didn't understand . . . I mean . . . I didn't appreciate what she did. I was an idiot and I fucked up that friendship. Now, Jeannie's gone." I held her stare. "I can't change that, but maybe I can . . . I don't know . . . atone, maybe? If I can somehow figure out what happened, understand who did this and why, maybe there's a chance I can find some justice for her."

Sara stared at me.

"And maybe some sort of peace for myself," I said. "Please?"

As I watched the woman, tears welled up in her eyes and when I pulled my hands away from the armrests, she turned her chair slowly away from me and rolled off a few feet. After a beat, she turned her chair back to me, a terrible struggle showing on her shrunken, wrinkled face.

"I wasn't a good friend," she said quietly. "Or maybe I was the wrong kind of friend."

I sat back in my chair.

"You talking about drugs?"

She gave me a surprised look.

"Jeannie's sister told me," I said.

I watched waves of emotions sweep over Sara's face: fear, sadness and what looked like regret. She raised her eyes up to look at me, her gaze then drifting over to the stack of papers on her dining room table and then she started rolling back.

"I started early," she said in a halting, quiet voice. "Middle school. It was a birthday party and I was feeling pretty shitty. Home-life sucked. A friend saw me, felt bad for me and slipped me a pill, said it was a love drug. Safe as aspirin, he said."

"Love drug?"

She gave a sad nod.

"I found out later it was ecstasy, you know, MDMA. He said it would make me feel better and, holy fuck, did it ever! That shitty little pill made me forget all about what was happening at home and feel better than I ever remembered feeling. It was fucking amazing. And I wanted more."

She gave me a sad smile. "I got more." She shook her head and shrugged. "Pretty typical story after that. Like a bad TV movie. Before I was a senior in high school, I was smoking, drinking, huffing and pill-popping."

Sara reached out to an overstuffed manila folder that was on the table, lifted it up and waved it at me. I recognized the logo of a major cancer research hospital on the envelope.

"Shoulda seen the warning signs of what would happen," she said, "but what kid understands mortality? My parents died young. Cancers, organ failures, heart disease. That should have been a warning." She let out a crisp cough of a laugh. "The only thing they left me was their shitty genes, so now my lungs, liver and kidneys are pretty much gone. And soon . . ." She drifted off.

She dropped the envelope back onto the table.

I stared.

"Choices," she said.

What do you say to someone who has just told you that they are dying? All I could think to do was place a gentle hand on her forearm.

"I'm so sorry, Sara," I said in a near whisper.

She nodded a tiny appreciation at me, then pushed my hand away.

"And you didn't see any of it," she said. "So strait-laced, so goody-goody that you couldn't tell that me and Shannon were high most of the times we were playing tennis." Her tone had a subtle, bitter edge.

"There was a lot I didn't see," I said, "which is why I was asking about Jeannie."

Sara nodded.

"We got together during our junior year, I think." She fiddled with the cannula as she searched for the memory then pointed a finger at me when she remembered. "Harvest vacation. That's when it was. We were working on a spud combine out on the Marlowe farms. During breaks, we'd hide behind the spud trucks smoking weed."

"What was she like then?"

"Quiet. Tired. Wary."

"Wary," I said. Sara was the second person to use that word. "Wary of what?"

"Everything."

"Was that before her dad died?" I asked.

"I think so," she said.

"Was Pete around?" I asked.

"He was driving truck for Marlowe. I think that's how Jean got the job on the combine."

"What was he like then?"

"The same asshole." She was recalling more. "Annoying. Always butting in when Jean and I were hanging out. Wanting to know what we were doing. What we were talking about. If he caught Jean with a doobie, he'd yank it out of her mouth and toss it."

"What did she do?"

"She'd just flip him off and as soon as he was gone, she'd light up another."

"She ever say why he acted that way?"

"I asked, but she always brushed me off, saying he was just an ass."

"Did she have many friends?"

Sara shook her head. "Not really. At least, not that I remember. Mostly hung out with her sister."

"Boyfriends?"

Sara stared blankly for a moment, breathing a little harder. I was worried that I was exhausting her.

"Look…" Sara said finally, "you gotta remember that you're asking me about stuff from like thirty years ago when I was too fucked up on booze and drugs to remember much. And we weren't like best friends or anything. We were friendly, got high together once in a while, but not a lot more than that."

"Sorry," I said.

"I just don't remember," she said, looking out the window. "There could have been guys, but I'm not sure."

"Who were you getting drugs from back then?"

The question startled her and she stared at me, then her eyes slid away once again.

"Too many to remember," she said finally. "They would get arrested, OD on their product, find Jesus and go on a religious mission to South America or get killed by another dealer."

"Remember any names?"

She looked back at me and gave a tight head shake. Something told me she wasn't being honest.

"You sure?"

"I hooked up with dealers in IF and Poky, but they would never give their real names, always some stupid code name like Cola Man or CrackPot." She coughed out a laugh at the memory. "You know, dope wasn't cheap and I didn't always have enough money and so I would have to sometimes exchange, uh, services for my score, but Jean usually had a supply."

"Meaning what?"

"Probably had a reliable dealer."

"A boyfriend who was a dealer?"

She shrugged. "That was a route I took a few times. Make your dealer your boyfriend. You always had the drugs you needed, even if you were broke. But it was a leash. You had to put up with abuse, intimidation and even beatings. They made sure you always owed them and were always in their debt." Tears were coming again. "I did a lot of awful, awful things for dealers who were boyfriends. Bad things . . ."

"But no idea who Jeannie's dealer or boyfriend could have been?"

Sara looked away again. "Like I said, she wouldn't talk much about herself. Maybe her sister knows."

I felt like I was hitting nerves with some questions, but Sara was holding back. Hurt? Scared?

"Having a hard time getting her sister to talk to me," I said finally, looking at her and hoping for more. She just gazed out the window again and I knew I wasn't going to get any more.

"Okay," I said. I sighed and stood up. "Thanks." I started towards the door, but stopped and turned back.

"Sara, the night Jeannie was killed," I started, "she got a call to meet a friend at The Dump. That wasn't you?"

"I was in North Dakota that week for a funeral," she said. "I found out about Jean's murder when I got back."

"The police never came to talk to you about it?"

She shook her head. "I think that after a few months, they just gave up."

I went back to Sara and pressed a hand on her forearm. "Thank you Sara. This has been a help." She nodded. I looked around at the room and at my former classmate, shriveled and exhausted, sitting in her wheel chair, sucking oxygen from a tube in her nose. Dying. I didn't know what to say. Finally, I asked "Is there anything I can do for you?"

She opened her mouth, like there could have been something. She looked up at me, tensed up struggling with something, then slumped back down into her wheelchair and shook her head.

"Just come back when you figure this thing out."

"I will."

"And hurry."

TWENTY-FIVE

By four-thirty that afternoon, I was back in the Brannon County
Court House conference room scrounging through Jeannie's case
files, page by page, trying to see if I had missed something. There was
no mention of a boyfriend and Julie and Pete denied that Jeannie was
in any kind of relationship.

Were they lying?

I pulled out my phone and snapped a picture of the list of people
interviewed. As I did, I noticed a smirking emoticon text from Ellie,
asking how my detecting was going. I emojied back with a Pile-Of-Poo.

"Meet tonight?" I thumbed.

"Nine? Got rehearsal," came the response.

"Marty's? I'll buy."

"Wow. Big spender."

The sarcasm emoji was not needed and we agreed to meet at Marty's
as close to nine as she could manage. Going back to the case files, I
pulled out a beat-up, coffee-stained folder labeled "Autopsy Report"
that I had avoided looking at before.

Fortunately, photos from Jeannie's autopsy were in a closed manila
envelope that I decided not to open. I didn't want to have that image
burned into my brain. I sat it aside and just dug into the statements,
forms and diagrams that took up the rest of the folder. Most of the

information I already knew, but seeing in print the cause of Jeannie's death was horrifying: asphyxia subsequent to blunt force trauma.

I pulled out the diagram of the human skull that was included. The coroner's description said that injuries appeared to have occurred while the victim was already on the ground, postulating that the attacker had pinned her to the ground during the assault. He, assuming it to be a male, had then dug into the plowed up ground and buried her. Had he thought she was already dead? Did he know that he was burying her alive?

I shook that thought off and flipped to the toxicology report. I scanned through the columns of items in the report. Most of them I could recognize, like levels of TCH, alcohol and barbiturates, but there were a few things that I needed to look up. Knowing I couldn't take the report with me, I snapped a picture of the report to google it later.

"Here again?"

I was startled by a voice behind me and turned to see the Sheriff standing at the conference room door.

"Scared me, Gil," I said.

"Sorry Richie," he said entering and dropping into a chair next to me. "Geraldine told me you were back here looking into that girl's case again. I was about to head home for the day and thought I'd see how you were doing."

I waved at the case files that were scattered around me. "I wanted to go back over these to see if there was something I missed."

"Or something we missed?" he asked.

I held up the pile of interview notes. "In all this, there is no mention of a boyfriend. No one like that was even interviewed."

"Yeah?"

"But I've talked to people, credible people, who were pretty sure that Jeannie did have a boyfriend."

"Maybe the people you talked to were wrong, Richie. I mean, it was thirty years ago."

"I don't think they were mistaken, Gil," I said. "They gave me too much detail about people and places and events."

"If it was true, why didn't someone tell the detectives about it?"

"They were never asked," I said.

Gil gave me a sideways, skeptical look.

"That's gotta be bullshit. . ."

"Gil, there wasn't any pressure to ask."

"C'mon. . . "

"The detectives did their due diligence," I said, pointing again to the notes, "they asked the basic questions and chased down the basic leads. After all that, they didn't have a single lead to follow and they didn't have any pressure to keep looking."

"What do you mean?"

"You know how it is, Gil," I said. "An unsolved homicide gets less and less attention over time, unless someone is pushing it. In this case, no one was. Her parents were dead, two siblings were dead and the other two, Pete and Julie were missing in action."

"Okay, yeah, I get that," he said. "But even if what these people told you is true, what's it matter? So, she had a boyfriend. That would be normal, right?"

"Then why is there nothing about a boyfriend in here?" I pointed to the case files. "The first person looked at is always the husband or boyfriend. Why did they all say she didn't have one?"

Gil just stared at me.

"I think they were hiding something," I said.

"Seriously?" He couldn't hide his skepticism.

"That's gotta be it, Gil."

"I really doubt it. Thirty years can mess with memory."

"This doesn't feel like that," I said. Gil sat back in his chair shaking his head. I placed a hand on the pile of papers in front of me. "Gil, can you get one of your guys to take another go at this?"

His forehead wrinkled into a frown.

"I'm no detective, Gil, I said. "I'm an old computer guy and I don't really know what I'm doing with all this. You guys should be doing it."

Gil sat forward, folded his elbows and arms on the table looking at the papers and then at me. "Richie, I'm short-handed and swamped. I can't spare anybody to go back over a thirty-year old case."

"Gil. . ."

He pointed to the collection of detective notes. "I'll bet half of the people they talked to back then are dead and the other half have moved away. That means somebody's gotta give up all the cases they're working on to track down who in these files is dead, who is alive and who is off on a church mission to Mongolia."

"What about getting a detective to talk to Jeannie's brother and sister? Just those two."

Gil pushed his chair back with a sigh and stood. "I'm sorry, Richie, but I don't have the manpower for this. I can free someone up in a couple months, but right now, I can't."

"Okay Gil," I said with a sigh. "Thanks anyway."

He moved to the door, but stopped as he opened it and turned. "Why don't you talk to the brother and sister?"

"I have," I said. "All I've gotten so far is a cracked rib and a bill from a bail bondsman."

"Sounds like you're asking the wrong questions."

And then he was gone.

"You should become a private detective," Tyler said after dropping off two plates of food for Ellie and I at our table at Marty's. He picked up the folder I had laid on an empty chair and sat down. I snatched the folder away. It was stuffed full of printouts from Jeannie's case file and I didn't want him snooping through them.

"There's no PI in Black River, so you would have the market to yourself," he said.

"Tyler. . ." I tried to stop him but he kept going.

"You could start a YouTube channel and film all your exploits." He drew an invisible giant banner in the air and waved his hands over the title. "The Adventures of a Small Town PI. Oh . . .wait . . . The Black River PI. That one sounds cool."

Ellie started laughing.

"And you'd need a crazy little sidekick for comic relief who is also an amazing cook," He continued while hooking his thumbs under imaginary suspenders and proudly puffing up his chest. Then he pointed at Ellie. "Of course, you'd need a love interest to get the female viewers subscribing."

Ellie laughed even harder.

"Okay, Tyler, that's it," I said. "You're fired."

"Hey!" he said.

"Or you can get your ass back to the kitchen where it belongs," I said.

Tyler stood, hands up as if I was pointing a gun at him.

"Okay, okay," he said.

"And hurry," I said, pointing towards the kitchen. "I'm sure there's a burger that needs flipping."

Tyler bowed, gave Ellie a wink -- who, I noticed, returned it -- and made his way back to the kitchen.

"The kid's crazy," I said, "but man, can he cook?"

Ellie mumbled a "Yes" at me through an embarrassingly large mouthful of burger.

We ate in near silence with me hungrily scarfing down my patty melt and fries, realizing I hadn't eaten all day.

Ellie watched me gobbling up food with an amused smile.

"Maybe he's right," she said, breaking the silence between us. I frowned at her. "You should become a private investigator."

I picked up a fry and jabbed it in the air at her. "No way."

"But you're going to keep investigating." She smiled.

"Yes."

"Privately."

"Yes."

"There you go. You're a Private Investigator."

Ellie pointed a ketchup-dappled finger at the folder with a mouth-filled grunt that communicated curiosity.

I flipped the folder around and slid it to her side of the table.

"Copies of some of the files the sheriff had on Jeannie's murder," I said.

She wiped the red tomato goo off her fingers and opened the folder, picking up the top bundle of printouts. She held it up to show me. I nodded.

"Medical examiner's report," I said. "There are items in the blood work that I don't understand. Thought I'd google them."

"Ah yes," Ellie said, her eyes scanning down the page.

"I should have paid more attention during chemistry class," I said, swallowing another hunk of hamburger and watching her read. Suddenly she stopped, re-read something, then looked up at me.

"What?" I asked.

"HCG, 34,700."

"Yeah, I needed to look that one up."

"You don't have to," she said.

"You know what it is?"

She was looking at the paper and nodding.

"How do you know what it is?" I asked.

"Because I'm a woman," she said.

She looked up at me and I was about to say something snarky, but luckily, she spoke first.

"Your friend was pregnant."

I'm pretty sure Ellie saw my jaw drop.

"No," I said.

Ellie pointed to my phone.

"Google it," she commanded. "HCG level and pregnancy."

I looked at her for another beat, then picked up my cell and started thumbing.

"Got it," I said when Doctor Google displayed a small chart of HCG levels that I held up for Ellie. She looked it over and then nodded at me.

"HCG is a hormone that gets cranked up when a woman is pregnant," Ellie said. "According to that chart, Jeannie was about two months along when she died."

"How the hell . . ," I mumbled.

Suddenly, our attention jumped to the front door as two laughing women made a noisy entrance. I was about to turn back to Ellie when I saw that one of the laughers was Rosa Grazzano. She noticed me at the same time.

"Richie!" she called out in a loud, alcohol fueled yell. She gave her girlfriend's arm a squeeze. "Go get us a couple beers. I'll be right there."

The girlfriend made for the bar and Rosa turned our way. Under her breath, I heard Ellie mutter a "Wow."

The 'wow' was seeing a slightly plump, middle-aged woman shoehorned into a pair of too-small jeans strutting towards us, her massive breasts bouncing in siliconic independence beneath a sheer cotton blouse. She came to our table, slid a chair next to mine and plopped down onto it, pressing up against me.

"I totally forgot that you own this place," she said, waving her arms as if revealing the room to me for the first time. "The place to be in Black River on a Friday night." She smiled at Ellie, suddenly cognizant of another female's presence and, noticing all the papers spread out on the table, twisting her head to try to read them.

"Rosa," I said, "this is Eleanor Fife. She teaches at ISU. Ellie, this is Rosa Clawson— "

"Grazzano," she corrected, still trying to see what all the papers were.

"Sorry. Grazzano," I said. "Her brother Robbie and I were mortal enemies during high school."

Ellie nodded a greeting. "I remember you talking about the fights."

"They don't fight anymore," Rosa said.

"Well," Ellie said, "the eight hundred miles separating them helps a little with that."

Rosa laughed a little louder than she needed to and then pressed up even tighter against me.

"You still haven't called," she said in a voice failing to sound sexy. She picked up the papers, starting to shuffle through them, reading. "Too busy with all these?"

I snatched the papers away, handing them to Ellie.

"That reminds me, Rosa, you said you knew Julie Sorenson, right?"

That threw her off her game.

"Well . . .yeah, uh . . . sort of," she answered.

"How well?"

"I guess like enough to say hello. Small talk and shit. Why?"

"Not close enough to like drop by for a friendly chat or go out for coffee?"

"No," she said, confused. "Why?"

"I'm having trouble getting Julie to talk to me. Thought an old friend of hers might help."

Ellie jumped in.

"Rich thinks his friend, Jeannie, might have had a boyfriend that the police didn't know about," she said.

Rosa pointed a finger at Ellie.

"You helping?" she asked.

Ellie smiled. "Moral support."

"The detectives back then were told she had no boyfriend," I said, "but I think she did."

Rosa was shaking her head.

"As much as I'd like to help you, Richie," she said finally, standing up and placing a hand on my shoulder, "that was a hundred years ago and I don't really want to be involved with that or even think about it. So, you'll have to count me out." She gave my shoulder a gentle squeeze and bent down towards my ear. "But if you need help with anything else," she said in a low voice, "you've got my number."

Rosa shot Ellie a smile that was one lioness warning another to stay away from the freshly killed wildebeest.

And I was the wildebeest.

Ellie watched Rosa join her gal-pal at the bar, tap freshly opened bottles of beer and start swigging.

"What the hell was that about?" she asked in a low voice.

"Happens to me all the time," I said pointing to myself. "A middle-aged, single woman smells a widower and they pounce."

She slapped my arm.

We went back to talking and eating as the music got louder and the Friday night crowd grew bigger.

"Why don't we get out of here and go for a walk along the river?" I asked when we finished our burgers. I tapped the folder of papers. "Forget about all this for a little while."

Ellie nodded. "Sounds nice. I didn't bring a jacket. Got something I could borrow?"

"In my closet," I said, starting to get up. She stopped me.

"I'll go up and get it," she said. "You bus the table."

"Deal," I said. I handed her the folder. "Could you toss these up there when you go?"

She nodded and headed for the stairs while I cleared the table. A few minutes later, she came back out holding a baggy, faded blue knit sweater. I looked at the sweater, at her and smiled. She held it up.

"You kept it," she said.

I nodded.

"Why?"

"It still fits," I said.

We started for the door, Ellie pulling the sweater on over her head. Rosa had settled into a table with her friend and I gave her a wave as I passed and caught up with Ellie on the front steps of the place, the door closing behind us.

"I can't believe you kept this ugly old sweater," she said, holding the loosely knit material out and giving it a light stretch. "This was the only thing I ever knitted. I totally screwed up the measurements. Way too big."

"I remember."

"But you kept it."

"Some things you just can't give up."

Ellie looked at me for a long moment, then smiled, nodded, took my arm and we started off for the river walkway.

The Black River coursed along the western border of the city not far from Marty's, beyond a nearly impenetrable band of trees where a pathway followed the river north and south of town. Ducking through a short, arched opening in the tight stand of trees, we popped out onto the path that followed the slow-moving Black River as it meandered along. A light breeze was skimming over the water, freshening the cool, autumn air on a cloudless October night. I looked up and down the gravel footpath.

"Which way?" I asked.

Ellie took in a deep whiff of the evening air, let it out and pointed to our right, upstream. We started off.

We followed the river, talking and laughing. After half a mile we stopped where the river dropped three feet over a natural rock dam that extended all the way across it. I pointed upstream.

"When I was a kid, my dad would take me fishing," I said. "Early in the morning, we would put his little old aluminum boat into the river about ten miles upstream and spend the day floating downstream until we got right there." I pointed across the river to the willow covered bank. "We'd pull the boat out there, thirsty and sunburned, but with a boatload of trout."

Ellie bent down, sorted through some rocks until she found a flat one and tried skipping it across the water. Two bounces and it was underwater.

"I used to be pretty good at that," she said. She planted herself and let another rock fly. She got three bounces.

"Eleanor . . ." I started.

"Uh oh," she said, tossing in a third stone. "He used my full name. Must be a serious question coming."

I sat down on the riverbank and scooped up a handful of rocks.

"Gonna let me talk or are you gonna give me shit the rest of the night?"

"I'll let you talk," she said. "Still gonna give you shit, though."

I growled and tossed a rock into the river, trying to hit the broken off limb of a willow tree that was floating there. I missed it. Ellie dropped down on the bank next to me.

"It's about you and me, right?" Ellie asked.

I nodded.

Ellie put her arm around my shoulder and laid her head against me.

"The honest answer to the question you were going to ask is . . . I don't know, Rich." She took a deep breath. "Matthew and I have been married for twenty-three years, but we have lived separate lives since my son was born. That was more than twenty years ago."

"Sorry. . . "

"No need to be," she said. "I didn't mind the situation at all. I got to raise my son the way I wanted, do my work while Matthew did his. We never fought or argued." She shrugged and glanced up at me with a sad smile. "Basically, we became housemates and I was content with that. Matthew and I get along fine." She paused, took a long breath and let it out. "But then, here comes Rich Willis into town."

"I feel like I'm supposed to apologize," I said.

"Let me finish, okay?"

I looked at her. "Of course."

Eleanor stood, walked a few steps away and tossed another rock into the river.

"Matthew has had more than a couple of flings over the years and I haven't minded. In fact, right now, he has a fairly serious female friend back in Chicago."

"Where he's attending a conference."

"It's okay. In fact, I had my own little dalliance a few years ago."

"Oh?"

"Big mistake. Grad student. Too young for an old lady like me. Ever try to explain prog rock to a guy who has a One Direction poster on his dorm room wall?"

"His dorm room?" I said in mock shock.

Ellie ignored me.

"It was a fling. Nothing more."

"Did Matthew know about it?" I asked.

"We have a sort of don't-ask, don't-tell pact," she said, "and it works. Looking back at my little liaison, it was like something I needed . . . I guess to know that I was still attractive."

"So, what about us?" I asked.

Ellie sat back down next to me, shrugged her shoulders.

"Is it possible that I'm trying to relive what we were in college? Or is it more than that?"

I stared out at the river.

"This last week has been so much fun," she said. "I had forgotten what that was like. It has been a sort of a re-awakening." She paused.

"But?"

"Is it real? Or is it an old lady's vain attempt to recapture her lost youth?"

"That's usually a guy thing," I said. "You know, red sports car, young, vapid blonde girl, hair plugs and lapsed gym memberships."

"That happen to you?"

"Not yet," I said with a smile. She smiled back, then looked away.

Silence.

"So, what do we do?" I asked.

"I wish I knew," she said wistfully.

"Just keep testing?"

She smiled and turned back to me, planting a kiss on my cheek. "Yes. Keep testing and enjoy it. C'mon. Let's head back. This old sweater of yours isn't warm enough."

We walked back down the path in silence, enjoying the sound of the rustling leaves in one ear and the burbling river in the other until I pointed to an arched opening.

"I think that's where we--"

I stopped abruptly.

Ellie stopped and looked at me, opened her mouth to ask a question, but I held up a finger. She furrowed a brow and I pointed towards the trees, leaning in close to her.

"I thought I heard my name," I whispered.

"What?" she said.

We stood motionless, listening.

"Uh huh," came a woman's voice from the other side of the trees. Then "Yeah."

"Someone on a phone," Ellie whispered. "You heard your name?"

I nodded.

Ellie bent down, trying to see through the thicket of trees and bushes.

"A car," she said pointing to the bottom half of a set of radials.

"I don't know how," the woman was saying, "but he knows she was pregnant."

"Who is it?" Ellie asked.

"Need to get through these trees," I said

"Where did we come through?"

"I thought it was here, but it's not. Where the hell is it?"

We headed further down the walkway looking for the opening and still trying to hear.

"It's not my job, asshole," the woman was saying. "This was your mess." A pause. "No, I won't." Another pause. "I told you all I know. You figure it out." An electronic beep told us she had clicked off. "Asshole," we heard her mumble.

A car started.

"C'mon!" I said taking off on a run down the path looking for the opening. Where was it? Ellie came running after me and I finally found the narrow path through the trees and dashed through in time to see the car speed away. Ellie emerged behind me.

"Damn," she said, watching the tail lights disappear. She looked at me. "You know who that was?"

"Yeah, I know."

TWENTY-SIX

"The woman with the big fake tits? Yeah, I saw her go back down the hall. To the bathrooms," Jia said. "You think she went upstairs?"

I nodded.

I was standing at the bar, relating what we had heard to Jia, who was on the other side polishing glasses. Marie and Camila were working the tables.

"I didn't hear anyone on the stairs," she said.

"I did," announced Tyler leaning over the service counter behind Jia, while drying his hands on a greasy white rag.

Jia turned to him. "What did you hear?"

"Creaking stairs," he said, pointing up at the ceiling. "At the top. They always squeak. I thought maybe it was Rich or his girlfriend going up there. Maybe forgot something."

We all turned hearing Eleanor tromp down the stairs and emerge from the hallway, dropping onto a stool next to me.

"You were right," she said. "I laid that folder on the edge of the bed but now it's on the table at the other end of the room. She was up there."

I sighed, shaking my head.

"She stole something?" Tyler asked.

"Should I call the police?" Jia asked.

Ellie touched my shoulder. "Maybe this will get your buddy the sheriff to re-open the case."

"What would I tell him?" I asked. "We heard someone talking to someone on their cell about someone knowing that someone was pregnant?"

"You're pregnant?" Tyler asked Jia.

She glared at him. "Don't you have something to burn back there?"

He smiled back. "No."

"An overheard conversation is useless," I said. "Gotta figure out who she was calling."

"How do we do that?" Ellie asked.

I turned to her. "We?"

She smiled.

"Hack her phone," Tyler said.

"You know her number? Is her phone here somewhere?" I asked.

"No . . ."

I just shrugged and shook my head at him.

Ellie pointed towards a corner of the ceiling and we all followed her eye to the security camera.

"Think there's anything on that?" Jia asked.

"Let's check," I said and started towards the hall, Ellie right behind me.

"Very cool!" Tyler said, following us. Then he stopped and turned as he heard the front door open and he saw a half dozen laughing kids flood in.

"Tyler?" Jia called. "Kitchen."

"Damn." Tyler turned dejectedly back toward the kitchen.

Minutes later, Ellie and I were up in the musty old storeroom, seated in front of the security monitor, scrolling back through the evening's recordings.

She pointed to the timestamp at the bottom right of the video and arched her eyebrows at me.

"Yes," I said wearily, "I know. The clock is twenty-four hours ahead. I'll get to it."

She just rolled her eyes at me and shook her head. Turning back to the screen, she watched people walking awkwardly backward as I re-wound, then she suddenly tapped the screen.

"There."

It was the point where Ellie and I had walked out the front door. I pressed play.

"She watched us leave," Ellie said pointing at Rosa on the screen. "The woman she is with is talking but your friend is watching us leave."

We saw Rosa turn back to her companion and say something.

"No sound, huh?"

"Old camera," I said.

"Read lips?"

"As well as you," I said.

"Shit."

About a minute after we watched ourselves walk out in the video, we could see Rosa say something to her companion, get up and walk towards the hall, out of view of the camera.

"Note the time," I said.

We kept an eye on the screen's time display and when she came back into view of the camera, more than five minutes had passed.

"Plenty of time," Ellie said. "Ran upstairs, found the folder, did a quick read of the autopsy report and then back down."

I nodded, watching the recording as Rosa sat, exchanged a few words, then pulled her phone out of her purse, scrolled, selected something on the tiny screen and pressed it to her ear.

"Who's she calling?" Ellie asked.

Rosa clicked off almost immediately.

"She got voicemail." Ellie said.

"Or changed her mind," I said.

Rosa stood and said something to her companion, who returned an expression of disappointment but stood and the women hugged. Then Rosa dropped a few bills on the table and hustled out the door.

I reached for the mouse to turn the playback off, but Ellie grabbed my hand.

"Look," she said.

Rosa's friend had sat back down to finish her drink when Camila walked over with her order pad. When the woman indicated that she wasn't going to order anything else, Camila laid the check on the table and then, to our surprise, pulled up a chair and sat, chatting.

"They're friends," Ellie said, tapping the screen.

I turned the camera playback off and the monitor went back to watching customers eating and drinking. The person Camila had been chatting up was gone.

"Maybe your server could tell you who that woman was," Ellie said. "And maybe she would know who Rosa was trying to call."

I turned to look up at her.

"Coulda been Pete," I said.

"Huh?"

"Jeannie's brother, Pete."

"Yeah?"

"She might have been calling him," I said.

"Why?"

"Rosa used to go out with Pete."

"Okay," Ellie said, "but that's a weird leap to be calling an old boyfriend."

"People say Pete was angry and abusive, territorial about his sisters. Like he owned them."

"But why call him to tell her that Jeannie had been pregnant?" Then her eyes got big and her jaw dropped. "No," she gasped.

Eleanor reached out and grabbed my wrist, her eyes bulging, shaking her head. "You can't think Pete knocked up his own sister?"

I stood, she released her hold and I stepped away, trying to think. She followed me. I could feel my pulse rate going up.

"And you think Rosa was calling him to tell him that you had found out about the pregnancy? That's another huge leap, Rich."

"It would explain a lot," I said, turning back to her. "Pete jumping me when I tried to ask him about Jeannie."

"But killing her?" she asked. "Just because she was pregnant?"

"Maybe they got in argument about it and Pete lost his temper. My ribs are proof of his temper."

"Then he beat her up and buried her in an old potato field?" She was incredulous.

"I've gotta talk to him."

I turned toward the door but before I got two steps, Ellie was in front of me, a hand pressed to my chest.

"Hold on, cowboy," she said. "You are making way too many leaps of logic there."

"But I've got too . . ."

"No," she commanded.

I stopped and stared at her, wide-eyed. She patted my chest and spoke with a forced calmness.

"You're pissed off that this Pete guy kicked in your rib cage and it's messing with your thinking. That silicon bimbo might have been calling somebody else, not Pete. We've got to figure that out. Before we do anything else."

I didn't say anything. Just looked at her.

"Well?" she asked.

"I just remembered what bugged me about you twenty years ago."

Ellie straightened, hands on her waist, daring me to give her an answer she didn't like. "What?"

"The fact that you are always right."

Again, I started for the door, but again she stopped me, but this time she was pointing to the security monitor. On the live feed I could see a man in work clothes talking to Camila. He must have come in while Ellie and I were talking. I went to the monitor to get a closer look.

"It's Rob Clawson," I said.

"That woman's brother?"

On the screen, he said something to Camila, then turned and left.

"What's that about?" Ellie asked.

"Let's find out."

"He was looking for his sister," Camila said when we caught up with her as she was getting ready to leave for the night. "The woman with the big watermelons on her chest."

"Did he say why?" I asked.

"He said he was supposed to meet her here," she said. "His sister had something of his or for him or something."

"But he didn't say what?"

"No," Camila said.

"Coincidence?" Ellie asked me.

"Or did Rosa call him?" I asked back.

"Did he say anything else at all, Camila?" Ellie asked.

"No. Just looking for his sister."

"The woman who was with the big boob lady," I said, "you knew her."

"Nessa," Camila said.

"Friend of yours?" Eleanor asked.

Camila waved her head back and forth, like she was weighing the relationship. "Not really. Just someone I know from church. We're both in the choir. But she sings with the soprano section. I'm an alto."

"Did this Nessa say anything about the woman she was with?" I asked. "Like who she had been trying to call?"

"I wasn't paying attention to what they were talking about," Camila said.

"What about the phone call," Ellie asked. "Rosa's call."

"Don't know anything about any phone call."

"Nessa didn't say anything?" I asked.

"Why would she?"

"Just hoping," I said. "Do you have Nessa's number?"

"No. Like I said, I just know her from the Sunday choir. I don't even know her last name."

"Okay. Thanks Camila. Sorry to hold you up."

"It's okay," she said, standing and gathering herself back up. "I hope you two figure out what ever it is you are trying to figure out." She gave Marie and Jia a wave. "Tomorrow girls."

As she left, Ellie and I dropped into chairs. I slouched, staring at the door.

"Well?" Ellie asked.

"Yeah," I said.

"So, what do we do now, Detective Willis?"

Jia stepped over to the table and laid two foaming glasses of beer down.

"Thought you might need these."

"Thanks," Ellie said grabbing one and draining half the glass."

"Camila couldn't help?" Jia asked.

I shook my head. "We need to figure out who Rosa was calling."

"Any way we could get her phone and look at her call list?" Ellie asked.

"You mean like hold her down while you rifle through her purse to get to her PIN protected cell?"

Ellie sighed dejectedly. "Yeah . . ."

We all sat silently for a few minutes.

I looked at Jia.

Jia looked at Ellie.

Ellie looked at me.

I shrugged.

"Okay," I said. "I guess the answer is obvious."

"It is?" Ellie tilted her head with a puzzled look.

"I'm just going to have to go ask her."

Twenty-Seven

Trudging through a plowed up old potato field, shivering with the cold, I'm stumbling over mounds of raised earth, smelling dirt and rotting plants.

In front of me, there's a ribbon of curly yellow hair blowing in the wind, then a hand emerging from the ground, then another, then hands pushing soil away and I see a face, almost recognize it, then something hits me from behind, knocking me down and I look back and see a big shadow moving closer and getting bigger and bigger and bigger.

"Rich!"

I jerked awake, looking around in near panic until I realized it was Saturday morning, it was my room above the bar and Ellie was lying next to me in the bed. I shook my head to clear away the fog.

"Sorry," I said hoarsely.

"It's okay," she said snuggling close and laying her head gently on my still bandaged chest. "That same dream?"

"A little different. In this one, it was like she was pulling herself out of the ground as I got closer and then there was a shadow of something behind me and then you woke me up."

"You were making whimpering noises. Scared me. I had to wake you."

"Sorry," I repeated.

She shrugged it off. "Been awake for a while."

"You okay?"

"Yeah." Ellie's long fingers were tracing the edge of the Ace bandage wrapped around my chest. I brushed her thick hair away from her face and she looked up to see the question on my face, then laid her had back down on my chest facing away.

"You've changed," she said after a moment.

"I hope so," I said. "Those boxers were getting pretty rank."

"God!" she said, giving my ribs a little jab.

I moaned. "Sorry."

"You know what I mean. I don't see much of that selfish guy I dated in college."

"I hope not," I said, caressing her soft shoulders.

"And it's making my life a little difficult."

"Is this all a mistake?" I asked. She didn't answer for a few moments.

"A few days ago," she said slowly, "I had thought that this was just a little fling with an old boyfriend."

"And now?"

"And now, I don't know."

"No?"

She sighed. "Hell, maybe it is just a silly dalliance, since you are going back to Bellingham next week."

"If I go back."

Ellie turned to look up at me. "Whaddya mean?"

"This is a leave of absence from work, not a vacation." Ellie pulled herself out of the blankets and sat up cross-legged, throwing me a confused, expectant look, waiting for more. I continued. "I have to let the department know if I'm coming back or not."

"Why wouldn't you go back?"

"Mid-life crisis?" I said with a half-smile.

"You're too old for that."

"Thanks," I said.

"Really. C'mon, why?"

I took a deep breath. "Bunch of reasons: my wife's been gone for more than two years; I've sold my business to my daughter who is thriving on her own without me and this job as a forensic technician has settled into a routine that is just . . . routine."

"Boring."

"There's no challenge to it. I'm not writing apps, not hacking, not doing tech security work."

"What would you do then?"

I shrugged. "Start another small business or join another company. I could write apps, but any twelve-year old can do that now using ChatGPT to write the code." Ellie laughed. "Maybe travel? Maybe not quit? Maybe move back here and run a bar."

Ellie straightened up. "Stay here?" she asked.

"Would that cause you problems?" I looked at her but I wasn't sure what I wanted her answer to be. Did she like the idea of me staying? Or would it complicate her life too much?

Ellie stared at me for a long minute, opened her mouth to speak, then stopped herself and laid down next to me, both of us staring up at the stained and cracking plaster ceiling. I heard her take a deep breath.

"You can't think about me, Richie," she said. "You decide what you want. Think of me as a one-night stand."

"It's been three or four nights."

She elbowed me in the ribs, then realized what she had done when I cried out in pain. "Sorry, sorry." She rolled over and gently rubbed where she had elbowed me.

"It's okay," I said. "It's time for me to get going." I sat up, trying to hide the pain it caused. "Whaddya say to breakfast?"

"Maybe coffee. And half a Danish."

"And a half-tab of oxycodone," I said, groaning in pain while pulling on some boxers. "Then how about we hit the library to talk to Rosa and then drive to Pocatello to see if we can get Julie to talk to us?"

"I can't." Ellie slipped off the bed, stretched and gathered up her clothes to get dressed. "We have a tech rehearsal this morning. It'll last most of the day."

"Can I pick you up after I talk to Julie?"

She shook her head. "No idea when we'll finish. How 'bout I meet you back here tonight?"

We agreed and headed out for caffeine and sugar.

It was nearly noon when I stepped into the Black River Public Library, but this time Rosa wasn't at the front desk. A pimply-faced, red-headed kid was there, with a small stack of books. I watched him open a book, stamp something on the inside front cover, then go to the back of the book and glue something in place there. I stopped at the desk.

"RFID tag?"

The kid jumped when I spoke.

"Hey, man," the kid said, "'bout made me crap my pants. Don't sneak up on me like that."

"Sorry kid," I said. "Wasn't trying to be sneaky. Rosa around?"

"Who?"

"Rosa. Rosa Grazzano?"

It was almost like he didn't understand the question. I waited a beat, hoping his brain would click into gear. It didn't.

"She works here," I said. "Middle aged woman?"

"They're all middle aged here," he said.

I was getting so frustrated with the kid, I wanted to reach across the desk and pop every zit on his face.

"Short. Dark hair." He looked at me, scrunched up his face, shaking his head. I sighed. "This woman," I said and threw him the universal gesture for large breasts. He snapped a finger at me.

"That old lady," he said. I nodded. "She's in back."

I stared. He went back to his book.

I slapped my hand down on the desk. He jumped and looked up at me. "Go get her!"

He jumped up. "Okay, man. Okay."

He headed into the back. I just shook my head and walked away from the desk, attempting to control a homicidal urge by wandering down a random aisle and finding myself between rows of bookshelves in the history section. I was lost in a photo book of early Eastern Idaho settlements when a pair of arms wrapped around my waist and hugged me tight.

"Hi Rosa," I said, grabbing her wrists to free myself.

"Shh," she whispered playfully, "this is a library."

"I know."

I wasn't in a mood to play and managed to pry her grip loose and then I spun around to face her, but she wrapped her arms around me again pinning my arms to my waist. She squeezed.

"Ever do it in a library?" she whispered.

"Twice in college," I said, working my arms loose.

"Third time's the charm," she said.

"God damn it!" I said, grabbing her arms above the elbow twisting her to the side and shoving her hard. Her heels caught the carpet and she tumbled backward onto the floor.

"Asshole!" she said.

"God, Rosa . . ."

Pimply-face heard the noise and peaked around the corner, staring at Rosa struggling to get off the floor.

"You okay?" he asked finally.

"Fine," Rosa growled.

"She slipped on a banana peel," I said.

The kid looked dumbly around the floor then said "Huh?"

"Back to your desk, kid," I said, with a sense of authority that surprised even me. It must have worked because he backed away while I helped Rosa to her feet.

"Didn't have to do that," she said, straightening her skirt and tucking her blouse in.

"Sorry, didn't mean to," I said.

"But you did it."

"Again, sorry. I just wanted to ask you a few simple questions and you come out here and start groping me."

"Ask me?"

"Yeah. Last night, after you left Marty's, who'd you call?"

A pause. She made a thinking-hard expression. "Last night?"

"Yeah. I heard you."

"Heard me?" She was shaking her head, avoiding my look. "I don't know what you're talking about."

"Rosa, last night, after you left Marty's, you got in your car, drove over by the trees along the river and then you called and talked to someone. You told them about what you saw when you snuck up to my room and read Jeannie's autopsy report."

She stared at me. She had been caught and she would either have to make up some story or would have to deny it all outright.

She chose the latter.

"I did not sneak up to wherever your room is and look at whatever it is you're talking about."

She tried to walk past me but I stopped her. "You did go up there. We have you on video. And then you called somebody to tell them that I had found out about Jeannie's pregnancy."

"Not true."

"I heard you."

"No, you're mistaken."

"Rosa, if you won't tell me who you called, my friends down at the sheriff's office will subpoena your phone records and get it for me." It was a complete lie, but my years as an actor paid off, because she believed me.

She looked at me, scared, speechless.

"They can't. . ."

I just looked her straight in the eye and lied. "Yes, they can."

She looked away, confusion, fear and anger battling until anger finally won out and she pushed past me.

"Get outa here," she said. "Or I call security."

She got to the pimply-faced kid's desk with me on her heels and she spun around to face me.

"Just tell me who, Rosa. Who did you call?"

She came one step closer, jabbed a finger at me and in a controlled, furious whisper said "Get out now or security hauls you out."

We locked pairs of angry eyes for a moment, with pimply-face reaching for the phone, but stopping when I nodded. I backed up and turned, heading for the doors. I opened them, stepped out, then looked back. Rosa was looking away, far away, like someone struggling to work out a math problem. Pimply-face was talking but she wasn't paying attention. It looked like she was mouthing some words, then her expression turned to confusion.

Then to fear.

TWENTY-EIGHT

I was in front of Julie's beaten-up little cottage by late afternoon. It felt
empty and her car wasn't in the driveway, but I went up to the door
anyway, knocked and got what I expected: nothing.

I stood on her porch, staring out at the ragged little neighborhood,
an unopened bottle of vodka in my hand that I had picked up as a
peace offering. What to do? I could drive back to Black River, wait a
few hours, then drive back. That would be a huge time-suck. I could
call her, but, of course, I didn't have her cell number. I sat myself down
on the steps to figure out what to do.

I wasn't sitting for very long when the decision was made for me:
Julie's crappy old Camry raced in and rattled to a stop in her driveway.
With a cigarette dangling from the side of her mouth and carrying a
plastic bag of groceries, she slipped out of the car and slammed the
door shut, stomping towards me. I held up the vodka bottle.

"Peace offering," I said.

Julie stopped. Looked at me skeptically, then at the bottle.

"Peace offering, huh?"

"Yup," I said. She exhaled, shook her head and joined me on the
steps.

I cracked the vodka bottle open, tipped the bottle up and took a
swallow. To be honest, I hated vodka. I was more a beer and cider guy,

but I figured us appearing to be vodka guzzling buddies might help things along, so I forced a mouthful down then held the bottle out to her.

"Worried about boy germs?" I asked.

She let out an exasperated huff. "Fuck no."

Julie took the bottle raised it in a toast gesture then took a long drink, followed by a satisfied sigh. She handed it back.

"Thanks," she said. "Needed that."

"Rough couple days, huh?"

She nodded. "Sorry I jumped all over you yesterday."

"It's okay."

"Bailing me out . . . I'll pay you back."

"Don't worry about it," I said. "Just helping out an old friend."

"Old friend," she said wryly. She snatched the vodka from my hand, took another long drink, then with a sweep of her arm she pushed the bottle back at me, but I wasn't ready and the bottle hit me in the chest. I screamed in pain, stood up and walked away, bent over in agony.

"Shit," she said. "What did I do? You okay?"

I turned back to her and straightened up. "I'll be fine," I moaned. "Cracked ribs."

"What happened?" she asked.

"Ran into your big brother."

"Pete did that?"

I gave her a painful nod, took a few deep breaths and carefully sat back down.

"I made the mistake of asking Pete about Jeannie."

Julie stared at me. "Shit, Richie. What did you expect?" She shook her head and looked away.

"Not that."

We were quiet for a while, watching a squirrel run across the brown grass lawn with a discarded apple core in its mouth. I declined Julie's offer for another swallow and she took a long swig. I decided that small talk might be a good tack so I asked her about what she did after she quit USP, about marriages and all the other non-threatening things old acquaintances talk about. We touched on how I ended up in computer forensics and how she ended up doing hair and nails. As she relaxed more and as the vodka did its work, the talk veered into children. I mentioned my daughter's struggles after her mother died and that seemed to hit a nerve in Julie and she looked off into the foothills, seeing nothing. She stared a long time, then muttered something.

"What?" I asked.

"Glad I never had kids," she said, still staring out.

"Why?"

"This world ain't no place for kids," she said.

"Whaddya mean?"

She just shook her head.

"People pressured you about kids?"

"Fuckers tried," she said. "Jeannie even tried."

"She did?"

"Yeah. You'd think she would know better."

"Why?"

Julie just shook her head.

"I'd like to ask you something," I said. "Was Jeannie happy?"

Julie swallowed her mouthful and gave me a sarcastic half-laugh, half-snort. The vodka was catching up to her.

"Happy. Funny fuckin' word," she said.

"What's that mean?" I asked.

"Home was pretty shitty for us, you know."

"With the deaths, yeah."

"Oh . . .well, yeah," she said, "there was that too."

"What else?" I asked,

"It was pretty bad for me and Jean. Worse for her, I guess."

"Worse how?"

"Farm work. No money. Useless mother, asshole brother . . . asshole father. . ." She snorted a snide little laugh then realized she was talking too much and stopped to take another drink.

"What about your dad?" I asked.

"Nothing. Not anybody's business."

"He do something?"

Julie stood abruptly, but a little shakily. "Time to leave, Willis."

"Wait. . ."

"Need you to go, Richie."

"What happened?" I asked.

"Leave me alone."

"Was someone hurting you? Hurting Jeannie?"

Julie stared at me, speechless.

"Was it Pete?"

Julie answered with another snort.

"Did he do something?" I pressed.

"Didn't do nothin'," she blurted out. "Go away, Richie! Leave me the fuck alone."

She started towards the door. I stood.

"What happened, Julie?"

"Go away." She opened the door.

"Julie!" I said in as commanding a voice as I could muster. She stopped; the door half open. "Didn't you love your sister?"

She slowly turned towards me, tears dripping and stared.

"Fuckin' stupid question, Willis."

"Did you?"

"Of course!" she screamed at me.

"Julie," I said. "Jeannie was pregnant."

Julie jerked back like she had been hit with a hammer. She stammered. "What?"

"Jeannie was pregnant."

Julie was wide-eyed. "How . . . how do you know that?"

"The coroner's report."

She was just looking at me like I was speaking gibberish.

"You didn't know?"

She just stared then turned slowly and walked into her house.

"Julie!" I yelled after her. "Julie! Was it Pete?"

The door slammed shut.

"Julie!" I yelled at the door. "Who got Jeannie pregnant?"

There was silence, except for the sound of the deadbolt locking.

At Marty's, I crashed for a few hours then stumbled down to the bar and plopped onto a stool. I must have slept longer than I thought. It was already early evening and the Saturday night crowd was trickling in. After sending Marie off to a table with beers and glasses, Jia came over to me.

"You look like shit," the redhead said with her crooked little smile. "Caffeine?"

"Please."

Jia pulled a mug from under the bar and began filling it.

"Hangover?"

"Just tired," I said. "Shitty, frustrating day." I told Jia about confronting Rosa and Julie and being repulsed by both.

"You were expecting something else?" Jia asked.

"There's something they're not telling me," I said.

"But you don't know what?"

I shook my head.

"I tried scare tactics on Rosa," I said, "and tried guilt-tripping Julie. Didn't work." I gulped down a few swallows of coffee.

"I wish I could help," Jia said.

"Me too, but I don't know how you could and my decision clock is ticking."

"What do you mean?"

"I may have to head back to Bellingham in a few days unless I decide to quit and stay here. I've got to let them know."

Jia looked at me like I was an idiot.

"Then let them know," she said.

I stared.

"Stay?" I asked. "And run Marty's?"

"Hell no!" she said. "I'm running Marty's. I'll let you live upstairs. Maybe even free of charge."

"You'll let me live free of charge, in my own place."

"Sure," she said. "I could probably even get you a job here." She laughed, then placed a hand on my arm. "Seriously, Rich, stay. You could live off what you get from this place couldn't you?"

"I suppose. . ."

"Or get a job with the cops around here like you had at home. Or, do like Tyler said."

"Become a private detective."

We just stared at each other for a moment.

"Yeah," she said finally, "that does sound really stupid, doesn't it?"

We laughed and then, after a silence, I told her that I would have to think about it.

"There's something else you need to think about," she said.

"Yeah?"

"Eleanor."

I sighed and nodded.

"She's in love with you, you know."

"She said that?"

"No, but I can tell."

I started to respond, but the front door opened and Ellie popped in and when she saw me, she pointed back out towards the parking lot.

"I think your buddy is back," she said.

"Who?"

"Your friend's brother."

Pete was back.

I followed Ellie out the door and pointed to where Pete was parked in his beaten-up old pickup.

"What's he want?" Ellie asked quietly.

"Maybe to warn me off again?"

She placed a hand on my shoulder. "Why don't you call your sheriff-buddy before you go over there?"

"And tell him what?" I shook my head. "Let's just go talk to him. If he starts to get aggressive, you'll protect me, right?"

"I guess I'd better," she said, "'cuz so far, you seem to be on the losing side in these fights."

Pete stepped out of his truck as we got closer and slammed the door closed.

"Somebody's pissed," Ellie mumbled as she watched him stomping towards us.

"I asked you to leave the fuck alone, Willis," he said approaching.

"What are you talking about, Pete?" I asked.

"Why'd you do it?" he interrupted.

"Pete . . ."

"You went after Julie, you threatened her, you scared the shit out of her," he said, "after I told you to keep away."

I gawked at him.

"I didn't threaten anyone," I protested.

Ellie stepped in front of me, trying to interrupt, raised a hand, palm out towards Pete. "Let's wait a minute, okay?" she said.

"Let's stay out of this, okay?" he snarled at her. "I'm talking to my old buddy here." He pushed past her and planted himself right in front of me, jabbing an angry finger hard into my chest. I instinctively let out a howl and backed up a step, ribs throbbing.

"Shit, Pete," I moaned.

Pete sneered. "What?"

Ellie jumped back in front of Pete blocking him. "Stop it. He's hurt," she said.

Pete wasn't listening. Angry at the interruption, he grabbed Ellie with both hands and flung her hard off her feet and to the side where she lost her footing, smashed head first into the bumper of a car, and with a cry, crumpled to the ground. She rolled onto her back, dazed, blood pouring from a gash on her forehead.

Enraged at seeing Ellie on the ground, my pain was forgotten as Pete stepped close and I pulled back my right arm to take a swing. He raised his left to block it but I smashed a surprise left jab straight into his nose and he staggered back as blood squirted from broken cartilage and then my right fist plowed into his left cheek and he staggered more and then I hit him once with my right and then threw a left into his jaw and he wobbled, dazed and I pulled back my right arm again and buried a handful of knuckles right in the middle of his face and he toppled to the ground on his back and I jumped right on top of him, straddled his chest and began pummeling his face left and right until a pair of hands pressed against my arms from behind and I heard Ellie's faint voice.

"Stop, Rich."

I turned just as I felt Ellie collapse against me. I twisted and took a hold of her, guiding her gently to the pavement, blood covering the left side of her face from a cut somewhere in her hair. I searched around for something to wipe her face off and heard footsteps running in my direction. Tyler, followed by Jia, ran up and knelt on the other side of Ellie.

"Christ. . ." Jia muttered.

"What the fuck happened, man?" Tyler asked, yanking a kitchen towel out of his apron. I grabbed it from him and pressed it to Ellie's forehead.

"I'll call the police," Jia said, starting back towards Marty's.

"No," Ellie said in a voice struggling to be loud enough. "No police."

"Wait, Jia," I said, waving her back. I gently dabbed at the blood on Ellie's face, her twitching with every touch as I worked my way across her forehead looking for the injury. "You sure, Ellie?"

She gave a tiny nod. "No police."

I cleaned off enough blood to find the gash just above her hairline on the left-front side of her head.

"There it is." I folded the towel up and looked at her. "This'll hurt a little." She nodded and winced as I pressed it over the cut and glanced at Tyler, gesturing for him to take over. He knelt next to me and replaced my hand on the towel.

"Keep pressure on this, Tyler," I said, giving Ellie's hand a squeeze. "Right back."

I flipped back over to Pete who had managed to drag himself a few feet away, his head propped up against a car's tire moaning. I sat astride him again. It startled him and he tried to push me off.

"What's wrong with you, Pete?" I screamed at him. I cocked an arm like I was going to take another punch at him and he threw his arms up over his face, palms out, like a child trying to ward off a father's blow. And then, unbelievably to me, he started crying. "Don't hit me again," he blubbered.

It was such an abrupt, shocking shift from the seemingly angry creature from just a few moments before, that I dropped my arm, sat back and stared down at the man who had once been a childhood friend.

"Pete. . ."

"Don't," he cried. "Please . . . "

"What were you doing, Pete?"

"I wanted you to leave us alone."

"Why?"

He was getting a better grip on himself and lowered his arms so I could see his face and what I had done. He had slices on his cheek and under his left eye, his lip was swelling and bleeding and it looked like I might have broken his nose. I was still angry but guilt was creeping in. "Why, Pete?" I repeated.

"Protecting," he mumbled.

"Protecting?" I asked. "Protecting Julie? What?"

"The family."

"Protecting the family? What family, Pete?"

"My sisters. . . Leave me alone." He tried to shove me off, but he couldn't budge me.

"Protecting them from what?" I demanded.

"From people."

"People?"

"From people . . . people knowing."

"Knowing? Knowing what? Knowing what you did to Jeannie?"

"Huh?"

"Knowing that you beat her?"

"What?"

"Did you hurt Julie? Did you beat Jeannie?" I felt myself losing control.

I felt Jia come up behind me and put her hands on my shoulders to pull me back but I shrugged her off.

"What did you do to Jeannie?" I yelled.

"What the hell are you talking about?"

"You were abusing her, weren't you?"

Pete's face turned white and he stared at me in utter horror.

"No . . ."

I grabbed him roughly by the shirt and pulled him up. "When Jeannie died, she was pregnant. Did you do it?"

His look of horror intensified, tears filled his eyes and he was shaking his head.

"No . . ." he said.

"Did you?"

"I couldn't . . ."

"You could and you did!" I yelled right into his face.

"No!" he cried, "I couldn't, Richie, I couldn't!"

"Yes!"

"No! You don't understand! I couldn't . . . no . . . no . . . balls . . ." he choked out between sobs.

"Bullshit. You had the balls to show up here and threaten me—"

"No!" he screamed at the top of his lungs, "No, god damn it! You moron. . . I don't have any testicles!" He then let out a sad, grief-filled howl and collapsed back against the tire.

The parking lot was silent.

I couldn't do anything but look at him, releasing his shirt to let him drop back to the ground. By then Eleanor was sitting up, Jia had grabbed one of my arms and Tyler took the other and pulled me back and off to the side on my knees, Pete blubbering like a baby.

"Back off, boss," Tyler said quietly.

Jia went around to the other side of Pete with a towel that she pulled out of her apron and began gently wiping the blood and tears from his face.

The parking lot was silent except for the exhausted panting of two men. I gawked at Pete. Looking at him in this new light, I could see it. He had a full head of hair, while the males in his family that I knew had gone bald by the time they had hit twenty. He had almost no facial hair, had a thin voice and didn't seem to have the same muscular build as his dad or older brother. I was no doctor, but I knew those things were proof of what he was saying. A sudden wave of sadness and guilt washed over me and I flopped down on my ass, watching as Jia helped Pete to sit up and lean back against the tire of the car behind him.

"Pete," I muttered, "I . . . I don't know what to say . . ."

Eleanor had managed to get to her feet with Tyler's help and sat down beside me, holding the towel against the cut on her head, her t-shirt drenched in darkening blood.

"Okay?" I asked her quietly.

She nodded. "You hurt?"

I shook my head, then looked back at Pete who was staring down at the ground. "What happened Pete?" I asked as gently as I could.

"Accident?" I tried to think of what else could cause someone to lose their testicles. "Cancer?"

"No."

Pete crumpled into uncontrolled sobs and fell against Jia's shoulder who placed a gentle hand on his arm and held it there while the man trembled. I opened my mouth to say something but felt Eleanor place a hand over mine.

"Wait," she whispered.

I nodded. A few people passed by on their way in or out of Marty's. Some stared, some asked if we needed help or needed them to call an ambulance or the police. We declined. Tyler disappeared into Marty's then came back out with damp, warm towels that he handed to Jia and me.

"Thanks Tyler," I said quietly and began carefully wiping more of the dirt and blood from Ellie's face. Pete sobs were subsiding and after a bit, I looked over and he turned to look at me.

I don't know if it's a guy-thing or a sports-thing or what, but there is something that happens after two people have survived a traumatic event together, competed vigorously against each other or fought in the ring or in the school yard. It opens a connection between the two of you because you have shared something very personal, something very primal, something honest. It doesn't last long, but while it is open, truth is easy.

"PeeWee," I said using his childhood nickname, "what happened? Who did this to you?"

Pete held my gaze for a long moment, then lowered his eyes.

"My father."

TWENTY-NINE

Exhausted, Pete and I both sat on the ground facing each other, his face a battered mess and my ribs pounding in pain as the adrenalin dissipated. I took as deep a breath as my ribs would allow and looked at the man I had just pounded into the ground and who, as a child, had been one of my best friends.

"What happened Pete?" I asked gently.

"My father was an angry man," Pete said. "He put on that fuckin' great-pal face in front of people, but the asshole had a vicious temper. Lotsa beatings."

"Pete . . .I had no idea," I stammered.

"No one did." He shook his head and looked down at the ground. "I was eleven or maybe twelve and we were fighting and he started beating on me. It got crazier and crazier. He was completely out of control and I was down on the ground and he was hitting and kicking me and he had those, those fucking steel toed boots on and I turned at the wrong time and he kicked me and the next thing I knew, I was in the hospital waking up after surgery." He choked up. "Motherfucker had ruptured both testicles."

"Shit . . ." Tyler gasped.

"He told the docs a horse had kicked me in the nuts and then said if I ever told anyone anything different, he'd kill me."

"God, Pete. . ."

"He woulda too. And back then there was nothin' they could do but offer me hormone pills. And guess what? We couldn't afford 'em."

"What were you fighting with your dad about?" I asked.

Pete looked off, like he was looking for something that was a long way away, then he began, in a voice so low, it was like he was talking to himself.

"Trying to protect them."

"Who?"

"Too late for the older kids."

"Jean and Julie?"

"Didn't do any good. Couldn't stop it."

"Couldn't stop the beatings?" I asked.

Pete turned to me with a look of profound sadness and regret as I heard Ellie's voice from behind me.

"Couldn't protect them from the abuse," she said softly.

Pete buried his face in his hands, heavy sobs racking his body.

"I tried, Richie," he cried, "I tried. But I was a kid and he was so big and he was gonna kill me and I couldn't do nothin' about it." He broke down in more sobs, Jia putting an arm around him and giving him the towel to wipe his eyes. She looked at me shaking her head, almost crying herself. After a moment, my throat tightening, I spoke into the silence.

"He was abusing Jeannie and Julie?" I asked.

A pause and then a slow nod.

That was a gut-punch. "How long?" I asked.

He shook his head. "I dunno. Since Jean was nine or ten, I guess. I don't know when it started with Julie."

It was getting hard for me to breathe and Eleanor saw that I was struggling. I got to my feet with Eleanor's help and she guided me to the front of the car Pete was propped up on. I leaned against the hood.

"What about your mother?" I asked quietly.

Pete snorted. "Mom gave up a long time before that. She was living in the medicine cabinet."

"Jeannie never told me," I mumbled, more to myself than anyone else.

"We couldn't say anything," he said. "You didn't talk about shit like that back then. Couldn't tell anyone. Couldn't tell you. Jeannie wouldn't let me."

I nodded. A lot of things suddenly made sense to me.

"You've been telling me to keep away from you and your sisters, but you weren't protecting them from me or from other people, were you?"

He didn't answer, but looked away.

"You were protecting the family secret."

He looked up at me, and the expression on his face confirmed it.

"I thought it was the right thing to do," he said, "but it didn't stop us all from being fucked up. Good ol' beer helped me. Worked for the girls for a while, but then, I guess they needed something more."

Ellie turned to me. "Now you know how drugs came into the picture."

"Yeah," I said, turning to Pete. "How'd they ever get into drugs?"

He snorted. "You were so fuckin' naïve Willis. How'd you not get into drugs? They were everywhere."

"I was an idiot."

"They had a dealer, right?" Tyler asked.

Pete shrugged.

"Who was it?" I asked.

He shrugged again, looking away.

I walked over and knelt down next to him. "You know who it was."

"Why the fuck does that matter now?"

"Is the guy still around?"

"It's stupid to go digging around in that kind of shit. Stay away."

"I can't. It's too important. So do you know?"

He hesitated. "It's dangerous."

"Who?"

"Please . . . I . . ."

"Give me a name!"

I could see him struggling, he wanted to tell me or couldn't tell me or was afraid to tell me.

"Who, Pete? Tell me!"

"Rob Clawson."

It was like I had been smacked in the face with a two-by-four.

"Rob Clawson?" I asked.

Eleanor looked at the expression on my face.

"Was that the guy at Marty's last night? The librarian's brother?" she asked. I nodded.

Jia snapped her fingers and pointed at me. "The guy who talked to you about buying the bar."

Ellie tapped my shoulder and I looked at her. "Could that be who the woman was calling on her cell phone?"

I stared at her.

"Could he be the boyfriend?" she asked me. Then she leaned toward Pete. "Was Rob Clawson your sister's boyfriend?"

He looked at me, then at Ellie, then shook his head. "Wasn't around much."

"Pete . . ." I started.

"I just don't know, Richie," he said. "I just don't. . ." He looked away, a man barely holding himself together. "I shoulda done more. ."

Pete pushed himself away from Jia as she helped him to his feet. I stepped closer.

"Pete . . . I'm sorry for all this, for all that's happened." It was clumsy, but it was all I had. I pointed up at his face. "I lost control. I'm sorry."

"Yeah," he said, "had it coming." He sighed, shrugged, turned and started limping towards his truck.

"Stay out of all this, Richie," Pete said. "It's bad."

"Something I've got to do, Pete," I said.

He struggled into his truck and slipped in behind the wheel. He looked my way, gave me an exhausted, defeated nod, a broken man.

We all watched him drive away, then realized we were all just standing around.

"Don't you have some burgers to burn, Tyler?" I asked.

"Subtle, boss. Subtle."

Jia grabbed Tyler by the arm and started marching him toward Marty's. "Let's go feed the starving masses, Tyler," she said.

"Hey, Jia," I called as they were walking away, "could you run up to my room and grab a t-shirt that Ellie could change into?"

"Sure."

"And grab the first aid kit so I can do a proper cleanup on the cut on her head."

"Yeah," she said.

"We'll be out back. Don't think Ellie wants to walk into Marty's covered in blood."

Ellie and I walked in silence around to the back of the building, where Ellie settled herself onto the back steps while I went to the Jeep to get a flashlight out of the glove box. At that moment, what I had just found out hit me hard. I froze, flashlight in hand, just staring. Ellie's voice emerged from behind me.

"Rich? What's wrong?"

I turned back towards her, leaning against the Jeep, trying to figure out how to answer her. Ellie could see I was having a hard time and came over to me, placing her hands on my waist.

"What is it?"

I held it together and finally got some words out. "I understand now."

Elle was puzzled. "Understand what?"

"Why she saved me."

"Who? Do you mean Jeannie?"

I nodded.

"Saved you from what?" she asked, pressing a hand to my cheek.

I gave her a weak smile and took a few steps away before turning back to look at her. She sat herself back down on the steps.

"I told you that our farm and the Sorenson farm were next to each other," I said. "Until just before high school, Jeannie and I were as close as two friends could possibly be. She was kind of a tomboy, we were the same age, in the same class and at the same school. She was across the fence to our place as often as I was across the fence to hers."

"Okay," she said, encouraging me.

"It might have been the summer between seventh and eighth grade. I guess I was twelve? Maybe thirteen. I don't know. My uncle Carl, my mom's brother, was helping with the hay. Carl was a mean, old drunk who couldn't hold down a job, so dad would hire him out of pity a few times a year."

"Was that the uncle in your dream?"

"Yeah. Carl and I were in the barn, stacking bales of hay. He was drunk and he was big and had always scared me with the way he talked and acted. That day he had been talking crazy stuff about women and then started asking me whether I had been jerking off or screwing girls at school and it got crazier and crazier and then he said something about wanting to check something out and he made me take my shirt off and then he made me drop my pants 'cuz he wanted to see if I was ready to be a man or something like that and then he laughed at me and pulled his pants down and pushed me down to my knees. I was so scared, I didn't know what he was doing, I was crying, begging him to stop and he was laughing and then all of a sudden, like out of the dark behind him, a bat swung out and smacked him on the side of the head and he went down and there was Jeannie standing above him and she brought the bat down on his nuts and he screamed and then she hit him again and again and he kept screaming at her and she was screaming at him, telling him to get out and never come near me again, saying if she ever saw him again, she would tell everyone he was a child molester and then she would kill him and then she hit him again and again with the bat and he was bleeding and he finally gave up and ran out of the barn promising to never come back."

"God. . ." Ellie said.

"And then there I was, half-naked, kneeling, crying, embarrassed and ashamed, with my best friend in the world looking down at me with such . . . sadness, such pity. I just couldn't take it. I pulled my pants back up, grabbed my shirt and ran. I ran and ran and ran until I was as far from the barn as I could get and I crawled down into a ditch and laid there. Laid there for hours. I don't know how many hours. Finally went back to the house, didn't eat dinner, just went to bed."

"What did you say to Jeannie after that?"

"Ellie," I said. "I was so stupid, such an idiot. I was so horrified about the whole thing, so embarrassed by it that I was too ashamed to say anything."

"It wasn't your fault," Ellie said.

"I know that now," I said, "and I know that she saved me from what could have been, but the stupid twelve-year-old me didn't understand that so I had to pretend it never happened. But every time I saw Jeannie and that look of pity in her eyes, it reminded me. So, I blocked her out. Stopped talking to her, stop doing things with her. I erased it."

"Oh, Rich . . ."

I pointed out to where Pete had been. "I finally understand why she did it."

"She didn't want what had happened to her, to happen to you," Ellie said.

"Now you see. I owe her," I said.

Ellie nodded.

I shook myself out of the moment. "Okay," I said, "enough of the self-pity crap. Let's take a look at that cut. I walked over to where she was sitting and pointed the flashlight at the wound.

"It's not very deep," I said, "but there's some hair caught in the cut and you are growing quite a lump."

"Hurts," she said.

The door opened and Jia stepped out handing me the small first aid kit and a blue Radiohead t-shirt.

"Anything else?" she asked.

"We're okay, I think" I said.

"Thanks Jia," Ellie said.

She turned to go, then stopped and turned back. "FYI . . .everyone in there has heard about the fight already and the description is getting wilder and bloodier with every retelling."

"Great," I said with as much sarcasm as I could manage.

Then she was gone.

I dug some wipes out of the first aid kit and cleaned the dried blood off Ellie's neck and face.

"Amazing how much a head wound bleeds," I said after going through half a dozen wipes.

Ellie looked down at herself. "Let me get rid of this shirt."

She carefully slipped the blood-soaked shirt over her head and off, then wadded it up and handed it to me.

"Toss," she said. I handed her the clean t-shirt and headed to the dumpster.

"Oh shit," she said, stopping me. She was looking down at her bra which had been white but now was nearly as stained as her t-shirt had been.

"Toss this too."

She reached behind her back, unsnapped her bra. slipped it off and threw it my way.

"Those stains'll never come out," she said. "Now you owe me a blouse and a new bra."

"I do?" I threw the shirt and bra into the dumpster.

"Oh yeah," she said with a smile. "This was your fight, not mine. I was an innocent bystander." She slipped the clean t-shirt on.

"Okay," I said. "We'll go shopping tomorrow. Now, let's clean up that cut."

After numerous yelps of pain from Eleanor and careful wiping, the cut was as clean as it would get. I rubbed an anesthetic cream over the wound then reassembled the first aid kit. I went to the Jeep to stash the flashlight, turned and leaned back against the Jeep thinking.

Ellie looked up at me. "You can't let this go."

I sighed. "Yeah, I know."

"You've got to get to your pal, the sheriff, and get him to look into this."

"If it's enough," I said.

Eleanor stepped over to me. "You've done all you can. Let the real detectives go after Clawson."

"Tomorrow's Sunday," I said. "Not likely to find anyone there."

"Try, Richie."

I looked at her. "I'll call him. But if he won't do anything, I'm going to keep digging."

"After all that's happened tonight," Ellie said, "if those assholes still refuse to help, I'll grab a shovel and help you dig."

THIRTY

"Damn it!"

I jerked awake to the blare of my daughter's ringtone and fumbled around until I was able to snag the phone from the bedstand.

"You couldn't let me sleep a little longer, Jess?"

"Good morning to you too, Dad," my daughter said.

"What's wrong?" I asked.

"You not answering my texts."

"Been busy, kid." I groaned, my ribs aching. I needed Tyler's magic pain pills.

"You alone?"

I looked to the other side of the bed, but was surprised to see that it was empty.

"I guess so," I said. "Why?"

"I was just hoping you weren't," she said. "You need to not be alone."

"I do?"

"Yes."

"Thank you, Doctor Willis," I said. "So, what's going on?"

"Calling with a head's up. Expect a call from your boss tomorrow. He said he hasn't heard from you."

"Uh oh."

"Says he needs that decision this week."

"Yeah . . ."

"You really might quit?"

"Uh . . . considering it."

"You wouldn't really move back to Black River, Idaho, would you?"

The door opened and Ellie pushed in juggling steaming mugs and day-old Danish. She had thrown on my Radiohead t-shirt and a pair of boxers to run downstairs and get us coffee. I pointed to the phone and mouthed "daughter".

"I haven't decided yet, Jess," I said.

"Time's running out, Dad."

"I know. I promise, we'll talk before I decide."

"Fine," she said. "Just don't buy a potato farm, okay?"

"I promise you that, kid."

"Love you, Dad."

"Love you, too."

I clicked off, then glanced at Ellie as she settled next to me on the bed, handing me a cup of caffeine.

"Decision time about the job, huh?" she asked through a mouthful of sweet roll.

"Yeah," I said. "Have an opinion?"

"Yes," she said. "These Danish are really dry."

"That's all you have to offer?"

"Well . . . the icing's good."

"Okay." I gave up and headed to the bathroom.

"How long you been up?" I asked from the bathroom.

"Couple hours."

"Did I wake you again?"

"Wasn't quite as bad this morning," she said.

"Maybe I was exhausted," I said, coming back out, grabbing my mug and sitting next to her. "I'm surprised that two old middle-agers can still go at it as long as we did last night."

"I was surprised too," she said. "Pleasantly surprised." We tapped coffee mugs in a toast to our sexual prowess.

"How's your head?" I asked. She dipped her head toward me so I could check it.

"A dull ache right now. How's it look?" she asked.

"There's a lump," I said. "No bleeding, though."

I took another swallow of coffee then went off searching for the clothes I had tossed off. Ellie swiveled to the other side of the bed to get dressed.

"Still seeing the sheriff today?" she asked.

"Yeah. What time is it?"

"After nine."

"Damn," I said. "Didn't mean to sleep so late." I slipped pants on, grabbed my phone and thumbed a text to Gil.

"I need to get back home for a few hours," Ellie said. "As much as I love playing detective with you, I've gotta get course prep done."

A beep from my phone interrupted her.

"It's from Gil," I said, looking at the screen. "He's in his office until eleven." I dug through a pile of clothes to find the least odorous t-shirt and socks.

"You go talk to him," Ellie said. "I'll drive home and then what say we meet up this afternoon? Because you owe me a shopping trip."

"I remember."

Ellie came around the bed, wrapped her arms around me and pulled me in tight. "Rich, I can't say where it's going with you and me, so don't let that affect your decision."

"I'll try," I said, giving her a peck on the cheek.

"But I will say one thing," she said, heading toward the door. "As crazy, stupid and dangerous as all this that we've been doing is, I'm enjoying the hell out of it."

"Sorry, Richie. We can't do it."

I had gotten to the sheriff's office to find Gil behind his desk with Detective Yankovic planted in a visitor's chair.

"Even though we know Jeannie had a boyfriend?" I pleaded. "That we know that Rob Clawson was probably her drug dealer and her boyfriend?" I looked back and forth between the two of them. "And that Clawson's sister Rosa knows it and called somebody – probably Robbie – to warn them?"

Gil was shaking his head.

"Lotsa maybe's, possiblies and mights in there," Yankovic said. "You can't open cases on probablies."

"No, you can't" I said, "but can't you at least start asking questions?"

"Not on a thirty-year old case," Yankovic said, his voice rising.

I turned to his boss. "Gil, just one detective?"

"Look, Richie," Gil said, leaning forward, folding his hands and setting them on the desk, "there's another problem with you pushing on this."

"What?"

"We've had a complaint about you," Yankovic said.

I stared dumbfounded at the two of them.

"About you harassing this Grazzano woman," Gil said.

"Rosa? Who filed the complaint?" I asked.

"You know I can't tell you that, Richie. But I was able to hold it down to a verbal complaint, nothing formal, just a promise that I would warn you off."

"Warn me off?"

"Or a real complaint will get filed," Yankovic said, "along with injunctions and restraining orders."

"I don't believe that," I said.

Yankovic stepped towards me. "Then you better readjust your belief system."

Gil put a hand up to him. "Enough Yank," he said.

I stared at him, shaking my head in disbelief. "You don't want me asking questions. And yet, you won't, is that right?"

"We are just too busy for cold cases right now," Gil said.

"Too busy with what?" I asked exasperated.

"In the spring, when things slow down, I'll free somebody up. Until then, back off."

I must have registered shock.

"Rich," Gil said, "You're not a cop, you're not even a relative and running around pushing people about this is going to make it harder for us when we actually get to this case."

"Like that'll happen," I said with serious snark.

"Willis," Yankovic said, standing, "I think it's time for you to leave. We're busy here."

"I ask again, busy doing what, Yankovic?"

"Knock it off, Rich," Gil said.

I looked back and forth between the two, not believing what I was hearing from two law enforcement officers. I finally put my hands up in surrender.

"Fine," I said. "I tried." I turned towards the door, then looked back at Gil, walked to his desk and dropped the security card and keys on it.

"Stay away from this case, okay?" Gil said.

Yankovic stepped over to me. "And Willis?

"Yeah?"

"If I find that you've been sticking your nose into this case, I'll toss you in jail for police interference."

I turned back to face him.

"If you don't want help solving this case, then get off your asses and solve it yourselves."

I smiled, waved and walked out.

If I had any hesitation about my next move, Gil's refusal to help and Yankovic's threats had removed it. There was no longer much doubt in my mind about what happened to Jeannie and I had an idea about where to go to confirm it.

I pulled into Sara Wilcox's driveway and watched her push through the door in her wheelchair, behind her yapping little mutt. When she saw it was me getting out of the Jeep, she sighed and tilted her head in a gesture for me to follow her in.

"I thought you might come back," she said as she rolled to her dining room table. I stopped inside the door.

"On Friday, you told me you didn't know your drug dealer's name. Or Jeannie's dealer, or her boyfriend."

Sara remained frozen, looking out the window over her dining room table.

"That's not true, is it?" I asked. "You know his name."

Sara didn't move.

"Sara," I said, "I need to know. It was Robbie Clawson, wasn't it?"

Like air slowly leaving a balloon, Sara sagged in her chair.

I walked into the dining room and she turned her chair to look at me. I knelt in front of the ill woman and gently took her right hand in mine.

"Jeannie's brother told me Clawson was a dealer," I said quietly. "He was your dealer, Jeannie's dealer and Jeannie's boyfriend, right? And she was pregnant with his child, wasn't she?"

Sara's head popped up in surprise, her pale eyes looking into mine. "She was pregnant?"

I nodded.

"Oh god," Sara muttered, eyes watering. Her skeletal hand was shaking. "She thought she might be and she didn't know what to do about it, because she knew Rob wouldn't like it."

I waited a moment, then asked, in as gentle a voice as I could manage, "Sara, was he your dealer?" Her look slowly changed from sadness and shock to what looked to me to be fear, a very old fear. "What's wrong, Sara?" I asked. "Are you afraid of Clawson?"

"It's hard to understand a woman's fear, why we keep bats next the bed and mace in our purses. It's in every crime show on TV, in every mystery novel. It's the woman as victim. For us, the fear of becoming that missing girl, that beaten daughter, that murdered girlfriend feels real." She sat back in her chair, her eyes drifting back out the window. "And then, when there is a real threat, a real fear for your life . . .it terrifies you more than could be put into words."

"Robbie threatened you?"

Very slowly, still not looking at me, Sara nodded.

"Go to the police," I said.

"The police," Sara said derisively, followed by a coughing fit as she shook her head.

"How did he threaten you?"

"Nothing overt, but we knew. He'd kill us."

I nodded, encouraging her to continue.

She looked at me again, stricken like someone who already knew the answer. "He killed Jeannie, didn't he?" she asked.

"I think so," I said.

She shook her head, letting out a tiny painful moan.

"Jeannie wasn't the first," she said.

I stared at her in shock, then stood and backed down into the chair facing her.

"Shannon," she said.

It took me a minute to understand. "Wait. Shannon Baumgartner? The girl in the drowning accident?"

"The sheriff was the only person in town who believed that was an accident."

"What happened?"

"Shannon had been as deep into drugs as me, but then her mom died. Remember that? It was our senior year, maybe the summer before. It changed her. She saw God, she said, and then quit the junk cold turkey, if you can believe that."

"Are you saying she was killed because she kicked the habit?" I asked.

"She was going to make it right, do her penance, she said, to protect other girls and was going to turn him in. Turn in Robbie."

"Robbie was her dealer, too?"

"And when they found her body in the river," Sara said, "we all knew he did it. Couldn't prove it and to be honest . . . we didn't want to believe it. But then he came to me and Jeannie and said if we ever said anything about him, there'd be another swimming accident."

"What about the girl Shannon went swimming with?"

I could see her struggling to remember. "Margaret. Margaret . . . something. She swore to everyone that Shannon hit her head on a rock in the river while they were swimming and was swept downstream. It wasn't true."

"Because she was one of Robbie's customers too?"

Sara nodded.

"Could we find her, get her to talk to the sheriff?"

"She OD'd years ago."

"Damn. And you never went to the sheriff with what you knew."

"I couldn't," she said. "We were scared teenage girls. Stupid and scared. Then, later, when I finally got clean, I had kids. I couldn't endanger them for something done twenty years before. It wouldn't have changed anything. Wouldn't . . ."

"But you're telling me now," I said. "But you weren't going to before, were you?"

"No, I wasn't," she said. "I was afraid, Richie, afraid he'd come after me. But then, after you left on Friday, I looked at myself and thought, what did I have left to lose?" She pointed to her wheelchair, the oxygen tank and the pile of medical bills. "What can he do to me now? I'm already dead."

Eleanor and I had arranged to meet at Pocatello's T.J. Maxx and I used the drive there from Sara's house to work out how to get the proof Gil needed to officially dig into Jeannie's case. By the time I got there, Ellie was already in the women's clothing section, checking out blouses and I had a plan figured out.

"What happened?" she asked seeing the look on my face.

I couldn't talk about it in the middle of a department store, so I just shook my head and pointed to the blouses she was holding.

"Blue or off-white?" she asked holding up two shirts. "I've got it down to these two."

I smiled, remembering that one of the things I had always liked about shopping with Ellie was that she knew pretty much what she wanted and she didn't waste any time getting it. I pointed at the blue.

"That one has the nicer trim and I like the V-neck," I said. "But I think the white one looks better with your hair."

"Really?" She held them both at arm's length and looked them over."

"Get 'em both," I said.

She looked at me, then the blouses. "You sure?"

I nodded.

"Thanks," she said with a wink. "Now, a bra," she said starting towards the lingerie section. "Did you talk to your pal the sheriff?"

"Yeah."

"And?"

"They aren't going to cut anyone loose to look at Jeannie's case until spring."

"You're kidding?"

"And they want me to back off."

Ellie stopped in the middle of the aisle and stared at me. "They can't do that. Can they?"

"They might try. And someone has filed a complaint about me talking to Rosa. Said I was harassing her."

"Who filed it?"

"They wouldn't tell me."

"Screw it then," she said with a flick of a wrist. "They can't stop us."

"There's that 'us' again," I said.

"I'm invested in this thing now," she said, pointing to the scalp wound. "We're gonna figure it out, right?"

I smiled. "Yes, we are."

"Good," she said. "C'mon."

We spent five minutes looking at bras, with Ellie picking out a simple, flesh-toned one.

I had just paid the cashier and was waiting for the receipt when we heard a voice call Ellie's name. Ellie turned to a tall, black woman in tight jeans and a pink cashmere sweater holding a winter coat.

"Micaela," Ellie said. "I thought you lived in Soda Springs. Move up here?"

"No, just shopping for cold weather clothes for me while my hubby is at Best Buy buying cold weather games for his PlayStation." She rolled her eyes. "Different priorities."

Ellie laughed, then pointed to me. "Micaela, this is Rich, an old college friend. Rich, Micaela. She teaches sociology at ISU."

We exchanged greetings and brief pleasantries, me explaining why I was back while avoiding any questions about why I was buying Ellie underwear.

"Is Matthew still off at that conference in Chicago?" Micaela asked.

"Supposed to be back Tuesday," Ellie said.

"Let's the four of us get together for dinner some night, how's that sound?" Michaela asked.

"Let's do that," Ellie said.

"Nice meeting you," I said as Micaela went in search of her game-playing husband and we went in search of the Jeep. Ellie was quiet, lost in thought as we walked and that guilt about our situation snuck back into my head, but I pushed it away.

"Where to now?" she asked, climbing into the Jeep and belting up.

I opened the glove box and threw my wallet into the nearly empty space, then pressed a recessed button and the back wall of the compartment dropped down to reveal a tiny, hidden compartment. I fished another wallet out, closed the hidden compartment up and locked the glove box.

Ellie gave me a very puzzled look. "What the hell?"

I just winked. "Where can I find a Walmart?"

Ellie navigated us to a Walmart that was ten minutes away and soon after entering, we were looking at a locked case of iPhones in the electronics department.

"I still don't get what we're doing here," Ellie whispered.

"Something that might be considered... uh... illegal," I whispered back.

"Illegal?"

"Well," I said, "unethical might be a better word."

Before she could ask another question, the clerk, a short, Hispanic kid with ear, cheek and nose piercings and who might have been as old as eighteen, stepped up asking us if we needed help. I picked out a smaller iPhone and a large backup battery that the clerk pulled out of the locked case and carried to the counter. Ellie and I followed. She opened her mouth to say something, but I gave her a head shake and a smile and pulled out the wallet I had kept in the Jeep and just as I extracted a credit card, Ellie snatched the wallet away from me with a look of victory and began rifling through it, pulling out cards and pieces of paper and looking at them, then looking up at me. I smiled and paid for the electronics.

"Do you need help setting this up?" the kid asked. "This phone is unlocked. It must be set up with Verizon or T-Mobile. I can do that for you."

I smiled as politely as I could. "Thanks, I can manage it," I said.

"Thank you, sir. You both have a nice day."

The clerk handed me my bag of goodies and Ellie, barely containing a laugh, grabbed the credit card out of my hand as we walked out of the store.

"Chuck Babbage?" she asked reading the name on the card.

"Uh huh."

"Well?"

"Well, what?" I started the Jeep and kicked it into gear, enjoying the tease.

"One of your hacker aliases?" she asked.

"I've kept a couple of them around for things like this."

"Things that are . . . uh . . .unethical? Things that I have a feeling you and I are going to be doing?"

"Yes."

"Is it dangerous?"

"Yes."

"Could we get in trouble?"

"Yes."

"With the sheriff?"

"Yes."

"And possibly ruin the reputation of this respected university professor?"

"Yes."

She smiled. "And you knew I'd go along anyway."

All I could do was smile back at her.

— • —

THIRTY-ONE

"What do you want to call it?" Ellie asked.

"Ada," I said

"Shoulda guessed," she said with an eye roll. "You're such a nerd, Richie."

We had planted ourselves in a booth inside a retro-fifties type diner outside Pocatello after ordering her a chocolate milkshake and me a root beer float. The bright red, tucked vinyl seating and the classic Formica table top was accompanied by tinny music left over from the Eisenhower era. Amidst the aroma of frying burgers and roasting onions, Ellie and I were setting up the cell phone we had bought at Walmart.

We were sitting near a power outlet and we had the iPhone and the battery pack charging as we worked. Though Ellie had been skeptical of the plan I was hatching, she agreed to help me set things up. We created a bogus Apple account under the name of Ada Lovelace using my Chuck Babbage credit card so she could sign the iPhone up with a service provider.

"You kept this fake ID and credit card from when you were a hacker?" she asked.

"Even when I went legit with my little security company," I said, "there were times when I needed anonymity for the work."

"What else do you have hidden in that sneaky little glove box?"

"Well," I said, "a couple credit cards, a stun gun, a lock rake, some latex gloves and a burner phone. That's in case I need to make a call that can't be traced."

"Weird," she said.

"Leftovers from my hacking days," I said. "I always had them with me. I haven't used them much lately, but it's nice knowing they are there. Finished with the card?"

She handed it back. "It's set up."

Next, we enabled the Find My Phone app so that I could use my phone to see where the one labeled Ada was located. It worked there in the diner but we would need to do a real test later. We sat the cell down to let it finish charging. I picked up the power pack, which was about the same size as a phone, but thicker and much heavier. Ellie gave it a curious look.

"A giant battery," I said. "This will keep the phone running three or four times as long as it normally would."

"Like a week?"

"Which will be more than we need," I said.

Ellie nodded and sipped on her shake. She was looking out the window with a slightly worried look. I noticed.

"Listening to you at night," she said slowly, "struggling with those nightmares . . . ." Her voice trailed off.

"What?" I asked.

"Tell me," she said, "you've talked to a lot of people, read the police reports, heard things. What do you think happened to Jeannie Sorenson?"

I took a deep breath.

"I think now," I said, starting slowly, trying to put the pieces together into a few sentences, "that the Sorenson family that I knew, was one screwed up family. Screwed up in a way that I didn't see. The children were battered and scarred by their parents and to escape they found drugs or alcohol or pills as the easiest way out. That's what killed the two older kids. Then there was Pete. Beaten and ruined for life by his father, and turned into an angry, barely functional drunk."

"And Jeannie?" Ellie asked.

"It sounds like she fell into drugs pretty soon after the abuse started, before high school and managed to get hooked up with dealers. My guess is that one of them was Rob Clawson, who took advantage of her drug use to control her."

"Then he became her boyfriend?"

I nodded. "Until something happened. Probably an argument or a fight."

"Over a pregnancy?".

"Possibly. Could be that she told him she was pregnant and he didn't want her to have the kid or maybe she had decided to get out of the relationship or maybe she told him she was going to quit drugs. Whatever started the argument, whatever it was that made him angry, I think she ran and he chased her out into that field, caught her, beat her into unconsciousness and then buried her right there where she dropped."

"God . . ."

"I don't know if he thought she was dead or what, but the ground was soft after being plowed and he dug a hole and stuffed her into it. She died in that hole."

Ellie watched the expression of horror on my face as I struggled to block out the image that still haunted me: a beautiful, childhood friend, buried alive in an old potato field.

"Why didn't anyone say anything about their relationship?" Ellie asked.

"Like any good drug dealer-slash-buyer relationship, it must have been a secret no one knew."

"Someone must have," Ellie protested. "Her sister, at least. Her brother, Pete?"

"Pete had moved away by then and I think Julie was as deep into drugs as Jeannie had been," I said. "It fucks up your judgement. I'm sure she suspected something, but she needed Clawson and couldn't live without what he supplied." I shrugged. "And then, there was fear."

"Fear?"

"This morning," I said, "I went back out and talked to Sara Wilcox, the old, dying classmate I told you about?"

"I remember."

"Clawson had been Sara's dealer, too and she guessed that he was Jeannie's boyfriend, but she couldn't tell investigators that back then. She was afraid that if she said anything, he'd kill her. And she needed him because he was her drug supplier."

"He would kill her?"

"As foul a human being as I thought he was back then, it looks like he was worse. Sara told me about another classmate that had been a user and was going to come clean about everything, but before she could, she was found dead. Drowned. Police called it an accident. Sara was sure Clawson did it, but had no way to prove it and she was scared that the same thing could happen to her if she spoke up. She kept quiet."

"Until now, " Ellie said sipping on her milkshake. "Because she's dying and has nothing to lose. Why no one else?"

"Same reason," I said, "fear and guilt. The police would wonder why they waited so long to say anything, the families would ask the same question and then there is the fact that Clawson is still around. What would he do to someone if they said anything?"

"Yeah . . ."

"He can't afford to let that happen. He runs a little security business on the side but would lose his license as well as his job at USP if it was revealed that he had been a drug dealer in the past."

"Or a murderer," Ellie said.

"He has too much to lose if there is a whisper of what happened, so people are still afraid of what he'd do to them."

"But then, you come back to town, asking about your old friend's murder."

I jabbed a finger at her. "Yes. And, you know, the same day that I happened to talk to his sister about Jeannie's death, Robbie shows up at USP to talk to me, then shows up at Marty's, all buddy-buddy with me, friendlier than he ever was before."

"Staying close in case you found something."

"Right," I said.

Ellie pointed to the cell phone and battery that were charging up.

"So, you're going to follow him until he screws up somehow?" she asked.

"First," I said, "I'm not going to follow him, I'm only going to keep track of him so I know where he is. And second, I'm not waiting for him to screw up, I'm gonna make him screw up."

"By making him think you have something on him?"

"Yes," I said. "He's going to find out that I have letters and a diary that Jeannie had where she mentions a dealer and a boyfriend and her fear that he could hurt her. He'll hear that I plan to use those items to force the sheriff to re-open the case. He'll know he's the boyfriend she named in her diary and he'll have to get those things from me."

Ellie wrinkled her nose at me. "But you don't have her letters or her diary."

"Of course not."

"Who's gonna tell him you have this diary?"

"His sister. Rosa. I'm going to go after her again, threaten her, scare her, make some throwaway comment about the letters and diary."

"And she'll tell her brother."

"Yes."

"And then he'll come after you."

"Yes."

"And then what?"

"With a little help from Tyler, Jia, some modern technology and my friend, the sheriff, on speed dial, I'm going to get him with breaking and entering." I said. "Then when he is locked up, I'll bring out Julie, Pete and Sara Wilcox. I think they'll feel safe with him behind bars and with a little judicial encouragement, they will come clean about what happened."

Ellie was nodding but looking very skeptical. "I hope the hell you are right."

"So do I," I said.

Ellie took a deep breath and exhaled, forcing herself to relax and then pointed at all the stuff littering the table. "Okay. So, what now?" she asked.

"Hold the Ada phone and the battery pack."

She held them out for me and I pulled out a tiny bottle of Super Glue that I had brought in from the Jeep's tool box. I spread some on the back of the phone and some on the battery pack. I took them from her and pressed them together, holding them, waiting for the adhesion to set.

"Won't that ruin the phone?" she asked.

"Probably," I said, "but we weren't going get this one back anyway."

"Have you done this before?"

"A couple years ago, for a private investigator working for a health insurance company."

"A fraud thing?"

I nodded. "Following a guy who was claiming disability, but the bean counters at the insurance company were sure he was faking it. The investigator couldn't follow the man twenty-four-seven, so he used a cheap cell phone planted in the man's car to track him."

"I see."

"Turned out, the man wasn't faking it."

"That's a twist."

"We ended up helping the guy sue the insurance company for harassment," I said smiling. "Kinda satisfying."

I checked and the glue seemed to have done its work: the battery pack was solidly attached to the back of Ada.

I smiled at Ellie. "Time for a test drive."

I dropped her off with the Ada phone where we had parked her 4Runner. She would take off for Black River on the back roads and I would be in the Jeep and go by way of the freeway back to Marty's. I'd use my phone to track her location as she drove.

She took off and I sat in the diner's parking lot watching the Find My Phone app on my cell. I watched the little blue dot that indicated Ellie's location and was able to follow it as she traveled through Pocatello and then onto an old road that would take her to Black River. The tracking seemed to be working, so I fired up the Jeep and headed north.

Ten minutes after I pulled in behind Marty's, Ellie pulled in behind me.

"Did it work?" she asked, leaning out of the driver's side window.

I stepped over to the Toyota and held my phone up for her to see a line marking her entire route from the diner in Pocatello to Marty's in Black River.

"Cool," she said, nodding.

"I only had problems when I passed through a few dead zones," I said.

"A bunch around here," Ellie said. "It's a nightmare for my students. Scared to death that they might be miss a Tik Tok or Instagram during those seconds they're in a dead zone."

"But we know it works," I said. I glanced up at the sky, then at the clock on my phone. It was early evening and we had hours of sunlight left. It was time to go. "Ready?"

Ellie looked at me for a few seconds and I felt like she might change her mind. But she didn't.

"Guess so," she said finally.

"Let's take your car," I said. "He knows my Jeep."

I grabbed a couple things out of the Jeep, jumped into the 4Runner and we headed out.

Being Sunday afternoon in Black River, there were very few cars on the road and even fewer in the parking lot at United States Potato when we drove into the complex. I guided Ellie to park near a small cluster of pickups and cars, one of them being Rob Clawson's old Corvette.

"There shouldn't be many employees here tonight," I said.

She looked around, then nodded.

I pointed to Clawson's Corvette and we walked over to it. I was carrying the cell and battery pack in one hand and was shaking a spray can in the other. Ellie pointed to it and arched her eyebrows in a silent question.

"Foam insulation," I said.

Ellie gave me her WTF look.

"Those old Corvettes are all fiberglass. That plastic rear bumper has a little lip underneath that I can set the phone into and then I'll seal it in with the spray foam. Its fast drying, a great adhesive and best of all, won't block a cell signal."

We made a casual glance around and didn't see anybody. I nodded at Ellie, then dropped down to the ground and slid under his car. On the inside of the back bumper, I found the little lip where I could place the phone. After brushing away dust and dried leaves, I pointed the spray foam at the back of the phone battery and squirted a bunch on it and then reached up and planted the phone inside the little lip where the foam would hold it in place. Lastly, I sprayed foam all over the phone, sealing it in.

As I watched the foam expand and dry, Ellie kicked my foot and then said in a loud voice "Did you find it yet?"

I couldn't figure out what she was talking about and was about to crawl out when she started talking to someone.

"I dropped my phone," she said in an unusually girly voice. "My husband's trying to find it."

I realized that the kick had been a warning and smiled at what she was doing. Somebody had walked by wondering why she was standing there while I was crawling underneath the Corvette. She came up with a good cover for what we were doing, but now I was going to need to come up with the phone that she supposedly dropped.

Ellie got down on her knees looking at me. "I think it bounced that way," she said in a louder-than-necessary voice.

A male voice spoke. "You sure it's under there?"

"Yeah," Ellie said. "I was texting my girlfriend and the phone slipped out of my hands and bounced right under there."

I suddenly figured out that I had my own phone in my pocket, so I grabbed it.

"Found it!" I said loudly and backed out clumsily from under the car and handed it to her.

Standing up and brushing dirt off, I looked at the guy she had been talking to. Luckily it wasn't Clawson or some security guy. It was an older man in work clothes, carrying a jacket, gloves and a lunch pail, looking like he was heading home for the day.

"Thanks sweetie," Ellie said, still in her helpless-girl voice.

"Glad you found it," the man said. "Take care."

He stepped away, going to an old, yellow pickup.

Ellie and I looked at each other and exhaled, straining to contain a laugh.

The man started his truck and drove out of the lot as we walked towards Ellie's car.

"That was a close one," she said.

"Nice bit of improv you did there," I said.

"See?" she said. "Those years of acting classes finally paid off."

We laughed as we reached the 4Runner, then heard a voice call out from behind us.

"Wilbur!"

Ellie looked at me, saw the startled look, then we both turned to see Rob Clawson striding our way.

"Did he see us?" Ellie asked out of the side of her mouth.

I gave her a tiny head shake, but she saw the anger on my face and felt me tense up. She put a grip on my arm to hold me back as he got nearer and as I turned and took a step toward him.

"Did you file a complaint against me, Robbie?" I demanded.

"It was a warning," he said, coming up to me and stopping. "To stay away from my sister."

"I can't ask her questions?" I asked. "Is there a problem? Something I'm not supposed to know?"

"What the fuck does that mean, Willis?" he said stepping in tighter.

"You tell me," I said.

"I think it means that you're not going to bother my sister with those questions," he said.

"I'm not?"

Like a flashback in a movie, I was suddenly back on a grade school playground, standing toe to toe with Robbie Clawson about to launch into the first of our numerous fist fights.

Fortunately, this time Eleanor was there and stuck an arm in between the two of us. She pushed me back and planted herself in front of Clawson.

"For God's sake, guys," she said. "Stop."

Clawson's right hand had hardened into a fist and I thought he might take a swing at her, but after a beat, his hand relaxed, but kept his anger pointed at me.

"What the hell you doing here, anyway?" he growled.

I opened my mouth, but Ellie chimed in first.

"He was showing me where he used to bring the trucks when he was helping his dad on the farm," she said.

"Yeah?"

"And we're leaving," she said. She turned to me, gripped an arm and shoved me towards the other side of her car.

I fumed for a moment, but then complied and got in the car, with Clawson just staring at me. When Ellie opened her door to get in, he yelled at me. "Stay away from my sister, Willis."

As we left the lot, Ellie turned to me, wide-eyed.

"What the hell is wrong with you?" she asked. "Another fight? Haven't you been beaten up enough in the last couple of weeks?"

I was shaking my head, because I couldn't believe it either.

"Sorry," I said exhaling. "It was stupid."

"Did he see anything?"

I looked back and saw Clawson walking toward one of the smaller buildings.

"Don't think so."

Driving back towards town, I could feel her stress dissipating.

"Thank you, Ellie," I said.

"You know," she said, "I thought all the shit we did in college was crazy, but this is batshit crazy."

She looked at me and rolled her eyes. "Life's never boring with you around, Willis."

"Is that a good thing?" I asked. "Or a bad thing?"

Ellie smiled, reached over, cranked up the Nickelback on her radio and we car danced all the way back to Marty's.

Thirty-Two

"Grab a beer, Tyler!"

It was evening at Marty's and the Sunday customers were all gone, dishes were washed and the kitchen was closed down. Camila had left and Ellie, Jia and I were sitting at a table munching on leftover fries and sipping on beers and ciders. Ellie and I had just returned from a run to Best Buy to pick up three motion-activated security cameras.

I had finished telling Jia about the day's adventures, with occasional snide comments from Ellie, when Tyler joined us, popping the top on a Bud.

"Overheard that you got beat up again," he said, eliciting a laugh from Ellie.

"Did not," I said.

"Almost," Ellie said.

"I may have to get you more of them pain pills," Tyler said.

Laughing hurt and I moaned, holding my still sore ribs and waving a stop gesture at them.

"If you guys don't stop giving me shit," I said, "I'm gonna laugh another rib loose."

"We'll try," Tyler said. "No guarantees, though."

"Thanks," I said with another moan. "Now can I explain what I would like your help with?"

Jia and Tyler looked at each other, then gave me a conditional nod. I started by explaining what I believed Robbie Clawson had done and went over my plan to get him to come after the evidence I had upstairs. I was going to set up cameras covering the front and back doors and one in my little apartment upstairs under the assumption that Robbie would try to get in after dark to snatch the documents. The cameras would catch him breaking in and then catch me confronting him upstairs as I speed dialed my old buddy, the sheriff.

"Then we wrestle the asshole to the ground and zip-tie him up?" Tyler asked, seemingly excited by the idea.

"God, no!" I said. "What I'd like you to do, if you're willing, is camp out in here at night, starting tomorrow night."

"Sleep here?" Jia asked.

I nodded and pointed to Jia. "I'd like you to set up near the front door and I'd like Tyler to camp out in the bathrooms by the back door. I'll be tracking Robbie, and when he heads our way, I'll wake you so you can hide. When he comes in, likely thru the back, just let him go. He knows I live upstairs and he'll head up. The second he does, Tyler, you go out the back door. Lock it and then throw a latch that I'm going to install outside the door. Jia, you go out the front, lock it and throw the latch on that door. Then call 911 and report a break-in. At the same time, I'll be speed-dialing the sheriff."

"The latches aren't going to stop him from getting out," Jia said. "He'll either break the door or a window."

"I know," I said, "it's just to slow him down while Tyler flattens all the tires on his car." I turned to Tyler. "He'll be driving an old Chevy Corvette. You know how to flatten tires, right?"

Tyler pretended to be puzzled. "Flatten tires?"

"Google it," I said. "He won't be able to drive away. Then both of you get away, lock yourselves in Jia's car or something, until the cops arrive."

We worked out the rest of the details, I answered questions and then I finally asked them if they would do it.

"Oh yeah," Tyler said. "Sounds fun."

"Fun? No," Jia said, "but I'll do it. If this guy did what you said, he should go away."

Ellie looked at the three of us and shook her head. "I hope you guys know what you're doing."

"Me too," I said.

We drank in nervous silence for a while until Jia decided to change the subject.

"Have you decided about Marty's yet?" she asked. "Keeping? Selling?"

"Giving it to us?" Tyler injected.

I looked around at the place and at the three faces watching me. "I wish I could tell you." I looked at Ellie. "A few more things to figure out, before I decide about the place, about staying, about going. . ."

"Well, I've made my decision about going," Ellie said standing. "I have classes all day tomorrow and if I don't get some sleep, I won't be worth shit."

"Walk you to your car?" I asked.

Ellie nodded and said her good nights to the others.

"Why don't you two go home," I said to Jia and Tyler. "I'll lock up."

"Thanks, boss," Tyler said swallowing the last of his beer. Jia smiled and nodded then gave an extra smile to Ellie, winking. "Talk to him about staying," she said.

Ellie smiled and I followed her out to her car. At the driver's door she turned to me and I wrapped my arms around her.

"Be careful tomorrow," she said into my shoulder.

"I will," I said. "Sure you can't stay here tonight?"

"I really can't. Gotta rest, shower, change, prep for classes. You know, be responsible?"

Unspoken was the fact that she had a home and as distant as she said he was, a husband returning soon. Still, I needed to ask something.

"Ellie," I said, "what if I decide to stay here?"

She looked up at me with a sad smile, leaned in and pressed her lips to mine, then turned, got into her car and drove away.

"What the hell are you doing here?" Jia asked.

It was six in the morning and Jia had come in the back door to start the morning shift at Marty's and spotted me in the kitchen.

"Scrambling some eggs with bacon," I said. "Want some?"

"Scared the hell out of me Rich," she said. "Thought Volkov might have come back."

"I don't think you have to worry about that," I said. "I'm sure he's resting comfortably in the luxurious accommodations at Guantanamo Bay. Eggs?"

"Yes, please." Jia stashed her purse and jacket under the bar and started prepping for the day. "Why are you up so early?"

"I set up the cameras," I said, pointing to the one I had mounted above the stage aimed at the front door. "And I put the latches on the outside of the doors. Anything I can do to help you open?"

"Lee should be here in a few minutes to help," she said, shaking her head. She was turning on lights, warmers, the espresso machine and filling napkin dispensers.

"Haven't see Lee here in the morning," I said.

"He'll be hung over and grumpy, but still able to cook amazing food." she said.

I slipped a small bowl of scrambled eggs across the service counter at her.

"Eggs are up!"

She snagged the bowl and stood at the counter gobbling them down. I brought my own bowl of eggs out and sat at the bar across from her. I had some strips of bacon on top of my eggs, which Jia noticed. She snatched one out of my bowl and stuffed it into her mouth.

"Want some bacon?" I asked sarcastically.

"Thanks," she said, grabbing another out of my bowl. "Think any more about what to do with this place?"

"No decision yet," I said.

"Well," she said, "I can decide for you."

"You can?"

"Oh yeah. Keep this place, don't sell it. Give me a raise. Quit that police job out there in Birmingham."

"Bellingham."

"Whatever," she said. "Quit that job and live here. Fix up the rooms upstairs, live there off the millions you make from Marty's, get Ellie to dump her boring husband, move in with you and live happily ever after."

"Anything else?"

"Did I mention a raise?" she asked through a huge mouthful of eggs.

"Don't think so."

We heard the backdoor open and Lee, stooped and half awake, lumbered in.

"Morning Lee," Jia said.

"Fuck off," Lee mumbled, finding his way into the kitchen.

"Coffee?" Jia offered.

"Six shots," he replied. "And twelve Advil."

By mid-morning, I had shaved, showered and dressed, ready to get going when my phone buzzed at me. I saw it was from the Bellingham police department. The chief was calling for an answer from me about the job, but I wasn't ready to give him one. I let it go to voicemail.

I checked the Find My Phone app to see where Clawson's car was. I had been watching it on and off all night. The car had been at USP until two in the morning, then it moved to a spot north of town and stopped. When I checked the location on Google Maps, I found out he was parked off Howell Road, which is where he said he lived. The car was still there.

I was out the door and slipping into the Jeep when my phone buzzed again. It was my realtor.

"Hey Randy," I said.

"Didn't I tell you it was a great time to be selling houses?" he asked enthusiastically.

"Yeah?"

"You got yourself some great offers on both properties over the weekend," he said. "When can you come in and look at these?"

I looked at the time. I needed to get to the library before it opened, then get to Julie Sorenson this afternoon and all while tracking Clawson. It was going to be a busy day.

"Can I come by around eleven?" I asked.

"Perfect," Randy said excitedly. "These offers are awesome so warm up your pen. Then we'll talk about getting rid of that shitty bar."

I clicked off smiling because good old Randy Bronco could smell a juicy commission coming his way on those two sales.

Five minutes after hanging up, I was pulling into the tiny, empty parking lot in back of the Brannon County Public Library. I killed the engine and waited. I didn't know where Rosa Grazzano lived, so I planned to catch her when she arrived for work.

A car pulled into a space not far from me and I grabbed the door handle to get out, but stopped when an elderly man stepped out of the car, locked it and then walked around to the other side of the building.

I relaxed.

After another ten minutes, a nice looking, Ford F-150 turned into the parking lot and I could see it was Rosa behind the wheel. As she pulled into a spot not far from me, I took a deep breath, got out and walked in her direction so that when she opened the door to get out, I was there.

Rosa got out, closed the door and turned but stopped suddenly seeing me. She backed up a step. I held up my hands, palms out to try to communicate that I meant no harm.

"It's okay," I said as reassuringly as I could. "Just want to talk."

"What about?" she asked. "You're supposed to stay away from me."

"Because of the complaint to the sheriff?" I asked.

She stumbled to answer.

"Robbie did that, right?"

She just stared.

"Yeah," I said. "Thought so."

"I have to get to work," she said and tried to get around me, but I held up a hand and blocked her.

"I only want to give you a warning," I said.

"About what?" she asked with deep skepticism.

"There is going to be some serious trouble for your brother in the next few days and to protect yourself, you need to steer clear of him."

"What the hell are you talking about?"

"I have found some letters and a diary that show that your brother was Jeannie Sorenson's drug dealer as well as her boyfriend and that she was pregnant with his baby."

She tried to slip by me again, but I blocked her.

"Your brother didn't want her to keep the baby. They got into a fight over it, she ran, but your brother chased her down and then killed her."

"No . . ." she stammered.

"Oh yes," I said, stepping right up to her. "I also now have a witness who confirms that Robbie was responsible for Shannon Baumgartner's accidental drowning." I had put accidental in air quotes.

Rosa looked startled.

"Didn't know about that, did you? Now, unless you want to be taken down with him, you keep out of all this. Don't contact him. After I talk to the police and they make the arrest, they will contact you. Then you can tell them everything."

"But I don't know anything," she said, without much conviction.

I just nodded. "Okay, Rosa," I said. "I was just trying to warn you as one friend to another. Think about it. For your own sake."

I gave her one more hard look to communicate that I was serious and then I turned, walked to the Jeep and drove away, watching her stand there, staring after me.

Once I was out of sight, I took a deep breath and pulled over. Most of what I told her was a lie. I didn't have real proof, I wasn't going to talk to the police and what I said had happened to Jeannie was just a guess. I was also guessing at what Rosa was going to do. In spite of my warning, I was counting on Rosa to contact her brother and tell him everything. That would scare him, then make him angry and then make him come after me.

Randy Bronco jumped up from his desk when I walked into the realtor's office. I was early, but I knew he wouldn't mind.

"Glad you made it," he said, shaking my hand vigorously and indicating a visitor's chair. "I think you'll be happy with these offers."

Randy sat and pulled a folder from a draw and laid it out so that I could see both offers. I gave a very brief look at both, nodded and held out a hand to Randy, gesturing for a pen.

Eyes wide in surprise, Randy fumbled through a mug full of pens until he found one that looked like it might still be working and handed it to me. Then he watched, totally shocked, as I accepted and signed both offers and handed the sheets back to him.

"You don't want to read these or make a counter offer or anything at all?" he asked in amazement.

I shook my head.

"Just want to be done with it," I said.

"That is fucking awesome!" he said reaching out and vigorously shaking my hand in both of his. "This is great. Just great! I'll get the escrow set up, the title insurance and get a closing date for you as soon as I can."

"Perfect." I stood to go.

"Hang on there, buddy," he said.

"What?"

"Let's talk about that piece of shit you call a bar," he said. "I have a restaurant franchisee who wants to check it out. I've also found a small LLC out of Idaho Falls that is looking for a new location for their Mexican restaurant. Either of those will bring us a wheelbarrow full of cash."

"Us?"

"I mean you, of course," he said.

I looked at him and then shook my head.

He looked like I had just smacked him across the face.

He finally managed a "What?"

"Not gonna sell Marty's," I said.

"Why the hell not?" he asked. "Think of the money you could make. You gotta."

I smiled at him. "No, I don't gotta."

He stared. "Richie," he pleaded.

I waved, said "Thanks, Randy," and walked out.

It was too early to get to Pocatello and talk to Julie, so I opted to double-check Rob Clawson's location just to make sure his car was where my app said it was. I pulled Google Maps up on my phone, located Howell Road and headed off in that direction.

Halfway there, my phone chirped and I glanced to see it was a message from the police chief in Bellingham. I slipped off to the side of the road to take a look.

"Rich, I need to have a decision about your position here," the text read.

I didn't know yet how to answer him, so I just thumbed in "Thursday."

I hoped that was enough and I watched my phone for a few minutes, but there was no response, so I dumped the phone onto the passenger seat and drove on.

When I reached Howell Road, I slowed down and searched the driveways and side roads for Clawson's Corvette. Finally, about a quarter mile down Howell, I saw it parked in front of a sun-worn, brown, ranch-style house.

It turned out that my app was accurate and his car was where the app said it would be. That made me feel confident that I would be able to see him coming when he made a run at me.

I was a block down the street, when Clawson suddenly emerged from his house, making for the Corvette.

Oh shit.

I didn't want to be seen and didn't want to draw his attention by gunning it out of the neighborhood. I looked all around and found a driveway just ahead and pulled into it as if I lived there and was going home. I pulled in, killed the engine, ducked down in my seat and listened. In the distance I heard his car start up, make what sounded like a U-turn and pass behind me.

Without knowing it, I had been holding my breath, waiting for him to go by. I finally exhaled when he was a block down the road. I sat up and backed out of the driveway.

Once out of the neighborhood, a look at my app showed Clawson on the highway to Idaho Falls, meaning he probably hadn't heard from Rosa yet. I was relieved. I wanted to have enough time to get to Pocatello and warn Julie about what was coming, just in case he decided to come after her.

Julie's car was parked in her driveway when I got to her house, but there was no answer at the door. I waited, hammered louder and waited. Still no answer. I wondered if something had happened to her and walked around the sides of the house, looking for an open window to see if I could see her. I got to the back of her house where a huge empty field bordered her back yard. Her bedroom window was there and the curtains were only partially closed. I shielded my eyes and looked in. I could see her bed. It looked like she was laying on top of it. A fear that she might be dead flashed through my mind. I knocked hard on the glass.

"Julie!" I called out. I knocked again, louder and yelled louder, "Julie!"

To my relief, the corpse on the bed moved, rolling over, apparently confused by the sound and then looking around the room, finally settling on my face, peering through the window at her. It startled her and it took her a few moments to figure out who was looking at her. When she did, I gestured for her to go to the front door. It took her a few more moments to figure that out, but she finally staggered to her feet and made for the other side of the little house.

I met her at the front door and was shocked at what I was seeing. She was even more pale than usual, smelled of stale sweat and urine and the pupils were tiny pinpricks in her eyes, a sure sign to me that she was on something.

"Julie," I said. "You okay?"

"Richie!" she slurred. "Yeah, fine. Wassup?"

She was wobbly and I was afraid she might fall, so I gently took an arm.

"Can we sit down for just a minute?" I asked. By the look and smell, I guessed that she had been high for a couple of days.

"Wassup, Richie?" she asked again as I walked her to an easy chair. I could feel her arms shaking as I helped her sit.

"How long has it been since you've eaten anything?" I asked.

She looked at me and shrugged.

"Okay," I said. "You sit there and let me see if I can find something, okay?"

She nodded and slumped back into the chair, watching me as I dug around in her kitchen cupboards. When I finally found a can of mushroom soup, I dumped it into a bowl and then into the microwave. By the time it had heated up, I had found a spoon, some crackers and had a glass filled with water sitting on the table next to her chair. When I brought the bowl of steaming soup to her, her eyes were half closed.

"Here you go, Julie," I said, holding out the bowl.

She looked at the bowl and gave her head a tiny shake. "I'm not really hungry," she said.

"Just a few bites," I said. I scooped out a spoonful and held it to her mouth until she reluctantly opened up and let me give her a swallow. She appeared to like it, so I fed her another spoonful. Then another, like she was a baby.

"How's that taste, Julie?" I asked.

She nodded and seemed to be gaining some strength from it, so I kept it up until the bowl was half empty. She relaxed back into the chair again.

"That was good soup," she said. "You make it?"

I shook my head.

"Good soup," she said to herself.

"How are you doing, Julie?" I asked.

"Doing really good," she said.

"Heroin?" I asked.

She smiled. "I'm good, though."

"Julie, can you go somewhere else for a few days?"

She frowned up at me. "Why?"

I explained to her what I had learned in the last few days from Pete and from Sara Wilcox and that I was sure Rob Clawson had murdered her sister as well as Shannon Baumgartner and that I was setting a trap that I hoped would put him away forever.

"You talked to Pete?" she asked.

"Yes. He told me everything about what happened to you and then Sara told me about Robbie and Shannon and the drugs. If we get all that to the police, they'll arrest him and we can give Jeannie some justice."

"We can?"

"Yes," I said, "but I'm worried about Clawson maybe coming after you because of what he thinks you know, so that's why I think you should go away for a few days. Could you?"

"Go away?"

"Stay with someone. A friend. Or Pete. Could you call Pete and stay with him for a few days?"

"Pete? Yeah, I suppose," she said slowly.

"Good."

"Tonight?" she asked.

"This afternoon, if you can," I said. "Would you like me to help you pack up a few things?"

She looked up at me and smiled. "No, I can do that."

"Could I drive you to Pete's house?" I asked.

She waved that off, too.

"Okay. Good." I stood and looked at her. "You'll call Pete, right?"

"I promise," she said.

"Okay." I pointed at the half bowl of soup. "Try to finish that soup. You need the strength."

"I will," she said, and scooped some into her mouth.

"I've got to get back to Black River, Julie. Finish up that soup and call Pete. Get yourself somewhere safe, okay?"

She nodded. "I will. Scout's honor."

I took another look at her, then turned and headed out to the Jeep. As I got in and started up the engine I glanced through the front window and saw her pull a cell phone out of a pocket and start thumbing in a number.

Good, I thought. She's calling Pete and he'll get her away from here.

Next, I looked at my phone. Clawson's car was back on Howell Road. He had probably just gone out for groceries and was back at home before heading into work later.

I took a deep breath. Everything was in place.

I hoped I was ready for it.

THIRTY-THREE

To my surprise, Clawson didn't look to be doing anything out of the ordinary the rest of the day. Based on what my app was showing me, he stayed at the Howell Road address until early evening, and then drove to work at USP. All that made me think that maybe Rosa hadn't called him yet to tell him about me.

It was a quiet evening at Marty's and I was sitting at a corner table, working on my laptop when my phone buzzed with a message from Jess, asking if I had talked to my boss. I texted back that I told him I would give him a decision by Thursday.

"What's taking so long?" she texted.

"Solving a murder," I texted back.

Jess texted a bunch of shock emojis.

I texted that I would explain as soon as I could.

"Grrrrrr" was the text I got back from her.

I had just put my phone down when Tyler plopped down into a chair at my table, slipping a basket of fries over to me. He had come out of the kitchen in his little black chef's hat and filthy white apron, sipping coffee out of a paper cup.

"Had some fries left," he said, "You look like you need some."

"I do?"

"Yeah," Tyler said. He leaned in towards me, speaking confidentially. "Between us guys, you gonna sell this joint to Jia?"

"Think I should?"

"Fuck, yeah," he said. "Better than selling it off to be like a Wendy's or a Pizza Hut."

"What if I don't sell it?" I asked. "What if I decide to keep it and hang out here in Black River?"

"Well, that'd be cool too," he said, surprised. "As long as you keep Jia around." He looked hard at me. "You really might stay?"

I shrugged.

"You should stay, man," he said enthusiastically. "Things have been pretty exciting since you got here and I like that."

"You do, huh?"

"Yeah. Stick around after we put this buddy of yours in jail."

"I'll think about it."

"Do," he said and with a thumbs up, he headed back to the grill. I went back to my phone to find that Clawson's car was still parked at USP. I started second guessing myself. Maybe I had been wrong about Rosa: maybe she wouldn't call to warn him.

I shook that thought off, reminded myself to be patient and trust my judgement. I went back to my laptop.

Closing in on eleven, I was checking my phone when Ellie pushed through the doors and, after seeing me, headed in my direction.

"Hey, sweet cheeks," she said, hooking her pouch on the back of a chair and plopping down with a big exhale.

"Long day?" I asked.

She nodded just as Jia came over and bent to give her a gentle hug.

"Glad you're back," Jia said. "Hungry?"

"Yeah," Ellie said. "Could I get a burger?"

"Of course," Jia said. "Fries?"

"Please."

"Could you make that two?" I asked. "And maybe a couple beers?"

"On the way," Jia said, walking back to the bar and giving Tyler the order.

"I'm a little surprised to see you," I said.

"We finished rehearsal and I got to worrying about you and this plan of yours."

"You could have called," I said.

"I know," Ellie said, "but I wanted to see you." She tapped a finger on my phone. "Where's your buddy?"

"Looks like he's at work," I said holding the phone up so she could see the screen.

"So, nothing's happened yet?" she asked.

"No move towards me, if that's what you mean."

She seemed to relax. "I'm glad, 'cuz I'm having serious concerns about what you're doing, Rich. You're no cop and you don't know what this guy might do." Ellie reached out and took my hand in both of hers. "Give up on this plan of yours. Give your loser of a sheriff all the stuff you've found and let him take over."

"No . . . "

"Even if it is next spring," she insisted, "they are trained for this and it would still get justice for what happened to Jeannie."

"I need to be part of that justice, Ellie" I said. "For my own peace of mind. I have to."

She looked at me for a long time, finally nodded and released my hand just as Camila dropped off our burgers, fries and beers.

"Had to try," she said after Camila was gone.

"I would expect no less," I said.

My phone alarm pulled me out of a shallow sleep at two in the morning. Ellie was lying next to me with an arm draped over my chest, deep in sleep and I managed to slip out from under her, sit up and click the alarm off. I rubbed the sleep out of my eyes and found the app to check on Clawson.

He was still at US Potato, just as he had been all night, but knowing his shift ended at two, I had set my alarm so I could watch where he went after work. I slipped into the bathroom to pee, then came back out and sat down on the side of the bed as gently as I could, phone in hand, waiting for Clawson to move.

I felt movement on the bed, then Ellie slipped up against my back, her legs straddling me, resting her head against my back. She wrapped her arms around me and nuzzled my neck.

"Any change?" she mumbled.

"Still at work," I said. "His shift should have just ended."

"Okay." Her breathing slowed and it felt like she was falling asleep again as I kept tabs on Clawson between checking emails and texts, seeing one I missed from my daughter about my boss calling her. I texted a response she wouldn't see until morning. I checked the app again and stiffened.

"Clawson's moving," I said, which woke Ellie up and she looked over my shoulder so she could see the phone. Every time the screen refreshed, his location changed and we could watch him as he left the USP campus and drove onto the main road back towards town.

"Where's he going?" she asked, straining her sleepy eyes to read the screen.

I pointed to the map with the Clawson dot on it and ran my finger along the road he was on, showing her that it went past Marty's.

"He's coming this way," she said, standing,

"Looks like it," I said, handing Ellie the phone. "Watch him."

I threw some boxers on and ran down to the bottom of the stairs. "Tyler! Jia!" I called out. "He's moving!"

I heard Tyler groan from where he was sleeping on an inflatable mattress and heard Jia in the kitchen.

"Already awake," she said. "Couldn't sleep."

"Get in your places!" I said, running back up the stairs to Ellie.

"Still coming," she said, getting her pants zipped up and snapped.

I sat back down next to her getting my own pants on.

She handed me the phone as she rushed around the room trying to find the rest of her clothes.

"Still moving!" I said, I yelled towards the stairs to Jia and Tyler. "He's coming this way!"

"Shit . . ." Ellie mumbled, struggling with her bra and blouse.

"Moving . . ."

I stood, looked at the phone and yelled so Tyler and Jia could hear. "Still moving!"

I dropped the phone on the bed to throw on a t-shirt. I could hear Tyler and Jia rushing around downstairs. I picked my phone up off the bed and looked.

"Hold on!" I called out.

"What?" Tyler yelled from below.

"Wait!" I called back.

"What's going on?" Ellie asked. She had found her socks and was hopping around the room on one foot slipping them on.

I stared at the phone.

"What's going on?" Jia called up from the bottom of the stairs.

"Wait!" I stared at the phone, then sat down on the bed.

Ellie dropped down next to me. "What?"

I showed her the phone. "Drove right by us. Damn . . ."

We watched the Clawson dot move through town and then start on a long road north. I walked over to the stairs.

"False alarm guys," I called down. "He drove somewhere else." I could hear Tyler cursing and making his way back to his sleeping bag, Jia likely doing the same thing. "Sorry guys." I turned to Ellie. "Probably going home," I said and laid back down on the bed, disappointed.

Ellie took the phone from me, watching the dot move.

"He's north of town now," she said. She slipped her shoes on and then looked at the phone again.

"He stopped," she said.

"What street's he on?"

"Uh . . . Howell?"

I nodded. "Home. That's where he lives."

She turned to me and gently rubbed my still sore chest as I lay there. "So, you can go back to sleep," she said.

"Probably won't be able to now," I said.

She nodded. "I know, but try. I am going to head home." She leaned down, gave my cheek a kiss and stood to go. I got up and went to her as she slipped on a light sweater and I pulled her into an embrace and looked deeply into those sleepy, but beautiful eyes. "Ellie, even though it's been twenty plus years since we were together, I've. . . I've never stopped –"

Ellie pressed a finger to my lips, stopping me. "Let's not say anything about that, okay?"

I opened my mouth to argue, but knew it wasn't a good idea, so I just said "Okay."

She slipped out of my arms and turned to the door, her back to me. "I won't say anything either," she said, "but I want you to know that I feel the same." Then, without looking back, she was gone.

I was actually able to sleep, though fitfully, the rest of the night, waking from time to time to check on Clawson, then forcing myself back to sleep. I finally gave up and spent the rest of Tuesday morning and the early afternoon working around the café. I kept an eye on my phone, but nothing was happening.

I was becoming more and more convinced that I had failed, when a little after three, I saw that his location had changed.

Clawson was moving. Finally.

I checked the time. It was about an hour before his shift at USP started. Could he finally be coming after me? I kept an eye on the dot, watching him move. He was coming south, coming south, then into town, coming south, getting closer, then turning onto the main street through town that would take him to Marty's.

Closer.

I started tensing up, wondering if he might try to come during the day.

Closer.

I called Jia over and pointed to the phone. I told her that we might have to close up and get people out.

Closer and closer.

Then . . . he passed right on by Marty's, heading west out of town, towards US Potato.

"Shit," I said out loud, throwing my phone down on the table. "He was just going to work early. God damn it."

I looked at Jia who just gave me a tilted head-shake and shrug and went back to work.

Frustrated once again, I followed Jia over to the bar and asked her to pour me a beer. She did and I took the glass and a handful of peanuts back to my table, settled in and began shelling. I glanced over at my phone.

I frowned and picked it up to look at the screen.

Clawson wasn't going to work. He had driven past USP and was on the highway heading west out of town. What the hell could he be doing out that way?

The dot kept moving west, then it disappeared.

"Damn. Dead zone," I said to myself.

I kept watching the phone, waiting for the dot to reappear.

Waiting.

Waiting.

Then it popped up, further west, but still on the same road, stayed there a while, then disappeared again.

Why are there so many damn dead zones? And where the hell was he going? There weren't any stores or businesses out there, hardly any homes and it was fifty miles to the next town on that road.

After a few minutes, the dot reappeared, but it looked like he had turned onto a side road.

"What the hell?" I said to myself.

I looked at the location and zoomed in on Google Maps to see what road he was on. It was Turner Road.

Holy shit!

I jumped up from my seat, phone in hand and started running towards the back door.

"What wrong?" Jia called as I ran past her.

"I fucked up!" I said, racing down the hall, out the back and into my Jeep.

"He's going after Sara Wilcox!"

Clawson must have found out that I had been talking to Sara. I couldn't think how, but I was deathly afraid of what he might do to keep her from going to the police. There was an outside chance he was on that road for some other reason, but I doubted it and I could not take the chance.

I glanced up at the threatening clouds as I jumped into the Jeep, but had no time to get the ragtop and put it back up. I burned rubber and got out of the parking lot and onto the road, just to come to a screeching halt behind a line of cars waiting as a huge tractor-trailer backed across the road to make a delivery. Frustrated and angry, I pounded on the steering wheel trying to figure things out.

I needed to call 911, and could remember Turner Road, but I couldn't remember Sara's address and I didn't have her phone number.

I clicked through my recents and my contacts until I found Sandy's number at the court house. I punched it in.

"This is Sandy," came the response.

"Sandy!" I said. "This is Rich Willis"

"Oh, hey Rich, how –"

"Sandy," I snapped, shutting her up. "I need you to get me Sara Wilcox's address again. Right now! And I need her phone number."

"What's going on?" Sandy asked.

"No time, Sandy!" I said getting angry. "I need her address and that phone number."

"Okay, okay. Gotta get logged on."

While I waited for Sandy, the tractor-trailer finally managed to get off the road and the line of cars began moving, but at a three-legged turtle's pace and I was boxed in by other cars. I was pounding the wheel, waiting for Sandy to come back on, infuriated that the cars were taking so long to speed up when I thought of another route, an old paved road through farm land, that might be faster, so I abruptly turned off the highway and raced off, just as rain starting coming down.

Sandy finally came back on.

"Got it," she said.

"Address."

"Box 128, Turner Road."

"Box 128! I couldn't remember the fucking box number," I said. "Good, thanks. Phone number?"

Racing along the narrow, pot-holed road, I reached over to open the glove box, but had to slam hard on my brakes to keep from hitting an old tractor pulling a hay baler down the road, the baler being as wide as the pavement.

"Here's the number," Sandy said.

"Just a sec," I yelled as I took the Jeep onto the shoulder of the road and into the weeds to get around the snail of a tractor.

Back on the road and gunning the motor, I reached into the glove box and pulled out the burner phone I had hidden in there. I needed to call Sara, but didn't want it traced to me.

"Number," I demanded, after I had the phone powered up.

Sandy gave me the number and I punched it into the burner.

"What's going on?" I heard Sandy asking.

"A sec, Sandy," I said as I listened to the other phone ringing Sara's number. Ringing and ringing until it finally dropped into voicemail.

"Fuck!" I yelled into the phone.

"What?" Sandy asked, sounding as panicked as I felt.

"She's not answering," I yelled angrily. "God damn it. Gotta go, Sandy."

"Wait!"

I clicked off and then, as I was racing down the old road at too high a speed, I one-handed my iPhone to see where Clawson was. The dot was stopped at what I was sure was Sara's house. I had to think a minute about what to say and then I dialed 911 on the burner phone.

I told the dispatcher that a house was being broken into and gave Sara's address, saying a man was trying to break in through the front door, hoping that my telling them that the burglary was going on right now might get a uniform there faster.

The dispatcher said that a car would be sent as soon as one was available and asked for my name. I clicked off.

As soon as a car was available? What the hell? Pedal to the floor and racing through neighborhoods on increasingly wet and slippery streets, I finally got to Turner Road, heading towards Sara's house, with rain falling on my head. I reached for my phone to check Clawson's location, but I was speeding around a bend at the same time and knocked the phone onto the floor out of reach. Cursing myself, I kept driving and when I thought I was about half a block from Sara's I screeched to a stop, jumped out and ran, my fear of what might happen to Sara pushing me faster. Luckily, the sudden rain had pushed everyone inside, so there was no one to see me running down the road to Sara's.

I stopped at the driveway and peered through the downpour. There was no sign of Clawson's Corvette.

Out of breath, I scrambled up her driveway to find her screen door ripped off its hinges, the front door partly open and lights on inside.

"Sara?" I called.

No answer.

"Sara!"

Still no answer and my gut told me that this was bad, but I had to look, so I used a knuckle to push the door open.

There she was.

Sara Wilcox was lying in a crumpled pile next to her wheelchair.

I let out a moan, looked back out to see if anyone could see me and then carefully stepped in after wiping my feet dry on her welcome mat. I knelt next to her.

I had only been at two or three crime scenes, but I knew a dead body when I saw it. Sara's pallor was gray and her body was unnaturally contorted, but to be sure, I pressed fingers against her neck.

Yeah, she was dead.

There was no obvious injury, so I didn't know what he had done, but she was so weak, it wouldn't have taken much.

I stood, staring at the poor woman's body. How could this have happened? How did he find out about Sara? Rosa didn't know. No one knew. No one except Ellie.

I stopped.

And Julie.

I had told Julie about Sara Wilcox.

"No!" I said in anger. "No!"

I turned and started running for the door, but stopped abruptly. Sara's annoying little yapping dog was lying behind the door that I had pushed open, it's neck visibly broken. Clawson had even killed her dog.

"Motherfucker," I mumbled and shot out the door.

The rain was getting heavier and I could hear a siren in the far distance. There wasn't anyone on the street so I ran back to my Jeep and turned it around, heading back down the same road I had come in on to avoid running into the cops coming to check on the burglary.

I had been wrong thinking that Rosa would call her brother and warn him. The person who warned him was someone who still needed him, needed her dealer.

Julie.

She had looked like she had been high for a couple days and I would wager that Clawson had gotten to her with a gift of heroin as soon as he had found out about me looking into Jeannie's death.

A quick look at my phone while I drove told me where he was going next.

The dark clouds, heavy rain and dim late afternoon sun made it feel later than it was when I skidded into Julie's driveway in Pocatello, thirty minutes later, dreading that, once again, I was too late. I grabbed my phone to locate him, but my screen wouldn't wake up.

The damn battery was dead.

I had been so busy the last few days that I had forgotten to keep it charged. Another screw-up.

I jumped out of the Jeep and ran to Julie's front door, knocking frantically. There was no response. Worried again that this could be a crime scene, I pulled my t-shirt out of my pants, wrapped it around my hand and grabbed the knob, which turned and I carefully pushed the door open.

"Julie?" I called. "Julie? It's Richie."

Lights were on and I could hear what sounded like a radio in the kitchen. From the few crime scenes I had been to, I had learned a few tricks and one of them was to put your hands in your pockets so that you didn't touch anything, so, hands in pockets, I stepped to the kitchen.

Empty.

A battered radio was propped up in a window sill, playing an oldies station.

I went back out into the living room and then around the other side to her bedroom. It was empty too, so I ran back to the kitchen and out the back door to look. There was a line of what might be footprints trailing across the small yard towards the field.

In the dark and the rain, it was hard to be sure they were footprints, but I followed them across the lawn to the empty field that spread out behind the house. There was nothing there. I looked out through the rain and couldn't see anything but brown. I started to turn, but a flash of orange caught my eye. I stopped, looked back out across the field and couldn't see anything. But then there was another flash of orange. The headlights of cars on a nearby road were reflecting off something out in the field.

I stepped into the muddy field, walking towards where I had seen the flash and found that there were other foot prints there, all filling up with rainwater, making it harder and harder to follow them, but after trudging a hundred feet into the soaked field, I saw her.

I froze.

On her back, rain pummeling half-open eyes, was Julie Sorenson, lying dead, in an old potato field, just like her sister. I took a breath, stepped closer and saw that there was a pistol in her right hand and a small red dot on her right temple. It looked like the same pistol I had seen in her kitchen and it all made it appear to be a suicide. I knew it wasn't.

I shook my head. Poor Julie, abused by her parents, most of her siblings dead and a slave to her habit, she never really had a chance. But still, it shouldn't have ended like this: dead in a wet, cold and lonely patch of earth.

I was looking at her, trying to figure out what to do next when I noticed a piece of paper sticking out of her shirt pocket. I tore off a corner of my wet T-shirt and used it to pull the paper out and take a look. In a crude scribble it read "I have gone to be with my sister."

My guess was that sometime after I talked with Julie, she called Robbie and warned him about the trap I had set and told him about Sara Wilcox. She trusted him, thought she was doing him a favor and saving her drug pipeline, but she didn't understand that after eliminating Sara, he was going to have to eliminate her. He must have come to her door, talked her into getting her gun out and killed her with it. Then Clawson scribbled the suicide note and stuck that gun in her hand to make it seem that she had gone out into an old potato field and killed herself. I decided that I was not going to leave it like that. I stuffed the fake suicide note into my pocket, then I ripped off another piece of my shirt and used it to take the pistol out of her hand. I wrapped the cloth around it to keep my prints off it and stuffed it into my back pocket.

I stood and looked down at what had been Julie Sorenson, furious at what he had done to her.

"I'll get him, Julie," I said. "I promise."

I ran along the same muddy steps back across the field to the house, knowing that the footprints will be nothing but muddy holes in a few hours and of no use to the police.

I plugged my dead iPhone into the car charger and splattered rainwater everywhere as I spun the Jeep around and took off for Black River, where I was sure Robbie would be trying to establish an alibi.

Twenty frustrating minutes later I screeched to a wet stop in the parking lot at United States Potato near where I saw Clawson's Corvette parked in a corner. There were only two other vehicles anywhere in the parking lot, which meant that the facility was almost completely empty.

Clawson would likely be in one of the cellars so I took off running down the fairway between the rows of giant buildings, looking left and right into each cellar. They were dark, with no one inside, so I kept running and looking and searching and then . . . I heard a pop.

I slid to a stop and listened.

Nothing.

I looked around and then ran towards the cellar I thought the pop came from, running down the driveway into the cavernous A-shaped space. It was lit by lights hanging from the top of the "A" and they illuminated the towering mounds of potato hills that ran to the ceiling at the peaks of their mounds and all the way to the back of the long building.

I stopped, trying listen and catch my breath and I still couldn't hear anything, but I knew that mounds of potatoes and the thick insulation of the walls muffled sound. The sound must have come from this cellar. As my eyes adjusted to the light, I looked up and thought I could see shadows moving on the ceiling of the cellar.

I stuffed the T-shirt wrapped pistol in my back pocket and scrambled up the hill of tubers, slipping and tripping, triggering tiny potato landslides moving at an angle across the mountain of spuds until I got to the top of the first mound and looked down at the little valley between the potato hills. There was nothing there, but I saw a shadow further back and then heard muffled voices.

I slid down from the first peak and ran up the second. Still nothing, but the sounds were nearer, so I dropped down into the next potato valley and then up the next peak, stopped at the top and looked down at the little plateau before the next peak.

Two men.

Rob Clawson was splayed out on his back, moaning and holding his stomach with a pair of bloody hands as a tall shape hovered over him, holding a gun. Clawson's face was bruised and bleeding.

"What are you doing?" I called out.

Startled, Pete Sorenson turned to look up at me.

I held my hands up. "What are you doing, Pete?"

"Richie," he said. "You shouldn't be here."

"Neither of us should be here, Pete."

"Richie. . . help me," Clawson groaned, in pain and breathing hard and fast. "Please."

"Tell me what you're doing, Pete?" I asked, stepping a little closer.

"I figured it out, Richie," he said tilting his head at Clawson. "He killed Jeannie, didn't he?"

"Yes, Pete, I think he did." I was at his side.

"It's a lie!" Clawson protested, then fell into a coughing fit. Pete made a threatening move with the pistol he was holding, but I waved him back and carefully stepped over to Clawson.

"That's bad, Robbie," I said pointing to his belly. "Looks like a gut shot. Know what that means? It means we gotta get you an ambulance right now or you're gonna bleed to death. It'd be a miserable way to die."

He was moaning, trying to get up but couldn't seem to move his legs. Pete might have hit his spinal cord with the shot.

"Let me do this," Pete growled.

I stopped Pete with a gesture and turned back to Clawson and knelt next to him. "I did something, Robbie. I put a tracker in your car. I've been following you and I know where you went tonight. I know what you did."

"No," he said, eyes wide.

"Now, I want you to tell Pete what happened. Tell us and I'll call 911."

"No," Pete protested. I turned and gave him a look. It took a second, but he understood.

"Tell me," I said turning back to Clawson. "And we get help."

He stared, wide-eyed at me, then at Pete and back to me, his fear intensifying.

"What happened, Robbie? What happened to Jeannie?" He stared, mouth open, struggling. "She was gonna have your kid, right?"

He glanced towards Pete, the gun, then back to me with a slow nod. A quiet moan came from Pete.

"She was gonna get clean and keep the baby? Is that right?"

"Yes," he snarled.

"What did you do?" Pete asked.

"Bitch wouldn't listen to me," Clawson growled. "I didn't want a kid around and I wasn't gonna let her dump me, so I told her she had to get rid of the baby or else."

"The 'or else' turned into a fight at her house," I said. "She ran but you caught her and beat her to death out there in that field, didn't you? And then you buried her. But you didn't know, Robbie. You didn't know she was still alive when you stuck her in the ground and left her to suffocate, with her mouth and nose stuffed full of the dirt that you shoveled on top of her."

Clawson was crying. "I thought she was already dead."

An even louder cry, like an animal in pain, came from Pete as he fell to his knees, blubbering like a child.

"I thought she was already dead!" Clawson yelled. "Get a fucking ambulance!"

I went over to Pete, kneeling next to him and put my arm around his shoulders.

"It's even worse, Pete," I said quietly. He looked up at me. "A few hours ago, Robbie went to your sister's house in Pocatello."

He stared up at me in horror. "No . . ."

"I'm so sorry. . ."

Pete fell back on his haunches staring at me, tears flowing from his bloodshot, tired eyes. "Julie?"

I nodded, then went back and stood over Clawson's struggling, weakening body.

"Julie called you and told you everything, didn't she?" I asked. "She's the one who called to tell you about me. And she's the one that told you that Sara Wilcox was going to confirm it all to the police."

I turned to Pete. "Sara's dead, too. He killed her tonight and then went after Julie because she was the one person left who could hurt him. He killed her and then left her out in a field along with a fake suicide note."

"God damn you to hell," Pete said standing.

"Richie," Clawson said pleading. "Please . . ."

I shook my head.

He coughed up blood, looking back and forth desperately between me and the pistol pointed at his head. His eyes came back to mine.

"You promised," he growled.

"My promise was on Jeannie's grave and over Julie's body. I promised I would make sure there was justice for what happened to them." Robbie cried out as I pulled the wrapped pistol out of my back pocket and pointed it at his forehead. But, as I took a deep breath to squeeze the trigger, I looked over at Pete, saw the pain in him, saw the life of abuse, the loss and a guilt that was far deeper and more personal than mine could ever be and then, I looked down at the dying man. I dropped the pistol to my side. "I think justice has been served," I said, wiping then re-wrapping Julie's revolver and handing it to Pete. "He used this on Julie."

Clawson stared, shaking his head back and forth eyes searching, hoping for help.

Pete wiped his eyes, then, pointing his gun at the terrified man lying on the blood-soaked bed of potatoes, he turned to me. "You better go now."

I placed my hand on top of Pete's and gently pushed his arm down. "Pete... we could still turn him over to the police and let the state dole out the punishment."

Pete shook his head. "I can't do that, Richie. Not doing this for the state. This is for me. I need this. You know why."

I looked at him for a long time and then nodded. "Yeah, Pete . . . I know why."

"Let me have this."

I looked down at Clawson, who was growing weaker; pain and fear streaking his face. Then I turned and put a hand on Pete's shoulder to say something, but there was nothing I could say. He nodded at me and I started back up towards the cellar entrance.

"You can't do this, Richie," Clawson croaked out, coughing. "You can't . . ."

I looked back as Pete stepped closer to Clawson, his gun aimed at his head. "Yes, I can, Robbie."

I stumbled over the mounds of potatoes and made my way out of the cellar. The rain had stopped and when I got back to the still nearly deserted parking lot, I walked over to the Corvette, made a quick scan for any witnesses, then crawled under the back bumper and ripped out the foam-encased cell phone I had put there. I would toss it into the river on my way back to Marty's.

I climbed into to the Jeep and had just put the key in the ignition when I heard the sound. It was faint, but I knew where it came from and I knew what it was.

It was a single, final pop.

Thirty-Four

It may have been called sleep, but it was too fitful of a night to be able to say I got any rest. I gave up trying as soon as the sun peaked over the eastern hills and I decided to do some Jeep work: change oil, put in new spark plugs and get the ragtop back on. By noon on Wednesday, after a long shower and a bowl of scrambled eggs, I was on my back, underneath the Jeep behind Marty's, watching dirty motor oil drain into a bucket, when I heard the back door open and heard Tyler say "He's out here."

I took a deep breath and got myself ready. I knew what this was going to be. I had been expecting it.

Someone kicked my foot. Hard.

"Ow!" I yelped.

"Willis! Get out from under there."

It was Yankovic.

I wiggled my way out from under the Jeep, propping myself up on my elbows to see Yankovic and a uniformed cop standing over me.

"Why the hell did you have to kick me, Yankovic?" I asked.

"Time to talk," he said, gruffly. "Get up."

"What's wrong?" I asked as I got to my feet, and grabbed a rag out to wipe the oil off my hands. "Problem with the Wendover case?"

Yankovic stepped closer. "Where were you last night?"

I looked at him, then the uniform, then back to him, making sure to register curiosity. "Here. Something happen?"

"Here? All night?"

"Yeah."

"Can anyone vouch for that?" he asked.

I tilted my head towards Marty's and nodded. "What happened?"

"You own a gun?" Yankovic asked.

"Never have. Why?"

Yankovic turned to the uniform behind him. "Check his Jeep." The man went around to the passenger side, digging through everything.

"Hey!" I protested.

"Shut up." Yankovic stepped closer. "This morning, your old friend Clawson was found dead in a cellar at US Potato."

I didn't say anything, just stared at him, then leaned back against the Jeep, as if I was trying to absorb what he had told me. I glanced towards the uniform, then slowly back to Yankovic. "And you two are here, which makes me think it wasn't an accident. What happened?"

"Some time last night, he was shot to death at USP and then buried under a pile of potatoes," the uniformed cop said.

"Shit . . ." I mumbled. "Buried?"

The cop nodded. "An employee found him this morning."

"What do you know about it, Willis?" Yankovic asked.

"Me? Why would I know anything about it?"

Yankovic pressed, "You come to town, bent on solving some ancient murder and suddenly the guy you've been telling us was involved in it is found dead from two gunshot wounds. Just a coincidence?"

I straightened myself up to glare down at the man.

"Or, detective," I said with as much disrespect as possible, "maybe me digging into it stirred things up and somebody around here decided to do what you assholes wouldn't."

Yankovic shook his head. "Not likely and I don't believe in co-incidence." He turned to the cop behind him, who shook his head, indicating he hadn't found anything in the Jeep. I had already made sure there wouldn't be anything. "Check his hands."

The cop nodded, slipped on disposable gloves then pulled out what looked like a Handi-Wipe you'd buy for cleaning and came toward me.

I just stared at them.

"Hold out your hands, please," he said.

I looked at the cop, then his boss. "GSR test? Aren't you supposed to get a search warrant or something?"

"You are willingly cooperating with a police investigation, aren't you, Willis?" He gave me a mean smile. "Get your hands out."

"Okay," I said, surrendering. I held out my grease covered hands for the cop who took a look at them and then turned to Yankovic, shaking his head.

"Do it anyway," Yankovic said, fuming at me.

I watched as the cop wiped my hands with the cloth that could be used to detect gunpowder residue, which would be there if I had recently fired a gun. I hadn't fired a gun since I was fourteen, but even if I had, all the grease on my hands would have made the test useless.

Finished wiping my hands, the cop placed the wipe in a plastic bag and sealed it.

"Don't plan on going anywhere, Willis," Yankovic said. "We are going to have a lot of questions for you." Yankovic stepped closer. "Think about getting a good lawyer."

"Wow, thanks for the advice, Yankovic," I said with heavy sarcasm. "I never would have thought of that."

The two turned and I watched them walk around the building out of sight and let out a huge sigh of relief. I knew Clawson's body would turn up at some point and that they would probably come to me first with questions. I had been ready.

The door pushed open and Jia peaked out, looking around.

"They gone?" she asked.

I nodded.

"What did they want?" she asked coming down the steps to me.

"Well," I said, "arresting me was probably what he wanted, but he knew that wasn't going to work."

"What?"

"The man that I warned you about the other day?" I said.

"Yeah?"

"He was found dead last night."

"Uh oh . . ." she muttered.

"The cops wanted to know where I had been and I told them that I had been here all night."

Jia looked at me, frowning. "But you weren't here all night." She searched my face, then her eyes got big. "Oh, God. . ."

I stepped close to her. "No, Jia. I didn't."

"You didn't . . .?"

"No, I didn't. It's important, though, that I was here, all night. Can you help me with that?"

She searched my face again, then reached out and touched my arm.

"I can."

I smiled, relieved.

"I'll talk to Tyler and Camila," Jia said. "They will vouch for you too. I hope that will be enough." She turned to go back inside.

"Thank you, Jia."

She stopped and turned toward me.

"Does this have anything to do with the justice you told me you wanted?" she asked.

I looked at her, but couldn't form an answer. So, she just gave me a sad smile and went back inside.

I did feel like some sort of justice had been meted out, but at a shitty cost. Sara Wilcox and Julie Sorenson were both dead. Clawson had killed them, but they would probably be alive if I hadn't come back to Black River, digging into Jeannie's murder. I felt a deep guilt about that and I knew it would haunt me for a long time.

Later in the afternoon, after exchanging long texts back and forth with my daughter about whether I was going back to my job or not, I settled onto a table in the corner of the cafe with my laptop. I needed to know what was going on, so I began searching local news blogs.

It didn't take long to find a brief note on a Pocatello television station's news blog mentioning that a woman's body had been found in a field just outside of town. Her name was being withheld, pending notification of next-of-kin, and her death was listed as suspicious.

I knew they were talking about Julie.

I sat back letting a wave of deep sadness sweep over me again, then shook it off to kept searching. I eventually found a post on a Black River Facebook page.

It read: "So sorry to pass on that our neighbor, Mrs. Wilcox died this morning in her home. She had been ill for a long time so it was not a surprise. She was a wonderful friend and will be missed by all of us."

I sighed. In the next few days, I expected that the police would discover that her death was not natural, but would they ever find a way to link her death and Julie's to Rob Clawson?

My phone beeped and I looked to see a text from Ellie.

"Anything happen with your friend?" she texted.

"Plenty," I thumbed back.

"What?!?!" she texted.

"Can you come by later?" I typed. "Can't explain over the radio."

"Yes." She texted.

"Okay. Tonight," I texted and clicked off.

By seven that night, Marty's was busy. Camila, Marie and Jia were shlepping trays of food and drink back and forth as Tyler and Lee struggled to keep up in the kitchen. I had thrown on an apron and was bussing a table when the door opened and my old guitar buddy, Sam, came in carrying his guitar case.

"Sam!" I called in greeting.

"Hey Rich!" he called out over the noise of the customers. "I brought you something."

Sam pointed towards the door and to my complete surprise, Cal, Zack and Kelly, the guys who had been in our band back in high school all trooped in. I couldn't believe it. There were happy shouts of greetings and hugs and jokes about how old we all looked as we laughed and talked, oblivious of everyone else in the cafe.

"This is great!" I said. "You got the guys all together. And after all these years?"

"It's been too many years," Sam said, "but we thought maybe we could still play some music together. How about it?"

"What? Here?" I asked.

"Here," said Cal, who had been the bass player.

"And now," said Kelly, our drummer.

Zack went out and a moment later came back in with a couple more guitar cases.

I beamed at the guys and nodded.

"We gotta do this!" I said. I turned and called out to Jia. "You okay with some live music?"

"Really?" Jia asked. She heard encouragement and hand-clapping from a few patrons. "Absolutely!"

I turned to the guys. "Go get set up on the stage and I'll get my guitar."

"Sounds good," Sam said. "Let's do it!" The four of them went to the tiny stage, moving things out of the way and arranging chairs while I started towards the back.

I came back down from my room with my guitar and joined the guys on the stage as they were pulling their instruments out of their cases, talking over some songs to try and comparing guitars. Kelly, our drummer, set up an electronic drum pad while the others tuned up. I was about to do the same when I glanced over at the door as it opened.

A uniformed policeman came in followed by Yankovic and the sheriff, Gil.

"Uh oh," I muttered, looking at their serious faces.

Seeing me, Gil led the other two over to the stage.

"Hey, Gil," I said, then nodded at Yankovic. "This about Robbie?"

Gil said, "Can we sit down somewhere? We need to talk."

The guys in the band moaned and protested, but I waved them down.

I looked around and saw an empty table in a far corner that would be as close to private as we'd get here.

"Over there," I said, pointing to it, then turned back to Sam and the others. "Why don't you guys go ahead and start playing something? I'll catch up."

Gil gestured for the uniform to stand by the door and then I led the two over to the table and sat, looking back and forth between the two. Jia came over as we settled down.

"You guys want something?" she asked.

"Could we get some coffee?" Gil asked. "Been a day,"

"Sure," she said. "Anything else?"

"Yeah," Yankovic said. "Answer a question. Where was Willis last night?"

She stared at him, puzzled. She paused, then said "Here."

"Is that right?" Gil asked, turning to her.

She nodded. "All night, until later, when he went upstairs."

"You're sure?" he asked.

"Oh yeah," she said. "Tyler was here too." She turned to the kitchen and called out. "Tyler, was Rich here last night?"

"All night," Tyler said. "I made him and his friend burgers and fries."

"Friend?" Yankovic asked.

"Eleanor," Jia said, walking back to the bar.

I wished they hadn't mentioned Ellie because I hadn't explained anything to her and I realized that she was going to be showing up before long.

"That the woman I met here last week?" Gil asked.

I nodded. Jia was back with mugs and a carafe of coffee.

"Where is Eleanor?" Gil asked me.

"Probably at ISU tonight," I said. "She teaches theatre. They're rehearsing a show now."

"We'll want to talk to her, too," Gil said.

"Okay," I said. I looked at the two of them, getting ready for them to grill me about where I had been, what I had been doing and what I knew about Clawson's death. "So . . . what's going on? More questions about Robbie Clawson?"

"A shitload," Yankovic growled.

Gil turned to him. "Let me do this, okay?"

Looking at the two of them, I could see that something new had come up. Something to do with Sara?

"I got a call from the police in Idaho Falls this afternoon," Gil said. "They found Pete Sorenson, dead, in the cab of his truck."

I gawked at the two of them, not knowing what to say. I finally came out mumbling, "Oh god . . ." I was genuinely shocked, I didn't have to fake it. "Pete . . . shit. What happened?"

"Shot himself," Gil said.

"Damn . . ." I muttered. "They're sure it was suicide?"

"He left a note," Yankovic said.

I turned to Yankovic. "What?"

Gil took over again. "He left a note, a handwritten note, taped to the window of his truck."

Gil said that Pete was found in the cab of his truck, in the trucking company's garage by the night janitor. The gun he had used was next to him on the seat and he had taped a suicide note inside the windshield. In the note, Gil said, Pete confessed that he had killed Rob Clawson and left directions on where Clawson's body could be found. The note explained about Clawson being Jeannie's drug dealer and the father of her unborn baby and that when Jeannie decided to get out from under Clawson, get off the drugs and keep the baby, he killed her. Pete then wrote that Clawson had found and killed Sara Wilcox and Pete's little sister, Julie, because they were going to come clean about what Clawson had done. Pete said he tracked Clawson down at USP, forced him to confess and then killed him. He explained that it was not self-defense. It was an execution. In the note, Pete said that justice had been done for what Clawson did to the three women and that Pete saved the last bullet for himself, punishment for killing Clawson and punishment for failing his sisters.

"The gun Pete used to kill himself was the same caliber as the one that killed Clawson," Gil said. "Forensics will probably verify that it's the same gun."

"What about Julie?" I asked. "Did you find her?"

"After we found out about the Sorenson suicide and note, we contacted the Bannock County sheriff. Julie was found dead in a field behind her house with a single bullet wound to the head. It looked to be a small caliber weapon and it was probably the gun we found with Clawson's body. Another job for the forensics guys."

"And Sara Wilcox?" I asked.

"They found her last night. She was terminally ill so it was assumed the disease had killed her. But now, because of what we've learned, the medical examiner will be taking a closer look."

"You have anything to say about any of this?" Yankovic asked.

I just shook my head. "I don't know what to say. The whole Sorenson family is gone." I looked at them. "Every single child of that screwed up household is dead."

Gil looked at Yankovic and then at me. "On top of this, we had a visitor this afternoon."

"Visitor?" I asked.

"Rosa Grazzano," Yankovic said. "The woman we told you to stay away from Willis. Apparently, you didn't."

"She file another complaint?" I asked.

"No," Gil said. "It looks like your visit on Monday morning scared the shit out of her. That and her brother being killed made her decide it was time to talk to us."

"About what?" I asked.

"Her brother," Yankovic said.

"She told us that she had been too frightened of him before to say anything," Gil said, "but with him gone, she could."

Rosa had told them all about Robbie's drug dealing and that Jeannie and Julie Sorenson had been customers as had Sara Wilcox and many others. Rosa told them that Jeannie was pregnant with her brother's child, and that she suspected he may have hurt her, but she couldn't prove it and was afraid to say anything.

"She also gave us one piece of information we didn't have before," Yankovic said.

"She told us that she believed Robbie was involved in the death of a girl thirty years ago name Shannon Baumgartner," Gil said. "She had been another one of Robbie's customers but was going to go to the cops about him. Rosa believes her brother might have killed this Baumgartner girl and made it look like an accident."

I feigned surprise and just shook my head. She was just confirming what Sara had told me.

"We'll be looking into that as well," Yankovic said.

"So," Gil started, "this suicide note from Pete Sorenson, the gun found with Clawson's body and then what Rosa told us seems to take care of almost everything, but we have to know. You came here, dug into this and two weeks later, an old murder is solved. But, some people are dead, Richie. Tell me you weren't involved in any of this, that you weren't out there in that spud cellar last night, helping Sorenson execute Robbie Clawson."

Our attention suddenly went to the door as it opened and Reggie came in, followed by Ellie. My pulse rate doubled. If they started asking Ellie about last night, I would be in trouble.

Jia saw her come in and opened her arms out wide yelling out "Ellie!" She ran to her and gave her a big, long hug, surprising me and probably surprising Ellie. Then Jia released her from the hug and led her over to our table, before going back to the bar.

"Reggie's Jeep crapped out on him again," Ellie said to me as she pulled out a chair to sit, "so I offered to give him a ride down for his shift." She looked at the men at the table. "What's going on?"

I started to say something, but Gil held up a hand.

"Were you here last night?" he asked.

Ellie looked at him and at Yankovic, then back to Gil. There was a pause. "Yeah. What's up?"

Yankovic looked at her. "You were here?

"Yes."

"Was Willis here?" Yankovic asked.

She glanced over at me. "Yeah? Why?"

"Was he here all night?" Gil asked.

"All evening," she said, "and then he and I went upstairs for the rest of the night. Is he in trouble or something? He get beat up again?"

Gil shook his head. "No."

Yankovic looked at Gil. "These people are his employees. They could be lying to protect their jobs."

"You asshole," I said to him.

"Gil, I think he was there, down in that cellar last night. It's just too convenient that he shows up to look into a murder and less than two weeks later, the killer has confessed and has been executed. He can't have been here."

"Would this be enough to prove it?" Jia asked, coming back from the bar and handing a VHS tape to the sheriff.

"What's this?" Gil asked.

"Yesterday's security tape."

Ellie and I stared at her.

"You'll see Rich on there. And you'll see him and Ellie there. From last night. I pull the tapes every morning. Check the timestamp on it. You'll see it was camera footage from yesterday."

Gil took the tape. "Good," he said actually sounding relieved. "Thank you." He stood.

Yankovic stared at the sheriff. "You going to accept that?" he asked, still angry.

"We've heard their statements, we have the tape," Gil said. "I'll take a look at it and then I think we'll be able to wrap this up."

"You can't do this, Gil" Yankovic growled.

"I am doing this, Yank," Gil said. "Now just shut the hell up about it, okay?"

The detective stormed out, followed by the uniformed cop.

"Need anything else from me, Gil?" I asked.

"Not right now, but we may have questions later," he said. "Gonna be around for a while?"

"Haven't decided yet," I said.

"If you decide to head back to Washington, just leave us an address and phone number, in case we need something."

"Will do."

I stood and Gil and I shook hands. He nodded at the others and left.

When the door closed behind them, Ellie and I turned to Jia.

"A security tape?" I asked.

She nodded.

"How?"

"You don't know?"

I stared at her, puzzled, then looked up at the security camera and then over to where the server would be. I figured it out and smiled back at Jia.

"Pretty smart, lady," I said to her.

"What?" Ellie asked the two of us.

Jia jerked a thumb in my direction. "This lazy bum has never fixed the timestamp on the security camera."

I started laughing.

"Huh?"

"The timestamp on the camera is off by twenty-four hours," I said. "It's twenty-four hours ahead."

Jia joined in the laugh. "They have a tape that will show what it says is Tuesday's activity," she said, then went in an exaggerated conspiratorial whisper. "But it will actually be Monday's tape."

Ellie stared for a moment as she caught on and she smiled and nodded.

"And based on everything you've said about these guys," Jia added, "they'll never even look at the tape."

I walked over and gave Jia a hug. "How can I thank you?"

"No need," she said. "I owed you, remember?"

I had to smile, then turned to Ellie.

"And how the hell did you know to go along?" I asked Ellie.

She pointed at Jia.

"Her."

"What?" I asked.

"When she ran to me with that big hug, she whispered in my ear to say that you and I were here last night. And that's what I did."

"I don't know how to thank you, Ellie," I said.

"I do," she said taking my arm. "Explain why I had to lie my ass off for you."

"I promise," I said, "I will, but first, I want you to meet the guys from my old band."

Jia went back to the bar and I led Ellie over to the stage where I jumped up next them, made the introductions and we started playing.

By midnight, we had played as many old songs as we could remember and were too exhausted and hoarse to play any more. The guys packed up their instruments, said their good nights and headed off to their homes. Reggie had gotten a ride back to Pocatello with another student and Ellie helped me clean up the stage. When we finished, I took her by the hand and we went out front, sitting on the steps of the patio, looking out at the empty parking lot.

Gathering up what I wanted to tell her, I began with how I had been wrong believing that Rosa would warn Robbie. Julie had called him. I described my desperate run to get to Sara and then to Julie, but then finding both dead. I exaggerated my struggles calling 911, I explained about my phone dying and then finally getting to USP only to find Pete Sorenson there, having already shot Clawson. I decided to leave Ellie with the impression that Robbie was already dead when I got there.

"Then, Gil showed up here tonight," I said, "and told me that Pete had killed himself and that he had left a note explaining everything. My involvement wouldn't have changed anything and might just muddy things up, which is why I told them I had been here last night."

Eleanor stared at me for a long time, searching, then asked, "If you had found Clawson first, would you have done what Pete did?"

I looked out past the parking lot, shaking my head, then turned back to her. "I don't know Ellie. I just don't know."

She leaned in, her arm around me. I hated not telling her everything and thought that one day, I might give her the details, but I wasn't ready to do that yet.

"Richie," she said after a while, "I'm not sure what to say." She looked at me. "You gonna be alright?"

"I don't know," I said. "Finding out Robbie was the one who hurt Jeannie. . . and then Julie and Sara? They didn't deserve what he did to them. And I feel like I failed them."

We sat for a long time talking about it all until Ellie, yawned and stood.

"I have to get home," she said.

"No chance you can hang out here tonight?"

She shook her head. "Can't."

"I understand," I said, standing.

I walked her to her 4Runner where we stopped, she turned back to me and I pulled her into my arms.

"I have to give my boss a decision tomorrow," I said as I held her. I pulled back and looked into her still youthful blue eyes. "Ellie, what would happen if I decided to stay here in Black River? What would happen with us?"

She looked at me for a long time, then said softly "I can't answer that. I want to, but I can't. You have to decide what you want. I can't have anything to do with it."

Eleanor kissed me on the cheek and got into her car.

"Whatever you decide," she said looking at me, "I know it will be the best decision for you. And for me."

Thursday morning, I woke late and laid there for a long time, realizing that for the first time in almost two years, I had slept the entire night without nightmares. I sat up in bed, looking at the happy pills that I had been taking for most of that time, took them into the bathroom and flushed them down the toilet.

After I got dressed, I sat on the edge of the bed with my phone, staring at it. Staring and thinking and second guessing myself. Then I sucked in a lung full of air, shook it all off and texted my daughter about what I had decided to do.

Finally, I searched through my contacts and found the chief's number in Bellingham. It rang once, twice, three times and I thought it was going into voicemail, but then, he picked up.

"Hey chief," I said.

"'Finally. Good morning, Rich," he said.

Silence.

"Well," he said, "have you decided?"

Another deep breath.

"Yeah. I've decided."

THE END

Congratulations!

You made it to this page which means there's a fifty-fifty chance you actually read the book. If that's the case, thank you! If you just skipped ahead and landed here, well . . .that's okay. I won't tell anybody.

Choosing to self-publish one's book is a major undertaking, requiring the author to play the part of Agent, Editor, Publicist, Tour Manager and Psychotherapist, all at the same time. Most of us aren't very good at that, which is why we use pages like this to ask for your help. In the current bookselling universe, reviews and word-of-mouth are more important than ever. Potential readers rely on reviews to decide what book to read, especially when it's a new book by a new author.

So, if you are able, please leave a review or a comment about this book, wherever you purchased it, And if you liked the book, share your thoughts with your friends and even consider passing the book along for others to enjoy.